TailSpin

ALSO BY CATHERINE COULTER

The FBI Thrillers
Double Jeopardy (2008): *The Target* and
The Edge
Double Take (2007)
The Beginning (2006): *The Cove* and *The Maze*
Point Blank (2005)
Blowout (2004)
Blindside (2003)
Eleventh Hour (2002)
Hemlock Bay (2001)
Riptide (2000)
The Edge (1999)
The Target (1998)
The Maze (1997)
The Cove (1996)

TailSpin

CATHERINE COULTER

**Doubleday Large Print
Home Library Edition**

G. P. PUTNAM'S SONS

New York

This Large Print Edition, prepared especially for Doubleday Large Print Home Library, contains the complete, unabridged text of the original Publisher's Edition.

PUTNAM

G. P. PUTNAM'S SONS
Publishers Since 1838
Published by the Penguin Group
Penguin Group (USA) Inc., 375 Hudson Street, New York, New York 10014, USA • Penguin Group (Canada), 90 Eglinton Avenue East, Suite 700, Toronto, Ontario M4P 2Y3, Canada (a division of Pearson Canada Inc.) • Penguin Books Ltd, 80 Strand, London WC2R 0RL, England • Penguin Ireland, 25 St Stephen's Green, Dublin 2, Ireland (a division of Penguin Books Ltd) • Penguin Group (Australia), 250 Camberwell Road, Camberwell, Victoria 3124, Australia (a division of Pearson Australia Group Pty Ltd) • Penguin Books India Pvt Ltd, 11 Community Centre, Panchsheel Park, New Delhi–110 017, India • Penguin Group (NZ), 67 Apollo Drive, Rosedale, North Shore 0632, New Zealand (a division of Pearson New Zealand Ltd) • Penguin Books (South Africa) (Pty) Ltd, 24 Sturdee Avenue, Rosebank, Johannesburg 2196, South Africa

Penguin Books Ltd, Registered Offices:
80 Strand, London WC2R 0RL, England

ISBN 978-0-7394-9474-5

Printed in the United States of America

**This Large Print Book carries the
Seal of Approval of N.A.V.H.**

**To my crackerjack spouse, Anton.
You are beloved.**

C.C.

To my nephew, David Steffens, M.D., MHS,
Professor of Psychiatry and Medicine at
Duke University Medical Center.
Thank you for the compelling suggestion.
I hope I dealt well with it.

TailSpin

ONE

Black Rock Lake
Oranack, Maryland
Friday night

She thought she swallowed because her throat burned hot, as if splashed with sharp acid, but she wasn't sure because she couldn't think clearly. Her mind felt dark, as heavy and thick as chains, and she knew to her soul there was violence just beyond it. She smelled something rancid, oil with a layer of rot and decay. What was that smell? What did it mean? Her brain wasn't clear enough yet to figure it out. But she knew she had to, had to fight it or—what? *I'll die, that's what. I've got to get myself together, I've got to wake up, or I'll die.*

The smell grew stronger, and she wanted to vomit. She knew she had to be awake or she'd choke to death. She had to move, to wake up.

She swallowed again, nearly heaved when the acid in her throat mixed with that rancid smell. She tried to breathe lightly, concentrated all her energy on opening her eyes, on feeling her body, on tearing herself out of the black shroud where she was unable to move or speak. Her head felt heavy, her throat burned, and her mind—where was her mind? There, gnawing at the edges of her brain, were sharp hits of pain and fear, sweeping away the confusion, coming closer, breaking through the numbness.

She heard voices. Mr. Cullifer's voice? She didn't think so; his voice was very distinctive, like wet gravel underfoot. But she couldn't make out who they were or what they were saying, if they were male or female. But she knew that what the voices were saying was bad. For her.

The smell was so strong it burned her eyes and her nose. *Suck it in, suck it in, get yourself together.* She breathed in deeply, ignored the nausea, and at last she felt her brain jitter, felt edges of consciousness spear up, tear through the black.

It was dead fish she smelled, overwhelming now, and the smell of boats, of diesel fumes overlaying wet.

They were picking her up—who were they?—carrying her, her feet, her arms, and she breathed in the fetid odor. *Keep breathing, keep breathing.* She heard wooden planks creak, heard night sounds—crickets, an owl, the lapping of water.

Her eyes flew open when she went airborne. She hit the water hard on her back. The slap of pain snapped her back into her brain and her body. Instinct made her draw in a big breath before the water splashed over her face, closed over her head, before she was slowly dragged to the bottom. *Move, move.* But she couldn't. Though her hands weren't tied, a rope was wrapped around her chest to hold her arms at her sides. Her feet were tied and tethered to something heavy—a block of cement, she knew that instinctively. Too many Mafia movies. They didn't just want her to drown, they wanted her to disappear forever, like she'd never existed, never come into their lives.

She didn't want to die. *I'm not going to die.*

She was tied to the cement with the same thick rope that bound her ankles tightly together. She could do this, she could. She quickly shimmied away the rope around her chest, then her fingers went to work. They were clumsy, but it didn't matter, she didn't want to die, and she worked frantically. Surprisingly, she could see in the water, knew it wasn't all that deep because she sensed the moonlight above, and it was enough. She dug her fingernails under the knot and patiently, so patiently, worked it loose. Her chest began to burn. She ignored it, concentrated on the knots.

Because she'd been the captain of her swim team in college, because she knew how to control her breathing to maximum effect, she knew her time was running out. The drug she'd ingested hadn't helped. She knew she couldn't last much longer. It was so hard to keep her mouth shut, to keep from breathing. Her eyes were blurring, the water shimmering, the pressure in her chest building and building until it nearly burst her open.

I'm going to drown, I'm going to drown. The knot came loose. She kicked off the cement block and shot to the surface. When her head cleared, she wanted to haul in a huge gulp of air, but forced herself to take short, quiet breaths through her nose. She had to hold very still, trying not to ripple the water for fear they were still there, staring down at where they'd thrown her in, watching for bubbles, waiting, waiting until they knew she couldn't still be alive. They'd wait, oh yes, they'd wait to make sure they'd erased her.

Her brain was in full gear again. She heard the light lapping of water against the pilings of a wooden pier. They'd walked out onto the pier and thrown her out into the water, believing it deep enough. She eased back under the water and swam under the pier to hide behind the pilings.

She surfaced very slowly, very quietly, wanting to suck in so much air she'd never run out again, but she only let her face clear the surface. She forced herself to take calm, light breaths. She was alive. Slowly, her breaths became deeper and deeper. She filled her lungs. It felt wonderful.

She heard voices again, but couldn't understand any words because they were moving away now. Men? Women? She couldn't tell, she only knew there were two of them. She heard feet clomping on the wooden pier, heard a car engine, heard the car drive away. She swam out from under the pier and saw the taillights of a car in the distance.

Good. They thought they'd killed her.

How had they drugged her? For a moment she couldn't think, couldn't remember, couldn't picture what she'd eaten or drunk earlier. She'd eaten dinner by herself, in the kitchen. The wine, she thought, the bottle of red on the table that she'd opened. Where had it come from? She didn't know, hadn't paid any attention.

She smiled. What none of them had realized was that she'd drunk only a bit of the wine. Any more and she'd be lying dead at the bottom of this lake. No one would know where she was. She'd just be gone. Forever.

She pulled herself out of the water, shivered as she slapped her hands against her arms and looked around. There were no houses, no lakeside cottages with narrow docks and tethered boats, only a skinny two-lane road winding off into the distant darkness. She shuddered with cold and shock, but it didn't matter. She was alive.

She came upon a sign: BLACK ROCK LAKE. Where was Black Rock Lake?

It didn't matter. She had two legs that worked fairly well. She began to walk in the same direction as the car.

It seemed like forever, but it was maybe only fifteen minutes when she saw the lights of a small town—ORANACK, MARYLAND, according to the small black-and-white sign.

It was late. She didn't know exactly how late because her watch had died in the water. She walked through the deserted town, her eyes on a neon sign that beamed out in bright orange—MEL'S DINER—all glass so you could see back to the swinging door to the kitchen.

Two people sat in a booth next to the glass, a limp waitress standing beside them, a pen poised over her pad. She saw a taxi sitting outside the diner, saw the cabbie at the counter drinking coffee, and she smiled.

When the cab pulled into Jimmy's driveway, she asked the driver to wait and prayed they hadn't taken her purse. The alarm wasn't set, thank God, and the window in her bedroom was still cracked open. She found her purse downstairs on the kitchen counter, where she'd left it earlier that night. Was it really only three, four hours ago? It seemed a lifetime.

Thirty minutes later, she took one final look at Jimmy's big redbrick Georgian house, built in the thirties, the centerpiece of this well-tended neighborhood, nestled among huge oak trees on Pinchon Lane. She'd never had the chance to think of him as her father, to call him Father; she wondered now if he would remain Jimmy forever.

She'd had only six weeks with him.

She drove her white Charger through the quiet streets until she reached the Beltway. She knew where she was going and also knew she'd be crazy to try to drive through the night, because she was so exhausted she was shaking. But she had no choice. She ate two candy bars, felt a brief spurt of energy. She had to think, had to plan. She had to *hide.* She forced herself to drive through the night, surviving on hot black coffee and a half dozen more candy bars and, at eight A.M., stopped at the Cozy Boy Motel off the highway in Richmond.

She awoke fourteen hours later, groggy at first, every muscle in her body protesting, but her strength was surging back. *Fear,* she thought, *an excellent energizer.*

She wasn't about to go to her mother's house. She wasn't even going to call her. No way would she put them in that kind of danger. She realized with a sort of depressed relief that she had no close friends to call, to tell them not to worry about her. She hadn't kept up with friends she'd made in Richmond. As far as she could think, there was no one to even wonder where she was. Mrs. Riffin, Jimmy's longtime housekeeper, was even gone now, having retired the week after Jimmy's death. No one, she thought, no one to worry, to wonder. Jimmy's lawyer might wonder in a sort of intellectual way where she was, but she doubted he'd press it. As for Jimmy's siblings, if they believed she was tied to a concrete block at the bottom of a lake, they certainly wouldn't say anything.

Could Quincy and Laurel have been involved? Jimmy's brother and sister—unbelievably, her uncle and aunt—hated her, wanted her gone—but murder? Yes, she thought, they were capable of anything. Maybe there were others who didn't want her around, but murder? She always came back to Quincy and Laurel.

She meandered along back roads in Virginia until she ended up the following morning at a small motel in Waynesboro. She knew where she was going, but then what? She watched local TV news, listened to the local radio, and thought. She heard a retrospective of Jimmy's political life on PBS. Even though he hadn't been a liberal, they'd been mostly positive in their assessment of him. They probably hadn't meant to, but Jimmy came across as a larger-than-life figure, charismatic, dedicated to public service. If only they knew, she thought, Jimmy had been so much more. And there was the other thing. No, she wouldn't think about that right now. She couldn't. It would wait.

She listened to the vice president speak of Jimmy's ex-wife, his two daughters, but nothing about her, nothing about his other daughter, the one he hadn't known existed until six weeks before he died.

She leaned down to rub her ankle where the rope had been bound so tightly, and for an instant, she couldn't breathe. She smacked her palm against the steering wheel, got herself together. She looked out over the dark Virginia fields, the line of trees, unmoving black sentinels in the night, and thought, *If you two maniacs tried to kill me, then I hope you're happy, I hope you're making toasts to each other on my removal, the one person who can make your lives very unpleasant. Yes, drink up.*

Until she was ready to take them down.

TWO

Georgetown, Washington, D.C.
Monday morning

Sherlock took Jimmy Maitland's call at 7:32 while she was pouring Cheerios into Sean's Transformers cereal bowl, Astro sitting beside his chair, tongue and tail wagging, ready for his share. The terrier loved Cheerios.

"It's about Jackson Crowne," Maitland said. "And it isn't good, Sherlock."

"What is it, sir?"

Sherlock began shaking her head, her face going pale. Savich's head snapped up. He poured milk over the Cheerios and talked to Sean to distract him, but he was aware of every expression on his wife's face. He gave Astro a handful of Cheerios in his dog bowl.

"But you don't know for certain, sir?" she asked, her voice thread thin.

Maitland said, "No, not for sure, but it doesn't look good, Sherlock. Add Dr. Mac-Lean to the mix—well, you can imagine how worried everyone is. A helicopter is waiting for you and Savich at Quantico. Get there as soon as you can. We're not sending out Search and Rescue right now, that would lead directly to the media and that would mean too much information about Dr. MacLean getting out to the wrong people. If you don't locate him, we have no choice but to call in Search and Rescue. Funny thing is, Jack's piloting a Cessna search-and-rescue plane. I know you understand. I'm counting on you two."

Sherlock understood all too well, but she didn't like it. She would have damned the media, said to hell with concerns for Dr. MacLean's safety, and launched a full-bore Search and Rescue in ten minutes. But Mr. Maitland could be right—if this wasn't a malfunction—an accident—then that meant sabotage. As she carefully laid down the kitchen phone, watching

Sean studiously plowing through his cereal, she got herself together, said calmly, "It's Jack. His plane went down in southeast Kentucky, his mayday was near a small town called Parlow in the Appalachians, an hour from the Virginia border. As you know, Jack's got Dr. MacLean with him. Mr. Maitland wants us there as soon as possible, find out what's going on. No Search and Rescue right now. It doesn't sound . . ." She swallowed, looked again at Sean when her voice cracked.

Sean's spoon stopped halfway to his mouth, and his head came up, his father's eyes staring at her. "Mama, what's wrong?"

"It's one of our agents, Sean, he could be in some trouble. Your papa and I are going to go find him and bring him home."

Sean nodded. "All right then. You find him, Mama. Bring him over, maybe he can play *Pajama Sam* with me."

"I will, sweetie," Sherlock said, and gave him a loud kiss, then ran her hand through his black hair, his father's hair. She couldn't help herself and kissed him again, this time even louder. Sean smacked his lips back at her. Astro barked. "Astro, too, Mama,"

Sean shouted. Sherlock let Astro lick the powder off her cheek.

"Maybe your mama will let me ride shotgun," Savich said, and hugged and kissed his son, then nodded to Gabriella, Sean's nanny. "We'll call you, Gabby, when we find out what's going on."

Ten minutes later Gabriella walked them to the front door. She laid her hand lightly on Sherlock's arm. "I met Jack Crowne once," she said, "when I brought some papers to your office. He asked me if I liked to throw a football as much as Sean did, and I told him my spiral rivals Tom Brady's. He laughed. I hope you find him. This other man, this Dr. MacLean, is he all that important?"

"I'd call him more a lightning rod," Sherlock said. "We'll find Jack, I promise," but she knew it didn't look good, for either Jack or his passenger.

THREE

Monday morning

Rachael stared at the sign, at the bright red script letters against the white background: PARLOW, HOME OF THE RED WOLVES.

Almost home, Rachael thought, and laughed at that thought. Home? Parlow, Kentucky, a place she hadn't seen since she was a stick-skinny twelve-year-old, with braces on her teeth and hair down to her butt because Uncle Gillette hadn't wanted her ever to cut it. Her visits had been to Uncle Gillette's now-magnificent home in Slipper Hollow, a stretch of land five miles northeast of Parlow, well off the beaten track, unknown even to many locals. Uncle Gillette liked his privacy, especially since returning home from the Gulf War in the early nineties. Maybe too much.

It looked like she was going to have to walk the last mile. Rachael didn't kick her Dodge Charger; it had gotten her this far, after all. It sat on the side of the road, dirty white with a muddied-up license plate, deader than a doornail, whatever that was.

She was closing in on the back end of nowhere, and that was a wonderful thing. She had only one ancient duffel bag stuffed with clothes she'd flung into it the night she drove away from Jimmy's house in Chevy Chase. She'd driven again all through the night and now, at seven-fifteen in the morning, she was getting tired. As far as she could tell, no one had followed her on her slow nighttime drives across Virginia. She looked back again at her faithful Charger, which hadn't given her a single problem since she'd bought it three years before—until now.

Calm down, you're nearly there—to Slipper Hollow, where Uncle Gillette lived, protected by the densely forested mountains ranging as far as you could see. Their peaks were wreathed in early morning fog, blanketing the light dusting of snow until the sun melted it away. They were comforting, those mountains, when, as a child, she'd hidden among the thick green leaves on a branch of an ancient oak tree, staring at that immense stretch of mountains and hillocks and towering boulders, wondering what was beyond. Only giants, she'd believed at age four, and maybe, if she was lucky, some dogs and cats.

She clearly remembered that summer day when her mother told her, *It's time we were on our own.* That was it. She'd helped her mother and a reluctant Uncle Gillette pack their old Chrysler with their most prized belongings, and they'd headed out at sunrise. She'd missed Slipper Hollow and Uncle Gillette to her bones, counted off days between visits, and there'd been a lot of them in the early days.

But it had been almost a year since she'd last seen Uncle Gillette. At least she knew he'd be there. Uncle Gillette never left Slipper Hollow.

Time to get a move on. She wanted to be there before noon—if she could get her car fixed that fast. Her stomach growled, and in her mind Rachael saw Mrs. Jersey, the best cook in Kentucky, according to her mother, and the owner of Monk's Café, and wondered if she was still there. She'd seemed ancient to a twelve-year-old. Ah, but those hot blueberry scones she made, Rachael could still remember the taste, and those hot blueberries burning her tongue. Monk's Café opened early back then, for truckers, and maybe it still did. If Mrs. Jersey was still there, Rachael prayed she wouldn't recognize her, prayed no one in Parlow would recognize the twelve-year-old girl in the woman, and hoped she'd let Rachael use the landline since cells didn't work out here in the boondocks, and tell her who the best mechanic was in Parlow. She wasn't going to call Uncle Gillette; she was careful now, very careful. She had no intention of leaving any trail, no matter that they believed her dead, no matter that as far as she knew, they'd never heard of Parlow, Kentucky, or Slipper Hollow.

I'm safe. I'm dead, after all.

She shivered, remembering the slapping cold of the water, and pulled her leather jacket closer. She'd forgotten how cold it was here in the early morning even in the middle of June. She looked around again at the fog-shrouded mountains, a grayish blue in the early morning light. But this morning she wasn't moved by the incredible raw beauty, she only wanted to get home. She wanted to plan, and Uncle Gillette would help her. He was very smart, a marine captain. There was no such thing as an ex-marine, he'd said once with a snap in his voice, and she'd never forgotten.

But her Charger had let her down on the final lap.

Rachael hitched her duffel onto her shoulder, looked toward Parlow, seeing houses dot the distance among trees and hills and narrow winding roads.

She'd taken three steps when she froze in her tracks at a distant noise, a sputtering sound, an engine coughing, and it was coming closer.

She looked up but didn't see anything. Maybe it was a car coming on another road, maybe it was . . . No, no way could it be them. She drew a deep breath, then continued to scan the sky. No, what she'd heard— well, she didn't know what she'd heard.

But still she didn't move. She stared toward the end of long, narrow Cudlow

Valley, cut like a knife slice through the mountains. She stood there, her hand shading her eyes from the slivers of sunlight trying to break through the fog.

And there it was, a single-engine plane coming over the low mountains at the far end of the valley, jerking and heaving, black smoke billowing out near the tail. The plane was in trouble, dear God, it was going to crash, no, the pilot was pulling the bucking plane to line up at the far end of the narrow valley. She saw flames shooting out through the smoke, moving up toward the wings. He wasn't going to make it. She watched, couldn't take her eyes off that plane even as she began to run toward it.

Was Cudlow Valley long enough and flat enough to land a plane? She had no idea, she'd never learned to fly. She watched the wings straighten, pictured the pilot willing his plane to a sloping trajectory, lower and lower. She held her breath, and prayed.

An explosion rocked the small plane, nearly flipping it over, and it began to spiral, out of control.

FOUR

Unbelievably, the pilot wrenched it back in line. The next second, the engine went dead and the small single-engine plane dropped like a stone. She knew she was going to watch him die, there was no way he could bring it in. But somehow, somehow, he caught an air current and managed to glide the dying plane forward and down until the wheels finally touched the ground. The plane bounced and lurched, the front came up, then slammed down again. It jerked and shuddered before coming to a rolling stop not fifty feet from where she stood at the very end of the valley. Smoke gushed out and the flames licked higher.

Rachael started running toward the plane even as she saw the pilot kick open the door and struggle to drag an unconscious man across the seat and out the narrow door. She didn't know how he did it, but he did. He hauled the man over his shoulder and began to run away from the plane.

He stumbled and went down. The unconscious man flew over his head and landed hard, his head striking a clump of rocks. He didn't move. The plane exploded into a bright orange ball, flames gushing high into the air, spewing parts of the plane in every direction. She saw the pilot pull himself up and stagger toward the unconscious man. What looked like part of the tail struck his leg and he went down, and this time he stayed down.

It was terrifying, Rachael thought—life or death, all decided in under two minutes. She'd had maybe another minute.

She reached the unconscious man first and dropped to her knees. He lay on his back, motionless, eyes closed. He was slight, and older, near fifty, and there was blood on his head and all over his chest. She pressed her fingers to his throat. He was alive, but his pulse was faint. She lightly shook him. "Can you open your eyes?"

He didn't move. She sat back on her heels. Without thinking, she took off her leather jacket and covered him as best she could.

Her head whipped up when she heard the pilot groan. She was at his side in a moment, looking down at his smoke-blackened face, blood matting the dark hair against the side of his head, a thick trickle of blood snaking down from his left ear. There was blood oozing out of a tear in his pants where part of the tail had slashed into him. He wasn't moving. *Please don't die, please don't die.* She couldn't stand any more death.

Rachael lightly laid her hand on his shoulder, shook him slightly, but he didn't move. She felt his arms, his legs. Nothing seemed broken, but inside he could be seriously hurt. He was much younger than the other man, around her age, big and fit.

He wore a black leather jacket similar to hers over a white shirt and tie, black pants, low black boots. She lightly slapped his face. "Please, wake up."

He moaned, jerked onto his back. She leaned close, slapped his cheek again. "Come on, wake up. You can do it. I can't lift you by myself and I'm alone. The other man is unconscious and he needs your help. Wake up. Please." She slapped his face harder.

A hand grabbed her wrist.

She yelped but he didn't release her.

Jack opened his eyes. Long straight hair brushed his face, hair the color of sunlight. Blond and brown and gold, with one skinny braid running down the side, and he tried to lift his hand to touch it, but he couldn't get his arm up there. He said, "I like the braid. I've never seen that before. You pack quite a punch."

"Yes, well, sorry, but you have to wake up. I've got to get you and your friend medical help. Where are you hurt? What happened?"

To her surprise, he actually smiled. "Am I dead? Are you an angel? No, you're not an angel, your hair's too pretty and that braid—angels don't wear braids like that. And you've got dirt on your nose."

"I'd like to be an angel but I guess that would mean you're imagining me, and thank God you're not. I'm Rachael." She swiped at her nose. "There's a cut that's bleeding above your left temple; it's only a trickle now. I saw part of the plane tail hit you, knock you down. Your right thigh is bleeding pretty bad. We need to put pressure on it."

"Use my tie."

She pulled off his bright red tie with little colorful squiggles on it and eased it under his leg. "Tell me when you think it's tight enough," and she pulled.

"That'll get it. Knot it good. Anything broken?"

"No, not as far as I can tell, but I'm not a doctor."

"Usually broken bones tend to be pretty obvious."

"There's your innards. Anything could be going on inside you."

He was silent a moment, communing, she supposed, with his insides. "Feels okay, so far."

"Good. I'm not a pilot, either, but I watched you bring that plane down. I have no idea how you managed it, but you did. That was amazing. I've never been so scared. Well, maybe one other time." *Just last Friday night, as a matter of fact.* Insanely, she wanted to laugh.

He looked up at her, managed a smile. "Hey, since I walked away—well, ran away—I won't call it a crash, but it was definitely what I'd term a forced landing." He frowned, and she realized he was barely hanging on. "I couldn't believe it when I saw this valley. I thought for sure we'd end up slamming into a mountain and some archaeologist would find us in a couple hundred years."

"I don't think you should count on that much luck ever happening again in your life. I'm sorry to tell you, but your plane's pretty much destroyed. So's your cool tie, now that it's got blood all over it."

He dropped her wrist. "A bomb." His voice was faint now.

"No, no, don't fade out on me again. You've got to wake up, you've got to help me." She leaned real close. "Look at me. What's your name? That's it, concentrate on your name. You can do it." *A bomb? He said there was a bomb?* Well now, wasn't that great, just great.

"My name's Jack."

"Okay, Jack. You hang in. We're going to get to my car, you'll at least be safe there and warmer than you are here."

Jack Crowne thought his head was going to burst, it hurt so bad. As for his leg, it nagged and throbbed, but he could deal with it. If he could have one more spot of luck, maybe that piece of plane hadn't sliced him all that deep. "The Marauder— she's a good plane," he said, then cursed under his breath. "Was."

His brain focused. "Didn't you say something about my friend? You found another man? Older, on the small side? Wearing a silly pink-and-blue bow tie?"

She lightly touched her hand to his shoulder. "Yes, he's over there. He's unconscious, but alive. There's blood all over his chest and on his head. I didn't check for broken bones. I'm sorry, but I'm alone. Once I get you to my car, I'll help him."

"No, no, I'm pulling myself together. We must get to him now. My cell, let me get my cell, I'll call for help."

"Sorry, that's not an option. Cells don't work out here what with all the mountains and no towers. We'll take care of him, don't worry. All right now, don't close your eyes. I really can't lift you by myself. We'll go over to help your friend."

Jack gritted his teeth and thought about Timothy, who could be dying right now, right here, in this empty valley in the middle of nowhere. With her help he managed to ease up onto his elbows. He looked around. "I'm still in Kentucky?"

"Yes, close to the Virginia border. You managed to land your plane in the Cudlow Valley, the only break in the mountains for miles and miles. If you hadn't made it here, well . . . it doesn't matter, you did. Best not to dwell on that right now. Luck and skill, you had both. Now, your friend—"

"Help me to him and I'll carry him to your car."

Rachael couldn't imagine his helping anybody, but she clasped him around his chest and pulled. He came up to his knees, plastered against her. She paused for a moment, his head dipped to rest on her shoulder. "You okay?"

"The world's spinning and I want to

vomit, but yeah, I'm okay. Give me another minute." Jack breathed slow and shallow. Thankfully, the nausea passed. His head pounded, sharp and heavy, but he could deal with that since it was no longer blinding him. "Okay, let's go. I've got to see to Timothy."

It took the better part of five minutes but he was finally standing, walking, Rachael taking as much of his weight as she could without dropping herself. "There's Timothy. He hasn't moved."

With Rachael's help, Jack knelt beside Dr. Timothy MacLean. He checked his pulse, checked his head, then ran his hands over his arms and legs. He handed Rachael her leather jacket. "The blood on his chest—he's got a good-sized gash, well below his heart, thank God. Doesn't look deep and the bleeding's stopped. I'd say he's also got a couple of broken ribs. As for his head, I know he was unconscious when I got him out of the plane."

"I saw him hit his head on some rocks."

He cursed. "It's my fault, I stumbled and he went flying."

"Yeah, right, blaming yourself sure makes sense."

He narrowed his eyes at her even as he took more deep breaths. She saw the fierce concentration on his face, watched him suck in a deep breath and lean down. He managed to pull the man up and over his shoulder. He staggered, but kept his feet. "I'm glad he's on the small side," he said, panting. "All right, Rachael, if you could ease yourself under my left arm, let's give it a go."

He wasn't all that steady on his feet, but together they managed one step, then another and another. "My car's on the side of the road, over there. She up and died on me and I don't know a thing about cars."

"I do," he said, gritting his teeth, wanting to puke again. Timothy didn't weigh much, but still it was nearly 140 pounds of dead weight. Jack stopped, waited until the nausea passed, which it thankfully did again. "Okay, what is it? Twenty more feet. I can do that."

He did. She opened the back door and he eased his friend onto the backseat. He shrugged off his leather jacket and handed it to her. She was able to nearly cover Timothy completely with the two jackets.

Jack leaned against the car, his eyes closed, the blood now caked on the left side of his face. "What time is it?"

"Going on eight o'clock."

He said, still not opening his eyes, "Loosen the tie around my leg."

She did. "Good, the bleeding's stopped."

His head listed to the side, then he straightened. "All right, let me take a look at your car. Maybe it's something easy I can fix."

Probably not, Rachael thought. Nothing was easy in her life.

FIVE

As Jack straightened, he grazed his head on the raised hood and thought he'd pass out. He grabbed the dirty fender, closed his eyes tight, and let the world spin. Maybe it wouldn't be so bad, being laid flat again; it might save his head from exploding. He felt her arms come around his chest to prop him up. She said, "Hold still for a moment. That's right, I've got you."

When he finally got himself together and pulled away, she said, "Are you okay?"

"Better days," he said, "like yesterday. Thanks."

She grinned up at him, and wanted to

say, *Me too.* "Can you tell what's wrong with my car? Can you fix it?"

"Any chance you're out of gas?"

"Nope. I filled up in Hamilton."

"Okay, the hoses look okay. Crank the car."

She turned the ignition, but nothing happened. She tried again, still nothing.

"Okay, there's no fuel coming out of the fuel line. Your fuel pump's busted. It's got to be replaced. I wish I could jury-rig it, but I can't. That sign says we're in a town called Parlow. Is it big enough to have a decent mechanic?"

She nodded. "Yeah, population's maybe three thousand. It's only a mile up the road. Is a fuel pump major?"

"Nah, and it's not too expensive."

"I was starting to walk to Parlow when I heard your plane coughing and sputtering. You said it was a bomb. I don't understand."

Now didn't he have a big mouth? "I was probably wrong. It's over, don't worry about it." He tried his cell again, knowing there wasn't magically going to be a signal when there hadn't been one the last dozen times he'd tried.

Sure enough, no signal.

She said, "Right, I won't worry my pretty little head about it. You moron."

He somehow managed a grin over the grinding pain in his head. "No one's called me a moron since I forgot the condoms and Louise Draper walked out on me."

"Well, there you go," she said. "Forget the cell phone. It's the mountains, and too few towers out here, like I said."

"Okay, then, Parlow, Kentucky, here we come." He looked once again at Timothy, still unconscious on the backseat, his face ghostly pale. But Timothy was alive, thank God, and Jack just had to keep him that way. At present, that was a pretty big joke—he was nearly ready to fall facedown onto the blacktop.

This was all she needed, Rachael thought, but what else could she do? She couldn't leave this man here to fend for himself. Okay, so she'd arrive at Slipper Hollow later rather than sooner, no problem. Since Uncle Gillette didn't know she was coming, he wouldn't worry. She said, "I don't think there's anything more either of us can do except make it to Parlow and get some help."

"Have you been here before?"

For the barest instant, her face froze before she said, "No, I haven't."

He studied her through a haze of pain, watching her hair curtain her face as she looked down, that braid cupping her cheek, then slowly nodded. "It's okay, I haven't, either." He wasn't stupid, he'd seen the shock of panic in her eyes, heard the lie, and wasn't that strange? Who cared if she'd been in a little town in Kentucky? He ran his fingers through his dark hair, making it stand on end. "Parlow's bound to have medical facilities, an ambulance."

"Seems likely," she said, and the way she said it—too studied—another lie.

Parlow would have a police chief or a sheriff, Jack thought. He really didn't want to involve local law enforcement, but given his and Timothy's current condition, he doubted he'd have a choice.

Walking beside the two-lane road was slow going. Jack was a big man and she had to take a lot of his weight to keep him upright and moving. After twenty steps, Rachael, now panting, said, "Stop a moment." She leaned him against an oak tree beside the road. "This rest stop is as much for me as it is for you. Okay, okay, we don't have much farther to go, we can do it."

"Sorry, I forgot, what's your name again?"

"Rachael—ah, well, last names aren't really important, are they?"

His cop antennae flashed red again even though the Devil was pounding nails into his head. At least his leg was hurting a bit less so his brain could function a bit more. He wanted to ask her who she was and what she was afraid of, but he said, "I guess that would depend on why you don't want to tell me. Do you think I'm going to hit on you and you don't want me to follow you home?"

Hit on her? *Her?* "I guess your head injury is making you blind."

"Oh no, a man is never blind when it comes to a woman. Well, unless he's dead."

She laughed, shook her head at him, pushed her hair behind her ear. The braid fell forward to dangle alongside her cheek again. He'd have told her it was sexy, if he'd had the strength. She said, "I saved your bacon—drop it. Well, to be honest here, you saved your own bacon, but then you dropped it and I picked it up. I figure you owe me."

"Yes, ma'am, I surely do. I wonder if Parlow has a hospital."

"Oh no—well, who knows? There's probably a community hospital not far from here. We'll see, won't we?"

Got you on that one, kiddo.

"I hope you're not dangerous," she said, looking straight ahead, her shoulders and back hurting now from supporting so much of his weight. She looked up to see an amused look on his face. "If you weren't leaning on me, like a drunk, you would look dangerous with your face all black like a night-ops soldier."

"Nah," he said, swallowing down bile and wishing he could simply fall over into those nice soft-looking bushes on the side of the road. No, he had to get help for Timothy, but the dragging pain was pulling him under. Concussion, he knew, remembering too well getting his brains knocked stupid in a college football game. Not pleasant, but he'd get through it.

She said, "Hey, I see a house. We're nearly there, Jack. Hold on. I don't suppose you're going to tell me your last name?"

"Nope. Can you help me another fifty yards?"

She was panting hard. "Sure, I was on the high school wrestling team."

He laughed, the pain in his head flashed hard and hot, and he thought he'd bite the big one right there.

They finally reached the small white house she recognized very well. Two goats eyed them with little interest as they shuffled up the weed-choked drive. She remembered dogs, mongrels, a good half dozen, lazing in the sun. Jack said, "Thank the good Lord, I see phone lines."

Rachael wanted to tell him not to hold his breath, that in her childhood Mr. Gurt had been known for not paying his bills until his creditors camped on his doorstep.

There's no way Mr. Gurt will recognize me and blurt out my name, none at all. Trouble is, dammit, I've never been a good liar, and from Jack's reaction, I must really suck at it. I've got myself back on track, I've got to try to sound honest and straightforward, I've got to think before I simply bleat out everything. I can do this, I've got to, no

choice. If it gets back to them somehow that I'm alive, that I've been seen, they'll come after me again.

Rachael didn't think there was much likelihood of this happening, but they had such power, so many resources, she was afraid to take the chance. No, she would remain dead until she was ready to take them on. Well, first she had to make sure it was Quincy and Laurel, then she'd get them. As for right now, she was safe. You couldn't get safer than dead.

Showtime.

Her knock was answered by Mr. Gurt, now a very old man indeed. He was still wearing ancient blue jeans tucked into scuffed army boots. The same ones? He stood in the open doorway and squinted at them out of suspicious old eyes that didn't have a hint of recognition. Thank you, God, thank you, God.

But how could he not recognize her when he looked exactly the same to her, down to the sour look on his seamed old face? She looked into those rheumy eyes and realized he had no clue who she was.

"Yeah? What do you two want?"

Seems pretty obvious to me, you old coot, she thought, but since Jack was hanging on by a thread, she pushed her hair back from her face and said, "We've had an accident. Could we use your phone? We left our friend unconscious in the car. He's hurt pretty bad."

"What'd your husband do, missus, drink too much and drive you off the road?"

"Actually, he fell out of the sky at my feet. Please, sir?"

Mr. Gurt huffed, waved them in. Well, this was something. As a kid, she'd been in his house only once, with her mother, to bring Mr. Gurt Christmas cookies.

They stepped into deep shadows and smelled oatmeal and vanilla. She heard a dragging sound that had her heart galloping until she saw a very fat pug trotting toward them, his leash clamped in his mouth, the leather strap dragging along the floor.

"Don't get yourself in a dither, Marigold, and don't piddle on the floor. Let's get the folks on the phone, then I'll take you out." He led them into a living room where the smell of fresh lemon wafted in the air. Every surface was covered with old-fashioned lace doilies and antimacassars, yellow with age. He said, "Marigold hates the out-doors, weirdest thing I've ever seen. Just doing her business makes her nervous so I gotta be with her. Even Oswald and Ruby scare her."

"Oswald and Ruby?" Rachael asked.

"Two goats chewing on God-knows-what in the front yard. There's the phone. I paid the bill no more than six weeks ago so the buggers can't have turned it off yet. I threatened to get me one of them newfangled cellular phones, but the gal at the phone company laughed, said there might not be a signal here until the middle of the century, aeons after I'm croaked. Don't do no long distance, all right? Marigold, hold your water, I'm coming."

Jack took the phone out of her hand. "I'm sorry, but this is priority." He dialed Savich's cell.

"Savich here."

"Savich, it's Jack."

There was a brief pause. "Jack, let me say it is very good to hear your voice. You okay?"

"A little banged up, but I'll live."

"Dr. MacLean?"

"He's unconscious, smacked his head

good when he fell. He's got a gash on his chest and I think a couple of broken ribs. We had to leave him in the backseat of Rachael's car. We're in Parlow, Kentucky, close to the Virginia border."

"Who's Rachael?"

"She watched me bring the plane in, helped me get it together." He looked over at her as he spoke. She was twisting the skinny braid.

"All right. It turns out Parlow is where we're heading, that was where they marked your mayday."

"That's a helicopter rotor I hear. Where are you?"

"We left Quantico fifteen minutes ago. It'll take us a couple of hours to get to you. Bobby's heading to a private airfield owned by a Judge Hardesty just off Route 72, close to Parlow. There'll be a car waiting for us there so we'll be able to get around. Now, let me give you over to Sherlock before she rips the phone out of my hand."

"Jack? It's Sherlock. Mr. Maitland called us around seven-thirty this morning, said you went down—you bozo, do you swear to me you're okay?"

Jack smiled. "Oh yeah, an angel saved me, but . . ."

"But what?"

"It's Timothy. He could be badly hurt. Like I told Savich, he's lying unconscious in Rachael's car, which is broken down on the side of the road. We had to leave him there to get help."

"All right, I'll make a call, set up getting him medevaced to the closest trauma center. I'll get back to you. Jack, please tell me there was some sort of mechanical malfunction."

He was aware that Rachael was studying his face, listening to every word he said. He said only, "Very probably not."

Savich came back on. "Okay, we'll figure it out. I'll call Mr. Maitland. He'll get an expert out there to take a look at the plane. You need a doctor, don't you? Wait, Sherlock's got the medevac people, and they need to know exactly where Dr. MacLean is. Jack, you there?"

Jack felt his brain wafting away, and what was worse, he welcomed it. "Sherlock? I guess you'd best have Rachael tell you."

Rachael took the phone from Jack and

watched him collapse into one of the ancient, nubby gray easy chairs. She listened, then told the woman the location of her car, adding, "I'm very glad you're coming because Jack needs help. As he told you, my car broke down, so we're walking. We'll meet you in whatever medical facility they have in Parlow. He's got a concussion, he thinks, and his leg was hurt by a piece of debris from the plane. I'll stay with him until you get here."

"Thank you very much for helping him. We're still a couple of hours away. What's your name?"

But Rachael had hung up. Jack was barely conscious.

SIX

Parlow Clinic
Rosy Bill Avenue
Monday morning

Dr. Post straightened as Nurse Harmon ushered a man and a woman into the small examining room.

Sherlock stood in the doorway, staring at Jack, who was stretched out on his back with a sheet pulled to his waist, his shirt hanging open. A young woman was leaning over him, her long hair hiding her profile, carefully soaping the black off his face. There was a braid hanging down from her side part.

"Jack?" Sherlock took a quick step forward.

"Is that you, Sherlock? You look hot in

that black leather jacket. Excuse me, but I'm not really with it," and his eyes closed.

Dr. Post said, "Don't worry, he's asleep again, mostly from the medication. Let's let him rest, all right?"

Sherlock drew a deep breath, smiled at the doctor. "I'm Agent Sherlock, this is Agent Savich, FBI. And this is Agent Jackson Crowne."

"I know. He was awake enough to tell me when I found them on my doorstep."

The woman standing over Jack straightened. "I'm Rachael," she said. "I've been helping Jack." She didn't say another word. When Jack had identified himself to Dr. Post, she knew she was cursed. This was all she needed. And now there were three feds, all in the same small room with her.

Sherlock asked Dr. Post, "Tell us exactly what's wrong with him."

Dr. Post said, "He's got a concussion and he isn't going to feel too happy about it for a while. We don't have an MRI in town, but the CAT scan didn't show any abnormalities.

"He had a nice gash on his leg, but he was lucky, didn't hit anything major, just needed some of my pretty stitches. I've put him on antibiotics and some pain meds. I'd like to let him rest for a while, but he should be all right. I'd like to keep him overnight, to make sure nothing else develops.

"I've invested lots of time in him and I don't want him to leave the clinic and collapse on his face, undo any of my excellent work."

Dr. Post looked curiously at the two FBI agents, who looked so relieved they were ready to high-five him.

"I guess you guys work together? Maybe you're here on a case?"

Savich said, "Yes."

Dr. Post pointed at Rachael. "She told me she isn't his wife."

Sherlock said, "No, she isn't, but he's going to think I'm his mother when he wakes up, because I'm going to chew his butt for scaring us so badly."

Dr. Post laughed. "Okay, are you going to tell me what's happening? The reason I'm asking is right after these two staggered into my clinic, I heard an ambulance heading through town, sirens blasting. Is someone else hurt?"

"Yes, I'm afraid so. Thank you for taking care of him."

"You're welcome," said Dr. Post.

Savich looked at Rachael. "So you're Jack's savior."

Rachael still couldn't believe it. FBI agents, all three of them. When she and Jack had stumbled up the steps to the clinic, Dr. Post was unlocking the front door, balancing a cup of coffee in his free hand. Jack had pulled out his ID and flashed it to the startled doctor.

And she thought again, why couldn't Jack have been a nice rent-a-pilot? No, he was an FBI agent, a fed whose bosses could be all chummy with Quincy and Laurel, who might be bought or influenced, defer to them because of their power—no, she wasn't going there. *They believe I'm dead. They've got to keep believing that.*

As long as these three federal agents didn't find out her full name, she was safe, she'd be okay. She'd still be dead.

She knew every bureaucracy leaked like a sieve, the FBI included. No, she'd be very careful, she'd lie well, a novel experience for her. She smiled. "I'm Rachael." She shook their hands.

Savich said, "I understand you watched Agent Crowne's plane come down and you helped both Jack and Dr. MacLean." He stepped forward, stuck out his hand. "We'd like to thank you for seeing to them, Ms. . . ."

I'm the most fluent liar in the world, I'm the coolest, the smoothest—"Rachael Abercrombie."

A lie, Savich thought, and wasn't that strange? He said, smiling at her, "Yes, thank you, Ms. Abercrombie. The medevac took Dr. MacLean to Franklin County Hospital about twenty minutes ago. We don't know his condition yet. I called your sheriff."

"Oh no, he's not my sheriff, Agent Savich. I've never been to Parlow before. I'm only passing through."

Savich nodded, but his head cocked to the side, and he studied her face closely. Looking at that small clever braid, he decided Sherlock would look very sexy with one. "Well then, we're all strangers here. Hopefully the sheriff will come soon."

Dr. Post saw the big tough-looking man look down at—of all things—a Mickey Mouse watch, and frown.

"We owe you big-time, Ms. Abercrombie," said Sherlock.

"Oh no, please," said Rachael, "Jack saved both of them. He pulled Dr. MacLean out of the plane before it exploded. I didn't do all that much—call me the mule."

Dr. Post said, "Deliah—that's Nurse Harmon—told me Dougie—that's Sheriff Hollyfield—had a septic tank problem this morning and that's why he's running a bit late. But he'll get here, he always does." He looked at them all closely. "I've never met any FBI agents before."

Sherlock said, "He eats Cheerios for breakfast with our son, Sean," and smiled. "I eat a slice of wheat toast with crunchy peanut butter."

Dr. Post laughed. "Just plain folk? Maybe, but not to me. The two of you, you're both FBI agents and you're married, and you work together?"

"That's right," Savich said.

Dr. Post picked up Jack's gun, which was sitting on top of the counter, next to his dirty, ripped slacks. "My dad owned a Kimber Gold Match 11. It's a fine gun."

"Agent Crowne believes it's efficient," Savich said easily, and held out his hand. Dr. Post gave him the Kimber, butt first.

"A ten-round magazine?"

"Yes," Sherlock said. "And one in the pipe for eleven rounds at your fingertips."

Rachael tuned them out. She looked hungrily at the gun now in Agent Savich's hand. She'd wanted to steal it the moment she'd seen Dr. Post unclip it from Jack's belt, but now it was too late. She couldn't figure out why she hadn't noticed it earlier, felt it, for heaven's sake, when she was walking beside him, supporting his weight. It had been a rather hectic morning. She didn't need a gun. All she needed to do was to keep her head. These agents had no idea who she was, where she lived, what she was doing when she'd come across Jack, and she had no intention of telling them anything. She had to remain anonymous, she had to remain dead. At least the two agents were focused on Jack.

But she didn't like the way Agent Savich had looked at her, like he knew she was lying but wasn't going to call her on it, and why should he? She wasn't his concern, not any of their concern. As soon as she got her fuel pump replaced, she'd be out of Parlow and hiding in Slipper Hollow, deep in the forests lacing the rolling Kentucky hills that stretched out like an accordion.

Time to take charge, time to get moving. She smiled at the two agents and said brightly, "Well, since you're here, I'll be off. I have to get my car fixed. Then I've got places to go, deadlines to meet. Like I said, I don't live here—Parlow, is it?—my car had just broken down when I saw Jack land the plane in Cudlow Valley. It's not been particularly fun, but at least it turned out okay."

Let's hear it for a gigantic dose of overkill—keep your mouth shut.

Sherlock cocked her head, but didn't say anything.

Nurse Harmon stuck her head in the door. "Dr. Post, we've got patients piling up out here, and Dr. Reimer called. Her little boy is throwing up and she doesn't know when she's going to make it in. Jimmy Bunt hurt his leg falling off his daddy's tractor, looks broken. He's making a racket, disturbing Mrs. Mason, who's telling everyone she's about to go into labor, although she shouldn't, not for another three weeks."

Dr. Post was out the door, saying over his shoulder, "I'll be retiring in twenty years."

Sherlock saw Rachael take one more long look at Jack, frown at a clump of bloody hair. She watched her grab the washcloth and begin carefully wiping away the blood. Well, she had saved him, it made sense she'd care enough to clean him up.

Rachael was a name Sherlock had always liked, but Abercrombie? As in Fitch's partner? Hmmm. She saw a faint line of freckles marching across Rachael's nose. That beautiful hair of hers, all long and smooth with streaky highlights, very nicely done, and that clever braid on the side. She'd have to ask Dillon what he thought of the braid. As for Rachael's eyes, they were dark blue and—what? Afraid. Yes, she was afraid, and her chewed nails took away any doubt. But afraid of what? Of them because they were cops? Was she running from an abusive husband? Sherlock knew their plates were full, but still, this woman had saved Jack. Whatever was wrong, she was ready and willing to help her.

She said to Rachael, "Do you know Jack's been injured only once before this? He was stabbed in the side by a crazed heroin addict. Amazing, really, since he spent four years in the FBI's Elite Crime Unit. He's already faced more horrific situations than most agents do in a lifetime. He burned out, no wonder, but instead of leaving the FBI to go practice law, Dillon talked him into transferring to his unit, the CAU—the Criminal Apprehension Unit."

"Ah, well, that's very interesting," Rachael said, and tossed the washcloth back into the sink, her eyes now on the door. She gave them a big smile. "It was a pleasure to meet both of you. I'm off now, good-bye," and she started walking around them.

Sherlock lightly laid her hand on Rachael's arm. "Jack's a very good agent and a very good man." Rachael was wearing a soft beige cashmere V-necked sweater with a white oxford blouse beneath it, very expensive, Sherlock thought. The boots she was wearing looked so soft you could butter toast with them. But she looked strung out. Sherlock smiled.

Rachael looked down at Sherlock's hand, her long fingers, buffed nails, the wedding band. "Yes, I can imagine Jack is very good at what he does."

"Before you handle car repairs, we'd really appreciate it if you would tell us exactly what happened the moment you saw the plane, all right?"

Rachael was so close to the door she could touch the knob. She realized she was cold and wondered if she'd ever see her leather jacket again since she'd covered Dr. MacLean with it.

Savich said pleasantly, "We would really appreciate it, Rachael. Since Jack will be asleep for a while, why don't I hang around and speak to the sheriff when he gets here? I also need to check that Dr. MacLean is all right. Then I'll arrange to have your car towed to a mechanic here in Parlow while you and Sherlock have some coffee and something to eat. You must be hungry."

"Would you look at that," Sherlock said, eyeing her own watch. "It's getting late. Come along, Rachael. I, for one, am starving. Dillon, we'll see you at that café across the street when you've got everything wrapped up." Sherlock turned to Rachael, smiling all the while. "I'm sorry, but I missed your last name."

"Abercrombie," Rachael said, voice stony.

"A nice name, very English, very retail," said Sherlock, thinking, *You are a really rotten liar.* "Let's go have some scrambled eggs."

She was trapped, very neatly. She looked back at Agent Crowne's still face. With all the black smoke and blood cleaned off, she saw a good-looking face with an olive complexion, all strong lines and good bones, stubborn bones, she'd bet, and an indentation in his chin. He'd been in the FBI Elite Crime Unit? She didn't know exactly what they did, but it sounded scary. He'd nearly been killed by a drug addict? Was this Dr. MacLean a criminal he was flying back to Washington? Or a friend who was in trouble? She didn't want to know, didn't want to get involved. She wanted the time and privacy to enjoy her death. The last thing she needed was more complications.

Agent Sherlock was still smiling at her. Well, no choice. She said to Agent Savich, "Would you mind bringing my duffel with you to the café?"

"My pleasure," Savich said.

"Thank you, Agent Savich," Rachael

said, as she fell into step beside Sherlock and left Dr. Post's clinic, the half-dozen people in the waiting room staring at them, some with curiosity, some with hostility since they'd had to wait so long.

Savich stayed with Jack awhile longer, watching him breathe, checking his pulse to reassure himself. He'd stepped back toward the waiting room door when a slender straight-backed man in his mid-forties came through, wearing bib overalls, a long-sleeved bright red flannel shirt, a holstered .38 strapped to the wide belt around his waist. Savich didn't sigh at this example of local law enforcement, but he wanted to. He knew this was very likely going to be a chore.

SEVEN

I'm Sheriff Hollyfield," the man said, and stuck out a slender hand hardened with calluses. Savich shook it, introduced himself, showed him his creds.

"A pleasure, Agent Savich. Sorry I'm late. That dratted septic tank of Mrs. Judd's busted again. The first time, that damned dog of hers fell in and we had to pull him out. Come along outside, we can talk more privately."

"Maybe you could send a tow truck out to the crash site to fetch Rachael's car?"

"I've got a tow on my truck. Let's go. We can talk on the way."

Savich nodded and followed the bib overalls out the door.

The day was warming up nicely, the sun bright in the morning sky. "I appreciate your coming over, Sheriff," Savich said as he climbed into the passenger side of a big white Chevy Silverado.

A pale eyebrow shot up nearly to his hairline. "This is the last place I'd expect the FBI to come visit. I heard from Benny—one of the paramedics who met the mede-vac helicopter at the crash site—he told me the guy was in pretty bad shape. What's going on, Agent Savich?"

"I'll be happy to tell you when my agent who was flying the man to Washington wakes up. He's suffering a concussion and lacerations on his leg."

"What happened?"

"Agent Crowne crash-landed, managed to walk away, more or less. That's all I know at present, Sheriff, I'm sorry. We haven't gotten the status on the other man yet."

"You wouldn't be holding back on a local cop, now would you?"

"I might, but the fact is, I don't know how or why the plane came down."

"Very well. I'll tell you, Agent Crowne must have had an angel sitting on his shoulder since Cudlow Valley's the only flat stretch of land for miles around. Even our two-lane road is all twists, impossible to land on it. If he'd crashed in the mountains, it would have been the end of him and his friend.

"Incidentally, I'm a detective from Boston PD, so you can hang up thinking I'm a backwoods hick who doesn't know his butt from his pinkie finger."

Savich had planned to politely shuffle aside this sheriff named Dougie who tended septic tanks wearing his .38 over bib overalls. Time to reevaluate. He said, "I'll bet worrying about septic tanks wasn't in your job description in the BPD. How long have you been down here in Kentucky?"

"About ten years, sheriff of Parlow for nine. My wife was born here, missed it, so we moved here. You're real smooth, Agent Savich. You don't want to tell me a blessed thing, I get that. You thought you'd get away with a nice courtesy call, blow me off, and go about your fed business. But I am the sheriff, I'm not stupid, and, praise be, I'm not the stereotypical tobacco-spitting jughead who runs a still in his backyard." Then he looked down at himself and laughed. "Regardless of the picture I'm currently presenting, you might discover I've got a good brain, and it's at your service since we had a plane come down in suspicious circumstances in my jurisdiction. You don't want to come clean with me—well then, maybe I'll just have to do some checking on this myself. Who's the guy in Franklin County Hospital?"

Savich saw clearly now that this man not only had a good brain, he also wouldn't stop, he'd do exactly what he said, he'd check into this himself. Well, all right, he also knew the terrain, both people and geography. Savich gave Dougie Hollyfield a long look. He said, "I like the .38 over the overalls, nice touch."

Dougie Hollyfield grinned. "My wife was laughing too hard to tell me what she thought. Now, you going to level with me? Let me do my pitiful best to help you?"

"Yes," Savich said, "I think I am. The man in Franklin County Hospital is Dr. Timothy MacLean, originally from Lexington, Kentucky. His family owns the MacLean racing stables; perhaps you've heard of them."

Sheriff Hollyfield nodded.

"His family knows Agent Crowne and his family, and so they asked for his help, told him Dr. MacLean believed someone was trying to murder him in Washington, where he's a psychiatrist to some big-name patients. MacLean's wife got him to come back to Lexington, to his family. There was another attempt on his life, so Agent Crowne flew to Lexington to fetch him back to Washington for protection, and to get to the bottom of this."

A pale brow shot up, fingers hooked the wide belt over the bib overalls. "You gave me a lot more than I thought you would. Let me remark that the FBI doesn't do things like fly planes to fetch a non-criminal citizen back to Washington, Agent Savich."

Savich said, "Since Agent Crowne knows the family, it was personal."

Sheriff Hollyfield said, "Why don't you add that the main reason the feds are in this is because some very big, high-profile names are involved? What did this Dr. MacLean do to really piss off one of his high-roller patients?"

"Now that I can't tell you."

"All right, I'll buy that for the moment. So we keep things even here, Agent Savich, let me tell you Dot—she's Parlow's other paramedic—told me about the downed search-and-rescue plane. She figured the pilot was from a law enforcement agency since they're the ones who usually use those planes. She said the pilot was good, bringing the plane down in the valley. She should know—Dot's a pilot herself, as well as a paramedic. She wondered why Agent Crowne was flying it since she hadn't heard about any accidents."

"I believe it was the only plane available."

"So after they medevaced Dr. MacLean out, Dot examined the plane."

Savich waited. He knew there wasn't much left after it had exploded on the ground. He also knew he wasn't going to like what the sheriff was about to tell him.

"Dot didn't have the time or the expertise to do a thorough check, but from the look of what was left of the fuselage, it looked to her like the luggage compartment was blown outward by some sort of explosion, maybe a bomb. Seems like it didn't work too well, since the plane wasn't blown out of the sky. So, I'd appreciate it, Agent Savich, if you don't try to pawn off the crash on some sort of a malfunction." Sheriff Hollyfield was rocking back and forth on his toes. He was wearing galoshes, Savich saw, though very clean, thankfully, as if they'd been hosed down.

"Yes," Savich said, "that's what Agent Crowne thinks. We've got an expert coming to verify. If you wouldn't mind keeping a deputy at the crash site to protect it until our people arrive."

Sheriff Hollyfield nodded. "All right, then. You'll keep me in the loop, Agent Savich?"

Savich nodded. You never knew when you were going to find good law enforcement, he thought as he shook the sheriff's hand, thankfully as clean as his galoshes.

Savich looked over the scattered wreckage while Sheriff Hollyfield hooked up the tow to Rachael's Charger. "Hard to imagine surviving that," Sheriff Hollyfield said, straightening to look out over Cudlow Valley, his hand over his eyes to shade against the strong morning sun.

"Believe me, we are very grateful."

Before the sheriff dropped him and Rachael's duffel off at Monk's Café, Savich said, "Could I come to your office a bit later, Sheriff, and use your landline to call the Franklin County Hospital? See how Dr. MacLean is doing?"

Sheriff Hollyfield nodded.

First Savich wanted to speak to Sherlock, see what she was doing with Rachael Abercrombie. He tried his cell again, but couldn't get a signal. Mix mountains with the boondocks, and technology didn't mean squat.

Monk's Café was on Old Squaw Lane, a small skinny white building with an apartment on the second floor, sandwiched between May's Cleaners and Clyde's 24/7. It was kitty-corner from the Parlow Clinic on Rosy Bill Avenue.

Savich set Rachael's duffel next to her on the seat.

"Thank you, Agent Savich. Where did you have my car towed?"

"We'll talk about that in a moment." Savich picked up a menu. "What's good?"

A waitress with impossibly ink-black hair sprayed up in a cone walked briskly to their table, her bright yellow high-top sneakers thumping on the worn linoleum, wearing a huge apron over jeans and a man's white dress shirt.

She stopped, looked him over, gave him a big smile showing teeth as white as her dress shirt. "Well now, Deliah—she's my sister, the nurse at the clinic—she called me about the federal agents being here, one of them bloody and nearly dead in an examining room. But that isn't you, thank the good Lord." She paused a moment, tapped her pencil on her chin, and eyed him. "Aren't you ever a hottie, that's what Deliah said. She didn't know about the other one 'cause he was in such bad shape. You're all dangerous-looking, not a single soft edge on you. I'll bet you're a real bad boy. Of course, that's what makes the women perk up when you're around— even my sister, who never even noticed her own husband before he passed. Just look at you—two pretty girls here, ready and waiting."

Sherlock snorted. Suzette, the waitress, ignored her.

Suzette was old enough to be his mother, Savich thought, and gave her a big smile. "Nah, I'm only dangerous when

I don't get my Cheerios for breakfast. May I please have some very hot tea ... Suzette?"

"You can call me Suz," she said, licking the tip of her pencil before writing down the order. "We only got tea bags, that all right?"

Savich nodded. He could already see the tea bag floating in the lukewarm water.

"I know it's still early, but Tony just took his meatloaf out of the oven. Or, if you're into healthy eats, I've got some fish sticks, nice and deep-fried."

Savich ended up with scrambled eggs and wheat toast with some gooseberry jam Suz promised was the greatest. She nodded at Sherlock and Rachael. "Your two pretty ladies sure thought so."

He looked up to see Rachael grinning at him. "Something tells me you don't eat many deep-fried fish sticks, Agent Savich."

"No, but our kid would eat them every day if we let him, between tacos and hot dogs."

Rachael's eyes flicked over them. "What's your kid's name again?"

"Sean's our boy, big into computer games and football, wants to help the Redskins build a dynasty, though he doesn't really know what that means."

"Married FBI agents. I never imagined such a thing, and Sherlock tells me you work together."

Savich nodded.

Sherlock turned to him. "When you came in, Dillon, Rachael was refusing to tell me what's going on with her. You'd think what with sharing a lovely brunch that I offered to pay for, she'd have a bit more trust in me, would't you?"

"It's tough to trust someone, Sherlock," he said slowly, "when you're scared to your toes. I'll tell you one thing, though, we can't let her leave because she's clearly a material witness."

Sherlock looked straight at Rachael. "Who's to say she wasn't more directly involved in bringing down Jack's plane? You know, the spotter on the ground?"

Rachael banged her fist on the table, making her spoon jump. How could they know so quickly that she was in trouble? It wasn't fair. She was an idiot, dead for only two and a half days. If she wasn't more careful, she wouldn't make being dead to the end of the week. "What did you say? A material witness? I know more about the plane crash? Listen, you can't hold me, I was only an innocent bystander, you can't—"

Sherlock leaned forward to touch her ring finger. "Maybe you're running away from your husband?"

Husband? She choked down a hysterical laugh and felt panic shoot through her. She grabbed her purse and duffel bag, slithered out of the booth, and was out of the café in under five seconds.

Suz, carrying Savich's plate, the scrambled eggs steaming, stopped to stare after Rachael. "Isn't this par for the course—a sexy guy with two girls—I'll just bet the little redhead here threatened to whomp the blonde with that cute braid, right?"

"You're very observant, Suz," Savich said.

Sherlock rolled her eyes, tossed her napkin down over the one cold bacon strip left on her plate, and headed after Rachael.

"At least if there's a catfight, it'll be in the street and not in here. Tony would hate that, remind him too much of his mother-in-law."

EIGHT

Sherlock caught up with Rachael at Bobo-link's Bakery on the corner of Old Squaw Lane, leaning against the display window, her old duffel beside her, staring down at her scuffed boots.

Sherlock lightly touched her shoulder. Rachael didn't move. "You know," Sherlock said, "when things get tough, it doesn't mean you have to deal with everything alone. I'm a fed. I do tough really well. Dillon and Jack do tough well, too. That means it's your lucky day since I figure we all owe you."

Rachael said, "I don't need tough, I don't

need help. All I need is to have my car fixed so I can leave. I've got to go . . . There are people expecting me. I want Agent Savich to tell me where he had my car towed."

Sherlock smiled. "Well then, let's go back to the café and ask him."

"I couldn't get away from you, could I? Maybe coldcock you?"

"Probably not. Dillon pulls his moves on females. I don't."

"Since I don't have any transportation, I don't have much choice but to go back with you." She could walk to Slipper Hollow if she had to, but it'd be stupid not to have a means of escape—just in case. She prayed Agent Savich hadn't cleaned off the license plate. He could run the plate and find out exactly who she was, probably in under a minute. She was worrying herself nuts over this when Sherlock asked, "Where were you headed, Rachael, when your car broke down?"

"Cleveland," Rachael said brightly. "All the way to Cleveland."

Sherlock thought, *Another big whopping lie.*

Monk's Café was filling up with the early

lunch crowd. Conversation stopped dead when they walked in. Sherlock had no doubt the gossip winds had blown directly into the café when the federal agents had arrived.

When they sat down opposite him, Savich said, "I spoke to Dr. Hallick at Franklin County Hospital. He said Dr. MacLean's still not conscious. They have more tests to run before they can give a halfway decent prognosis. I asked Sheriff Hollyfield to send a couple of deputies to guard Dr. MacLean until federal agents arrive."

Rachael raised her head at that. She wanted to pin him immediately, ask him where her damned car was, but what came out of her mouth was, "Jack—Agent Crowne—said something about a bomb, then he clammed up."

"Could be. An expert will be arriving sometime today to see what brought down the plane. If it was a bomb, he'll be able to tell us why the Cessna didn't explode into a fireball when it detonated, not that it should have mattered, given the terrain."

"Why would someone want to kill this Dr. MacLean?"

Why not? Sherlock thought. It wasn't a state secret. After all, trust was a two-way street. "Well, let me just say that Dr. Timothy MacLean, psychiatrist, has lots of very high-profile people scared of what he might say about them."

"You mean, he was breaking patient confidentiality? A shrink?"

"So it seems," said Savich.

Rachael sat forward. "Agent Savich, truly, it's been a pleasure to meet you and Agent Sherlock, but I must leave. Please tell me where you had my car towed."

"I'll take you over to the garage when we're done here. But the thing is, Rachael, the way I'm figuring it is that we need you. You're the only witness to Jack's forced landing. You saw everything. You'll remember more details, trust me. Are you willing to stay with us for a while?"

Rachael looked from her duffel bag to the two agents. For the time being, until her bloody car was repaired, she was stuck in Parlow, and all she could do was pray that no one recognized her. Secrets never stayed secrets, even in the boondocks. At least, she thought, she would be safe with a pack of FBI agents. "I'd planned on getting to where I was going by now. I don't have much time left, or money."

"Where do you need to go?"

"Like I told Agent Sherlock, I was driving to Cleveland, a job interview, family, you know the deal."

Savich thought, Yeah right, and said easily, "A day or two then, if that's all right with you. Now, Suz tells me there's a fine B&B over on Canvasback Lane. The FBI will pick up the tab."

As Suzette toted up their bill, Sherlock asked, "What's with all the strange street names in Parlow?"

Rachael opened her mouth, then snapped it shut. This was, after all, her first time in Parlow.

Suzette said, "Horace Bench, the rich guy who founded the town back in the thirties, he bred and raised ducks—hookbills, rouens, runners, calls—the calls are real small, I'm told, like toy ducks. He figured not many folks would recognize those names, so he threw in some common ones, as well, like canvasback, rosy bill, old squaw. He himself lived on Runners Road, and his daughter, whom he didn't like so it's said, lived on Old Hooknose Lane."

Sherlock's eyebrow went up. "Hooknose? I thought the duck was called a Hookbill."

"Yep, that's right," said Suz, and grinned.

"Where'd the name Parlow come from?" Sherlock asked.

"Parlow was an Indian chief back in the eighteenth century who sought out any settlers he could find to celebrate Thanksgiving with him and his people every year. He always brought trout for the feast. Isn't that a kick?"

"And where is the sheriff's office?" Savich asked.

"Oh, that's on the main drag, First Street, one block over. Sheriff Hollyfield, now he's so honest you could put your money under *his* mattress. Smart, too."

"Duck names," Sherlock said as they walked out of Monk's Café, Savich carrying Rachael's duffel bag. "It always amazes me what strikes people's fancy."

The three of them were checked in by the manager, Mrs. Flint, thankfully not a longtime native who could recognize Rachael. She told them Greeb's Pond was the best of Parlow's upscale lodgings. It was also the name of the current owner's grandfather's favorite duck.

They found their rooms decorated with a duck motif, from the wallpaper, to the hooked rugs on the floor, to the bedspread, to three small stuffed duck heads on the walls. "The only one I recognize is the mallard," Sherlock said, shaking her head. "Imagine stuffing a duck's head. And look at that little tiny one—you think that's a toy duck, what's the name—a call? And what do you bet the alarm clock will start quacking to wake us up?"

Since Sherlock had no intention of letting Rachael out of her sight, the two of them went back to the Parlow Clinic, waded through half a dozen patients to the desk, where Sherlock flashed her FBI shield at a very young receptionist who had short spiky red hair tipped with black and was vigorously chewing gum. She waved them back to the small room where they'd left Jack sleeping. Sherlock stopped by the door and tried her cell again. No luck. When she walked into the room, Rachael was saying, "You look better, Agent Crowne, and that's a relief. We thought you'd still be out of it."

Jack smiled. The debilitating headache was only a dull throb now, what with Dr.

Post's magic pain meds. "I slept a good hour, and I was still out when this gum-chewing teenager came in to draw some blood—just like a hospital. I was thinking, Rachael," he continued, "that you need to stick around awhile, at least until after we get things squared away. What do you think?"

Rachael maintained a stony silence.

"Well now, moving right along. Sherlock, where's Savich?"

"Here he is," she said, and smiled as Dillon came into the examination room.

Savich said as he shook Jack's hand, "Well, lad, you're not looking so green around the gills anymore. How's the leg and head?"

"I'll live."

"And that's the best news."

"Please, Agent Savich, where is my car?"

Savich said, "They towed your car to the best and most honest mechanic in Parlow—you can't trust the others worth spit, so Mort, Sheriff Hollyfield's dispatcher, told me. Anyway, that excellent mechanic can't get to your car for a couple of days. He's really backed up."

"Yeah, right," Rachael said. "I'll bet you

terrified him down to his socks, threatened him if he didn't say that."

"I suppose that's possible," Sherlock said, and gave Rachael a sunny smile. "He can do anything."

"She likes to suck up to the boss sometimes," Savich said. "As I said, Parlow's got other mechanics, most attached to gas stations, but the sheriff strongly recommended against them. So did the dispatcher. These guys must know, Rachael."

"There's got to be another honest mechanic."

"Well, all right, there is one, but he's down with a bad back." She watched Agent Savich shrug, the jerk. He continued without pause to Jack. "Dr. MacLean's still out of it, so they don't know yet what's going on with him. They're calling his condition guarded.

"Tommy Jerkins should be here anytime to check out the plane. Okay, Sherlock, if you come with me, I've got more calls to make from Sheriff Hollyfield's office. I want to make sure, too, that his deputies have arrived at the hospital to do guard duty. You really are better, aren't you?" he asked Jack.

Jack said, "Well, I don't want to moan anymore, so that's something."

"Good. All right then, you can question Rachael, sift through more of her memories of the crash. Remember, Rachael, anything you might remember could be of great help. We'll see you guys a bit later."

What Savich had really meant was *keep Rachael close,* Jack thought. Once alone, he said, "You ready to tell me your last name?"

NINE

It's Abercrombie." Why had that ridiculous name popped into her head? "How's your leg?"

"It will heal, thank you for asking. I can't go to the gym for a week, then I've got to go easy for a while." Jack buttoned his shirt, then threw back the single sheet before realizing he was wearing only his boxer shorts. He quickly pulled the sheet back to his waist. "Since my head isn't going to explode, I'm ready to get up now. Dr. Post said it was okay as long as I don't attempt a marathon," and he smiled. "Would you hand me my pants, Rachael?

They're on the hook on the back of the door."

She handed him his dirty, ripped pants and left the room, saying over her shoulder, "You're going to look like the leftovers from a drug war."

"Nice image."

They left the Parlow Clinic with the nurse muttering under her breath about macho men with muscles in their heads, Jack clutching a prescription for pain pills in his hand.

She eyed the prescription and said, "First let's go to Peabody's Pharmacy."

"Nah, I don't really need any more pain meds right now."

"You will soon enough."

"No, I think—"

"Shut up, Jack." And so Jack shut up, cupped her elbow, as if afraid she'd bolt, knowing he couldn't catch her.

"I think Agent Savich got you a room at the B&B where we're all staying. If you're wondering, everything is ducks around here. I was thinking Old Squaw Lane over there was a tacky insult, but no, it's a duck."

"Well, of course it is," Jack said, aiming

her toward Peabody's Pharmacy. Once he had a bottle of Vicodin in his pocket, and one in his mouth, they walked to the sheriff's office at the top of First Street, next to the firehouse. "I wonder if the firefighters have lots of business—look at all these old wooden buildings."

"Hey, are you the pilot of what's left of the Cessna rescue plane?"

Jack smiled at the tall, fit fiftyish woman with cropped salt-and-pepper hair and a drill sergeant's voice. She stood right in front of them on the sidewalk by the big glass window of the sheriff's office. "Yes," he said, and raised an eyebrow.

"I'm Dot—Dorothy Malone—silly name my parents fastened on me, but my daddy loved her, the actress, you know. I spent a little time looking over your plane. I'm thinking bomb, but the sucker didn't do the trick, thank God."

"Actually," Rachael said, "thank God for Cudlow Valley."

Dot nodded. "That's for sure, but still, that must have been some flying you did."

"Thank you."

"Sheriff Hollyfield's assigned a deputy to guard the wreckage."

"Good thinking," Jack said, shook her hand, and opened the door to the sheriff's office. Jack knew Dot Malone was right. If the bomb had worked as expected, both he and Timothy would be memories. Fortunately, he'd had time to send the mayday and to spot Cudlow Valley stretching narrow and straight between that impossible mess of mountains.

There was no one at the front desk, so he and Rachael walked through a large room that held ten or so cubicles, three occupied by uniformed deputies who watched their every move. Jack nodded to each of the men, no women, and continued to follow the sound of Savich's voice to Sheriff Hollyfield's sparse office. Jack saw Savich on the phone through the open door. Rachael shoved Jack into a chair, eyed him. "Here I thought you were well enough to make this little trek, but you're not. You're hurting again. Stay put and don't you move. Give the pain med a chance to kick in."

"Nah, I'm—"

"Be quiet. What you really need to do is crawl into bed for a while and sleep. Lean your head back, close your eyes, and rest your mouth."

No sooner had Savich hung up than Tommy Jerkins poked his head in.

Things moved quickly. Savich and Sherlock and Sheriff Hollyfield went with Tommy out to the crash site. Even better, ten minutes later, after the blessed Vicodin was happily swimming in his bloodstream and Jack could see straight, he and Rachael walked over to Greeb's Pond, the finest lodging in Parlow.

Rachael held him up while Mrs. Flint checked him into the last available room.

Mrs. Flint said, "You're the federal agent whose plane was shot down and landed on the highway, right?"

"Close enough," Jack said.

Rachael helped him up the stairs to the second door on the right. It was a lovely room, with high ceilings and windows overlooking Canvasback Lane.

It could have been a closet for all he cared. "More ducks," Jack said as he eyed the duck border wallpaper and eased down onto the bed. "I feel fine now, Rachael. We can go out to the plane. Oh, man, this bed feels really nice and—"

Rachael pushed him onto his back. In under three seconds, he was out.

She poured a glass of water and left it and the bottle of pills on the nightstand next to his bed. She covered him with a duck-themed afghan and went back to her room.

When she left ten minutes later, she looked as good as she could with what she had in her duffel bag.

Mrs. Flint called to her before she could get through the front door. "Miss, are you a federal agent, too? I didn't get your last name."

"Abercrombie, Mrs. Flint. No, I'm not an agent. I'm happy to report that Agent Crowne is asleep. Ah, do you know where I can find Tip Top Overhaul?"

She walked straight to the car repair two blocks over on Long Neck Lane, set off by itself, the big lot in the back closed in by a high chain-link fence. Only one person was around, a youngish guy wearing a tatty T-shirt, jeans, and black sneakers, and he was sitting on a folding chair, back chair legs against the wall in the single garage bay, chewing gum and flipping through a tattered old *Playboy*.

Playboy. Now that was good, that was really quite hopeful, Rachael thought as she stepped over an ancient radiator and into the dim space. When he looked up, she nearly turned and ran. She recognized him straight off—Roy Bob Lancer. He'd been a senior when she was twelve, captain of the football team. He blinked up at her, and blessed be, there wasn't a hint of recognition in his eyes. It was obvious he didn't remember the skinny twelve-year-old with braces.

Rachael gave him a smile designed to curl his toes and churn up lust in his belly, and prayed to the tight sweater gods. "I wonder if you towed my car in, Mr. . . ."

He lunged to his feet. "Lancer, ma'am, it's Roy Bob Lancer. Ah, you're the Charger?"

"Yes, but I don't see it." She gave him another blinding smile.

"It's out back, ma'am, all safe and sound."

"Do call me Rachael. And I'll call you Roy Bob." Another toothy smile. "If I knew anything about fuel pumps, and indeed I don't, I'm going to need you to fix it or replace it for me," and she kept that delicious smile on her face, her shoulders back, breasts forward. "You're the expert, everyone says so. And you're honest, that's what the sheriff says, and the dispatcher. So, what do you think?"

"Well, ma'am, I haven't had a chance to look at it yet. I'm all backed up, you know?" Roy Bob quickly dropped the *Playboy* and toed it beneath an open toolbox. He looked back at the most beautiful girl he'd seen up close since Ellie had waltzed out on him nearly four months ago, off to the big city of Waynesboro where her cousins lived, she'd said, with a little wave. Rachael was giving him a helpless look that made him want to lay the world at her feet, but what could he do? Agent Savich was an FBI special agent, and it was Roy Bob's duty not—

"You know what, Roy Bob? In addition to paying for your services, I'd sure like to add my own personal thank you with a cup of coffee over at Monk's Café, or maybe even a drink somewhere—you know, a cozy little out-of-the-way place?"

He glowed, but then, he was shaking his head. "Oh yeah, well, no, shit—forgive my French—I'd sure like that, ma'am, you know, a beer, but I'm so dratted busy right now." He waved his hand around.

Yeah, right. Savich had indeed gotten to

him. It was time to find another mechanic. No, she would give it one more try.

"Listen, Roy Bob, I've got a super important deal I can't miss up in Cleveland. I've got to leave as soon as possible. Maybe you and I could work something out, maybe—"

A loud bang sliced through the air near her shoulder, ricocheted off a tire rim, and thudded into an oil can, spewing 10/40 in a fountain. Another bang, this one sharp and loud, gouged into the wall a foot over their heads.

TEN

Hey—what was that?"

Rachael grabbed Roy Bob's arm and pulled him down behind a stack of old tires. "It was a bullet. Stay down, someone's shooting at us."

"Nah, that can't be, I mean, who—"

Another two shots slammed into the wall behind their heads.

"Holy shit—pardon my Irish—you're right, but why? Who would do that?"

"I don't know." But of course she did. They'd discovered she wasn't dead. But how? "Roy Bob, you got a phone in your office?"

"Yeah, sure."

"Don't move."

She managed to look around the side of the tires through the glass into his small office, saw the black phone on his banged-up desk, the door not more than six feet away. Still, she pulled out her cell first, dialed 911.

No signal.

"Listen, Rachael—"

A bullet sank into an old car seat hooked to the wall beside his head. He ducked back down fast. "Oh man, what's this all about? You FBI, too, Rachael, and someone's after you?"

"Roy Bob, I've got to get to your phone."

"No, look, I'll go." He eased up enough to peer around the tires.

The next bullet struck a support column two feet from his head, spewing concrete shards and thick gritty dust. One spear of concrete sliced Roy Bob's upper arm, and he yelped.

"Stay down, Roy Bob. I don't suppose you have a gun?"

"Sure, my daddy's old Remington. It's propped up behind my desk against the wall, right under his favorite calendar. No, wait! I'll get it, I'll shoot this idiot's head off—"

He paled, grabbed his arm, and fell onto his side, gasping.

"Tell me it's loaded."

"Yeah, yeah, two bullets." No time, she thought, no time. Even if someone had heard the shots and called the sheriff— there just wasn't time. They'd both be long dead. The only reason they were still alive was because the shooter simply hadn't walked in and mowed them down. Why? Maybe he'd been warned she might have a gun with her. And she wondered again whether they'd checked to see the block of cement didn't have her attached to it at the bottom of Black Rock Lake. No matter, someone had seen her, simple as that. But how had they found her, and so quickly? Get a grip, they knew she was here and they wanted her dead. She had to hurry. "You stay here, Roy Bob. Keep pressure on your arm, and keep down. Don't give him a target."

Both of them would be slaughtered if she didn't do something fast. Before she could second-guess herself, Rachael crawled behind an ancient mop bucket, a stack of oil filters. Nearly there. She rolled through the open door into the office. A shot rang out, not a foot above her head, sending splinters flying out of the door frame. The shooter was firing from directly behind her, and that meant he was right in the middle of the bay opening. They were down to seconds. She felt rage shoulder aside fear. She rolled between the wall and Roy Bob's desk, came up to her knees, grabbed the Remington, identical to her uncle Gillette's that she'd learned on, and slammed down on her stomach onto the dirty linoleum as two more shots sprayed dust and clumps of Sheetrock over her head. Rachael jumped up, pumped it once, and fired toward the bay opening. She heard a man yell, curse.

Got him. She felt powerful, invincible in that moment. She shouted, "Drop that gun and step out where I can see you or I'll shoot your head off!"

She heard heavy running footsteps. She scrambled to her feet, ran to the bay opening, saw him rounding a corner, and fired again. She missed, but it was close. The footsteps faded into the distance. Rachael ran after the man, saw him get into a black Ford pickup and burn rubber onto the street. She started to run after him, but realized there weren't any more bullets in the Remington, and he might see her in the rearview and decide to stop and have another go at her. She lowered the rifle, a fierce smile on her face. She'd forgotten what it was like to feel strong and in control.

How had they found her so quickly?

"By gawd, ma'am, that was good, real good. You got the sumbitch—pardon my Italian—I saw a brief glimpse of him holding his sorry arm and running away as fast as he could."

"Call me Rachael," she said as she ran to Roy Bob's phone and dialed 911. The dispatcher Mort asked her to state her emergency. She nearly laughed. She sucked it in and asked for Agent Savich. He wasn't there . . . wait a minute, he and the sheriff just walked in.

"Hello? Savich here."

Rachael shouted into the phone, "A guy tried to kill us! Roy Bob's place, hurry!"

When Sheriff Hollyfield, Savich, and Sherlock came running, every deputy in Parlow racing behind them, she yelled,

"He's in a black Ford pickup—that way! The first three letters on his license plate are F-T-E!" She wanted to go with them, but the last thing they needed was to haul along a civilian with an empty Remington. It was hard, but she stood still and watched them take off after him.

Sheriff Hollyfield yelled, "I saw that wuss car you're driving. Take my Chevy, it'll get you anywhere," and he tossed the keys to Savich. He looked after them, and sighed. He turned to look at Roy Bob and Rachael. Roy Bob was holding his arm, his eyes nearly whirling in his head, not from pain but from excitement. And Rachael looked pretty pumped herself. Sheriff Hollyfield said, "Roy Bob, that was fine shooting. You said you shot him in the arm?"

"No," said Roy Bob, "it wasn't me."

The sheriff's left eyebrow arched as he looked at Rachael. "Sorry, that's my bib overalls talking. All right, you shot him. Tell me exactly what happened."

She laughed, couldn't help herself. "That was funny."

"Yeah, well." The sheriff was embarrassed he'd been sexist, and it calmed her, even made her smile a bit. She said, "Roy

Bob and I were discussing how speedily he could get my car fixed when a bullet whizzed by our heads. Roy Bob would have shot him, but he got hurt, as you can see. I crawled to his office, got the rifle, and shot the guy. Fact is, Sheriff, he could have run in and shot us both dead, but he didn't. Maybe he was afraid Roy Bob had a gun handy and so he waited and shot from the bay door."

"I didn't realize," Roy Bob said, still riding so high on adrenaline he couldn't hold still, didn't even pay any attention to the blood still dripping between his fingers and down his arm, "it was bullets. Then there was another shot and she pulled me down behind those Goodyears. The guy kept shooting, I got hit in the arm with a piece of concrete, and Rachael crawled into my office and got Daddy's Remington. Boy, she knows how to use a rifle, good as my grandpa, and she stood right up and fired, hit the bastard—pardon my Russian—her first shot. She fired again but he was moving fast so she missed." He paused for a moment, grinned real big. "Would you marry me, Rachael? I don't want Ellie, she can't shoot worth spit." He paused, looked down, and paled. "Oh, dude, I've got blood running down my arm."

Rachael tore the sleeve from Roy Bob's shirt and wrapped it around his arm. "It's nearly stopped bleeding, you'll be okay." She thought of her Charger and knew it was all over, she'd have to leave it here.

"And you, Miss Abercrombie? How're you doing?"

"I'm purely fine, just fine." She felt flushed with victory, lit up like a neon sign. "I got him, Sheriff, I got him."

"You shoot often with a rifle, Miss Abercrombie?"

"Not for a long time. It's nice that you don't seem to forget. It felt natural, you know what I mean?"

"Yes, I do. So you were raised around guns?"

"Where I was raised, everyone knew how to shoot and shoot well."

"I see. And where was that?"

Roy Bob burst out before she had to come up with a believable answer, "A Remington as old as my daddy, I haven't seen anybody so smooth with that sucker since Grandpappy died back before the turn of the new century." He beamed at

Rachael, not a single bit of macho irritation showing in his proud face. He added, "And would you look at how pretty she is, Sheriff. Can you imagine how good our kids would shoot and what they'd look like doing it?"

The sheriff wanted to laugh, but instead he turned a dark eye on Roy Bob. "So someone waltzes right in here and starts shooting. You gambling again, Roy Bob? You stupid enough to take on old Mr. Pratt after what he did to you last fall? You know he explodes like a firecracker."

Roy Bob drew himself up. "No, sir. I haven't gambled since Ellie walked out on me. I've been too depressed, just sitting home, beer and baseball my only pleasures."

The sheriff sighed. "All right then, Roy Bob, Deputy Glenda is going to help you over to the clinic."

"No, Sheriff, not Deputy Glenda, she's not too pleased with me right now. Besides, I ain't no wuss, I can get there under my own steam. Hey, Rachael, I'm thinking you look familiar."

"That's because I shoot well," she said, and poked him in his good arm.

The sheriff said, "Okay, Roy Bob, you go on over, see Dr. Post. As for you, Miss Abercrombie, I need you to come back to the office with me and we'll talk this all over, you can give me a formal statement. Hopefully Agent Savich and Sherlock will bring this fellow down."

"Roy Bob, about my car—"

"You gonna hurt my other arm if I don't fix your fuel pump right away, Rachael?"

Rachael pointed gun fingers at him. "I just might. Then you might think I look like your mother."

Roy Bob laughed, then moaned as he jerked his arm. "I'll get to it then."

But not in time. Now, how was she to get away from Sheriff Hollyfield?

The sheriff turned to see his youngest, greenest deputy come running into the bay.

Deputy Theodore Osgood, called Tooth because one of his front teeth was chipped half off, just turned twenty-one, was big, beefy, and panting. He wheezed out, "That guy in the black truck—he nearly hit old Mrs. Crump—missed her, but scared her so bad she fell into a hydrant. We're getting her over to the clinic."

Rachael wasn't listening. She was thinking, *He'll get away, monsters always get away.* Two and a half days since they'd tossed her into Black Rock Lake tied to a concrete block. Didn't matter how they knew she was here, they'd found her, and now things were critical. She had to get out of Parlow, now. She had to get to Slipper Hollow.

But how?

ELEVEN

The sheriff was right, Savich thought as he sped the powerful Chevy to Judge Hardesty's airfield. Bobby, their pilot, was sitting beneath a pine tree, puffing on a pipe, reading a Juan Cabrillo adventure.

He had them in the air in under five minutes.

Sherlock said into her headphones, "I bet he's going to head back to the main highway, Bobby. He needs traffic to get lost in, and he's not going to find it on this road."

Savich said, "Agreed. We're looking for a black Ford pickup, the first three letters of the license plate are F-T-E."

Bobby swung the helicopter in a tight circle and headed toward the junction of 72 and 75.

Sherlock said as she scanned the highway below, "He's also hurt, shot in the arm, so depending on how bad it is, he might drive erratically, maybe pass out, but there's no way he'd stop."

Bobby cruised at three hundred feet over the highway. Savich said, "Let's not go any lower yet. People have seen enough attack helicopters in movies. We don't want anyone to freak, cause an accident. Okay, traffic is getting heavier."

Five minutes later Sherlock said, "There—there he is. He just turned off 75 onto a parallel access road. He's in and out of sight, with all those trees canopying the road, and he's having to go real slow what with all the ruts."

Savich said, "You sure?"

"Yep, the license plate begins with F-T-E," Sherlock shouted.

"Continue on about five miles, Bobby, then bring us down. Sherlock, make sure he stays on the access road."

She grinned at him, gave him a thumbs-up.

The landscape was littered with dense clusters of oaks and pines, and rolling hills between higher peaks. About six miles up the road, Bobby brought them down not more than fifty feet from the access road. Savich and Sherlock jumped out of the helicopter, bent low, and ran toward the road.

Only seven minutes passed before they heard the Ford coming. SIGs drawn, they stood in the shadow of a trio of skinny pine trees.

When the truck was beside them, Savich fired three bullets into the front passenger-side tire and Sherlock blew out the back tire. When the truck swerved to a stop, Savich yelled, "Federal agents! Come on out now, easy!"

The driver's-side door opened slowly. A man yelled, "I'm coming out, don't shoot me!"

"Lock your hands behind your neck," Savich shouted. He couldn't see the man clearly, but he did see one hand go up to grasp his neck. That was okay, Rachael had shot him in the other arm. Then, so fast Savich barely had time to react, the man raised a pistol and fired off six fast rounds over the top of the hood. Savich fired back even as he hit the ground and rolled.

The man ducked behind the door, and Savich shoved a new magazine into his SIG and came up to his knees behind a big maple. He saw Sherlock out of the corner of his eye making her way around the back of the truck. She looked back once to see that he was all right, then crouched down and ran.

Keep his attention on me. Savich shouted, "All right, you've had your go at me. You missed. There'll be six cop cars here in about a minute. Do you want to die here? If so, then keep firing at me and I'll oblige you. If not, throw your gun onto the road so I can see it. Now!"

Aeons passed, perhaps ten seconds, before the man finally called out, "All right, I'm coming out. Don't shoot!"

Sherlock pressed her SIG against the back of his neck.

"Drop it now. Don't even twitch or you're a dead man."

The man jerked in surprise, then dropped the gun at her feet.

"Glad to see you're not a complete moron. Dillon, I've got him."

Savich came around the front of the truck, his SIG trained on the man's chest.

Sherlock pulled off the man's sunglasses.

They stared into the eyes of a man whose face was gray with pain. "Rachael got you good, didn't she?" Sherlock said.

He moved quickly, a small derringer in his hand, and grabbed Sherlock. But Savich was faster. He shot the man in the forearm of his gun hand.

The man screamed, the derringer went flying, and he dropped like a stone at Sherlock's feet. He wasn't unconscious, but his breathing was hard and strained. He was moaning, holding his forearm. He'd tied a dirty oil rag around his other arm. Savich picked up the derringer. "You were fast."

"But not fast enough," Sherlock said, and kicked him in the ribs.

"Bitch," the man whispered.

"Yeah, that's what all you losers say," Sherlock said and went down on her knees to handcuff his wrists in front of him. She gave him a handkerchief. "Here, put some pressure on your forearm. You okay, Dillon?"

"No problem." He wasn't about to tell

her his heart had dropped to his heels when the guy pulled out that derringer.

Sherlock said, "I can't wait to find out who this moron is. Hey, buddy, you got a name for us?"

He mumbled something, still enough anger and venom in him to hear in his words.

"I don't think that's anatomically possible," Sherlock said, and gave him another light kick with the toe of her boot.

Savich said, "Who trained you? You have been trained. You're for hire, right?"

The man didn't say anything, only moaned and pressed the handkerchief against his forearm. Savich dug into the man's pockets but only came up with half a pack of sugarless gum and a Swiss Army knife.

Sherlock said, "You were afraid we'd catch you so you tossed out your wallet, didn't you? Well, that's the only thing you got right today. I bet you stole this truck, too, didn't you? But you know, jerkface, I'll bet you've got priors, so you're in the system. We'll know all about you in no time at all."

Forty-five minutes later, the man was in

surgery at Franklin County Hospital, two floors down from where Dr. Timothy Mac-Lean lay in a coma.

Sherlock called Sheriff Hollyfield's office, spoke to Jack, told him to keep Rachael close. She and Savich met Dr. Hallick in Dr. MacLean's room.

Savich and Sherlock had never met Dr. Timothy MacLean, had only seen photos of him. Jack had spoken of his kindness, his wit, his extraordinary insights, his empathy. MacLean and Jack's dad were friends from way back, and the families had always known each other. MacLean had once played a mean game of tennis, and had one grandchild by his second daughter. They both looked down silently at his waxy gray face. With all the tubes that tethered him to life, they wondered if there was any way he could pull through. He looked withered, a decade older than his forty-nine years.

Dr. Hallick listened to Dr. MacLean's heart, took his pulse, then straightened. "We almost had to put him on a respirator when his breathing became erratic. Strange thing is, there is no obvious trauma to his brain on the MRI, except perhaps some slight edema. Bottom line, we don't know why Dr. MacLean isn't awake. The fact is, the brain is still something of a mystery to us.

"What we did notice was atrophy—shrinkage—of the front lobes of his brain. Your colleague Agent Crowne called me and helped us get in touch with his doctors at Duke University. Unfortunately for Dr. MacLean, they'd concluded he has frontal lobe dementia, even before this happened. It's a hell of a thing, a man as distinguished as Dr. MacLean, losing his mind so early."

Sherlock said, "Yes, we were aware of that, Doctor. Could Dr. MacLean's frontal lobe dementia be contributing to his not waking up?"

"Unlikely, but according to Dr. Kelly, our neurologist, there's very little experience with that question." He shrugged. "Nothing more to be done except to wait and see. He's got two broken ribs and a gash on his chest we've sutured and will need to keep an eye on."

As for their shooter, he was still in surgery. They'd taken his fingerprints before he'd gone in and they'd find out soon who he was. Neither Savich nor Sherlock had a doubt he was in the database.

When they walked out of Dr. MacLean's room, they saw Sheriff Hollyfield leaning against the opposite wall. He'd changed out of his bib overalls and into black slacks, a white shirt, a wool jacket, and boots. He was a slender man, fit, with a pleasant face and dark eyes that had the awareness and intensity shared by most cops. "What do they say about Dr. MacLean? Is he going to make it?"

"It's complicated," Savich said. "Hey, I miss your other duds."

"Yeah, that's what Jack said. Listen, Agent Savich, I do complicated real good. Why don't you call me Dougie?"

Savich looked at him. "I can't."

Sheriff Hollyfield grinned. "Yeah, I understand."

"But Dougie went real well with the bib overalls," Sherlock said.

"Yeah, yeah, why don't we have a cup of coffee in the cafeteria and you can tell me what's going on with this guy. Jack and Rachael are both okay, so don't worry about them. I had to leave them in Parlow since Jack still wasn't looking too hot. I got the impression, though, that he wasn't going to let her out of his sight. They went back to the B&B."

While Savich sipped his tea, the sheriff said, "Before I left Jack and Rachael to drive up here, Tommy Jerkins, your FBI expert, reported in. He found remnants of an explosive—Semtex, he thinks—but the detonator malfunctioned, didn't set off all the plastic explosive.

"After the wheels hit the ground, the fuel exploded the rest of the Semtex. Tommy said Jack is a very lucky man. Even without the bomb detonating, the Cessna was disabled enough to send him right into the mountains.

"Given how inaccessible the mountains are, even if the bomb had blown them out of the sky, the chances are Search and Rescue wouldn't have found enough of either of them or the wreckage to determine anything. It probably would have been deemed pilot error.

"Jack said he was going to miss that plane," the sheriff continued. "He told me she's gotten him out of a few tight spots. I told him a wreath might help."

Sherlock said, "The person behind this murder attempt will come after Dr. Mac-Lean again. This was his third try, no reason he'll stop now.

"Maybe he'll come after Jack, as well, if he assumes Dr. MacLean told Jack about a patient's illegal activities, maybe even where to find proof."

Savich said, "Our lab will examine what's left of the bomb and the Semtex, see if they can tell where it's from. Our people in Lexington are all over the private section of the airport, questioning everyone. Somebody had to see something."

Sheriff Hollyfield said, "Jack said Dr. Mac-Lean didn't tell him any specifics like that. And that's when Jack said he wasn't capable. I asked him how that was possible, and he said Dr. MacLean didn't remember."

Sheriff Hollyfield looked suddenly very tough. "Anyone going to explain this to me?"

Sharp and clean, Savich thought, that was Sheriff Hollyfield's brain. He looked over at Sherlock. She nodded. Savich said, "Dr. MacLean has an increasingly debilitating brain disorder called frontal lobe dementia. The prognosis for anyone who's unlucky enough to get it isn't good."

"Dementia? But this man isn't old."

"No, he's not," Sherlock said. "Frontal lobe dementia can strike middle-aged people."

"What are his symptoms?"

Savich said, "The disease reduces his inhibitions, makes him say and do uncharacteristic things—like telling the minister after church services that he's a sanctimonious prig, telling a woman she looks fat, attacking a guy for eyeing his wife—social gaffes like that. Sometimes he remembers saying these things, sometimes he doesn't. If he does remember, he tends to dismiss them, doesn't think there's anything wrong with saying them.

"As his disease has progressed, Dr. MacLean has started telling tales about his famous patients, even to his tennis partner. Privileged doctor/patient exchanges. Again, he doesn't necessarily remember what he's divulged, and if he does remember, he doesn't think it's any big deal.

"As you can imagine, Sheriff Hollyfield, this is not good since many of his patients are very famous and very powerful. And since he's in Washington, we're talking lots of politicians, some corporate bigwigs."

Sherlock said, "Dr. MacLean has a huge reputation, he's known for his bone-deep discretion before this disease struck him."

Sheriff Hollyfield said, frowning at a dustpan propped against the wall in the corner of the cafeteria, "Thank you for filling in the blanks. That makes it all very straightforward. Someone decided to take him out to protect himself."

Savich nodded. "Depending on what Dr. MacLean divulged, and to whom, it could ruin patients' reputations and careers, even send them to prison.

"One person we know for certain Dr. MacLean talked to was, as I already told you, his longtime tennis partner, Arthur Dolan, who died two Fridays ago, after driving off the road and over a cliff near Morristown, New Jersey. The case is still open, but the local cops are leaning toward an accident. The FBI began questioning MacLean's family and friends. He did indeed speak to several friends, revealed juicy tidbits. However, he didn't give out any patient names to those particular people."

Sherlock said, "But still, whoever is behind this was worried Arthur Dolan would spill out names sooner or later, so he or she killed him."

"A preemptive strike," said the sheriff, "and that bespeaks a powerful motive, doesn't it?"

"I'd say so," said Savich.

The sheriff said, "Did Dr. MacLean remember enough of what he'd said to his tennis partner to be frightened?"

Savich said, "No, but Dr. MacLean's wife Molly doesn't believe for a minute it was an accident. She knew, you see, what Timothy was doing, and was frantic. She called his family, in Lexington, told them what was going on. Then someone tried to run him down in Washington, near their house. They flew him back to Lexington, then traveled to Durham to get him diagnosed by a physician at Duke University. After an attempt on his life in Lexington, Mrs. MacLean called Jack to ask for help. The FBI cleared it, and Jack flew out to get him. Then this happened."

Sheriff Hollyfield said, "Is Dr. MacLean now on any medication? Something to control the symptoms?"

Sherlock said, "Unfortunately, there isn't

any treatment for this disease. It will continue to progress until he dies."

Sheriff Hollyfield's beeper went off. He looked down at the number, excused himself, and went off to find a hospital phone to use.

He was back in five minutes. "That was Jack. He said Rachael is threatening to go down to Roy Bob's and steal one of his cars. He said he's not really feeling up to chasing her down and tying her to a chair so he wants you guys to come back and talk her into telling us the truth."

Sheriff Hollyfield looked from one face to the other. "I don't think you guys are going to sleep for a good while yet. Let's go back to Parlow and have Rachael tell us why someone walked into Roy Bob's garage and tried to shoot her." He paused for a moment. "Why wouldn't she want to level with you? I mean, she's Jack's girlfriend, isn't she?"

TWELVE

Jack said to Sherlock as she walked into the sheriff's office, Savich and the sheriff following her, "I think she wants to hotwire a car. I've threatened to lock her in a cell, but I really don't want to since she saved my neck. I need reinforcements."

Savich said, "If she hotwires a car, that'd be okay, then we could arrest her."

Sheriff Hollyfield took the chair behind his desk, motioned for them to sit down. He looked at each of them, shaking his head. "I never knew the feds could be so much fun."

Rachael was wringing her hands. She

noticed it and wanted to kick herself. How had she fallen so low so quickly? She looked at the expectant faces surrounding her. "I don't know how to hotwire a car," she said.

Sheriff Hollyfield said, "I'm the sheriff of Parlow, Ms. Abercrombie. I would like you to tell me why this yahoo who is currently residing in the Franklin County Hospital tried to kill you."

Rachael knew anyone in this office could run her license plate, find out who she was in a flash. What with the shooting, she had no doubt that now they'd do it if she didn't level with them. Well, obviously Quincy and Laurel already knew she was alive, since they'd already tried to kill her again.

She supposed if she had to trust someone, it might as well be three FBI agents and a sheriff.

She nodded slowly, looking at each of them. "There's no rea-son to keep my mouth shut now. I don't know what you can do, but maybe you can help me. If there are FBI leaks, well, it doesn't matter now, does it? They know I'm not dead. I'm sort of like Dr. MacLean, I guess you could say. The people after me aren't about to stop until I am."

"Well then, Rachael Whatever Your Name Is, tell us everything," Jack said.

"Last Friday night when I got home I found a bottle of red wine on the kitchen table. To be honest here, I was depressed, tired, and I think I would have downed the whole bottle if I hadn't had a roaring headache. Lucky for me I only had one drink, because the wine was drugged.

"The effects of the drug were wearing off while they were carrying me out on a dock. There were two of them, one carrying me under my arms, the other, my feet. They hadn't tied my wrists together, simply tied my arms down to my sides. But they had tied my ankles together. I guess right before they threw me into the lake, they must have attached the rope to a block of concrete, though I don't remember that specifically.

"They threw me into the water as far as they could. When the block hit, it dragged me down to the bottom." Her voice started shaking, her whole body was shaking. "I'm sorry."

Sherlock stuck a cup of water in her hand. "Drink, take deep breaths."

Rachael drank. "I'm okay, sorry. I had the brains to keep quiet so they didn't realize I'd woken up. I sucked in a lot of air before going under, instinct, I guess. I didn't want to die. They obviously didn't know I'd been a big-time swimmer in college, and I had great breath control. I managed to get my arms free, then get my ankles untied and swim to the surface."

She heard Jack curse and looked at him. She didn't think she'd ever seen naked rage before, but now she did and she recognized it for what it was. It warmed her, gave her balance.

Savich said matter-of-factly, "You're quite amazing, Rachael, I hope you realize that. You didn't panic and drown. No, you got yourself free. You survived."

"I was terrified, truth be told, but I didn't want to die. I made it back up, yes, managed to clear the surface because I knew they'd still be standing on the dock, looking down for any sign that I was still alive, you know, bubbles. I swam underwater to the pilings and hid there. I heard them talking, but I couldn't tell you if they were male, female, or both. I heard them leave. I saw the taillights drive off into the distance. I walked to a little diner in Oranack, Maryland, and from there got a taxi home.

"I got out of there as fast as I could. I drove only at night, took two and a half days to get here because . . . Well, truth is I was scared. I wanted to get lost on the back roads. I wanted to know in my gut that it was over, that they believed me dead and weren't like some bogeyman ready to jump out and kill me.

"I was wrong. They found out—how, I don't know."

Sherlock said matter-of-factly, "Somone saw you. Did you see anybody at all when you arrived back at your house, or when you left?"

Rachael shook her head. "No, but I was focused on packing my stuff and getting out of there. You're right, Sherlock, that makes more sense than diving into the lake to see if the block and I were still together. Whatever happened, they found out I was still breathing and figured out where I was heading. They moved very fast."

She paused, looked at each of them now. "Do you believe me?"

"Oh yes," Sherlock said, "oh yes."

Savich said, "Would there be anyone who would report you missing?"

Rachael shook her head. "The man who tried to kill me in Roy Bob's garage, do you know who he is yet?"

Sherlock pulled a small notebook out of her jacket pocket, glanced at it and said, "Our shooter's name is Roderick Lloyd, thirty-nine years old, a supposed freelance journalist—har har—not married, lives in an apartment in Falls Church. He started his bad ways early—juvenile record for ag assaults, multiple car thefts, robbing a convenience store, you get the idea. His mother cut him loose at sixteen. She re-married and moved to Oregon, smart woman.

"It was the attempted murder of a DEA agent during a drug bust that finally nailed him. He spent a measly eight years in our fine facility outside Detroit—not enough, but the prosecutors cut him a deal, netted two bigger drug dealers.

"Mr. Maitland is getting a warrant as we speak and our people will go over his apartment with tweezers. Dillon has MAX checking on possible employers, property tax records, offshore accounts, whatever.

"The staff at Franklin County Hospital said when he came out of recovery, all he did was moan and demand a lawyer. So that was it.

"He'll leave the hospital in two or three days—and be accompanied by our people back to Washington. His photo should be coming through your fax, Sheriff, any minute."

Sheriff Hollyfield nodded. "Good work. For what it's worth, I checked on Roy Bob because of his gambling issues. Nothing there. Dr. Post stitched up his arm. He's okay."

Rachael said, "This man, Roderick Lloyd, I have no idea who he is. I don't know his name, I never saw him before in my life. For heaven's sake, sit down before you fall over, Jack. You should have stayed in bed, you idiot."

"Me? An idiot?"

"Yes, you. Your head's beginning to hammer again, I can tell. You need another pain pill." Jack wasn't overly surprised when Sherlock tapped his arm and handed him a cup of water, but he didn't want any more pain meds. They fuzzed his brain.

"Pay attention, Jack," Rachael said. "Pain isn't good for the healing process, so quit being so macho."

"That's right, Jack," Sherlock said, "down the hatch."

He kept his eyes on Rachael as he swallowed the pill. "You didn't want to tell us anything because you were so afraid this man, woman, whatever, would hear about your being alive and come after you again? Well, you kept quiet and they still found you. I agree with Sherlock. It makes more sense that someone saw you; probably one of your would-be killers was at your house or arrived as you were leaving."

"Or," Savich said, "there was something they wanted to get from the house, saw you, and probably freaked."

"Really, I didn't see anyone when I drove back to my house, not a soul. And I was in and out so fast."

Sheriff Hollyfield said, "They knew you were headed this way. You said you weren't from around here. Where do you live?"

"I lied. I did grow up here—well, not

right in town. They must have known about Parlow, Kentucky. But this wasn't my final destination. I was going to hide out in Slipper Hollow until I figured out how I could get them."

Sheriff Hollyfield sat back, crossed his arms over his chest. "Well now, even the folks who live here don't know much of anything about Slipper Hollow. I don't even know where it is exactly. I never had a call to go there."

"Slipper Hollow?" Savich's eyebrow went up.

"It's where I grew up. It's hidden, only my uncle Gillette lives there. I'd be safe there, with him, figure out what to do."

Jack perked up. "You want revenge, do you?"

"Oh yes. I want to nail them. I just have to figure out how. Now it's a different ball game again."

Savich said, "You keep referring to *them*. You know who tried to kill you?"

"Oh yes."

"Who?"

Rachael drew in a big breath, ready to shake her head. Then she grinned. "No more secrets on my part. I think it's the Abbotts."

"Abbotts?" Jack repeated, eyebrow up in question.

Sherlock said, "Are you referring to Senator John James Abbott of Maryland? Are you referring to the Abbott family?"

"Yes."

"Who are you, Rachael?" Jack asked, sitting forward in his chair.

"Well, the fact is, I'm a bastard."

They heard Mort the dispatcher hiccup a laugh from just outside the sheriff's door. Sheriff Hollyfield frowned toward the door, but didn't say anything.

Sherlock said, "And who is John James Abbott to you?"

"He's my father."

After a moment of stunned silence, Jack said, "I, for one, am glad it's not some Mafia don, that's just too clichéd. Or a wild-eyed terrorist, a *jihad* wouldn't make anybody's day. That would have made me wonder why Timothy and I couldn't have been saved by a local soccer mom. You're a senior senator's bastard daughter?"

"Yep, that's me. I didn't know anything

about my dad or who he was until about two months ago, when my mother finally told me."

Savich said, "And you're saying Senator Abbott's family is trying to kill you?"

THIRTEEN

Yes, that's exactly what I'm saying."

"Whoa," Sherlock said. "Let's back up a minute. Where's your mom?"

"She lives in Richmond with her husband and my half brother, Ben. Like I said, my uncle Gillette's the only one who lives in Slipper Hollow now. Actually, I was raised there, with Parlow the closest town, until I was twelve and my mom and I moved to Richmond."

Jack said, "Rachael, you're almost thirty years old! Why did your mom wait so long to tell you John James Abbott was your father? You said she only told you two months ago?"

"She said she wanted to wait until *his* father died—that's Carter Blaine Abbott—which he did finally, four months ago."

"*The* Carter Blaine Abbott?" Sheriff Hollyfield said, his jaw dropping. "That's right, I forgot Senator Abbott was his son."

Savich said slowly, never looking away from Rachael's face, "The old man was a legend. Word was he had ropes of power around the throats of many world leaders, both in business and in government. I think the president heaved a sigh of relief when the old robber baron finally died."

Sherlock nodded. "I read he ruled his family like he ruled his empire—you got out of line, he crushed you."

"He didn't crush Jimmy—my father."

"No, he didn't, did he? I wonder why?"

"Jimmy said his father actually came to believe his eldest son would make a fine president, but only if dear old dad—Carter Blaine Abbott—was still alive to tell him how to run things. Jimmy said that was the only time he could remember his father ever changing his mind about anything."

"Damn, Rachael," Jack said, "my hair's standing on end. You're really related to these people? Their blood runs in your veins?"

"Unfortunately, yes," Rachael said.

Sherlock said, "You said your mother wanted to wait to tell you until after the old man died. Why?"

"She told me she hated to admit it, but she was still afraid of the old bastard. She said that even though she knew intellectually all that was left of him was a moldering carcass, she would swear she could still sense him—a malevolence that gave her nightmares."

"Tell us what happened," Savich said.

Rachael stared at the big tough federal agent who looked like he ate nails for breakfast. All his attention was focused on her, and it was formidable. Then he leaned over, patted her hand. "Stop worrying. Everything will be all right." It broke her. She leaned against the wall, looked at each of them in turn, pausing a moment longer on Jack's face. He looked too pale, she thought. She said, "Needless to say, my mom was afraid of Carter Blaine Abbott. When he found out his eldest son—his ticket to immortality—was dating my mother, a small-town girl with no pedigree, no money, a backwoods hick, in his mind, he wasn't happy. He was big into bloodlines."

"What was your father doing here anyway?" Sherlock asked.

"My mom told me the local mill owner's son was one of Jimmy's good friends. That's when there was a mill here. Mr. Abbott swooped into town and took them both off to vacation in Spain. As you would expect, the mill owner's family didn't object to that."

Jack nodded. "All right. So your mom was pregnant. She never told your father?"

"No, she didn't tell anyone. Well, she had to tell Uncle Gillette, her brother. By this time, her folks, my grandparents, were both dead. She told me she was bitter, for a very long time, bitter and very angry. And scared. She was shocked when she got a letter from Carter Blaine Abbott some five months later, telling her he'd heard she was pregnant and there was no way he was going to let her blame it on his son, no way he was going to let her drag his family into it. If he ever heard a word out of her, if she ever tried to contact his son, he'd see that both she and her brat were taken care of. What did he mean by that?" Rachael shrugged. "Mom was sure he meant he would kill her and her baby. He enclosed a check for five thousand dollars." Rachael added, "Mom tore the check up, gave birth to me, and, as it turned out, I didn't look like either of them until I was a teenager. By the time I was eighteen, though, I was the spitting image of Senator John James Abbott, although no one ever seemed to notice the resemblance. I guess you wouldn't, if you didn't know the history. But I think that until two months after old man Abbott died, she was still afraid of him.

"So Jimmy never knew about me until I showed up on his office doorstep at the Capitol, a couple of weeks after my mom finally told me about him.

"I'll tell you, at first I didn't want to go. I guess I was angry at him, too, even though Mom swore he never knew about me. I remember way back when I was maybe five or so, I asked her about my father, if he died, if he ran out on us. She wouldn't tell me anything, but I saw her crying in her room, and so I never brought it up again.

"She convinced me to give him a chance. She didn't know, she said, what kind of reception I was going to get from him, but wasn't it worth a try?

"I agreed with her. It was time I met the man who sired me. I didn't have a clue where he lived and neither did she, so like I said, I went to his Senate office. He was coming back from lunch with his aide, Greg Nichols. He saw me standing there, staring at him. He did a classic double take, then he broke into this huge grin, called out my mom's name, Angela. He didn't wait for an answer, just rushed me into his office, past all his staff, past people waiting to see him.

"I can still see that smile of his, it was radiant. He grabbed my hands and began dancing me around his office. Then he hugged me until I thought my ribs would crack." Her voice shook and she ducked her head down. "He never voiced a single doubt that I was his daughter. Believe me, I never expected anything like that even though the resemblance between us is strong. It . . . it was wonderful."

Jack asked after a moment, "Senator Abbott has other kids, doesn't he?"

"Yep, I got two instant half sisters. Jimmy and his wife divorced about ten years ago. His ex-wife lives in Vail, Colorado, and both his daughters are married. I got the impression there wasn't much love lost between Jimmy and Jacqueline—that's his ex-wife. He never remarried, never wanted to, he told me. He said he sees his daughters twice a year, usually skiing somewhere, and spends Thanksgiving with his brother, Quincy, his sister, Laurel, and her husband, Stefanos Kostas, and their two boys at Kostas's house—ha, it's really a mansion—outside Hailstone, Maryland. There's a gatehouse, extensive grounds all enclosed behind a high stone wall, and a night guard. Jimmy said Thanksgiving is always very cordial but really pretty sad.

"I told him all about Slipper Hollow and Uncle Gillette and how we'd all lived there together, except for his stint in the first Gulf War, until I was twelve and we moved to Richmond.

"Jimmy had never heard of the hollow. I

guess my mom had been too embarrassed to tell him, thought Slipper Hollow was too hick for the likes of his fancy rich self. He'd always known, he told me, that she lived in or around Parlow, but she'd never offered to take him to her house.

"He wanted to know everything about Angela—my mom. But he didn't want to call her, didn't want to disrupt her life. I agreed with that. My stepfather's a great guy, but having a wealthy senator suddenly stick his nose in wouldn't be pleasant for him. And my mom realized this, of course, and told me she was fine seeing us reunite without her involved. Jimmy would have enjoyed Ben, my half brother, but there was never the chance."

Sherlock said, "So you think the people who tried to kill you are Quincy Abbott and Laurel Abbott Kostas?"

"That's right. I wouldn't be surprised if Laurel's husband Stefanos was involved, too."

Jack said, "Your father died in a car accident three weeks ago, right?"

"Yes," Rachael said, "he did."

Jack said, "Wasn't there drinking involved?"

Rachael's voice turned hard. "That's what everyone believes. The police said he'd been drinking and driving, alone, and he lost control of his car, but I know that isn't true. There's no way it was an accident.

"He was murdered. I knew that immediately. I remember standing in the huge foyer after all the police, the federal investigators, and the people from the state department left, and I thought about how I'd never really believed in evil, in something cold to the soul. I knew they'd killed Jimmy—there was no doubt about it in my mind. But I didn't have any proof, and that's why I ran after they tried to drown me, why I didn't go to the police. I guess after Jimmy died so violently, I was in shock, as well. I was trying to figure things out, but I didn't have time."

"So you're saying that Laurel Kostas and Quincy Abbott killed your father and are now trying to kill you," said Sheriff Hollyfield. "Truth is, Rachael, I'd want to get your head examined for a tale like that, but hey, look what's happened right here in Parlow. I'd have to agree, that sounds pretty evil. I'll bet you everyone in this room has close-up and personal experience with evil."

No one disagreed.

Sherlock said, "Dillon and I met your father at a charity benefit at the Bentley Gallery in Georgetown not too long ago. You weren't there. Neither of us even knew about you."

"I don't remem— Wait, yes, it was a last-minute deal. One of Jimmy's lady friends took me to New York to shop because he was throwing a party for me; he was going to introduce me to everyone, including handsome young men who would trample each other trying to get to me." She smiled, shrugged. "There was never any party. He was dead the next week."

Sherlock said, "Did you know your father was a friend of Dillon's boss, Jimmy Maitland? He was one of the pallbearers at his funeral. Mr. Maitland always called him John, as I recall, never Jimmy. Given they're both Jimmys, I suppose Mr. Maitland didn't want to deal with the name confusion."

"I didn't know that. I mean, I stood in a receiving line with all the other Abbotts, including my two half sisters, to greet all the people who came to his funeral. I don't remember a Mr. Maitland. But that day was such a blur."

"After his funeral," Savich said, "you simply dropped out of sight. The funeral was nearly three weeks ago. Why would they leave you alone for three weeks, then try to kill you? Why not kill you right away, in another accident? How do you explain that, Rachael?"

"Well, in truth, there wasn't time for me to be on the radar. Jimmy and I only had about six weeks together before his death." She paused, head down. Jack saw her twisting her fingers in her lap. Then she raised her face and said, voice composed, "They didn't have a chance to kill me because I left Washington the day after Jimmy's funeral. I just knew I'd be next. I didn't tell anyone where I was going, not even my mom. I got back to Jimmy's house last Tuesday. Well, now it's my house, since Jimmy left it to me. It only took them three days to act."

"Where did you go?" Jack asked.

"To Sicily, to a little town on the coast, not yet discovered by tourists. I hunkered down, I guess you'd say. I had a lot of thinking to do, but I knew I had to come back to

Washington, I had to deal with his estate and his family—and his murder—and so I came back nearly two weeks to the day after his funeral. I wasn't even back a week before they threw me into the lake."

Sherlock said, "Let's back up a bit. You think your father was murdered, but his death was ruled an accident. But there was a thorough investigation, everyone was convinced. Do you have any proof otherwise?"

"Not hands-on proof, no."

"Tell us what you have," Jack said.

"Okay. Two days after I came back, Jimmy's lawyer, Brady Cullifer, called. He was rather upset with me since I'd taken off without telling him and he hadn't known where to find me. There was Jimmy's new will, you see. Jimmy left me his house and split the rest of his estate among his three daughters. Mr. Cullifer told me he'd already notified Laurel Kostas and Quincy Abbott about what was in Jimmy's will, told them Jimmy hadn't left them anything. Oh yes, I forgot—Jimmy adopted me. It came through only days before his death, so I was legally his, surely a record, Mr. Cullifer told me."

Sherlock said, "Was your father's divorce messy?"

"You're thinking his ex-wife could have killed him? I don't think so. I met Jacqueline and their two daughters, my half sisters, Elaine and Carla, and their husbands at his funeral. They were all very kind to me, very civilized. Jacqueline was very distant, as if she were bored with all of it. His daughters were in shock, quiet, withdrawn, but it seemed to me they were thrilled to leave Washington, which they did the very next morning, and I left three hours after they did.

"I returned from Italy last Tuesday night. Friday night I drank a bit of the red wine that was evidently drugged. When I came back to the house later that night, the wine was gone."

Jack said, "Do you you think the lawyer, Brady Cullifer, was part of it too?"

"I thought he was for maybe ten seconds. But it just didn't make any sense. He'd been with Jimmy for years and years. He had no reason to hurt me. Laurel and Quincy put the drugged wine there, I know it."

Savich said, "Okay, let's get to the root.

You were telling us why you believe your father's sister and brother murdered him. Keep going, Rachael. Convince us."

"It's a long story, and it's not *my* story. Since it isn't about me, that's why I didn't say anything right after his death." She looked miserable. "I don't know, I just . . ."

"Too late for that," Jack said. "Come on, Rachael, spill it all. This is about your father, isn't it?"

She nodded.

"And a major disagreement with his siblings?"

She nodded again.

"You call your father Jimmy," Sherlock said, backing off a bit.

"Yes. I wasn't comfortable yet calling him Dad. Look, the rest of it, I simply don't know if . . ."

"Anything you tell us doesn't go out of this room," Jack said. "Everyone agrees?"

She looked at each of them as they nodded.

Still, it was difficult. To even think about what had happened was hard, but to speak about it, openly, she didn't know if she could. But, finally, she knew she had no choice. "All right, I have to trust someone, and you guys seem like my best bet. But it's got to remain a secret. You've agreed, right?"

They all nodded, Jack's head to the side, frowning at her. "What's the big secret, Rachael? Senator Abbott was a spy or something?"

"No, no, but . . . all right. If I can't trust you folks, then I might as well hang it up."

FOURTEEN

I told you that Jimmy overwhelmed me with his welcome, his generosity to me. He was open, he was loving, he wanted to hear every detail of every year of my life." She smiled at that. "But I began to notice that he would fall silent at odd moments, that he seemed disturbed and despondent about something. When I pressed him on it, he finally told me what he'd done. I believe he wanted to tell me, that I was like this miracle, and if he told me maybe he'd at least partly make up for this bad thing he'd done. And he was so desperately alone, so desperately afraid.

"About a year and a half ago, Jimmy was driving through Delancey Park on his way home. It was late, sunset, he'd had a couple of martinis with colleagues. He was talking on his cell, not really paying much attention. A little girl on a bicycle came pedaling in front of his car. He hit her, killed her. He panicked and drove away, called his senior aide, Greg Nichols, who came to him immediately.

"His aide—you need to understand about him. Greg is maybe in his late thirties. He's very smart—intuitive, I guess you'd say—and driven. His ambition was to see Jimmy in the White House. Jimmy trusted him, admired his brain, his drive, his *commitment.* Greg convinced Jimmy to keep it quiet, that if it got out he'd killed a child—accident or not—his career, his life, his family, would be ruined, he could even go to jail, convicted of vehicular homicide and leaving the scene of an accident.

"I'm not trying to excuse what he did, but Greg is the king of persuasion; he could convince the Pope to convert to Islam. Fact was, Greg himself would also be ruined if Jimmy confessed to killing the little girl. He'd be done in Washington, that's for sure, and so he worked very hard to convince Jimmy that the best thing, the smartest thing, the only logical thing, was to keep his mouth shut and simply leave the little girl right where she was. Bottom line, Jimmy told me, he wanted to be convinced, and so he was. And yes, he knew very well that Greg was being self-serving, but who cared? He was too concerned about his own future.

"He told me how hard he tried to excuse himself—you know, if the girl's parents had been with her, as they should have been, it wouldn't have happened. What kind of parents let their kid ride alone in a public park anyway? There were predators in public parks, were her parents idiots? But he said no matter how hard he tried to make excuses for himself, it never worked.

"He spoke of the personal consequences—unrelenting guilt, recurring nightmares of his hitting the little girl, over and over, he said, how he found himself disengaged more and more from Capitol Hill, from his colleagues, his family, his staff, that even therapy hadn't helped. He'd lived with this for so long, it seemed like forever, it was eating him up inside. He couldn't stand it any longer. He told me he was thinking about going to the police, telling them what he'd done, announcing it to the world. He wanted to know what I thought.

"I saw what a wreck he was, how what he'd done was debilitating him, but now that I had found him, I didn't want to lose him, to have him plunge himself into a scandal. But I could see what it was doing to him, and so I said he should do what he believed was right, that no matter what he did, I was behind him one hundred percent, and I would always be at his side. Let the world do its worst, I told him, I wasn't going anywhere. But it was up to him. His decision, his life."

Rachael paused for a moment, her eyes unfocused. She swallowed, said, "I can see so clearly that twisted smile he gave me. He said the shrink he'd been seeing had never spoken about confessing what he'd done; the shrink had only spoken of forgiving himself for an unfortunate mistake. *Unfortunate mistake,* he repeated, the little girl was nothing more than an *unfortunate mistake.*"

Sherlock's eyebrow shot up. "A shrink?"

"Yes, he went to a psychiatrist for maybe six months. Jimmy told me Greg hadn't believed it smart to see a local psychiatrist—too much chance for it to get out since there were probably three news sharks hanging around every doctor's office to see if any of the great and famous paid them a visit."

She took a deep breath, looked at all of them. "Jimmy finally decided to call a press conference. He was going to confess what he'd done, then go to the police. Only thing is, he didn't have the chance. He died."

Sherlock said, "Since you believe the Abbotts killed him, he must have told his sister and brother what he was going to do, right?"

"Yes, he told them."

"Did he call his ex-wife and his daughters?"

"I don't know. Maybe he did since the fallout would affect them. I'm sure he gave everyone close to him fair warning, probably begged for their understanding and forgiveness since they'd have to deal with the consequences. I believe his brother

Quincy told him to plant a tree in her memory, in Delancey Park, where he'd hit her."

Savich looked up from MAX's screen. "The little girl's name was Melissa Parks. Her case remains open. A hit-and-run."

"Anything else about her we should know?" Sherlock asked.

"A year ago, Melissa Parks's family received an envelope containing one hundred thousand dollars in untraceable small bills with a note that said only 'I'm sorry.' It revved up the investigation again, but since they couldn't trace the money, or the note, it once again went cold."

"Jimmy didn't tell me about that," Rachael said. "I remember a couple of days after he told me about the accident, I walked into his study and saw him staring at his phone. I knew he wanted to call Melissa's parents, call the police, simply end it all, right then. Unfortunately he waited a few more days, warned those who would take a hit, and then he was dead."

Sherlock said, "Rachael, you know for sure your father told his family and Greg Nichols, right?"

"Yes."

"Okay. I have to tell you, I have a hard time believing that his confession would enrage his family to such a degree that they'd kill him."

"There's more. The reason his death was declared an accident was because when the two patrolmen found Jimmy's Beemer at the bottom of a cliff, Jimmy was alone in the driver's seat. They said they could smell the alcohol on him. They said it was apparent he'd had too much to drink and lost control of his car, and hurtled down a steep embankment just off the Beltway, near Bethesda Navy Medical Center."

"Yes, I remember that," Sherlock said.

"Jimmy told me after he hit the little girl, he simply couldn't make himself get behind the wheel any longer. The fact is, he stopped driving. It was manageable because he had a car and driver available to him. Not only that, he hadn't had a drink since the night he killed the girl. That's what he told me, and I believed him."

"Then why didn't you tell the police the truth?" Jack asked.

"I couldn't," Rachael said. "It would have meant telling them why he'd stopped drinking and hadn't driven a car for the past eighteen months. I simply couldn't bring myself to do it. All of it would have come out. It would have destroyed his legacy." She drew a deep breath. "That was the main reason I took off for Sicily. I had to decide what to do. For two weeks I chewed it over every which way, and I came to a decision. I was coming back to Washington to tell the truth. Of course, I was going to discuss it with my mother, but I knew she would agree with me and it was what Jimmy would have done, what he was fully prepared to do. The least I could do for him was honor his wishes. After I nail Quincy and Laurel, I can and will do what Jimmy wanted to do. I will clear his conscience for him."

Sheriff Hollyfield was tapping a pen on his desk blotter. He said thoughtfully, "Your father's dead, so is his conscience, so is his guilt. I'm thinking like his aide did— why ruin Senator Abbott's name? Why ruin his memory? Why destroy what he stood for, what he was as a man for most of his lifetime? And that's what would happen. The sum of his life would be forgotten— he'd end up being remembered for killing a child in a park, and hiding it." He sat forward, his hands clasped.

"Rachael, do you want what happened in the final year and a half of your father's life to define him? That he go down in history as the rich guy who killed a little girl when he was drunk?"

Rachael jumped to her feet, began to pace the small office. "I've used the very same argument to myself, but I know he wouldn't! When I tell everyone how he'd planned to confess, surely they would see how moral he was, how ultimately honest."

Jack said very gently, "I've known since I was twenty years old that the human mind doesn't work like that. Sheriff Hollyfield is right—your father would be cut to pieces, all the good he ever did in his private life, in his political life, distorted, questioned, erased. As for you, there would be no recognition that you were simply following through on his wishes. You'd be the bastard daughter who destroyed her father's name."

"I know you're trying to help, but again, I've thought about all this, and it doesn't matter what anybody thinks or says about me. I think you're wrong, Jack, you have to be." She shook her head, then tucked her long hair behind her ears.

Savich looked up from MAX. "Did you tell anyone you were going to make your father's confession for him since you've been back?"

"I told Mr. Cullifer, Jimmy's lawyer. I'd have thought Jimmy would have filled him in on his plans, but he hadn't. He was pretty emotionless about it, told me he'd suspected something was very wrong with Jimmy, asked if I had any proof, like fingerprints or witnesses, which of course I didn't. He then said if I made Jimmy's confession for him, I would find myself in a snake pit—people vilifying me, accusing me of lying be-cause he left my mother all those years ago, that I was doing it to get back at him, and he wasn't even here to defend himself. I'd thought about most of those things, but I'll tell you, the way he spoke, the utter certainty in his voice, I was nearly ready to flip-flop on my decision. Then I found Jimmy's journal. It was filled with his misery, his guilt, his hatred of himself for what he'd done, and that's what made me decide to go ahead, no matter the fallout. I felt I owed it to him.

"I told Greg Nichols. He heard me out, then said he wasn't about to help me destroy Senator Abbott's name and drag the rest of his family through the muck. Of course, he'd be pulled into the muck himself, maybe even do some time in jail, but neither of us mentioned that.

"I didn't want to talk to Laurel Kostas and Quincy Abbott since I believe to my toes they killed him, and why. I guess I felt deep down that they'd look at me the same way, as something to be kept silent, or like I was crazy or some sort of rodent who'd crawled into their beautiful, perfect lives."

Jack leaned forward, his hands clasped between his legs. "It's not difficult to connect the dots here. The Abbotts—their holdings and wealth are up there with the DuPonts, the Barringtons, the Jetty-Smiths. I can see they'd hate the scandal, the questions, the media probes about their family ethics, and all the rest. And a possible lawsuit by the little girl's family, of course. Sure, they might have lost some of their A-list status, but it would have blown over, as every scandal does. But I can't see them losing much of their money over it, and after all, their brother wasn't some loser schmuck; he was a United States senator.

"I'm sorry, Rachael, but I can't see one or all of them murdering him to keep him quiet. The motive isn't there."

Rachael said, "As an outsider, I saw them very clearly. I cannot tell you how very proud they are. Their sense of entitlement, their sense of worth, their arrogance—it's off the scale. They worship their name, their lineage, worshipped their father, the founder of the Abbott dynasty. Laurel Kostas's children attend the finest prep schools, and they'll attend the finest colleges, both of them destined for power, destined to marry into other prominent families. And Jimmy's two daughters attest to that. Both their husbands are from wealthy families as well.

"In their eyes, a scandal like this would ruin the family, and they wouldn't accept that. They would determine that the removal of this threat was not only justified, it was rational. That's why they killed Jimmy and have tried to kill me."

FIFTEEN

And then three days later, you ended up drugged and thrown into Black Rock Lake," Jack said.

"Yes."

Savich added, "But bottom line, Rachael, all you have in the way of proof that he was murdered is your belief that your father had given up both driving and drinking."

"If I'd managed to come up with any proof, I would have camped out at the gate of the White House while I called the *Washington Post.* I wouldn't have run like a rabbit after they tried to drown me. Not that it mattered. They found me fast enough."

Sherlock rose and stretched, nudged her husband's shoulder. "Well, boss, what now?"

Savich grabbed her hand, gave it a squeeze. "First, Rachael, I want you to write all this down: Senator Abbott's accidental killing of Melissa Parks, his death, your attempted murder—both times. Put in every detail you can think of. Do it fast. Make six copies. We'll take a couple. I'm thinking it might be best to simply go public now. That should stop any more attempts on your life."

She shook her head. "I'll write everything down, but I don't want to go public. Not just yet."

"What? You like being bait?" Jack said.

She replied, "I don't need your sarcasm, Agent Crowne. I'll tell you, when I climbed out of that lake, I saw everything very clearly. I agree that going public might stop them, but they'll get away with killing Jimmy, their own brother. I have to find proof, don't you see? I want to bring them down, and if it means my neck is out there, then so be it." She looked at each of them. "Maybe you can help me do this, maybe you can't. But it's my only goal at the moment. Then

I'm going public and telling the world exactly what kind of man Jimmy was. After all, only an honorable man would feel such devastation about accidentally killing a child.

"I know you're all concerned about the repercussions, but I firmly believe that people are forgiving.

"Now that I've spilled my guts to you, I'm going to get my car fixed, and I'm driving to Slipper Hollow. I've got lots of thinking to do, lots of planning, lots of writing things down, as Agent Savich wants."

Savich said, "Rachael, what is the state of your finances?"

She blinked. "I suppose I'm very rich, at least in theory, since Jimmy left me one-third of his estate. In actuality, what I have is some money in my duffel I pulled out of Jimmy's petty-cash box before I ran Friday night. I haven't counted it, but there's maybe a couple thousand. As to the disposition of the rest of his estate—I don't really know. I intended to call Mr. Cullifer next week, ask him what to do about it."

Savich typed something into MAX, then looked up. "I think it's a good idea you disappear into Slipper Hollow for a while.

Jack, can you escort her there, check everything out, make sure she's safe?"

"Hold on, Savich. What about Timothy? I've got—"

"He's still unconscious," Savich said. "We're moving him to Washington tomorrow, easier to protect him. Another thing you need to do is put your head together with Rachael's, make sure she gets all the details down. We'll look for proof on our end. A few days. All right?"

"For a few days, then," Jack said. "Rachael?"

"For a few days," she repeated. "Then I want to come back and take them down."

"Sounds like a plan." Savich rose, shook Sheriff Hollyfield's hand. "Thank you for all your assistance. I like Parlow, Kentucky. The sheriff of Maestro, Virginia, Dix Noble—he's not more than three, four hours away—is a good friend. You two would have a lot to talk about—he was a detective with the NYPD before he moved to the boondocks. Don't tell him I said so, but I'd put your brain right up there with his.

"We'll keep in touch. Sherlock, you and I are going to spend the night near the hospital. Besides seeing Dr. MacLean, I want to see if our shooter, Roderick Lloyd, still wants a lawyer."

"And here I'd counted on spending the night at Greeb's B&B," Sherlock said, "falling asleep with that stuffed duck's head staring at me."

Roy Bob was the wounded hero of Parlow. By the time he stepped out of the clinic, arm in a sling, both he, Rachael, and the gunman who'd shot up his garage were major celebrities.

Everyone wanted him to tell what had happened in the garage that day. He was strutting around in his bay, fiddling with Rachael's Charger despite having his painful arm in a clumsy sling, half a dozen citizens marveling at his strength and stamina, when Jack and Rachael walked in.

"Hi," he called out, buzzed on pain meds, happy as a clam. "Not much longer here, Rachael. I was telling all the guys you said you'd shoot me if I didn't get it done fast. You know, Ted has offered to give you a free car wash."

"Not enough time. We want to leave in an hour. Can you do it, Roy Bob?"

"Sure thing."

"Did you really shoot that thug, ma'am?"

"Yes, I really shot him. He's in the hospital, but he's evidently not as stupid as I thought, since he won't talk at all."

They were quiet a moment, listening to the helicopter flying overhead.

"The FBI agents are leaving?"

Roy Bob nodded. "Yep, two of them. Agent Crowne here is staying to protect Rachael." He paused, frowned. "I don't think she needs it, though, like I was saying, the way she handled my pa's Remington."

Jack checked Roy Bob's progress under the hood. "Looking good, Roy Bob. Why don't we have Tony's meatloaf at Monk's Café, Rachael, then come back here in about an hour?"

"Sounds good," Roy Bob said, and he started singing about a man and his hunting dog, Ralph. His audience seemed to like it.

An hour later, Rachael was driving out of Parlow, Jack belted in beside her, only a dull ache in his head. "We have about an hour of daylight left. That's more than enough time to get us to Slipper Hollow and Uncle Gillette's house."

Jack found he appreciated the mountains more on the ground than he had with his plane on fire in the air. The road that led to Slipper Hollow was a well-maintained two-way blacktop. It rose and twisted back on itself, skirted boulders and cliffs, but continued to rise into the heart of the mountains. It was slow going because of all the sharp turns and steep falloffs.

"This is the end of the road," Rachael said as she pulled the Charger onto the shoulder and steered carefully into a thick mess of cottonwoods. "You'd have to be looking hard to see the car in here. We're pretty well hidden. This is why I wanted to keep the Charger dirty—better camouflage."

Jack grunted, got out of the car, and picked up fallen branches and leaves. He covered the car as best he could. He turned to smile at Rachael. "Even if the bad guys know about Slipper Hollow, I doubt they'd find it anytime soon. We're losing sun fast. Lead the way."

They walked for about a hundred yards, deep into the woods, winding their way between trees, climbing, then leveling off.

With no warning, they broke into a fairly flat clearing some forty feet wide, maybe sixty feet deep. In the middle stood a gem of a house, all logs and glass, two stories high, with a sharply raked roof, two chimneys, a huge wraparound porch, and four rocking chairs in a grouping around a small circular table.

"I never expected this," Jack said.

She grinned at him. "Yeah, I know."

What he'd expected, Rachael imagined, was some sort of shack, car parts strewn in the front, smoke billowing out of a dilapidated chimney, but not this. "It's a work of art," he said. "The yard and the house, framed by the thick forest, it looks like a postcard. And the flower bed. In a month or so there'll be a rainbow of color." He saw the two outbuildings standing off to the side. "Food storage for the winter?"

"Yes, and other supplies, as well. Uncle Gillette hates going into town. He stocks up six months at a time."

"Is he expecting us?"

"Oh yes. I called him right before we left Parlow, told him I was coming and bringing a guest. Still, maybe it's best to wave a white scarf. That'll keep him from shooting us." Then she poked Jack in the arm and laughed. "Gotcha."

A tall man came out of the house to stand on the front porch. He waved at them as he trotted down the half-dozen wooden steps.

Rachael ran to him. Jack watched the man gather her into his arms, hold her tight, his head touching hers.

When Jack got close, the man looked up, smiled. "Welcome to Slipper Hollow. I'm Gillette Janes."

"I'm FBI Agent Jackson Crowne. Call me Jack. I'm protecting Rachael." Gillette didn't let Rachael go, merely stuck out his hand. It was a competent hand, long-fingered, like a musician's, Jack thought as he shook it, but strong and calloused, to be expected since it appeared he did everything needful in his hideaway.

Jack could only shake his head at his willingness to jump to conclusions. Truth be told, he'd been expecting a stereotypical hillbilly in a flannel shirt with a big beer gut—was he ever an idiot. "You've got a beautiful home," he said instead, and meant it.

"Thank you. Rachael drilled, hammered,

mowed, you name it. I'm glad you got here okay, sweetie. It's getting dark fast. Come inside. I'll feed you both, then you can tell me what's going on."

"I don't suppose you've at least got a still out back?" Jack asked hopefully.

Gillette Janes laughed. "No, but I'm told my grandmother did."

SIXTEEN

Slipper Hollow
Monday night

Why is it called Slipper Hollow?" Jack asked as he spooned up the last bite of vegetarian stew. It was loaded with every vegetable under heaven, a recipe he should get for Savich.

Gillette Janes chewed a moment on a saltine cracker. "The story goes that two young lovers met here in the deep of summer when wildflowers carpeted the ground, for even then no trees grew in this hollow. Alas, her father found them one day, shot the boy, hauled off his daughter kicking and screaming to go back to her dead lover. In her struggles, her slipper came off.

"Years later, it was said you could hear her crying for her lost slipper—not her unfortunate dead lover—thus the name attached itself to the land."

"Any proof of that tale, Uncle Gillette?"

"Not a whiff, as far as I know," Gillette said. "I've never heard her crying for her slipper, and I've been here nearly all my life."

Rachael played with her crystal wineglass. "We're safe here. No one knows about Slipper Hollow except for a few old-timers in and around Parlow. And none of them would give directions to a stranger."

"Glad I made the decision to keep the place private," Gillette said, rising to stack stew bowls in the dishwasher. "After you and your mom moved to Richmond, I even began doing most of my shopping in Heissen's Dome, about an hour's drive north of here—people know my face, maybe my name, but not where I live.

"Jack, these people after my girl, it's doubtful they'll find her here since she's not been part of the area for years. So tell me, Rachael, you believe in your heart of hearts that Senator Abbott's siblings murdered him, then have tried to murder you twice?"

Rachael said simply, "There is no one else."

"They acted so quickly. Tell me about them."

"Most of what I know is from Jimmy since I was only with them three times before he died. Their names are Laurel and Quincy. They're brother and sister and they give sharks a bad name. Jimmy told me that right after his election to his first Senate term, Laurel managed to oust Quincy from the CEO position of the Abbott corporation. They're quite diversified, but their primary interests are in commercial real estate development worldwide—malls, skyscrapers, those sorts of projects.

"The fight between Laurel and Quincy was real nasty, Jimmy told me. But the old man—his father, Carter Blaine Abbott—came down on Laurel's side. She ran things after Carter Abbott loosened his grip on the reins five years ago.

"Fact is, I think Laurel and Quincy are equally grasping, condescending, and arrogant. I can also see the two of them joining forces to remove the bigger threat—their brother—probably right after he told them about killing Melissa Parks and that he was going to come clean, resign his Senate seat, go to the cops, the press."

"Laurel Abbott," Gillette repeated slowly. "Didn't she marry some Greek shipping magnate? What's his name?"

"Stefanos Kostas. Now there's a guy who's suffering from ego inflation. He thinks he's slick and stunning, that women can't resist him. Jimmy said he was unfaithful even after he proposed to Laurel. The way he looks at women—me included—it made me want to go take a shower."

"I've seen photos of him," Gillette said. "He's quite the fashion plate, looks smooth and tough, quite a combination. So you weren't interested, huh?"

Rachael shuddered. "If a shower weren't available, I'd go for a hose. They've got two boys, both off at Standover, this fancy prep school in Vermont. Stefanos owns a Greek island, Scorpios, but he spends most of his time here."

"Tell us about Quincy," Jack said, joining Gillette at the counter. "No, Rachael, you stay put. My head feels fine, so does my leg. I make good coffee. It's so good some say it's a gift."

She laughed. "Okay, Quincy. He's a clotheshorse, spends a couple months a year in Milan having new threads made for himself while he struts in and out of La Scala. He's divorced, three times now, and from a snide comment Laurel made once, I gather his alimony payments could feed a small country for a week. He's as self-centered and arrogant as Laurel, and wears a ridiculous toupee, like Donald Trump's. One night it nearly slid onto his steak and mushrooms, and no one said a word."

"Old man Abbott wanted Laurel to run the empire. So Quincy's not as smart as she is?"

Rachael thought about that. "It's not brains, really. They're both smart, but he doesn't have the force of will, the personality for it. He does what she tells him to do. With Quincy, I think he'd have trouble finding the jugular vein, whereas Laurel was born sucking blood from it."

Jack said, "So Quincy can do the war dance, but he can't take the scalp?"

"That's it. Another thing: he's extraordinarily sexist, and since being outsharked by his sister, Jimmy said he'd gotten more vicious toward women. I heard him say to Jimmy once that a woman is at her best on her knees with her mouth well occupied."

"Whoa," Jack said.

Gillette said, "Tell us more about Laurel."

"She knows where all the skeletons are buried, knows which buttons to push. She's the real deal when it comes to getting what she wants. She's a closer, no scruples at all. All of that's according to Jimmy, of course."

Gillette said, "Doesn't sound like there's much affection there."

"No, there isn't. I asked Jimmy about that, all the sniping beneath the civility, all the public pretense, and he said it had been like that for so long he couldn't remember if it had ever been any different."

Gillette continued. "I read the other day in the *Wall Street Journal* that Abbott Enterprises, both international and domestic, has increased in wealth, prestige, and influence under her leadership."

"So Jimmy told me," Rachael said. "You can bet that burns Quincy to his heels."

She sighed, ate a cracker, then twisted the bag closed. "Proof. Where am I going to find proof?"

"We will," Jack said with no hesitation at all.

She gave him a grin. "Do you know Uncle Gillette's a computer hound, maybe even as good as Agent Savich? You told me he was amazing, Jack."

Gillette did a double take. "Agent Savich? You mean FBI Special Agent Dillon Savich?"

Jack nodded.

"I've read about him, read several of the protocols he developed for the FBI. He adapted that facial recognition program from Scotland Yard. I'd really like to see it in action."

Jack laughed. "Do you happen to have a name for your computer, Gillette?"

"A name? No, I hadn't considered that. Hey, I've got three computers."

"It's a question to ponder," Jack said. "Savich has only the one laptop—MAX or MAXINE—it's transgender, changes sex every six months or so."

Gillette laughed so hard he spilled coffee onto the floor. And what a floor it was,

Jack thought, nicer than his, and that burned him since he'd selected the Italian tiles and laid them himself. He looked down at the various shades of gray with lines of milky white snaking through the marble squares.

"I wonder why I never read anything about MAX," Gillette said, hiccupped once, then leaned down to wipe the coffee off the floor. "Or MAXINE."

"I'll have to see if I can get you and Savich together, at least in cyberspace. Your home is incredible. I was thinking maybe it's about the right time to do some more work on mine."

"You already own a house? At your tender age?"

"I'm not all that young," Jack said, "nearly thirty-two."

"That's thirty-one," Gillette said. "That's young."

"Young enough," Rachael said as she blew on the coffee that Uncle Gillette had just poured in the big stone mug with her name on it. "You've only got thirty-six months on me."

"Thirty-six months and lots of years," Jack said.

Rachael sneered at him. "Oh yeah? You ever spend any quality time at the bottom of a lake with only a block of concrete for company?"

"Okay, I spoke too fast, but you've got to admit, that little phrase sounded profound."

She couldn't help it, she poked him in the arm and laughed. "All right, you're loaded with hard-nosed experience. Now, tell us about your house."

"It's old and needs lots of updating, but it's mine. I'm still living in my apartment since there's so much major work to do. My folks loaned me the down payment. I pay them ten percent interest. My dad told me to take my time paying them back, they like the interest rate too much. You built this house yourself, Gillette?"

Gillette nodded and walked to the shining silver Sub-Zero refrigerator. "After I came home from the marines—"

"Wait a minute," Jack said, staring at the man who looked like he should have been playing polo, his valet waiting in the wings. "You're a marine?"

Gillette nodded. "Yeah, I spent ten years in the Corps before I hung it up. I grew up here in Slipper Hollow, went to school in Parlow, couldn't wait to go out into the big bad world. Since home appears to be embedded in our genes, I came back here when I got out. Rachael and her mom lived here until she was twelve or so, I believe, when they moved to Richmond."

Rachael added to Jack, "My grandparents were killed in an avalanche while cross-country skiing when I was about eight. I never knew them very well, they were always bumming around. 'Hike the world' was their motto."

"Yes, that's right. After you and your mom left, it was tough being here alone, but I didn't want to leave. That's when I tore down the house and started building this one. It was a work in progress for a long time. Been finished about three years now. I've enjoyed every project, Jack, and you will, too, so take your time and don't cut corners. I made a cheesecake. Who wants strawberries with that?"

This handsome, fit man who looked like an Italian count in his pale blue cashmere V-neck, white shirt, black slacks, and butter-soft loafers, was a down-and-dirty marine? He made vegetarian stew and cheesecake and laid that incredible kitchen floor; he built this entire frigging house?

After his first bite of cheesecake, Jack said, "I have a sister who'd hunt you down like a dog, so great would be her desire for you."

"Hmm. She likes cheesecake, does she? Is she a lawyer like you?"

"How do you know I'm a lawyer?"

"The way you process information, the way you speak. It helped, too, that after Rachael called me, told me your name, I Googled you. You were second in your class at the University of Chicago. Good job. That's a tough program. You went directly into the FBI after graduation?"

Jack sat back, folded his hand over his belly. "No, I started out in the Chicago DA's office, stayed only a year and a half before joining the FBI. My sister was first in her class, also at Chicago, eight years before me. Plus, she's a vegetarian. So is Savich."

"Funny," Gillette said, frowning at a laptop that sat next to a bowl of green apples on the long kitchen counter, "for an FBI agent."

"Yeah, I'd have to say that most of us are predators." Jack thought about Gillette

Googling him, about the state of privacy now, and knew anyone could find out he'd made a B in Torts in his second year.

At ten o'clock that night, Rachael led Jack into her mother's old room, which, naturally, Uncle Gillette had prepared for him.

"I was wondering, Rachael, how does Gillette make his money? It's obvious he isn't hurting, plus he built this house and it's really high quality."

"He does computer troubleshooting for several large international corporations. Exactly what this involves, you'll have to ask him. I remember once he started talking about a tax scam he was hunting down in Dubai, and my eyes started glazing over. Go take a pain med, Jack," she added. She raised her hand to lightly cup his face. "Thank you. You fall out of the sky at my feet, then you become my bodyguard. Add to that you're fixing up your own house and I've gotta think you're quite a miracle."

"I like being a miracle," he said, and stared at that sexy braid before he left her. Jack took his pill and settled between lavender-scented sheets, unconscious in two minutes flat.

As for Rachael, for the first time since Friday, she felt safe to her bones even though she knew intellectually that anyone with the proper motivation and a certain degree of skill could locate her and Slipper Hollow without much fuss.

She lay on her back on her narrow childhood bed and looked up at the high-beamed ceiling that she couldn't see in the dark, and wondered how she was going to prove Jimmy's brother and sister murdered him before they added her scalp to their belts.

She wanted more than anything in the world to make them pay. She'd had only six weeks with Jimmy because of them. Talk about miracles, Jimmy had been the biggest miracle in her life, and he was taken from her. After so little time. She fell asleep thinking that Jack was a pretty nice miracle himself.

SEVENTEEN

Washington Memorial Hospital
Washington, D.C.
Tuesday morning

Chief of Neurological Services Dr. Connor Bingham said to Savich and Sherlock, "Dr. MacLean regained consciousness an hour ago. He was in considerable pain from the broken ribs and the cut in his chest, so he's medicated, a bit on the drowsy side. Maybe all the physical stimulation, the noise and activity of the helicopter ride, helped speed his awakening. But he is by no means a normal man, as you'll see. With his dementia, he'll never be.

"When you speak to him, keep it short. If you have questions afterwards, I'm available."

As a matter of course, Savich and Sherlock showed their IDs to the agent posted outside Dr. MacLean's room, even though they knew one another.

Agent Tom Tomlin was tall and rangy, his dark eyes alight at the sight of Sherlock as he said, those eyes of his never leaving her face, "Agent Sherlock, my mom sent me a photo from the *San Francisco Chronicle.*" He reached into his jacket pocket, pulled out his wallet, and unfolded the newspaper clipping. "See, here you are standing in front of a burning house, your face blacker than mine, your clothes torn and dirty, and I can tell you're wearing a Kevlar vest. My mom told me to ask you out. She was really bummed when I told her you were married." He beamed at her.

Her father had sent her the same photo. Sherlock grinned. "It took forever to get all the black smoke off. And the smell. It's still like a faint perfume."

Savich gave Agent Tomlin a terrifying smile before taking Sherlock's hand and leading her into Dr. MacLean's room.

Dr. MacLean moaned. They moved to stand on either side of his bed, staring down at gray eyes darkened with confusion.

"Dr. MacLean?" Sherlock waited until the gray eyes focused on her face. "I'm Agent Sherlock and this is Agent Savich. We're FBI. We work with Jack Crowne. Don't worry about a thing. You're safe. You're protected. We won't let anyone hurt you."

The gray eyes, a bit blurred, blinked at them. "You're friends of Jackson's? I want him to marry my daughter, you know, but my wife thinks he's too old for her. She's a freshman at Columbia this fall."

"He might make a better uncle," Savich said. "Remember, that's about the same number of years that separated Prince Charles and Diana. Look what came of that."

"Maybe so. Oh my, I never had such great drugs, even back in college. I feel like flying right off this rock-hard excuse for a bed and out that window, maybe buzz the White House. Is the weather nice?"

"Yes, bright sunshine, and it might hit eighty-five today."

"I have a real good friend who's a pharmacist and a killer at bridge. After I buzz over his house in Chevy Chase, hopefully ruin the bridge hand he's playing, I think I'll fly clear to the West Coast. I don't want to go back to Lexington—my family are a bunch of nags and doomsayers. And my wife Molly—I tried to make her listen to reason, but she's got her own rules for reason and won't listen to mine. Molly kept pushing me until we were on a plane back to Lexington. And then I had to come back here again—but wait now. What kind of sense does that make? Oh, I remember. There was a plane wreck—Jackson was piloting. Is he all right?"

Savich saw his sudden alarm and said, "Jack is fine now, just headaches from the concussion and some pain from a gash in his leg."

"Good, good, he's okay then. I'll tell you, even with these excellent pain meds, I still feel like I'm hurting all over."

"Understandable. You got thrown around quite a bit. There was a bomb on board the Cessna, but Jack managed to bring it down in a narrow valley. He pulled you out before the plane exploded. You are hurt all over, sir."

Sherlock said, "Dr. MacLean, we need to ask you some questions, to try to get a better handle on all of this."

MacLean closed his eyes, appeared to

go to sleep, but he didn't. He said, eyes still closed, "Jackson had questions, too. He wanted me to tell him the names of my patients who live locally, as the majority do since my practice is here, so the FBI could interview them. I couldn't do that, of course. My patients must have their privacy. They don't deserve to be singled out, to have others find out they're seeing me, and speculate why. I didn't—"

"Dr. MacLean," Savich said, interrupting him smoothly, "the fact is, with this disease—do you remember that you have frontal lobe dementia?"

He nodded. "How do you like that for a crappy roll of the dice? The disease starts in the front lobes, then continues all the way back, wrecks everything in its path. I'll end up like an Alzheimer's patient, lying in the fetal position, waiting to die, all alone in my own brain, the most terrifying thing I can imagine."

That was the truth, Savich thought, and wondered how he'd deal with something as devastating as that if it hit him. He said, "I wouldn't like it at all. You know this disease causes you to say things that are inappropriate?"

"I'm a doctor, Agent Savich. I'm not stupid. I know all of this. I did a lot of reading about it after I was diagnosed at Duke."

Savich continued. "Sometimes you remember what you've said and other times you don't."

"Sorry, what did you say?"

"Sometimes you—"

"That was an attempt at a bad joke, Agent Savich," Dr. MacLean said, grinning up at him. "But please understand, no matter what was wrong with me, I would have sworn on the grave of my grandpa that nothing could make me say anything to anyone about my patients. It's my goal to help them, not harm them." He paused and sighed. "But I know I have. Jackson told me."

"You've already spoken about three of your patients to a friend and layperson, in public. It would appear that one of your patients found out about it, and you scared him or her so badly that he or she has made three attempts on your life. Two attempted hit-and-runs, here and in Lexington, and then the bomb on your plane on your flight back to Washington. If it weren't for Jack's piloting skills, you'd be dead, as would he."

"It's so bloody difficult to believe I could do something like that."

"I imagine it is," Sherlock said. "We need you to tell us about the patients you spoke about to your tennis partner, Arthur Dolan. Perhaps we'll eventually need the names of all your patients, but it's likely the person who wants you dead is one of the three, particularly since Arthur Dolan was killed shortly thereafter up in New Jersey."

His haggard face suddenly looked austere. "That's ridiculous. I never said anything to Arthur about my patients. He died in an auto accident, always did drive too fast. Molly was screaming murder, but I told her to take a Valium, everyone said it was an accident." He suddenly seemed to calm, and said, his voice light, "Do you know, Arthur had a great backhand, but he was slow. I usually won our matches. Still, I'll miss playing with him. It was such good exercise. He'd come down here one week, I'd go north the next. He was also a golfer, better at it than at tennis. Arthur and I only talked about sports, he didn't know anything else.

"Now, as for that car nearly hitting me in Lexington, I know it was a drunk driver.

The cops agreed." He sighed. "Poor Arthur. At least for him, it was fast and clean and over with."

"And the first attempted hit-and-run here in Washington, sir?" Sherlock asked.

"It was the Plank area, lots of drugs there. Maybe it was someone whacked out on heroin. The guy split. I would, too, after being such a jerk."

Why all this denial? Savich wondered. Or had his brain simply reduced it to nothing, only a footnote, and who cared? Savich said, "And the bomb in your plane?"

There was dismissal in his light voice. "That's a no-brainer. Jackson's a federal cop, he has enemies, don't you think? Bad guys who want revenge?"

Savich met Sherlock's eyes for a moment, then focused again on Dr. MacLean's face, those gray eyes clear now, filled with sharp intelligence, insult, and fear. "You don't remember speaking about three of your patients to Arthur Dolan?"

His clear, smart eyes focused solidly on Savich's face. Anger washed color over his pale face. "What the devil do you mean? Tell tales of my patients to a friend? Naturally not. What kind of professional ethics do you think I have? Besides, I told you, we only talked about sports."

Down the rabbit hole, Savich thought. He said patiently, "No, sir, it has nothing to do with your ethics, it has to do with your disease.

"When we were investigating the first attempt on your life, we found a bartender at your golf club in Chevy Chase who's known you and admired you for years. He said he remembers listening to you speak to Arthur Dolan over martinis. He remembers you speaking about three of your patients, all well known, and that's why the bartender listened, and didn't forget." Unfortunately, the bartender had been working so he didn't hear all that much, but enough to know something was very wrong.

Dr. MacLean looked affronted, then, inexplicably, the anger and insult died out of his eyes and he began to laugh. The laugh must have hurt his ribs or his chest because he drew up short, breathed lightly for a moment, then said, his voice suddenly confiding, deep and rich, like a storyteller's, "Was one of the names Lomas Clapman?"

"Yes," Savich said. "Why don't you tell us about him."

Dr. MacLean's eyes glittered; he looked suddenly revved, excited, and there was something mischievous in his manner, like he was flirting with make-believe and being drawn right into it. "Clapman's an idiot, a buffoon, all puffed up in his belief he's got the biggest brain in the known universe. He worships himself, lives happily mired in self-deception. Ah, how he hates Bill Gates. He always calls Gates 'a little bugger.' I mentioned that many people think Bill Gates is not only extraordinarily smart, he's a stand-up guy, what with his foundation doing more good for people than any of the so-called relief agencies. Why not see if he could outdo Gates's foundation? He could certainly afford it.

"You see, I was trying to pull him away from this obsession he has with Gates, trying to channel his energies toward a positive goal. It didn't work. He yelled at me. You know what? I leaned back in my chair and laughed back at him. He threw a paperweight at me and stormed out." Dr. MacLean shook his head, still laughing. "What an unprincipled yahoo. I didn't see him again after that. He didn't even call to cancel his weekly appointments."

Before the disease had struck him, Sherlock doubted she would have ever heard Dr. MacLean speak in that sneering, dismissive, mocking voice about a patient. Had he really laughed at his patient? She doubted it. She wondered if he would remember speaking like this to her and Dillon. She said, "Did Mr. Clapman tell you anything that, if made public, could hurt him?"

"Yes, certainly," MacLean said, no hesitation at all, not a single protest about physician ethics or scruples. "Lomas built his company on the back of his supposed best friend and partner. He sold his first plane design, some sort of low-flying tactical aircraft, to the government back in the early eighties—fact was, Lomas stole his friend's idea and schematics right out from under him. His partner was an inventor, his head in a different reality, and he didn't even notice when Lomas put the patents under his own name. As for the partnership agreement, it didn't cover the patents. The poor schmuck killed himself maybe fifteen years ago, dead broke. Can you believe that?"

Sherlock said, "Was Mr. Clapman seeing

you because he felt guilty about what he did?"

"No, not really. He thought he deserved every unethical dime in his coffers. Nah, he saw me once a week because he wanted to brag about how great he was, and I was forced to sit there for fifty minutes and listen to him. His wife left him, you know, and I can't say I blame her."

Savich said, "If that got out, I imagine it would have considerable negative impact on Mr. Clapman personally and on his company, not to mention lawsuits from his partner's widow and family."

"You think Lomas tried to kill me? Excuse me, *is* trying to kill me? To keep me quiet?"

"Possibly," said Savich. "But you know, it just doesn't seem enough to me."

MacLean laughed. "Lomas also falsified performance trial data, massaged the stats on his fighters to meet government requirements. I told him to put a halt to that, that it would come to light, things like that always did. I remember he actually giggled, said it was all history now, anyway."

"Bingo," Sherlock said.

MacLean stared at them, a drug-happy

smile on his face, his eyes glittering, a bit manic. "You think old Lomas would try to knock me off for that? He told me straight out that everybody does it, that the Pentagon knows everyone does it, and so they simply make allowances, they even have tables that show the range of acceptable deviations, that sort of thing. He said it was all a big game."

Sherlock said easily, "Could you tell us exactly why Lomas Clapman was seeing you, Dr. MacLean?"

"He was impotent. After all the tests and a couple of tubs of Viagra, his doctor recommended he see me, see if his inability to sustain an erection was mental or emotional."

Savich said, "Did you help him?"

"I'll tell you, Agent Savich, Lomas is so filled with envy and arrogance, I think it would take God himself to help him." MacLean closed his eyes, leaned his head back against the pillow, and sighed.

EIGHTEEN

Savich said, "The bartender our agent spoke to said you also talked about Dolores McManus, a congresswoman from Georgia." And Savich waited to see if he would continue to talk with candor and cynicism, or would revert to the psychiatrist renowned for his discretion.

MacLean closed his eyes for a moment, hummed deep in his throat, carefully rearranged himself a bit to ease his ribs. They watched him give his pain med button a couple of pushes. Several minutes passed in silence. MacLean sighed and said, "Sorry, I just wanted to float about for a little bit, such a lovely feeling. These drugs are first-rate. Ah, Dolores—you strip away all the glitz and glamour and the attention her position has brought her, and what you've got is one simple basic human being—not many frills or mental extras, if you know what I mean.

"I wanted to sleep with her, I knew I could please her, but she wasn't interested."

Sherlock's mouth dropped open. This was a kick. She said, "Dr. MacLean, you propositioned a patient?"

"Oh no, I merely thought about it. I could tell she'd never see me that way." He sighed. "Even though she's nearly as old as I am, she still has gorgeous breasts, nicer than Molly's. Three kids'll make your breasts sag, Molly tells me, and then says to count my blessings. Molly's always been big into counting blessings. Even with all this crap, she still tells me I'm her biggest blessing." He continued without pause, "It was difficult to keep my eyes on Dolores's face, to listen to all her crowing. She was so proud of being on the A-list, wouldn't shut up about all the famous people who call her by her first name. Then she'd switch gears and crow for the umpteenth time about how her background hasn't slowed her down. She'd been a housewife with a college degree in communications, no work experience of any note, raising two kids, but she had one major asset—her mouth. She never hesitated to mix it up with the mayor, the governor, the newspapers, the phone company. It was her successful assault on the EPA that got her elected to her first term. She cut them off at the knees about a local cleanup project they weren't funding.

"Being elected to Washington simply gave her a bigger canvas. I have to admit, watching her take on all comers—it's a treat. She can spin on a dime, make you believe you just left the room when in reality you were actually coming through the door. It's her only talent, and makes her the perfect politician. As for substance, I guess she has about as much as any of her colleagues."

Sherlock asked, "Do you remember telling Arthur Dolan if she had anything in her past that could harm her if made public? Something so grave she'd feel threatened?"

"I never told Arthur a thing, I've already told you that. I wouldn't. Would she feel threatened enough to kill me? Of course not.Everythinginherpastisnickel-and-dime stuff—really nothing much at all, except that she murdered her husband."

They stared flabbergasted at MacLean, saw his eyes go vague, the manic light die out. He was about to go under. He'd given himself one too many doses of the pain meds. This congresswoman murdered her husband? The bartender hadn't heard anything about murder.

As if on cue, the door opened and Dr. Bingham looked in. He listened to MacLean's vitals, but didn't attempt to engage him in conversation. They all stood by his bed and watched him drift off.

Dr. Bingham nodded, then straightened.

Savich said quietly, "Do you have a moment?"

Sherlock shut down the small recorder in her bag as she left the room.

Once outside in the wide hallway, Dr. Bingham asked, "Was he alert? Did he make sense?"

Savich thought about how to describe

one of the strangest interviews he'd ever tried to conduct. "He was alert, yes, and he made perfect sense, for the most part. But it was how he spoke of his patients, his family, his tennis partner—it was like there were no brakes between his thoughts and what came out of his mouth. He didn't seem to realize he was saying outrageous things, vicious things, and he spoke so matter-of-factly. Without the requisite social buffing, I suppose his descriptions of his patients are painfully accurate."

Sherlock said, "But his disdain, Dillon, his contempt for them—I simply can't imagine that's how he normally thinks of his patients. Then he'd become himself again, I guess you could say. Serious, ready to fight to the death for the privacy of his patients. It was an amazing interview."

Dr. Bingham said, "Given his reputation, I would agree with that. It's a very sad thing that's happening to him, this dementia, and the resulting loss of self. It's a horrible thing, in fact, horrible." Dr. Bingham shook their hands, walked away, his head down, hands in the pockets of his white coat, and Sherlock would swear she heard him humming.

Sherlock said, "Dillon, do you think it's possible Dr. MacLean's having us on, maybe making a lot of this stuff up?"

Savich shook his head. "He might have exaggerated part of it. I don't know." And to Agent Tomlin, he said, "Take good care of Dr. MacLean. This guy's a huge target."

"No one gets past me," Tomlin said. "You can count on that, Agent Savich."

Savich was aware of Tomlin staring at his wife until they entered one of the elevators at the end of the long corridor.

Sherlock said as she pressed the lobby button, "Are you inclined to believe that Congresswoman McManus murdered her husband?"

"We'll find out soon enough."

"I wonder if that was why she went to see a shrink—you know, bad dreams, guilt, remorse."

"There's that," Savich said, and pulled her against him, kissing her until the elevator stopped at the third floor and a bleary-eyed intern staggered in.

NINETEEN

Slipper Hollow
Tuesday

It's a beautiful day," Rachael said, shading her eyes and staring up at the clear blue summer sky, the thready white clouds. Shepushed her hair behind her ears, tugged at the skinny braid. "Hard to believe there's so much actual bad out there in Uncle Gillette's world."

"I fear bad is rampant in the land," Jack said. "But it's not right here."

"Unlike Uncle Gillette, I never thought of Slipper Hollow as confining, never considered it a place to escape from. It was always a sanctuary, a haven where I'd be safe. Of course, I was a kid. Looking back now, I recognize that Mom was restless, wanted to go out on her own."

He looked at the braid in her hair, plaited closer to her face this morning. When she leaned her head to the side, it cupped her cheek. He said, "I really like the braid."

"What? Oh, thank you. Jimmy liked it, too." Her voice shook a bit on his name.

"For the most part," Jack said, "I agreed with your father's politics."

"I did, too. Can you believe Uncle Gillette washed and ironed our clothes?"

"I nearly kissed him for it, but drew back at the last minute."

"I kissed him enough for both of us. I believe he's gathering all the reports he can find about Jimmy's death. There are even film clips from the funeral. He said he'd have it all together for us by this afternoon."

Jack nodded. He felt suddenly itchy, felt his left elbow ache, something that tended to happen when something wasn't right, but he couldn't figure out what it could be. Slipper Hollow was a sanctuary, Rachael was right about that. It was cut off from the world; it was safe. Here they could enjoy the peace before they hunkered down to examine all the details of this psychotic situation. Psychotic? Jack thought about that for a moment. Odd, but *psychotic* was what came to mind. His elbow shouldn't be itching, but it was, big-time. He chose to ignore it. "You're not married," he said.

"I was close, once, but I found out he liked to gamble, and that was a deal breaker. My grandfather had that problem. I remember hearing my mom and my grandmother talk about it.

"I told my mom about the guy I'd thought I loved and wanted to marry, told her I'd found out he gambled, and you know what she said? Not a single thing. She only listened."

"Wise woman."

"Yeah, the last thing a twenty-seven-year-old woman who thinks she knows everything needs to hear is that she's an idiot and this is what she should do."

Jack wanted to know everything about this man, but now wasn't the time. "How old is your half brother?"

"Ben turned ten last week. He's a pistol, that kid, a pro quarterback in the making, fast, agile, strong throwing arm. His dad is thinking he's the next Joe Montana."

"What have you been doing, Rachael? I mean, did you go to college? What?"

Her chin went up. "I'm an interior designer."

She waited for him to laugh, to poke fun, to make a snide remark. He said, "I really like how Gillette did the house, particularly the kitchen. The tile job is incredible. Did you help with that?"

She nodded. "I remember drawing him a sketch of what I saw in my head, and he liked it."

"You've got to be the most popular girl in your group."

Rachael laughed. "It's been so long since I've been around friends—you know, people you trust and like and don't have to watch what you say when you're around them? The kind who won't hold it against you when you drink too much and act like an idiot." She tucked her hair back again. "Since I went to Washington to see Jimmy, I've simply let them go by the wayside."

"Did you work in Richmond?"

"After I graduated from the Everard School of Design, I joined Broderick Home Concepts. I was one of six designers on staff. I learned a lot, made a lot of contacts, and received a lot of glowing reports from clients. I had seed money lined up and was ready to go out on my own when my mom told me about Jimmy. I took a leave of absence, then Jimmy talked me into quitting Broderick, said he'd like nothing better than to set me up in Georgetown." She swallowed. "He was so excited, maybe more than I was. He . . ." She turned and walked away.

Jack grabbed her hand, pulled her against him, and wrapped his arms around her back. He realized they both smelled like the same soap, sort of sweet and tangy, like lavender, maybe. "It'll be okay, Rachael."

She leaned back. He saw she wasn't crying, she was shaking with rage. "Six weeks, Jack. I only had a father for six weeks! It's not fair, not fair." She slammed her fist into his shoulder. "I want to bring them down. Dear Jesus, I even have their last name now, legally I'm a bloody Abbott."

"Your father adopted you really fast."

"I was just getting used to introducing myself as Rachael Abbott."

"Keep his name. Do it to honor him. It doesn't tie you to the others. We'll get them,

Rachael, we will. I'll call Savich, see how much longer he wants you kept under wraps. Besides, you and I have a whole lot to discuss. I want every detail, Rachael, beginning with when you met your father for the first time. Have you finished writing up the detailed account of everything that Savich asked you to do?"

"No, I haven't even started yet."

"We'll get to it. Come over here, let's sit under that oak tree. Tell me again about the first time you met your father."

She sat, wrapped her arms around her knees, and began talking. "Did I tell you what he said when he first saw me? He shouted, 'Wait a minute—my God, a man can't be this lucky.' And he grabbed my hands and pulled me into his office, past his staff, people waiting. Like I told you, he never doubted for an instant I was his daughter. He was amazing. He had the most beautiful smile. It lit up his face, made these little crinkles at the corners of his eyes. He didn't want to let me out of his sight. We talked for hours. He told me about what had happened all those years ago, how his father took him and his friend to Spain to get him to forget my mother, only he didn't, not really. I told him what his father did to my mother, and he was tight-lipped. Of course I told him my mom didn't tell me about it until after his father died because she was afraid."

Rachael sucked in the fresh sweet summer air, and continued when Jack nodded. "He told me the first time in his life he really stood up for himself was when he made the decision to run for the Senate. He said he'd never felt so free as when he told his father to suck it up, it was his life and this was what he wanted. He said toward the end of the campaign, his father poured money into the coffers, probably put him over the top, got him elected.

"Then he laughed, shook his head. Right after Jimmy took his Senate seat, his father announced that he would now call the shots. Jimmy said he received detailed memos from the old man, telling him exactly what he wanted done. Naturally, he paid no attention. Jimmy told me his father had to manipulate and control everything and everyone until he died, supposedly issuing orders with his last breath. Jimmy said his mother probably died young just to escape him."

Jack asked, "How did Laurel and Quincy react to their father?"

"They both worshipped and feared him, like he was a god, one who was omniscient, one who could smile upon you or crush you."

"And how did they react to you?"

"The first time I met Laurel, her husband Stefanos Kostas, and Quincy was at dinner at Jimmy's house. He'd told them only that he had a big surprise for them." She looked up to see a rabbit sitting at the edge of the woods, seemingly content to stare at them. "I remember Laurel looking at me like I was a termite that just crawled out of the woodwork. Her niece? She couldn't believe it. All she could do was gape at me, and then at Jimmy." Rachael could hear Laurel saying, *"Pardon me? What did you say, John?"*

"This is my daughter, Rachael Janes, soon to be Rachael Janes Abbott. I'm adopting her so she'll be mine legally, as she should have been from the beginning.

"Rachael, your uncle Quincy and your aunt Laurel and my brother-in-law Stefanos." And he rubbed his hands

together, he was that happy, that excited. He hugged her against his side, kissed her forehead. "Rachael Abbott—now that has a nice ring to it, don't you think?"

Quincy cleared his throat, looked beyond Rachael's left shoulder. "She does perhaps resemble you a bit, but you must be responsible here, take your time to do things right. You must have DNA tests, make certain she is who she says she is."

Jimmy said simply, "She's my very image. Come on now, Quin, admit it. And there are simply some things you know to your soul. Listen to me, this is an evening to celebrate. I have another daughter I never knew about. I remember her mother, Angela, have thought of her often over the years. There is no doubt, and just looking at her, you know there's no question as to her paternity. Now, let's have some champagne."

Rachael sipped the French champagne as she eyed the braised French snails and the French sauced beef tips. The only thing French she liked was baguettes, but there wasn't any baguette. Laurel and Quincy were civil, but she knew they weren't happy, knew they distrusted her, believed she'd suckered their brother. As for Stefanos Kostas, he looked at her like he'd just as soon have her sitting naked astride his lap, her tongue down his throat.

"What does Jacqueline have to say about this?" Quincy asked.

Jimmy shrugged. "Who cares what she thinks? I would like Rachael to meet her half sisters. I think they'd all get along well." To Rachael, he said, "Elaine and Carla both live in Chicago, as I told you. They're both married. I'm a grandfather twice over now."

A long, long evening, Rachael thought, and felt her face had frozen into a rictus of a smile by the time Jimmy closed the door on his two siblings.

"They'll come around," Jimmy said, hugging her. "Don't worry," and he gave her a big sloppy kiss. "Fact is, they've got no choice."

It seemed so long ago, a different life, but it wasn't. She felt the sun warm on her face now as she looked over at Jack. "I remember thinking we could simply ignore them if they didn't like me. As long as I live, I'll remember how Jimmy never doubted me. Sure, I looked like him, but still he was powerful, rich, and famous, and I was nobody.

"Even if he'd been a serial killer, I'd have readily forgiven him."

"What'd your mom say?"

Rachael smiled. "She was surprised because it never occurred to her he would even remember her. She'd warned me that a DNA test would be the proper thing to do, didn't matter that I looked like him, and that when it was brought up, I shouldn't be insulted."

And Rachael told Jack again about the night Jimmy broke down and told her about the little girl on the bicycle. "I don't think I've ever seen such desolation in a person's eyes, such misery, such despair—"

There was a yell.

"Rachael, Jack, come here!" It was Gillette and he was shouting from the front porch. "Hurry! Now!"

Without a pause, Jack drew his gun,

grabbed Rachael's hand, and they ran in a crouch, back to the house.

A spray of gunfire erupted as the three of them dove through the open front door.

TWENTY

Gillette slammed the door, crawled to the side, and reached over to shoot the dead bolt through.

Bullets tore through the door, sending splinters flying. The beautiful high arched windows shattered, spewing glass shards everywhere. They heard bullets gouging the walls.

"Cover your heads," Jack yelled, pulling Rachael beneath him. "Gillette, stay down."

Round after round struck the house. No front window was left unshattered. Rachael struggled to breathe, and finally, Jack leaned up. She yelled over the shots,

"Uncle Gillette, how did you know they were here?"

Gillette was panting as he pulled a wooden splinter out of the back of his hand. "There was a break in the perimeter alarm. I wasn't expecting anyone, so I knew it had to be trouble. Well, malfunctions some-times happen, but I wasn't about to take any chances, not with your situation, Ra-chael."

Glory be, Jack thought, an alarm. The gunfire stopped for a moment. Jack said, "Both of you stay down, don't go anywhere near that door or the windows."

Gillette was already on his hands and knees. "I've got weapons upstairs. I'll get them."

"All right, but keep down. No marine hot-dogging."

Gillette laughed as he elbow crawled toward the stairs. Another spray of bullets tore through the line of front windows, strik-ing a side wall, shattering a beautiful gilded mirror.

"Don't you move a muscle, Rachael," Jack said, elbowing his own way over to the window. At a break in the gunfire, he peered out, saw a shadow of movement and returned fire with his Kimber. He had only one extra clip so he had to pace himself.

"They're destroying this beautiful house," Rachael said.

Gillette returned to the foyer, bent nearly double, clutching two rifles. He fell to his knees and crawled between two front windows to get to them.

Jack said, "Gillette, do you shoot as well as Rachael?"

"I'm a marine," he said. "Who do you think taught her?"

"Good point. The two of you keep the guys out front contained. There are more, I know it, and I don't want them coming in behind us. Back entrances, Gillette?"

"There's only one back door. In the kitchen."

"Keep your heads down," Jack said, and kept low to the floor. He felt the heat of some of the bullets flying over his head on their way to thud into the walls. The gilded mirror finally crashed to the floor, wood and glass flying everywhere.

When Jack was out of the line of fire, he jumped to his feet and ran down the hallway toward the kitchen. He felt a stab of exquisite pain in his thigh, ignored it. He stepped into the kitchen at the exact moment a man came in the back door. Jack fell to his knees and rolled, four bullets stitching the cabinets behind him. He heard one dig into the beautiful marble floor.

And that really made him mad. He came up on his side and yelled, "Hey!"

The man fired again, but he was off by a good foot. Jack shot two rounds, both of them missing. The man was crouched behind the washing machine just inside the back door.

"What are you doing here?" Jack yelled over the pumping gunfire coming from the front of the house.

The man fired off another half-dozen rounds. Jack felt a sharp spear of wood hit his left arm. He gave a huge cry of pain and slammed his Kimber against the floor. He lay there, still and silent.

The man fired again. Then he slowly rose and looked beyond the kitchen table to where Jack lay, nearly under one of the kitchen chairs. He took a step, then realized he didn't see the gun, but it was too late.

Jack reared up and shot him.

The man grabbed his shoulder and sank to his knees. His gun dropped onto the floor and skidded against the wall. He toppled over, moaning. Jack walked to the man, struck the back of his head with the gun butt. One down, but of course there had to be one more. Whoever ordered this wasn't about to take any more chances with only one shooter. No, this was a full-scale assassination squad. He heard two shooters in the front, and likely there was still one more in the back.

Jack pulled a wallet out of the man's jacket pocket, then looked at the expanse of green lawn that went back for perhaps thirty feet to the forest, a seemingly impenetrable thick, vibrant green. He looked for movement, shadow play, anything to help him locate the other shooter. Or shooters. He was patient. He waited. Finally he saw a flash of movement. A man was trying to slide between two oak saplings, being careful because he'd heard the shot and the yell. By now he had to realize his partner was down.

The man held something in his hand—not a gun or a rifle. Jack realized he was speaking on a walkie-talkie, telling the team leader one was down in the kitchen. Jack saw the dark blue of his shirt when he shifted forward, probably to get a better look at the house, to try to see him. Big mistake, Jack thought. He lined up the shot and fired, but the man was good. He'd seen Jack's shadow, seen a whisper of movement, he supposed, and dove to the ground. Jack's bullet went into a tree and spewed up a whirlwind of leaves.

No way was he going to let that man go back around front to join his team. He stretched his arm up and grabbed an apple from the bowl sitting on the breakfast table. He took aim at the trash can container off to his left and threw the apple. It struck hard. He saw the man jerk around, his gun arm swinging smoothly toward the container. Jack stood and fired.

The man didn't make a sound.

Jack watched him pitch forward out of the forest and onto the grass.

He heard gunfire intensify at the front of the house. He prayed his one civilian and one marine were being careful. He thought the two of them could handle the front. He waited, listened. He was as convinced as he could be that there were no more shooters lurking in the forest. He ran flat out across the backyard, fanning his Kimber, so pumped with adrenaline he could hear his own heart thudding against his chest.

How had they found Slipper Hollow? Not hard, really. With the Internet, nothing was secret for long.

He fell to his knees and checked the man he'd shot. The bullet had gone straight through his heart. He pulled out his wallet, stuck it in with the other one in his pocket. He picked up the fallen walkie- talkie and clicked the speak button. He lowered his voice, crumpled leaves in his left hand to create the impression of static, and prayed. "Hey, it's not going good here. What do you want me to do?"

"Clay, that you?"

He wasn't expecting a woman's voice. "Yeah, it's me."

He crumpled more leaves. "Hard to hear you."

"What about Donley? You said he went in the back and you heard a shot. What happened?"

"He . . . got . . . clocked."

"All right, all right, dammit, we'll have to wait until dark to go in. They're hillbillies, of course they've got weapons, probably coon rifles, so a frontal assault is out. Do you think you can get in the back?"

He rubbed his palm over the receiver. "It's tough, I . . ."

"Clay? Hey, wait, you're not Clay—"

He heard her cursing, then the walkie-talkie went fuzzy.

Jack quickly began making his way around to the front, in a wide circle, hoping to come in behind the shooters, but truth be told, he wasn't holding out much hope.

He heard a few more rounds of gunfire, then silence. He pictured the woman and her partner—they were pros, they wouldn't panic, but they were facing a full-blown screwed-up fiasco. They'd know enough to get out of there fast. Somehow they'd been spotted, and their prey were armed and shooting back. They'd probably believed it would be easy, even though the shooter they'd sent to Parlow was presently residing in Franklin County Hospital. Did they know that? Probably. But what they couldn't know was that an FBI agent was here with the *hillbillies.* And one of the hillbillies was a marine, the other a crack shot. What a nice surprise.

If they had a contingency plan, it was shot to hell now. He ran, hunkered down, ignoring the leaves whipping his face, ignoring the pain in his thigh, the blood seeping from the cut in his left arm, and tried to move as quickly and quietly as possible.

He heard something, and stopped on a dime. It sounded like a footstep, a single footstep.

Sunlight speared through the leaves overhead. Silence. Nothing. Then he heard an animal, probably a possum, running away, running from him, he knew.

No footfalls, no one was near. How much farther?

He heard some fresh gunshots coming from Gillette and Rachael, but no return fire.

They were gone.

He ran straight out toward the edge of the forest until he saw the front of the house. He had to be close to their last position. They could still be nearby, see what he was going to do, kill him if he showed himself. Jack didn't want to get shot. He nearly ran over their former position—saw the flattened leaves, the shells.

They were gone.

He ran all the way back to the road. When he burst out of the woods, he saw two figures in a late-model black Ford Expedition burning rubber down the road.

They'd had to leave their companions. Not a good idea—but they didn't have a choice.

He ran back as fast as he could, yelled before he broke through the woods in front of Gillette's house, "It's Jack! They're gone. Don't shoot! I'm coming out!"

Rachael flew out the splintered front door. "Jack! Are you all right? They ran?"

"I'm fine. You?"

"Some glass in my arm and neck, nothing bad. Gillette's okay, too. He went to check out back."

"One of the guys is alive. I left him on the kitchen floor. Let's get in the house," he said, and grabbed her arm and pulled her inside.

Gillette came running out of the kitchen. "There's blood on the floor, Jack, but the guy's gone."

He was a moron. He should have shot the goon in the leg. "He won't get far," Jack said. "There were two of them, actually. One's dead at the back of the yard, right at the tree line. I took both their wallets. I'll bet you these guys are in the system."

Rachael said, "I'll call Sheriff Hollyfield, tell him what happened and get him out here."

"I'm going to look outside."

When Jack walked into the kitchen five minutes later, he said, "The body's gone. Our wounded guy carried him out. They must have another vehicle."

"The sheriff will be here in thirty minutes, tops," Rachael said.

"I forgot, I've got some critical information for him," Jack said, and dialed him up, managed to catch him on the point of leaving his office. Jack gave Sheriff Hollyfield the license plate of the Ford Expedition.

Rachael ignored the objections of the men and went with Jack to track the shooters through the woods, the rifle pointed down at her side. Jack wasn't happy, even though he knew she was a good shot.

"There's got to be blood," he whispered. "Keep as quiet as you can."

They found the blood trail quickly enough. "Look," Jack said, going down on his knees. "He's carrying his dead buddy. They can't be too far ahead."

The blood trail led back to the road, some thirty feet farther beyond where the Ford Expedition had peeled out.

Jack said, "They were careful enough to have two vehicles. The guy I shot in the shoulder, he needs major help fast."

When they returned to the house, Jack called the nearest hospital. They'd already been alerted, he was told, by Sheriff Hollyfield.

"Gillette, are there any physicians close by that our wounded guy could find easily?"

Gillette shook his head. "No, unless he knows of one personally. Or has a phone book. Parlow's the closest town. Everything's so spread out around here, someone not familiar with the area couldn't find his elbow."

Jack phoned Dr. Post at the clinic, just in case. Nurse Harmon agreed to alert all the hospitals in the area. Then he called Savich.

Rachael listened to him with half an ear as she swept up the glass from the shattered front windows.

"We're beyond lucky," Jack was saying to Savich. "Without that perimeter alarm the shooters tripped when they came in, we'd have been in bad trouble since Rachael and I were out in the open.

"They didn't know I was here, probably didn't know Gillette was a marine, or that Rachael can shoot a quarter out of the air. Sheriff Hollyfield should be here soon, so everything seems covered." He listened, then said, "I got wallets out of both guys I shot, but it's like the shooter at Roy Bob's garage—they removed all ID, credit cards, likely left everything in their vehicles. I can get some blood from the kitchen floor and from some leaves in the forest, get us some DNA. Yeah, all right." Jack hung up. "Savich says enough is enough, said he never liked the idea of third time's a charm. He wants Rachael back in Washington. And he wants you, Gillette, to take a vacation."

"Yeah, like that'll happen," Gillette said.

He sighed and looked around. He bent down, picked up a large hunk of glass. "I guess I'm not through with my house."

"They're going to put me in the same hospital room as Dr. MacLean, are they?" Rachael wondered aloud. "Well, forget that. I've got to call my mom. If they didn't do a pretty good search to find out about Slipper Hollow, then they could have gotten to her."

Gillette said, "I called while you and Jack were tracking blood in the woods. Everyone's fine. I didn't tell your mother about any of your trouble."

Rachael said, "But shouldn't we warn them? Shouldn't they take a vacation?"

Jack shook his head. "Whoever ordered this hit doesn't want more collateral damage than absolutely necessary. Parlow must have scared them but good. Limit the risks, limit the exposure. They knew it'd be beyond stupid to go after your mom and her family. And so they did something else."

Rachael said, "Fine, aren't you brilliant. Just what did they do? I didn't think anyone knew about Slipper Hollow."

Gillette sighed. "It wouldn't be hard, Rachael, think about it."

Jack said, "Gillette's right. Not hard at all. They researched you, Rachael, found out about Gillette and where he lives. After the failure in Parlow, they must have looked for another destination, and found it."

Gillette said, "I guess I wanted this place to be off the map. Nothing's off the map in this day and age. I'm an idiot." He shook his head. "Oh yeah, there would be FedEx records, property records, asking at the local post office where my P.O. box is, any number of ways to track me down."

Jack said to Rachael, "I should have hauled your butt to the Arizona desert."

Gillette looked over at his bullet-riddled front door, at all the beautiful windows, now shot to pieces, the gouges in the walls, the shattered hall mirror.

Jack said, "While we're waiting for Sheriff Hollyfield, let's start fixing that door and boarding up the windows. You gonna use FedEx to deliver new windows?"

"Probably, but I might take myself off their database," Gillette said.

"I'm so sorry, Uncle Gillette," Rachael said. "It's all my fault."

"Don't piss me off, Rachael," Gillette said, and tugged her braid.

It wasn't until that evening, right before dark, that Jack discovered the gunmen had found and disabled Rachael's Charger.

TWENTY-ONE

Washington Memorial Hospital
Washington, D.C.
Wednesday morning

Dr. MacLean's eyes weren't drug-bright anymore; he was alert and laughing with a nurse when Savich and Sherlock came into his room.

He looked over at them, smiled. "I remember you two from yesterday. You're the FBI agents who work with Jackson." He shrugged. "Jackson told me the young lady with him—Rachael, I believe her name is—saved our hides after he brought the plane down. They left ten minutes ago, said you were on your way."

The nurse, Louise Conver, gave Dr. MacLean a smile and left. "Yes," Savich said, "we saw them in the lobby. They told us you're feeling much better this morning."

The neurologist had told them the disease was unpredictable and everyone was different. Savich prayed Dr. MacLean would remember enough of their conversation the day before so they wouldn't have to begin all over.

MacLean said thoughtfully, "I always told his daddy I never liked the shortened version of his name, so he'll stay Jackson to me. Fact is, I threw footballs with him, taught him how to pitch a curveball, gave him pointers on how to psychoanalyze his sister's lemonade customers. He set up a stand right next to hers. Unlike Charlie Brown's Lucy, Jackson charged ten cents for a three-minute reading and, ah, dispensing advice. He was ten years old, I believe."

"How did he treat his customers?" Sherlock asked.

"I believe he looked at the men's palms, and for the women, he swished the remains of the lemonade in the bottom of their paper cups and studied the arrangement of the pulp.

"That was the first time I realized how

intuitive he was. His mother closed him down after he counseled a neighbor to stop sleeping with Mrs. Hinkley, who lived two blocks over. He and his sister Jennifer made a bundle that summer.

"Listen, I can tell something's going on with him and that young lady—Rachael—but he claimed everything was fine, all the bandages were for dippy stuff, all the result of our plane crash. I told him my injuries hadn't made me stupid, but evidently his had. Rachael laughed. Jackson said she was an interior designer. She told me since I'm not going to be in this room for much longer, she wouldn't bother coming up with a new color scheme. She managed to distract me, and then they left, so I'm asking you: What's going on with Jackson? Don't try telling me it's only about me and my problems."

Savich nodded. "You're right, he is involved in some pretty hinky things. But you know he's good. He'll be fine. Try not to worry. The staff told us your wife stayed with you all last evening. You must have been very pleased to have her back from Lexington. Are you expecting her this morning?"

Sherlock realized, watching Dr. Mac-Lean's face, that his wife was the ultimate distraction.

MacLean said in a huff, "I told Molly not to come back today, that I'm not going anywhere and she doesn't have to worry—she'd just piss me off with all her nagging, her never-ending litany about finding us a little beach house in Bermuda. At least the rest of the family is still in Lexington. That crew would bring down the hospital. I threatened them on pain of death not to come here and drive me nuts." He grinned real big. "Hey, I guess I already am nuts."

Time to get to it. Sherlock dove right in. "Dr. MacLean, do you remember what we spoke about yesterday?"

"My brain might be executing a big-time tailspin into never-never land, but I do remember our conversation from yesterday. It's true, sometimes I don't. But yesterday, yeah, I remember everything. I told you about two of my patients, something I shouldn't have done. But you're FBI, so I suppose I have no choice since some jerk-face is trying to murder me. I'd sing it to you in an aria if I had to.

"Actually, telling you about those particular

people was amusing. And you can call me Timothy." They nodded, and he continued. "By the way, the FBI agent guarding my door, Tomlin, he's come in a couple of times, told me I'm not to worry because he never snoozes on the job and he's one tough bud, raised by a mom, a police lieutenant, who, according to him, shut down a gang in Detroit." He grinned as he looked from Savich to Sherlock. "He also told me you guys were in San Francisco a couple of weeks ago, playing with psychic mediums. Talk about weird yahoos."

"Agent Tomlin is a crackerjack," Sherlock said. "I didn't know his mom was such a hotshot."

Timothy laughed. "I'll tell him that next time he comes in to see me."

Sherlock asked, "How are you feeling this morning, sir?"

"I still feel like I'm busted up all over, but I took a hit of pain meds maybe five minutes ago, so soon that will translate into feeling mighty fine, thank you." He frowned, then said with all the innocence of a child, "I remember it clearly. I was telling you about Congresswoman Dolores McManus."

"Yes," Savich said. "And how she murdered her first husband."

Timothy sighed, then smiled beatifically. "Fact is, she popped out with it under hypnosis—you know, surprised the crap out of me. I couldn't believe it, didn't want to believe it. At first I thought she was pulling my leg, but no, that wasn't possible, she was indeed well under.

"I only wish I'd instructed her to forget everything she'd told me when I brought her out of it, but I was so flustered by what she'd said, I didn't."

Sherlock said, "Why don't you tell us exactly what she said so we can follow up on it."

For several moments MacLean looked uncertain. Even after saying he'd tell them everything, they could see him battling with himself. Then the disease must have blunted his concerns, or his sense of self-preservation exerted itself, because he said, his voice smooth, like a man carrying on a superficial social conversation, "Like I told you already, Dolores was married young, to a trucker, had two kids, and managed to get herself a communications degree before she was twenty-five. Life happened, as it always does, but with her it took an interesting twist. She had a big mouth, you see, and she wasn't afraid of anything. She started getting a reputation for taking on the big dogs, sometimes even bringing them down. This made her adjust her thinking about what she wanted and how she was going to get it.

"Her trucker husband, however, didn't want to get with the program. He wanted his wife waiting for him at home, a beer for him in her hand. He threatened to hurt her, to take the kids, whatever.

"She believed, she told me, that he would beat her. But the kids? The last one was out of the house in another six months so that wasn't a problem. But he was—a great big honking problem.

"So Dolores got to thinking. Who would vote for a congresswoman with a macho trucker for a husband? She knew this guy wouldn't rocket her to the stars, which she felt she deserved. For her that was winning a political office, one that paid her. He would only underscore her lack of any working credentials and what had been, to date, a worthless education.

"Then, all of a sudden, this middle-aged

woman proceeded to tell me that her husband was eighteen-wheeling on one of his regular runs through Alabama. When he pulled into his favorite truck stop to eat at the small diner, someone stepped out of the shadows and shot him dead.

"Then Dolores said, 'Watch this,' and she manufactured instant tears, told me this was how she acted when the cops came to her house—you know, 'Oh, how horrible, it must be a mistake, not my Lukey, oh God, what am I going to do, what about my poor fatherless children,' that sort of thing. Then she told me she swooned—the shock, you know. Then suddenly, she started laughing. She nearly hyperventilated she laughed so hard. She told me between hiccups how she'd hired this thug from Savannah to shoot Lukey, paid him five hundred bucks, told him where to do it. She was very pleased with herself, with her ultimate solution to getting elected to Congress. I was so shocked I brought her out of it. She remembered exactly what she'd said, of course, and so there it all was, the eight-hundred-pound moose in the middle of my office. I told her she was my patient and I would never break confidentiality. Still, I could tell she was spooked. I never expected to see her again, and I didn't. You think Dolores is the one out to kill me?"

"She sounds like a better possibility than Lomas Clapman," Savich said. "What she came to see you about professionally, any motive there if revealed?"

"Probably not, her stepfather sexually abused her, and she was having night-mares about it on and off during the past year. It was driving her nuts, and so she came to see me. What brought it on? She didn't know but that was the reason for the hypnosis—to take her back, to relive it, I guess you could say, in a controlled environment. But this is what popped out."

Savich nodded. "Okay, there was an-other patient the bartender heard you talk-ing about, right? Pierre Barbeau."

"Ah, yes, Pierre. I nearly forgot. Pierre is very smart, knows his way in and out of the intelligence community. I've known him and his wife, Estelle, and his son, Jean Da-vid, for years. Molly and I played golf with them, socialized a bit with them. We weren't best friends, but we had a pleasant ac-quaintanceship, I guess you could call it.

"Anyway, Pierre's a high-up liaison between the French National Police and our CIA. He's arrogant and rather vain, but you'd expect that because he's French, and over the years I just laughed at him when he'd go on and on about the superiority of the French. Blah blah blah, I tell him.

"Then, out of the blue, he called me, said he was in *turmoil*—that was his word—and he needed my help.

"Turns out it was about his son, Jean David, who, interestingly enough, was an American citizen, born unexpectedly three weeks early on vacation in Cape May, New Jersey, twenty-six years old, a Harvard graduate, very analytical, very bright, a nice guy, maybe even smarter than his old man, a strategic information analyst for the CIA, with a focus on the Middle East.

"Yeah, I can see you're getting the picture here. About six months ago Jean David got involved with a young woman who said she was a graduate student and worked part-time for a charitable group funding education in the Middle East. Of course, the group was only a cover, and she was actually gathering money here in the U.S. for terrorist groups, and recruiting. She found the gold at the end of the rainbow in Jean David.

"It wouldn't have been all that big a deal if Jean David had, for example, been a Maytag repairman, but since he was an analyst in the CIA, we're talking a major problem for him.

"About a month and a half ago Jean David let her see some sensitive material pinpointing the whereabouts of some of our operatives in Pakistan—showing off, I guess, to impress her.

"The CIA realized they had a big-ass problem almost immediately, what with the murder of two operatives, and went on full alert. Jean David realized he was in deep trouble, so he told his father about the woman he'd met and fallen for."

"Do you recall the name of this woman, Timothy?" Sherlock asked.

"It was something really sweet, like Mary—no, it was Anna. I don't know her last name. Pierre didn't know what to do. He came to me as a friend and in confidence to ask about the possibility of my defending his son legally from a psychiatric standpoint, maybe argue the boy was delusional or brainwashed and not legally responsible, and because he was worried about his son's mental health. I told him that no psychiatric diagnosis would keep Jean David out of prison in a case like this. I agreed to see him, of course, but only if Jean David confessed his crime to the authorities. Many operatives might still be in danger, and the authorities needed to know about the security breach. In fact, I told Pierre it was ethically impossible for me to keep it a secret under these circumstances and that I would tell the authorities if Jean David did not."

TWENTY-TWO

MacLean paused, closed his eyes, and Sherlock asked, "What happened, Timothy?"

"Now I've got to speak about Jean David in the past tense. I can't tell you how I hate that. You already know about his death, don't you?"

"Yes. Tell us what happened."

"All right. A week after I spoke to Pierre, Jean David drowned in a boating accident on the Potomac. Bad weather hit—a squall, I guess you'd call it, vicious winds whipping up the water. The bad weather was expected but still Jean David and his father went out fishing for striped bass. Pierre always believed you caught more fish in the middle of a high storm. They were heading back because the fog was coming in real thick when the rocking and rolling got to him, and he got real sick and vomited over the side of the boat. Then it gets sketchy. A speedboat evidently didn't see them in the rain and fog and rammed right into them. Pierre was tossed overboard. Jean David jumped in to save his father. So did one of the guys from the other boat. They managed to save Pierre, but Jean David drowned. They searched and searched, but they couldn't find his body.

"Pierre was distraught, and as sick as he was, he kept diving and searching, but it was no use. Jean David was ruled dead, and his death was ruled accidental two weeks ago. Was it really an accident? I know what you're thinking—Pierre and Jean David set it up between them to get him out of Washington. But, you see, there was the speedboat, and the people on board witnessed everything. They'd never heard of Pierre Barbeau. I believe that. I spoke to Pierre before he called me a murderer and hung up on me. He was grief-stricken. His son was dead and he blamed me for it. I strongly doubt Pierre could feign grief like that, at least not to me. I spoke to some mutual friends, and they agreed that both Pierre and Estelle were wrecks. He was their only child, and now he's dead at twenty-six. Because of me."

Sherlock said pleasantly, "You know that's ridiculous, Dr. MacLean. As a psychiatrist, you also know that when people are grieving, particularly when they've lost a loved one in a stupid accident, they try to apportion blame. You know it's natural, you've doubtless seen it countless times in your practice.

"Now, if you say something like that again, I will tell Molly and she'll deal with you."

He was frowning at her words, but at the threat about his wife, his mouth split into a grin. "Oh, all right, I guess I'm just feeling sorry for myself. Damn, I sure wish Pierre had never asked to see me. I've waded in quagmires before, but I've never been sucked down quite so deep."

Savich said, "So you told Pierre Barbeau that Jean David had to go to the authorities and confess or you were constrained morally and ethically to report him to the police?"

"Yes. It's like being a priest in the confessional. If the person making the confession is planning to do imminent harm, the priest has no choice but to go to the authorities. Would I have gone to the police? Actually I forgot all about it once I was in Lexington. I would hope they know exactly what Jean David did by now, but tomorrow, maybe I'll check in with the CIA, make sure nobody else is at risk."

Sherlock said, "You don't actually know if the CIA has tracked the information leak back to Jean David?"

"No. I haven't spoken to the Barbeaus, either, since that afternoon when I called to express my condolences and Pierre screamed at me.

"But whatever the CIA has found, trust me, it won't make the evening news. The CIA'll keep it under wraps, particularly now that Jean David is dead. They'll simply bury it."

They would, of course, Savich knew, but perhaps he could find out what they knew and what they didn't know, make sure for

himself that all the other vulnerable operatives were safe. He said, "This is a tragedy
that devastates, Timothy; it can make people act out of character, make them insane. I didn't feel a motive with Lomas
Clapman or Congresswoman McManus,
but here, it's bright and shiny, this beacon
of grief. Do you think Pierre Barbeau could
come after you, revenge for what he believes is your fault?"

MacLean squeezed his eyes closed
and whispered, "This utter consumption
of self by inconsolable grief—I've seen it
before. But Pierre? I don't know; I doubt it,
though. I'll tell you, any murder attempts
from that quarter would come from Estelle. She's the one who'd want me dead,
not Pierre. Estelle would bust the balls off
a coconut.

"I read people very well, agents, and I'll
tell you, what Pierre knows, Estelle knows.
She's the driver on that marriage bus. I'll
bet you Pierre didn't tell her he was coming to ask me for help. But if he told her
afterward, Estelle would see me as a danger to both her and her husband. Even
with Jean David dead, she'd be afraid that
I'd stir up talk. And of course there's her

family in France. I met them a couple of years ago. I'll tell you, I wouldn't want to be on their bad side.

"I have other patients with what you might call embarrassing incidents in their pasts, but not with any more juice than these three."

Savich said, "If you recall, Timothy, you blocked us from getting a list of all your patients. I hope you've since changed your mind. I really don't want anyone to kill you on my watch."

MacLean nodded. "You'll have the list as soon as I can get my receptionist to go into the office and make you a disk." They listened to him make the phone call. When he hung up, he said, "In a couple of hours she'll bring it here. I'm seeing the specialist from Duke again this afternoon. I don't know why he's making the trip since there's not a thing he can do but nod and try to look both wise and sorrowful about my condition. He's going to tell me what to expect in the future. Isn't that nice of him, the insensitive clod? As if I don't already know what my life is going to be like before I croak—which might be soon, if the person out to kill me succeeds. Maybe that would be a good thing. Then this mess—namely me—would be history."

Sherlock said, looking him straight in the eye, "Here's what I think: none of us knows what medical science will come up with next. Whatever weird diseases we contract could be helped or even cured next week or maybe next year. We simply don't know.

"I have a friend hanging on by his fingernails hoping for better antirejection drugs so he can have a pancreas transplant. And the thing is, it could happen. I know he wants to live. He has hope, boundless hope. As a doctor, sir, you should have hope, too."

She paused, her voice a quiet promise. "We will do our very best to keep you safe. If someone knocks you off after we've worked our butts off to keep you alive, I'll be extraordinarily pissed, Timothy. Forever."

He stared at her for a moment, then grinned hugely, showing silver on his back teeth, before pressing his head into the hard hospital pillow.

When they left, Agent Tomlin's sexy

smile wasn't returned. It fell right off his face when he realized Agent Sherlock was upset.

Sherlock looked straight ahead as she and Dillon walked to the elevator. "Given this horrible disease, given there's no cure, and finally, given what will happen, without fail—I think I might kill myself if I were him. All the rest is hooey."

"No, you wouldn't," Savich said, as he pressed the button in the empty car. "You believe exactly what you told Timothy. Life gives and life takes. The thing is, you simply never know, can never predict, and given the pace of science, you put up with what's on your plate, you do your best with the hand you're dealt, and you hope."

She leaned into him, sighed. "Some things are so sad. I hate feeling helpless."

"I do, too."

When the elevator doors slid open Savich and Sherlock stepped into the lobby to see Jack and Rachael walking toward them.

Jack said, "I just got a call from Ollie, and was on my way up to you guys. You won't believe this. Timothy's office was torched early this morning, his computer toasted, hard disk destroyed, all his hard-copy files burned to a crisp."

Sherlock raised her eyes to the heavens. "Why can't things ever shake out easy?" She kicked at a big ceramic flower pot with fake red geraniums in it.

"You don't even seem concerned, Jack," Savich said. "What do you know that we don't?"

"It so happens Molly gave me his laptop, and it has all his patients on it."

"Make note of this, Rachael. Jack here's a prince," Savich said. "I was looking forward to a lovely eggplant po' boy for lunch, and now you've made that possible."

"Eggplant?" Rachael repeated, and looked astonished. "An eggplant po' boy?"

"Oh yes," Sherlock said, smiling, "grilled in only a soupçon of olive oil, available only in our cafeteria on the seventh floor of the Hoover building. Elaine Pomfrey makes the best vegetarian sandwiches in Washington, and this one she prepares especially for Dillon. Thank you, Jack, for having that great news."

Savich said to Rachael, "You and Jack

need to go to Senator Abbott's house—
your house—get all your stuff. Then we're
going to put you in a safe house."

Rachael smiled at all three of them.
"Nope, no safe house in this lifetime. I'll
tell you what I'm going to do: I intend to
have a chat this very afternoon with Aunt
Laurel and Uncle Quincy, after I have some
nice crispy fried chicken, maybe a biscuit
and mashed potatoes in your famous cafeteria. But I don't want to hear any more
about hiding."

Jack said to Savich, "I've got some more
convincing to do, evidently."

Sherlock said, "By the way, the blood
samples from two of the shooters from Slipper Hollow are in the lab. We'll soon know if
those bozos are in the system. Still no word
from any medical facilities about the guy
you shot in Gillette's kitchen, Jack."

"Maybe they're both dead," Rachael
said, and pushed her hair behind her ears.
"Wouldn't that be nice?"

Savich held up his hand. "It's one o'clock.
I'm starving. Let's discuss this over my
eggplant po' boy." He looked at Rachael.
"And your fried chicken."

Jack said, "What about the guy Rachael shot in Roy Bob's garage? Roderick Lloyd?"

"He's got himself a lawyer, still refuses to say a word," Sherlock said. "Our agents searched his apartment, found some credit card receipts that might give us the gold. Lloyd has been to the Blue Fox restaurant over on Maynard four or five times in the past two weeks.

"Our agent found out Lloyd brought a Lolita with him the past three times, according to one of the waiters, who said she gave him her cell number. We should know who she is anytime now. As for Lloyd, at least he's no longer a danger to anybody."

Rachael said as they walked to the hospital parking lot, "I need a gun. Do you have one to lend me, Sherlock?"

"Look, Rachael, I know you're a fine shot, I know your life is on the line here, but I'd be breaking the law if I gave you one."

Not wonderful news, but Rachael said, "Okay, I understand. Hey, I wasn't thinking—I bet Jimmy kept one at home."

Savich and Jack both opened their

mouths but Sherlock held up her hand. "No, guys, if there's a gun at home, then what's wrong with her defending herself? It's not as if she's not trained and might shoot somebody who doesn't deserve it."

"Thank you, Sherlock."

"I don't like this," Jack said. "I really don't."

"Get over it," Sherlock said, and looked at her husband. "No, no, bad dog, keep quiet."

They stopped by the Criminal Apprehension Unit on the fifth floor, introduced Rachael to all the agents present. Ollie showed her a photo of his wife and his little boy. In the cafeteria, while Savich was eating his eggplant po' boy and Rachael was chewing on a fried chicken leg, Sherlock's cell rang. She swallowed a bite of taco, then answered.

She hung up barely a minute later. "We've got the name of Lolita—the young girl who was with Roderick Lloyd. The cell phone number she gave the waiter is for a phone that belongs to a married grad student who admitted giving the phone to a hooker in exchange for her services. He gave us her name."

Sherlock beamed. "Angel Snodgrass is in juvie over in Fairfax."

Twenty minutes later, she and Savich were in his new Porsche, zipping out of the Hoover garage.

TWENTY-THREE

Angel Snodgrass was sixteen years old, blessed with long, thick natural blond hair, soft baby-blue eyes, and a face clean of makeup. She did indeed look like an angel. An undercover vice cop had busted her for soliciting outside the Grove Creek Inn at the big Hammerson mall in Fairfax.

"Angel? I'm Special Agent Savich and this is Special Agent Sherlock. FBI. We'd like to speak to you."

She folded her very white hands on the table in front of her and stared at them. Her nails were short, clean, and nicely buffed. "Why are you special?"

Savich grinned. "The way I hear it, up until the time Hoover took over, the FBI was a mess—no background checks, no training, a playground for thugs. Hoover changed all that, announced his agents would from that time on be special, and so it became our title. There are lots of other special agents now, but we were the first." Savich wasn't at all sure if that was entirely true, but it sounded like it might be.

Angel thought about this for a while as she studied his face. "Who's Hoover?" she asked.

"Ah, well, he was a long time ago. Where's home, Angel?" he asked her.

"Since I'm not going back there, I'm not saying."

"Why were you turning tricks?" Sherlock asked.

Angel shrugged. "I wanted a Big Mac. Lots of businessmen are in and out of the Grove Creek Inn, and there are lots of guys at the mall. Since I'm so young and pretty, they usually tip me real good, too. If that cop hadn't nabbed me, I could have had a dozen Big Macs. Now, it's just the crap they claim is food in this pit. What do you special guys want anyway?"

Had she been abused before she finally ran away? Savich knew this girl would get counseled here, that there would be a shot at straightening her out.

Sherlock sat forward in her chair. "We need your help, Angel. The waiter you gave your cell number to at the Blue Fox restaurant told us you were with Roderick Lloyd. We need you to tell us about him."

"Why? What'd Roddy do?"

Savich studied her, her eyes, her body movements. "Thing is, Angel, Roddy's a very bad man. He's in a hospital in western Virginia right now because he tried to murder a woman. It's good for her that she's smart and fast, got herself a rifle and shot him instead."

Angel nodded, tapped her fingers on the tabletop, tossed her head, sending all that beautiful blond hair swinging away from her head to settle again on her shoulders and down her back. "Well, I can't say I'm surprised. Roddy is always blowing hard, bragging, like that, telling me how important he is, how when there's a problem, he's the one folks call to solve it. He was all puffed up when he told me he had to go out of town for a couple of days, take care of this *situation* for a real important dude. He didn't give me a name, if that's what you're wondering.

"I was wondering why Roddy hasn't called me, then I realized my cell is dead and I can't charge it since Roddy locked me out of his apartment. Is he going to die?"

"No," Sherlock said, "but he's not in terribly good shape. Lost the use of both of his hands for a while."

"I was thinking he was a hit man, like that," Angel said, looking over Savich's right shoulder, her voice calm. "I can see him blowing it, too. I mean even in bed he was always too fast off the mark, didn't really think things through, you know? No surprise he'd screw up a hit."

"Did he tell you about this *situation* he had to handle?" Savich asked. He pulled a pack of sugarless gum from his pocket, offered her a stick.

She took it, peeled the wrapper with long white fingers, stuck it into her mouth. She chewed, then sighed. "Well, this isn't a Big Mac, but it's not bad. Thanks, Special Agent."

"You're welcome." They chewed in companionable silence, then Savich said, "About the situation Roddy had to handle—we'd sure appreciate your telling us exactly what you know about it."

A flicker of alarm widened her eyes.

Savich said easily, "The woman he tried to kill, the woman who shot him instead, she's still in danger, from the people or person who hired Roddy. Did he tell you anything?"

Angel began tapping her fingers again on the scarred tabletop. Savich wasn't blind, he saw the gleam in her innocent blue eyes. Ah, so they had a budding deal maker on their hands. "Nah," Angel began, "he didn't tell me a thing, and I don't know anything—"

Savich interrupted her smoothly. "If you help us, I'll make sure you get the reward. It's . . . ah . . . I'm not really sure, maybe five hundred bucks, depending on the information."

"That's bullshit," Angel said.

"Well, yeah," Savich admitted, "but the thing is, it'd buy a lot of Big Macs and a new charger for your cell phone."

"Hmm," Angel said. "How do I know I

can trust you? I mean, you're pretty hot, but you're still a federal cop. It'd take weeks, maybe years before I'd get the reward."

Savich pulled out his wallet, saw her eyes were glued to it. He slowly peeled out five one-hundred-dollar bills, the entire amount he'd gotten from his ATM that morning. "To prove you can trust me, I'll advance the reward. It's yours if what you tell us is useful."

She never looked away from the stack of bills.

"The first one's on account," Savich said, and pushed one of the bills to her, "to prove my good intent." Angel grabbed it and stuffed it in her bra.

"There's nothing like green next to your skin," she said, and gave him a huge smile. "Okay, I can give you useful stuff. After three bourbons, straight up, Roddy started bitching, told me he should be paid more to handle this *situation.* Roddy always talked like that—you know, making words sound important. He said it was pissant dough for his talents, like that. I almost shouted at him, 'Dude, you're old and nasty, who'd want to pay you anything?'

But I had a nice place to stay and Roddy was easy and fast in bed, so I kept my trap shut. Roddy said it was a real rush deal. He was going in and out of this hick town like right now, and so he didn't have time to check anything out, said he hated going in blind, but from what I could tell, that's what he always did, just waltzed right in somewhere and hoped for the best. What a dumbass. Is that useful?"

"Not very," Savich said, and fingered a second hundred, his eyes on her face.

Angel's hands fluttered toward the second bill. She said, "Okay, I'll admit I was listening when the phone rang—that's how I knew he got the job. He knew whoever it was, and he was real respectful, assured whoever it was that he could handle anything, to trust him, lame stuff like that."

"He didn't say a name?"

"No, he listened, then kept telling whoever it was that he'd take care of it, no problem."

"When he hung up, what did he say?"

"He said he had to move fast, that he had to drive to this hick town in Kentucky tomorrow, he had to leave real early Monday morning. Oh yeah, he wrote down lots of stuff. Directions, I guess. Then this photo came through his fax machine."

Savich pushed the second hundred-dollar bill across the table. It disappeared into her bra.

"Okay, the fax—it was a woman, young, pretty, okay blond hair"—she tossed her head again—"but she had this real cool braid. So I asked him what he was going to do to her and he said, nothing much, just put out her lights, and he slogged down another shot of bourbon. While he poured, I picked up her photo—it was off a driver's license, but like I said, I could tell she was pretty even though the picture was lousy. When I get a driver's license I'm going to sleep with the guy taking the pictures so I can get me a good one."

Savich began to smooth out the third one-hundred-dollar bill.

"He grabbed the fax from me, started talking to himself, like, 'I need a full clip, maybe two, that'll do it. Cheap bastards,' on and on like that, you know?"

Bastards. Plural. Savich nodded. "Angel, by any chance did Roddy ever use your cell phone?"

She thought about that, and Savich could see her mental wheels spinning. "Well, yeah, maybe, a couple of times."

"How long ago did the graduate student trade your services for a cell phone?"

"Well, I guess I should tell you I gave that grad student a smiley face when I was living with Roddy."

"And you still have your cell?"

"Yeah, sure, but like I told you, it's deader than the fish my uncle Bobby shot out of the water when he was aiming for my little brother."

No, Savich thought, *don't go there.* "I'd like to borrow your cell phone, Angel. I'll return it. In fact, I'll pay you a rental fee. What do you say?"

Greed gleamed in those innocent eyes. "How much you willing to pay me? It's a good phone, lots of fancy things on it. Well, to be honest here, and that hurts real bad, I don't think it's got many minutes on it now."

"However many minutes you've got will be perfect," Savich said.

"You know, a cell phone's like a guy; if you don't plug him in every night, charge him good, you got nothing at all."

Savich slid two bills across the table as Angel dug her cell phone out of her pocket. "I need some lipstick, but they wouldn't give me my purse. They didn't take my cell because it's dead, I guess."

"Don't worry, I'll return it nicely charged." Savich rose, left the last hundred-dollar bill on the table. "Sherlock, why don't you give Angel your lipstick. It's a real pretty shade. See if you can't make her earn that last hundred."

He said to Angel, "I'll see you soon. I think your information was so valuable that I'm going to speak to the people in charge and have all charges dropped."

She gaped at him.

He held up his hand. "Wait, Angel. I will do this if you swear to me you'll call this number." He handed her a card. "This guy helps kids like you. Will you call him?"

He saw the lie in her eyes. "Oh yes, Mr. Special Agent, I'll call . . . Mr. Hanratty right away."

He shook her hand and left her and Sherlock to look at the lipstick. He joined the assistant director of the facility, Mrs. Limber, in the hallway. "It's going very well," he told her. "Thanks for letting us deal with her alone. I'm going to see if I can't get her released."

Mrs. Limber, soft as a pillow and wearing huge glasses, patted his shoulder. "Angel has guts and brains, but she's got a larcenous soul. Some do, you know."

"Yeah," he said, "I know, but—"

"She's also a freight train—she won't stop. I see you've got Angel's dead cell phone. Would you like to borrow a charger?"

Inside the small interview room, Sherlock smiled at the lovely shade of dark pink Angel smoothed on her lips. "Very nice. Yep, you keep it, the mirror, too."

"I want a Big Mac," Angel said, and tossed her hair.

Sherlock fingered the last hundred. "Why don't you tell me how you met Roddy."

When Sherlock found Savich, he was sitting under a tree in front of the detention facility, humming and playing with Angel's cell.

He looked up. "Did she earn the last hundred?"

"Yep, and now our budding Donald Trump owns my lipstick, mirror, and a comb. Oh yeah, she told me you should keep her cell; with all the cash she got off you, she's going to buy herself a Venus. She can't wait to leave this place in the dust. I don't know, Dillon, I just don't know."

"Sometimes you gotta cut the fish loose. You're not going to believe what I found on the cell."

TWENTY-FOUR

Baltimore, Maryland
Wednesday afternoon

This has got to be heaven."

Rachael stared around the large reception area on the thir-tieth floor of the Abbott-Cavendish building on the corner of South Calvert Street. Her breathing quickened. "Oh my, would you look at those beauties. Jimmy told me Laurel is an expert on Chippendale furniture and filled the place with originals, but he never brought me here, said he couldn't stand the stuff." She looked around at the mint-condition Chippendale chairs and tables and felt her pulse race. "He was wrong," she said, lightly running her fingers over a chair back. "How could anyone hate these? They're exquisite. Just touch the wood, Jack, so smooth and perfect. It's mahogany from the West Indies. And this chair leg—it's called the cabriole leg, his signature form."

Jack looked at the elegantly curved chair leg, at the turned feet, then back at her. He said slowly, "I knew you could come into my house and do this and that and it'd look a lot nicer than it does now, but you also know all about antiques?"

"Particularly Chippendale. Would you look at that lowboy, at the elaborate carving. It screams eighteenth century. Do you know he never used a maker's mark? To prove authenticity, you need to be able to trace the piece back to the original invoice."

What was a lowboy? Was she joking? An invoice from the eighteenth century?

Jack said, "No, I didn't know that." He listened to her talk about how Americans like Queen Anne splats and kidney-shaped seats, how they prefer cherrywood to mahogany. Those fancy cabriole legs sank at least three inches into the thick, expensive carpeting. You couldn't pay him to sit in one of those chairs.

"And the three Turners," Rachael went on. "Jimmy did like those paintings. I remember him telling me about them. They belonged to his mother." She looked around the reception area, lust in her eyes. "To have a huge budget to decorate a space like this—wouldn't that be something? I decorated a half-dozen commercial spaces in and around Richmond. I had to work my butt off to be both creative and cheap."

"Did your clients appreciate what you did?"

"They all did, and that's nice. Actually, I prefer being in on the design process itself, though, creating a space for a specific look and a specific function. My client list was growing nicely before I went to meet Jimmy."

They heard a throat clear and looked over at two young women and two young men seated behind a huge swath of highly polished mahogany, each seated at an individual computer station, all nicely dressed, all working industriously on keyboards or speaking in hushed voices on phones. Except for one young woman, who had a raised eyebrow and beautiful fingernails.

Jack smiled at Rachael, nodded toward the young woman. "Let's go hassle that bright-eyed young lass at reception, see where our prey is."

The young lass—her tag read Julia—looked suspicious at first, then fell victim to Jack's smile, a phenomenon Rachael had already observed a couple of times. It seemed Julia couldn't help herself, she loosened up, smiled back at him. "Good afternoon. How may I help you?"

Jack opened his wallet, showed her his creds.

Julia's smiled wavered.

"We'd like to see Ms. Kostas, Julia."

"Ah, well, yes, may I tell her what it's about?"

"No," he said. Then he smiled that lethal smile again, lowered his voice. "National security."

Julia immediately rang a number and spoke quietly.

"I'll show you to her office," she said. They followed her down a wide hallway with Stubbs horse paintings on the walls. There were half a dozen niches along the way holding antique vases filled with lush trailing ivy, warmed by small circular overhead lights.

Julia knocked lightly on a set of mahogany double doors, opened them, and they stepped into a large rectangular room furnished with spare, plain blond Scandinavian furniture, not a single antique in the place. Lots of windows filled the room with afternoon sunlight and views to die for, but still the office felt cold.

"Ms. Kostas, this is Special Agent Crowne and, ah . . ." Julia turned brick red because she'd neglected to ask Rachael her name.

"I know who she is, Julia. You may leave us now."

Jack had read all about Laurel Abbott Kostas on the drive over to Abbott Enterprises International headquarters in Baltimore. He'd studied several unflattering photos of her. She wasn't by any stretch a beauty. Still, given the wealth factor, he'd expected her to have at least a hint of glam, designer everything, but there wasn't a scintilla of pizzazz in this woman. Her eyes never left Rachael as she slowly walked toward them. Her hair was neither short nor long, salt-and- pepper, not a sophisticated salt-and-pepper like his mom's, whose hair was cut in a swinging bob, but flat, drab, and coarse. She wore no earrings, no makeup to soften the sharp angles of her face. Her eyes beneath thick black brows were cold stone gray, her mouth pinched and small. She was wearing a plain gray suit and low-heeled pumps, her sole jewelry a wedding band. She didn't look fat or thin; what she looked like was a cold and hard matron, or a prison warden. She wasn't smiling. She looked older than her fifty-one years. He wondered what she'd looked like at twenty-one, what she'd looked like when she married Stefanos Kostas at age thirty-five.

"Hello, Aunt Laurel."

Laurel Abbott Kostas looked at Rachael with a combination of distaste and indifference, and there was something else, something feral in those stone cold eyes of hers. "You are a bastard, Ms. Janes. It's very possible you are not even my brother's unfortunate mistake. I am not your aunt, nor are you and I on a first-name basis."

Rachael said, "Actually, I'm no longer a bastard, which means you are indeed my aunt. Didn't Jimmy tell you and Quincy that he adopted me? I became his legal daughter five days before his death. His lawyer, Mr. Cullifer, said the entire process took only five weeks, less time than it took the mechanic to fix his Jag, and then he smiled and said money and influence are very fine things."

"A fine tale, Ms. Janes. You will not call the senator by that ridiculous low-class name. His name was John James Abbott Junior."

"He told me until I could get used to the idea of calling him Dad, I was to call him Jimmy. And now I'll never have that chance."

Laurel Kostas's hands clenched at her sides. "He did that to get back at us." She sucked in a breath, calmed herself. Jack saw the take-no-prisoners iron in her, the formidable opponent who'd tear your heart out before breakfast, or, like Rachael had said, he could easily see her sucking the blood from your jugular. Old Man Abbott must have been proud of her. She looked briefly at Jack, dismissed him, then back at Rachael. "All right, you bullied your way in here. What's this nonsense about national security? What do you really want?"

"We're here about Jimmy's death."

Her eyes turned colder, if possible, and her mouth seamed as she said in her very precise voice, "What about his unfortunate death?"

"He didn't just die, he was murdered."

"That is absolute nonsense. Senator Abbott's death was a tragic accident. It was ruled an accident by the police."

"Greg Nichols, his senior staffer, knew it wasn't an accident."

"Everyone spoke to Greg Nichols. He was shocked and saddened by the tragedy. He believed it an accident, as well.

"It has nothing to do with you, Ms. Janes—yes, I will call you that until I have proof you have told me the truth. Brady Cullifer would have called both Quincy and me if you had been legally adopted; he would have warned us. But he did not."

"Perhaps," Rachael said, "Mr. Cullifer didn't call you because he considered it a confidential matter."

"There are no confidences in a family, Ms. Janes. However, regardless of any legalities, I will never recognize you as an Abbott. I want you to get out of here. I never want to look at your face after today. You managed to bilk my brother out of his money and his property, that wonderful house in Chevy Chase where we all grew up. It's in your hands, a stranger's hands. Bastard or not, you have won. Get out of here before I call security."

Rachael said easily, "I brought security with me, Mrs. Kostas. Don't you remember? This is Special Agent Jackson Crowne, with the FBI."

Laurel put out her hand. Short buffed nails, clear polish, but the thumbnails were chewed to the quick. Jack handed her his shield, watched her study it for an aeon before handing it back. "So," she said, "this pathetic girl managed to talk the FBI into revisiting this national tragedy. Has she accused us of murdering Senator Abbott?"

"Actually, ma'am, we have a lot of questions, not only about Senator Abbott's death."

"You won't for much longer," Laurel said, reaching for her phone, and she turned her back to them. Jack hoped she wasn't calling her lawyer. He really didn't want to have to deal with that.

Jack had faced down monsters during his years in the FBI's Elite Crime Unit, and remembered every single one of them with utter clarity, but in this woman's presence, listening to her low, clipped voice, he felt a sort of black coldness in her.

He purposefully turned away and led Rachael to the huge windows that looked toward the Inner Harbor, lined with shops filled with tourists, the blue water of the harbor dotted with pleasure craft, ferries, and fishing boats. It looked intensely alive, very different from this frozen world so high above it. He was losing it.

He said, "I know a little restaurant right on the Inner Harbor where I'd like to take you for dinner."

Rachael nodded.

Jack couldn't wait to get away from this cold, driven woman. It was very likely she wouldn't talk to them. Had she held the family's reputation so dear, had she believed her brother's confession to the world would not only destroy her brother but cause irreparable damage to the family and to the Abbott holdings so much that she murdered her own brother? He couldn't imagine it himself, it was too over the top.

They heard Laurel Kostas hang up the phone, and turned.

By the look on her face, she hadn't gotten what she wanted. Jack was tempted to applaud, but he didn't. He watched her face smooth out, and he knew to his gut that when this woman managed that slick-as-glass expression, she was in full control again.

She radiated power and malice.

"I spoke to my lawyer. He said he would call your superiors, who would deal with you, Agent Crowne. You will leave now. I will not speak to you."

Rachael said, "But Mrs. Kostas, don't you want to know if your brother's death really was an accident? Don't you care that someone might have murdered him and gotten away with it? Didn't you love your brother?"

Jack saw feral rage on her face. She leaned forward, her palms splayed on the long expanse of smooth blond birch. "My brother's drinking was unfortunate. Quincy and I told him many times to stop—at least not to drive when he drank too much—but he never listened to us, or to anyone. Quincy and I have wondered why he would drink to such an extent when his supposed precious daughter had magically returned to him. Both of us have wondered if he didn't change his mind about you, if he was about to demand DNA tests, but didn't have the chance—he died. Greg Nichols agrees it is strange, all of it, your appearance, my brother's death.

"You should be thanking me that we didn't push the police to investigate you, particularly since *you* are the only one to gain by his death. Why have you involved the FBI? You think they wouldn't consider you a prime suspect?"

TWENTY-FIVE

She was good, Jack thought, very good, a deft manipulator. She'd managed to turn it all around, and what she said made sense. It was obvious to Jack that Rachael had never considered this. She looked pole-axed.

Jack said, "Ms. Kostas, I understand your father was quite the autocrat, that Rachael's mother was so afraid of him she didn't tell Rachael who her real father was until after Carter Blaine Abbott died."

"That is nonsense. Absolute nonsense. My father was a great man, a brilliant man, a man with extraordinary vision. Look around you—he founded Abbott Enterprises fifty years ago with a small strip mall, and look what it is today: a power not only in the U.S. but in the world. Abbott is both respected and admired, and that is because of my father's legacy.

"To his family he was kindness itself. But I will tell you this—he couldn't abide fools or liars; he protected his children, took care of them. When he saw your mother, young as she was, he knew what she was, and so he saved his son from her.

"Did you show up on my brother's doorstep because that scheming mother of yours needed money and you were the one who was to get it for her?"

Rachael wanted to kill her on the spot, to put her hands around her neck and . . . but she said, her voice calm, even pleasant, "That was very well done, Mrs. Kostas. You put me on the defensive, a skill Jimmy said you have in spades. I would not like to own a company you wanted to acquire.

"But finding out about my father's death isn't about your spite, isn't about your dislike for me. It's about getting justice for a very fine man."

Laurel slammed her fist on the desktop. "I know the truth, and it's quite horrible and needless enough, without implying anyone else was involved. If you didn't kill him, then the senator was drunk and he lost control of his car."

"Surely you knew your brother didn't have a single drink since he killed that little girl, Melissa Parks, in Delancey Park eighteen months ago, nor did he drive a car after that evening.

"You had meals with him, saw him in social settings. Surely you noticed he no longer drank, never drove? This is the truth. I know it to be the truth. Actually, he always drank club soda. Therefore, he couldn't have been drunk, nor could he have been driving. Someone else was."

"I will not speak further about this."

"I know Jimmy told you and your husband, and Quincy, about what happened eighteen months ago. Moreover, he told you he couldn't stand living with the guilt anymore and that he was going public with all of it. He said you and Quincy were both furious when he told you what he planned to do, that even though he would be the one ruined by his confession, you and Quincy didn't agree. You felt it would blacken the family name, call into question the family honor, make business partners question the Abbott honesty. He said you and Quincy were enraged. He was disappointed because he wanted you both to understand, to support his decision to go public."

Laurel drew herself up to her full five-nine height. She looked faintly bored. "Whatever aberrations my poor brother suffered from at the end of his life, they are no longer of any concern to anyone. I loved my brother very much. I admired him, but he wasn't a strong man."

"Not strong? I didn't know him very long, ma'am, but I'd say he was one of the strongest people I ever met."

"I want you to go now. I have nothing more to say to either of you."

Rachael said, "There is something else, Mrs. Kostas. Did you and your brother, perhaps that lecherous husband of yours, drug me and tie my feet to a block of concrete and throw me in Black Rock Lake because you knew I was going to tell the world what my father had done?"

"You leave my husband out of this, you

little bitch! You claim someone tried to kill you? Threw you into a lake?" She laughed, tossed her hands. "How very melodramatic you are. Who would possibly believe someone like you? You are nothing more than a temporary annoyance. Get out."

Rachael said as she turned, "Actually, I'm far more than a temporary annoyance, Mrs. Kostas. I own Jimmy's house. I have a third of his money, a third of his stock. I hope you contest the will. I hope you demand DNA testing. Yes, let's do it, as publicly as you like. It will give me a chance to announce to the world what vipers you and your brother are."

Laurel leaned forward on her desk, her hands fisted on the desktop. "Get out of here now!"

"I know why you're trying to kill me. You're afraid I'll make Jimmy's announcement for him. You've had three tries—three!—and yet here I am, standing in your office. Jimmy's death was no accident, and you well know it. Just think about the reporters sleeping in your front yard, Mrs. Kostas, once everyone knows the truth.

"Enjoy this cold, soulless office while

you can, ma'am, because you're not going to be in here much longer."

"What is going on here, Laurel? Julia told me the FBI was in your office. Oh, it's you. What are you doing here, Ms. Janes?"

"She looks a bit red in the face, Quincy," Stefanos Kostas said, stepping around his brother-in-law.

Jack and Rachael turned to see Quincy Abbott and Stefanos Kostas. Quincy was what Jack expected an Abbott to look like—very expensive Italian suit, black with very thin red stripes, a white shirt, a red tie. He was elegant, polished, and at that moment he looked more bewildered than angry. But there was one thing that was off—it was the toupee he wore. The color was perfect, but the style didn't quite fit the shape of his head.

As for Kostas, Jack thought he looked like a dissipated playboy, a man who lived only for his own pleasure, for his own whims. He was handsome, Jack supposed, fit, well-dressed, but there was something off about him, too, and it wasn't a toupee. He didn't know at that moment what it was.

Rachael turned and said pleasantly,

"Uncle Quincy, this is Special Agent Jackson Crowne. He's here to find out what happened to my father and who tried to kill me last Friday night, Monday, and—goodness—yesterday, as well. But I'm sure you know all about that, don't you?"

Quincy Abbott laughed, then looked sideways at his sister and said, "Sounds to me like a boyfriend gone nasty. Who have you been sleeping with?"

Rachael thought about her one-time fiancé from Richmond. What a fiasco that had been.

Stefanos waved his question away. "What's this about killing you?"

Jack said pleasantly, "Perhaps you, sir, Mrs. Kostas, and Mr. Abbott could tell me where you were on Friday night."

Quincy raised a brow. "I was at Mrs. Muriel Longworth's welcome party for the new Italian ambassador. Stefanos, you came in later, as I recall."

Stefanos nodded and looked at Rachael's breasts.

"I will not dignify your question with a reply," Laurel said.

Rachael said, "Uncle Quincy, Jimmy told you about killing that little girl."

"Perhaps he did. I wasn't much interested, to tell you the truth. Oh well, who cares now? The senator is dead and buried. I just wish he hadn't left you our house. As for the stock, at least you don't have enough to cause trouble." He brightened. "You said someone is trying to kill you? Well then, have this FBI agent go find him and throw him in jail." Quincy Abbott nodded to both of them, gave his sister a long look, turned on his designer heel, and left Laurel Kostas's office.

Stefanos leaned against the door, arms across his chest, and said to his wife, "I've been shopping. Guido called me about this very lightweight wool I'm wearing. What do you think?" He looked at Rachael's breasts again, knowing his wife was watching. If she'd been Laurel, she'd have shot him dead. But Laurel said nothing, didn't appear to notice anything amiss.

The three of them, Rachael thought, didn't appear to live on the same planet.

Rachael walked out, Jack right behind her.

Jack's last memory of Laurel Abbott Kostas was of the cold, ripe malice in her eyes, her husband leaning against the door, like a beautifully suited lizard. He thought about Jukie Hayes, owner of a junkyard in Marlin, Kentucky, a good ole boy who visited neighboring towns. He killed people and buried them under ancient wrecks of cars, between stacked tires, stuffed inside car trunks. He told Jack he liked the smell of the decaying bodies. Jack still had nightmares about Jukie, and the stack of bones he'd uncovered beneath a tarp thrown over a dozen steering wheels. Odd that a wealthy Greek playboy would remind him of Jukie, but he did.

Both of them breathed in the sea air as they walked down Calvert Street to the Inner Harbor. Jack laughed. "She's a terror, Rachael, scares the crap out of me. Quincy doesn't like her, but he knows she has the power. Is he afraid of her? I wonder."

"I need to take a shower," Rachael said. "That Stefanos Kostas is a dreadful man. And she didn't appear to even notice he was eyeing me."

Jack stopped in the middle of the sidewalk, put his hands on her shoulders, and said, "You held it together. You went after her. That was well done. I'm proud of you."

Rachael stood very still, aware of people moving around them, aware that she felt good, and what he'd said. "Thank you. You said Quincy is afraid of his sister. Why?"

Jack dropped his hands and he and Rachael moved back into rhythm with the crowds of tourists. "He's smooth as silk, terrified someone won't believe he's God's gift to the world, and weak. He's not in his sister's league. As for the toupee, nothing said is too much. This was only the first salvo, Rachael."

Madonna's voice blared out "Like a Virgin."

Rachael's eyebrow went up when Jack pulled out his cell, flipped it open. "Yeah?"

He listened. His hand tightened on the phone. He listened for a very long time.

When he slipped his cell back into his jacket pocket, he said, "That was Savich. The guy I shot in the shoulder yesterday in Gillette's kitchen—the woman on the walkie-talkie called him Donley—they ID'ed him from a blood sample from the kitchen floor. His name is Everett, Donley Everett. Turns out he showed up in Clapperville, Virginia, went to a local doctor's house and forced the doctor to treat him. He didn't kill the guy, thank God. Evidently Donley thought the doctor lived alone, and so he left him bound and gagged in the basement. Turns out the doctor's wife had been on a business trip. She arrived home an hour after Everett left. They called the police, who put out an APB on him."

"What's Donley Everett's physical status?"

"The doctor said he was running a fever when he showed up, that if he'd had that bullet in his shoulder for another day or so without treatment, he might very well have died. Everett forced him to remove the bullet with only a local anesthetic, which he did. He told Savich the guy didn't make a sound.

"The doctor gave him a week's worth of antibiotics, some heavy-duty pain meds. He said Everett would feel rotten for a while, but he thought he'd pull through. The doctor wasn't very happy about that.

"Savich said the doctor was very relieved when Everett only tied him up in the basement."

"What about the other guy at Slipper Hollow, the one you shot dead? You said the woman called him Clay?"

"Yes. There's no word yet on his whereabouts. Savich thinks, and I agree, that Everett buried him somewhere deep in the sticks. Savich said they ran Clay's first name through the system. He's sending photos on my cell of two guys who seem promising, both with the first name Clay, one of them is a known associate of Everett, so he's the most promising."

They waited next to a Starbucks, both staring down at the cell screen.

In another second, Jack was looking at a guy named Clay Clutt. But he wasn't the man Jack had shot at the edge of the forest in Slipper Hollow.

He called back. "It's not Clay Clutt."

"Okay, Clutt was my warm-up. Here's the second one. He's worked with Everett in the past. Coming through now," Savich said.

"Bingo," Jack said to Savich a few minutes later. Clay Huggins. Rachael listened to him tell Savich about their meeting with Laurel Kostas, her husband, Stefanos Kostas, and Quincy Abbott. When he pocketed his cell, he said, "Both Donley Everett and Clay Huggins have sheets reaching to Kalamazoo, including suspected murder. Neither has been convicted. Savich is sending out agents to both gentlemen's places of residence. He said he and Sherlock are going to Everett's apartment, since it's likely he's holed up there, nursing his wounded shoulder and popping pain pills. Savich said it sounds like we stirred up the snakes, which is good. Let's call it a day, Rachael. Let's have that lobster."

TWENTY-SIX

Washington, D.C.
Late Wednesday afternoon

When Savich pulled his Porsche to the curb half a block from Donley Everett's apartment building, the sun was low in the sky, the June air soft and warm.

The apartment building was in the middle of a transitional neighborhood, where the old single-story houses from the forties and fifties were slowly being rehabbed or torn down. Unfortunately for the new, larger homes, the yards were still as minuscule as they'd always been. Everett's apartment building looked maybe ten years old, well-maintained, with a redbrick facade.

Sherlock waved at Dane Carver and Ollie Hamish, who were just getting out of Ollie's black Pacifica, behind them the two surveillance agents.

Savich and Sherlock watched as Ollie and Dane circled to the back of the building to check out exits. There weren't many tenants around yet since federal offices, the bread and butter of the Washington workforce, were just now closing down for the day. They heard a baby gurgling happily through an open window on the second floor, heard the new country singer Chris Connelly singing about his cheating love raking over his heart. Savich liked Chris Connelly.

The lobby was small, one wall lined with green-painted mailboxes, a live palm tree in a metal pot against another, its fronds stretching wide.

Sherlock double-checked the mailboxes. "Yep, D. Everett in 4C."

Savich looked at the two elevators. One was parked right there, the door open. He pushed the stop button, and they took the other one.

Donley Everett's apartment was on the corner of the fourth floor. Savich punched in Dane's number, said quietly, "Apartment 4C is on the east end of the building. I'll bet you there's a fire escape there."

"Yeah, I see it," Dane said. "There's only one back exit. We got it covered. Our two other agents are outside the front doors, keeping an eye on the lobby. Holler if you want us up there, you know, you being such a wuss and all, you might need some backup."

"That's okay, Sherlock'll take care of me."

Sherlock pulled a stick of gum out of her pocket, popped it into her mouth, and began chewing. Savich positioned himself at the side of the door. She rapped smartly on Everett's door and called out through the chewing gum, "FedEx for Mr. Donley Everett."

She smiled straight ahead into the peephole and blew a big bubble, letting it splat against her mouth.

A man's low voice said, "Go away, little girl. I'm not expecting anything from anybody." There was pain in the voice, she heard it clearly.

Sherlock's face disappeared from the peephole for a moment as if she were checking something. "It says here on the package, sir, that it's from Gun Smith Euro, whatever that is. It's sort of heavy. Wow, do you think it might be a gun? Did you order one? I've never seen a gun up close before. But hey, if you want it, I can't leave it without a signature."

"But I didn't order a . . . Wait a minute, you don't want to touch that package, you hear me?" Everett released three locks, then jerked the door open to stare at the redheaded woman who'd blown such a big bubble before it popped, holding a SIG Sauer aimed at his chest. "FBI, Mr. Everett. Nice and easy now, hands behind your head and step back, one step."

"Hey! FBI? Whoa . . ."

Sherlock slowly lowered her SIG until it was aimed at his stomach. "A gut shot isn't pretty, Mr. Everett, but hey, it'll go nice with your shoulder."

Everett stumbled backward, twisted suddenly, dove behind the black leather sofa, and fired.

The bullet was wide, struck and shattered a lamp.

"You idiot!" Sherlock yelled, and fired at his foot, which was showing from behind the sofa, missing his big toe by an inch. "The next bullet will go in your calf, then your knee, and you'll be crawling around for the rest of your sorry life! Throw out that gun! Now!"

Savich moved around to the other end of the sofa. "Now, Everett, or when she shoots you in your left knee, I'll get your right. Yep, there are two of us. Throw out the gun right now or you're going to be in very great pain."

They heard Everett cursing behind the sofa, then there was some back-and-forth discussion, blurred and contentious, as if he and his evil twin were arguing his odds.

"Gun out now!" Sherlock screamed.

The gun came flying out, skidded across the hallway floor. Sherlock stepped on a nice Kel Tec PF9 9mm. "Betcha when they dig slugs out of the Slipper Hollow house, we're going to find a match. Now, Don, come out nice and slow."

"Don't shoot me!"

"Show me your face in two seconds and I'll consider it."

When he finally crawled out from behind the sofa, using only one hand, he looked clammy and pale, his eyes a bit dilated, and he was cupping his right arm, held up and close in a blue sling.

"Stand up!"

He managed to hoist himself to his feet. He held out his good hand, palm open, toward them. "Who are you? What is this?"

"Pay attention, Mr. Everett. We're FBI," Savich said, and pulled out his shield, waved it at Everett. "Why don't you have a nice seat over on that La-Z-Boy? No stupid moves, Don. I don't want to have to kill you on such a lovely summer day." He punched in Dane's number and said, "No problem here. We've got him. Come on up."

Everett said, "It's not lovely, it's too hot, it sucks. Dude, can't you see me? Look at my arm. I'm sick, real sick. What do you want? I didn't do anything. I don't know anything about any Slipper Hollow."

Sherlock turned to see Dane step into the room from the fire escape, and Ollie standing in the front doorway, both with their SIGs drawn.

"All cool here," Sherlock said.

Dane and Ollie moved past them to look through the rest of the apartment. "Hey, what are you clowns doing? This is my place. Don't you go through my drawers!"

"Be quiet or they might do more than just go through your drawers," Sherlock said, and patted him down. "Now, to be honest here, Don, you did try to shoot me. However, I will say you look pretty down and out." Sherlock got right in his face. "Do you remember that very nice doctor you visited in Virginia? The one who took out the bullet, pumped you full of painkillers and antibiotics? You didn't even pay him. Nope, you hauled him down in his basement, all trussed up?"

"I didn't hurt him, now did I?"

"That was a good decision on your part," Sherlock said. "We got a lovely DNA match from that gallon of blood you left on the kitchen floor in Slipper Hollow. The FBI agent who brought you down also identified you. We've got you, Don. Your pitiful butt is now ours forever."

Everett said, "Fuckin' DNA."

"I'll forgive your French this time, Don," Sherlock said, "given your dismal situation." She studied his gray face for a moment. "Hey, you're hurting pretty bad, aren't you? I'll bet I can talk my boss here into taking you to the hospital if you tell us the truth about Slipper Hollow."

He weaved where he stood, moaned, and Savich pushed him down onto the La-Z-Boy. "I wasn't at no Slipper Hollow. I was huntin' ducks," Everett said, and looked up at Savich. "Mallards, a whole crap pile of them out at Eagle Lake. Look, I need another pain pill real bad. I was going to the bathroom to get one when you hammered on my door." He shook his head. "I'm in such pain that it ruined my judgment. I looked at you close, real close before I opened that damned door. How could I know a pretty girl like you was a rat cop?"

"Hey, Dillon, the man here thinks I'm pretty for a rat cop—what do you think about that?"

"The lowlife has good taste."

"There now, all of us agree. Why don't you tell us where you buried Clay Huggins. You're not in trouble over that since you're not the one who shot him. I'll bet you feel kind of bad about him being dead. He was a friend, wasn't he—well, at least a professional ally? And now he's rotting in a field somewhere like he wasn't important enough to even stick in a casket."

"I don't know what you're talking about. I don't know any Clay Higgins."

"Clay Huggins."

"Whatever." He looked at Savich. "Dude, I want you to get out of here, leave me alone. I don't know anything about any doctor in a basement, I was just agreeing with you to be cooperative. I want to take my pain pill and go back to bed. You didn't even have a box from Gun Smith Euro, did you?"

"Sorry, no box. It really hurts me, Don, but occasionally I have to lie in my job."

Savich said, "Okay, Don, listen up. It's either a small, uncomfortable jail cell with Big Bubba for a roomie, or a nice hospital bed, with clean sheets. Up to you."

"I want a lawyer."

"You know what, Don," Savich said, his voice slowing, becoming scary deep and as cold as ice, "I've found sometimes— well, rarely—that lawyers can really help a guy. In this instance, though, a lawyer isn't going to help you wiggle out of this. Now, if the lawyer's not a moron, he'll advise you to cooperate with us and tell the truth since we already have you dead to rights with your DNA. Neither of us is unreasonable. You want to deal? We'll deal."

Everett said, "I don't know anything, I—"

Savich slapped Everett's face.

Everett moaned, hugged his slinged arm against his chest. "Hey! Dude, what'd you do that for? I'm hurt here, no call for you to hit me."

"I want your attention right here, Don, right on my face. That's right. Look at me. I want you to tell me who hired you and the now-deceased Clay Huggins. I want you to give me the names of the other man and woman who were with you when you went to kill Rachael Janes in Slipper Hollow. I want you to tell me right now, or the only thing I'll guarantee you is a thirty-year stretch at Attica." Savich lightly laid the butt of his SIG across Everett's open mouth. "No, don't sing me your I'm-so-innocent song." He leaned closer, whispered in Everett's ear, "Something else I might enjoy doing, Don, and that's to let it out to the inmate population that you're a child molester."

TWENTY-SEVEN

Sherlock had rarely seen absolute horror on a person's face like she saw now on Donley Everett's. For the moment, it knocked his pain right out of his mind.

"Dude, it isn't true. You can't, dude. Oh, man, you can't."

Savich ran the muzzle of his SIG against Everett's ear. "When they're through with you, you'll sure wish you'd talked to us, Don. On the other hand, you tell us what we want to know, and I'll see to it personally that you're in a cell by yourself and there's not a single whiff of child molestation in your traveling papers. What do you say, Don? Tell me you understand all your options."

Everett sobbed into his one available open hand. Sherlock straightened. "You're disgusting," and she kicked him hard in the knee.

"Wha—?"

"Listen, you moron," she said, getting in his face. "You've done so much bad stuff in your miserable life you nearly fill up a computer disk. You've never shown an ounce of remorse about any of your victims, and now you have the gall to whine and cry? You make me sick.

"Now, you pathetic butt worm, you will tell us who hired you or I'm going to get ahold of some really appalling photos of kids who've been molested and write your name on the photos in big block letters. I'll have the warden paper the bathrooms and the cafeteria. I expect there'll be bets on how long you'll last. Can you imagine having a big bar of soap stuffed in your mouth, your jaws held together?"

Everett stopped crying, shut off like a spigot. He believed she was dead serious. "I heard about that," he said, and couldn't help the shudder. "You can't do that, there are rules you cops gotta stick to. You're constrained."

"Do I look constrained, Don?" Savich shook his head at him. "You don't get it, do you? You tried to kill our friends at Slipper Hollow. You think we wouldn't make up a story about you, that we'd hesitate to do anything we need to get the people you were with?"

Don shook his head back and forth, back and forth. "Oh, damn, this wasn't supposed to happen. It was supposed to be easy, in and out, that was it, then home again and I've got enough money for a nice vacation in Aruba. But there was this big guy and he walked into the kitchen and shot me right through the shoulder, then he went after poor Clay, shot him dead. Perky called me a couple of hours ago, told me she was glad I made it out, that even though everything went south, we should be okay if I didn't do anything stupid. I told her I was clean, no way they'd find out about me. I didn't leave any ID in my wallet—no driver's license, nothing. I had to tell her about Clay, that the big guy shot him dead. She told me to lay low, take care of my arm, that everything'd be all right."

Sherlock asked, "Did you tell Perky about leaving all your blood on the kitchen floor?"

He shook his head, muttered, "Fuckin' DNA."

Savich grabbed his chin and squeezed. "Watch your mouth. I won't tell you again."

"Who was the fourth member of your team?" Sherlock asked.

"T-Rex—he's down in Florida by now, runnin' in the surf at Palm Beach."

"And what would T-Rex's real name be?"

"Marion Croop. You can see why he likes his nickname."

"That's good, Don. What's Perky's real name?"

"No one calls her anything but Perky. It's the only name I know, honest. She always grins real wide and pokes out her tits, says they're as perky today as they were ten years ago."

"How old is Perky?" Savich asked.

"Maybe forty, in there somewhere. She's a real pro, knows exactly what she's doing. Got a big mess of blond hair, always wears it up with dangling curls, and she always wears opaque sunglasses. I've never seen her eyes.

"This job, dude, it was screwed up from the beginning. Perky bitched and moaned about how we couldn't be sure of anything, and it frosted her but good to be sent out to this backwoods place with no clue where anything was or who was where. Then she said she started counting the money and that made her think about it some more. She said there were four of us, and chances were that this Rachael Janes would be by herself, maybe with one family member, that was it. It'd be easy. Overkill, that's what we'd have. It wouldn't be a problem, and we'd have all that money. Perky was really pissed."

He looked at Sherlock, and tears trick-led out of his eyes. "Nothing went the way it was supposed to. There must have been a half-dozen people there, and all of them knew how to shoot. They had more weap-ons than we did. We didn't have a chance. How could that happen? Dude, I really hurt. Can I have one of my pills?"

"I'll give you two pills, Don," Savich said, "the minute you tell me who hired you to kill Rachael Janes."

"Damn, I knew you'd want that. You won't believe me, but it's the truth: I don't know, I don't know who hired Perky, who gave Perky all that money. She's always the lead, always, and she gets the contracts, briefs us, maps out the plan we're going to follow, hands out our shares. And then we split up until the next time. Clay wasn't one of our usual guys, but Gary's in bed with the flu, so there were only the three of us we could really count on. I'll bet you those were military people at that Slipper Hollow. It all went to hell."

"Did Perky tell you anything about Rachael Janes?"

"Only that she wasn't supposed to still be kicking around, said she should be lying at the bottom of Black Rock Lake, said those barbiturates were good. She laughed." Everett shrugged, then moaned. "Perky said Rachael Janes was some artsy-craftsy fluff head who arranged furniture and painted walls, and so she should be real easy to knock off. But look what happened. That Rachael Janes must have been another Houdini, getting herself free like that. Perky was pissed again."

"Keep it up, Don, you're doing good," Savich said.

"It was Clay who kept asking her questions

since he hadn't worked with her before. She finally let on that Lloyd Roderick—that dumb-ass rockweed who's into teenagers— he'd got himself shot while trying to nail Rachael Janes in Parlow, Kentucky. Who ever heard of Parlow, Kentucky? He was in the hospital, Perky said, so now it was our turn. This girl was a civilian, hiding out, thinking she was safe from the big bad wolf. And then Perky growled."

He sighed, the tears dry on his cheeks now, and itchy. "That damned girl, she wasn't alone. Surprised the shi—crap out of everybody, all those shots coming from inside that house. It was close."

He hung his head, scratched the fingers of his injured arm. "You're just trying to do a job and look what happens."

"What exactly happened?" Savich asked.

"Well, when we found our way through the woods to this Slipper Hollow, we saw the girl the first thing, but there was this big guy with her. Perky said it'd be okay, the guy would bite the big one along with her. But before we could get close, a guy comes running outside, yelling for them to get into the house. He obviously knew something was up—I don't know how he knew, but he did. Rachael Janes and this big guy made it through the front door just as we began shooting. Perky split us up. Clay and me slipped through the woods around to the back of the house to go in, get them in a cross fire. I decided it was best for Clay to stay back, since he was new to the team, to cover me, to shoot anyone who tried to get out the back.

"I come in the kitchen at the same time this big guy steps in. I thought I got him, he fell down, but he was only acting shot, the bastard. Then he clocked me in the shoulder. I'm down, then he's out the back and I know Clay doesn't have a chance, and he didn't.

"You can't believe how bad it hurt my shoulder to haul Clay back through the woods and out to our car, but I knew I couldn't leave him there. I buried him in a tobacco field about fifteen miles down the road. I don't know if I can find it, I really don't."

Everett started crying. He hiccupped. He looked up at Savich. "You promised me pills if I told you everything. I did. My pills, they're in the medicine cabinet."

Savich called out, "Dane, go into Mr. Everett's bathroom and bring out his bottle of pain pills."

They let him hiccup until Dane pressed the bottle into his hand, set a glass of water on the arm of the La-Z-Boy. Everett took two pills, drank the entire glass of water, some of it dribbling down his chin.

He wasn't bad-looking, Sherlock thought dispassionately, staring down at him, maybe late thirties, lots of dirty blond hair, a good build, but he hadn't shaved in too long, and didn't smell like he'd bathed recently, either, understandable given his shoulder. He was wearing dirty gray sweats, dark green socks, a hole in the big toe. He looked, she thought, like a man who'd been ridden hard and put away wet too many times in his short years.

"And now, Don," Savich said, "tell us where to find Perky."

Everett chewed his lower lip. This was tough, Savich knew, this was betrayal of the killing kind.

"Think of your future," Savich said, voice easy and smooth and scary.

"She lives a block over from that Barnes & Noble in Georgetown, off M Street, on

Wisconsin, I think, in a little apartment over a boutique. I don't know the name of the boutique."

"Address?"

"Dude, I don't know, I don't—"

"Fine, I believe you. You'll take us there." Savich pulled him out of the La-Z-Boy, ignored his moans and groans, and handed him over to Dane and Ollie. "Our hotshot here is going to direct you to Perky's apartment on Wisconsin. We'll be right behind you with the other two agents following, to cover us."

Savich turned to Sherlock, a black eyebrow hoisted. "Pathetic butt worm?"

TWENTY-EIGHT

Ten minutes later, Donley Everett pointed to a second-floor window above K-Martique, a specialized Goth shopping spot for the young fanged set. That, he said, was where Perky lived. Dane gave him another pill to keep him in the pain-med twilight zone. It would have looked like a regular shop from outside except for the lacy black curtains and the black door.

Once through the black front door at K-Martique, Sherlock, all smiles, nodded to the few customers as she wove her way through racks of gauzy black skirts, black dresses, black tops, some really interesting red plastic spikes, black boots, and lacy black underwear hot enough to sizzle a guy's eyes, to the counter in the far corner. It was stationed in front of a full-length mirror, doubtless to allow the sales clerk visual cover of the store. "Hey, I'm looking for Perky. Can you help me out?"

The young woman behind the counter had long straight black hair, a dead white face, and she was dressed all in Addams family black—her nail polish and lipstick black, too. Sherlock wondered what she looked like without all the paraphernalia.

She looked Sherlock up and down with a sort of vague contempt. "Hey, I can replace those bourgeois clothes you're wearing with something cool."

"You don't like my black leather jacket?"

"Well, it's okay, but you need some long gashes in it, you know, like with a knife, make you look more dangerous. I've got some you won't even need to slice up."

Sherlock looked interested, then regretful. "Sorry, don't have time to shop today." She pulled out her creds. "Special Agent Sherlock, FBI. Where's Perky?"

The young woman barely looked at her ID. She said, "Perky's gone."

"Gone where?"

The girl gave her a bored looked and shrugged; one of the gauzy black sleeves fell off her very white bony shoulder.

"And what's your name?"

"Me? I'm Pearl Compton. What's it to you? You really should let me help you— your clothes and hair are about as mind-numbing as it gets. You really could use some help, lady."

Sherlock said, "Listen up, Pearl. Tell me Perky's real name and where to find her or I'll get a big bucket of cold water and scrub your face in it."

The three other patrons, all teenage girls who'd obviously been listening, couldn't hightail it out of there fast enough. Savich held the door open for them and said, as they flew out the door, "Wise decision."

Pearl slammed a very white hand down on the counter. "Look what you've done! Three customers, and you ran them off!"

Sherlock leaned in, said, "Yeah, yeah, what's Perky's real name?"

Pearl shrugged. "Oh, who cares? Maude Couple. She's from Montana, says she grew up tending lambs."

"How old is she?"

"I don't know—old. Maybe forty, around there."

"How long has she lived upstairs, Pearl?"

"Since I came to the store to manage it."

"Where's she gone?"

"I don't know, honest. She gives me her key, tells me to water her ivy, then she just up and leaves."

"Okay. Good. I want you to come upstairs with us, let us into Perky's apartment." Sherlock turned and waved to Savich, who was standing in the doorway.

"Oh no, I can't do that. She's private, and I know Perky would be real angry if I took anyone up there. She and the owner, you know, they sort of sleep together when he can get away from his wife."

Savich walked right up to Pearl and towered over her, said absolutely nothing.

Pearl drummed her black fingernails on the counter, shrugged.

She pulled a key ring from beneath the counter, walked to the front door of the shop, flipped down the CLOSED sign inside, then locked the door.

"This way." She looked over her shoulder at Savich. "You'd look pretty hot with a nice set of fangs, maybe some light powder to get that tan off your face."

"Thanks," Savich said.

"Maybe a dribble of blood down the side of your mouth."

They followed her up the narrow back stairway, the wooden steps nine inches deep all the way to the top. They followed Pearl into a narrow, dim hallway, with a door at the end that had a sheet of black paper thumbtacked to it that said PERKY. "Here we go. This is her digs."

She unlocked the door, shoved it open. Savich quickly pushed her behind them. "Stay put," he said.

He and Sherlock, SIGs drawn, slowly walked in, Savich high, Sherlock low, careful to keep Pearl behind them. They were all the way in the small, shadowy space when the door slammed shut behind them and they heard the key turn in the lock, then the wild, fast flap of boots back down the stairs. Savich kicked the door open and, bending low, eased out into the small hallway. If he hadn't been nearly bent double, he would have been shot in the chest. The bullet whizzed over his head, barely missing him. He fell flat on the hallway floor and fired. Two more bullets slammed into the wall above his head, then he heard the sound of running. Sherlock came down beside him. "You're okay, aren't you?"

"Yeah, just humiliated."

"Well," she said, "I think we just met Perky. I gotta say, she's not bad. I didn't doubt her once."

Savich pulled out his cell. "Dane, a girl—all Goth black—just did us in. It's got to be Perky. No, no, we're okay. She should be running out of the K-Martique any second now. She's got a gun and she's good. One of you go around back, just in case. If she already came out, go after her. Like I said, all Goth—long black hair, black clothes, black boots, real young, maybe early twenties. Be careful. I mean it, she's dangerous."

He listened for a moment. "Excellent, yeah, that's her. Came right out the front door, did she? Pretty confident, our girl. Bring her down. Her real name is Pearl Compton. Maybe."

Savich heard running footsteps, heard

Dane shout, "Stop, Pearl! FBI, stop right there!"

There was a shot fired and Savich thought he'd swallow his tongue. He gripped his cell. "What happened? What's going on?"

Three more gunshots. People shouting, screaming.

Savich and Sherlock dashed out of the shop to see Ollie and Dane running a block away, ducking into a Barnes & Noble.

"Not good," Savich said.

They ran down the block and slowed only when they stepped into Barnes & Noble. They both knew the bookstore well, all three floors, the first floor a big open space, the clerks behind a counter extending along the left side, the books to the right. At that moment, the place was fast becoming a madhouse, clerks and customers shouting and yelling, some on the floor, a couple of bookshelves overturned, books tossed everywhere, and a man's voice—Steve Olson, the manager—yelling for everyone to get down. Dane and Ollie and the two surveillance agents were weaving their way in and out of the aisles, following the screams and yells, looking for Perky.

Savich saw her shoot at Dane from behind the travel aisle, then leap onto the down escalator from the second level and begin to run up, flat out, her black skirt flying, her boots thudding loudly on the treads, a gun in her right hand. He knew to his gut she was heading to the third floor, the children's section, to find herself the perfect hostage. Of course she could grab anyone. He called, "Sherlock, get everyone over here. Steve, buzz up to the children's area. Get the kids on the elevator, fast, or in the restrooms, just out of sight. Everyone, stay down!"

He heard Steve yell again and again, "They're FBI, everything will be okay. Don't panic, stay down!"

Perky turned as she jumped off at the top of the escalator and for one long moment, she stared at Savich. Then she grabbed a teenage girl by her long hair as she was crawling away and hauled her to her feet. "See what I got here, Mr. Agent?" She shook the girl like a rat. But while she spoke she looked over at Sherlock, who was approaching them, slowly, eyes on Perky, keeping real close to the books. "Say good-bye to the little cutie," Perky yelled, and fired not at the girl she was holding but at Sherlock.

Sherlock twisted against the bookshelf. A Linda Howard novel took the bullet. Three more shots, but Sherlock couldn't fire back, none of them could, not with Perky holding the girl in front of her.

Perky said, "Well now, this is what I'd call an impasse."

Savich called out, "Give it up, Pearl, it's over."

She brought up her gun, fast as a snake, and fired at Savich. He threw himself to the side, not wanting to fire back and risk hitting the girl. But that pale, terrified teenager leaned down and bit Perky's arm. Perky clouted her in the head with her fist, dropped her, whirled toward Savich, and fired again.

"Get down!" he yelled.

The teenager tried, but she fell onto the escalator and began rolling down toward him. She tried to flatten herself, but it was impossible. He yelled, "When you hit the bottom, run as fast as you can!"

Savich heard people yelling, saw parents clutching their kids, a teenage boy holding up his pants as he tried to shield his little brother behind him. The teenager hit bottom, rolled once, and came up running.

Perky stood at the top of the escalator and slowly raised her gun while she looked down. There were so many people—she had a fine selection.

No choice, no choice. Savich rolled and came up, moving faster than the teenager. He had to take her down, and do it now. He brought up his SIG.

He heard Dane shout, "Perky! Hey, girl, don't you love me anymore?"

TWENTY-NINE

Perky jerked around, her black hair lashing her face. She found Dane, crouched a dozen feet behind Savich, to his right. She raised her gun.

There were two little boys suddenly close to Savich, shrieking—he didn't know where they'd come from. One of them tripped over him and went sprawling. Savich rolled on top of the kid to protect him, twisted around to see Dane fire at nearly the same time that Perky did. The world slowed to a crawl. Dane's bullet slammed hard into her right shoulder, knocking her sideways onto the down escalator. Perky grabbed for the railing but her fingers couldn't make purchase. Dane watched her slowly sink down onto the moving steps. He ran up to her, grabbed the long flowy black sleeve of her dress but it ripped off in his hands as her body spilled out onto the floor, her black skirt twisting around her thin body, her long black wig pulled half off her head, long blond hair spilling out. She lay motionless. Savich knew she must be covered in blood from the wound in her shoulder, but he couldn't see any. The blood soaked into the black. Black on black.

Her gun, where was her gun? "Dane," Savich yelled. "I don't see her gun! She's dangerous. Everyone, stay put!"

Dane jerked back, but Perky was fast. She twisted up onto her back, gun in hand, to fire up at him. Ollie, coming at her from the other side, shot her in her gun arm. The gun went skittering down the science fiction aisle. She cried out, then fell onto her back and was quiet.

"Okay, okay," Savich said, "it's over. Everyone stay back."

Sherlock was on her knees beside Perky, flattening her hand against the wound in her shoulder. "She's alive, but we've got to get the bleeding under control. Give me your tie. Let's knot it tight over the wound. Come on, Perky, don't you dare die on me!"

Dane said, his words coming fast, tripping over themselves, "Backup is here. Ollie, you take care of that. I'll call an ambulance. Oh yeah, that was a great shot, thanks for saving my very grateful self."

Savich said, "Keep calming everyone down, help get them out. The manager, Steve Olson, is a friend, and he's solid. Help him, but let him handle what he wants to; it'll help focus him if he's in charge. Assure him it is indeed over. Sherlock, keep everyone back from this area."

Sherlock was now wrapping Dane's tie over the wound in Perky's arm.

Her black Goth shirt was soaked in blood, so much of it and she was so thin. How much blood could that thin body have in it? *All bones,* Sherlock thought, *she is all bones.*

Savich turned to look down at Perky. He realized the girl he'd thought was maybe twenty, twenty-two at most, hadn't seen twenty in a couple of decades. This was Perky, and she was forty, at least. He came down on his knees and tightened the tie around her wound. Okay, the blood was beginning to slow. He pressed on the wound though it was bleeding only sluggishly. She had a chance.

Where were the EMTs? She would be all right, she had to be. She was the only one who could tell them who hired her to kill Rachael.

When the paramedics arrived two minutes later, the FBI had the customers in pretty good control, but the EMTs still had to weave their way with their equipment through a crowd of people, some of whom were now crying.

Savich tried to keep the area clear, but some people were trying to crowd close, see the blood and gore, because that's the way some people were. More's the pity, there was plenty to see. He told the paramedics about her wounds.

An older woman, brisk, calm, her breath smelling of lemons, fastened an oxygen mask on Perky's nose. Then she studied Perky's shoulder, removed the tie, and wrapped a pressure bandage around it. "Bad," she said, "but with what you guys have done, she should make it." She jumped to her feet. "Okay, guys, let's get her onto the gurney." Savich had to smile because all the paramedics on this crew were female. Perky's black wig fell off when they lifted her.

The paramedics were soon out the front door with Perky strapped down on a gurney, her black skirts hanging down on either side, her black boots hanging free of the white sheet. Steve was directing his clerks to take care of the customers. One young girl, who looked pale and shocky, was wandering around the first floor, pausing to pick up a fallen book and trying to reshelve it.

The customers were walking slowly out of what would become a famous bookstore for the next three months. Savich walked over to Steve Olson, the manager, but he couldn't shake his hand, his were covered with Perky's blood. He turned to look around the bookstore. "I'm sorry about this, Steve, didn't mean for this to happen. You did good, thank you. Sherlock is calling our boss, and he'll send FBI people down here to handle the media. You need me, here's my card. Tell the media what happened straight out and keep repeating it. Remember, no one was hurt or killed and we got the bad guy. Hey, that teenage girl she caught as a hostage, take good care of her, she did good."

Sherlock said, "Please call me, Steve, give me her name and address. We want to thank her, speak to her parents, tell them what a heroine she is."

"You and Sherlock," Steve said, shaking his head as he took Sherlock's card. He pressed his palm over his chest. "Here I am trying to calm everyone down and my heart is suddenly ready to burst right out." He nodded to them once more, then turned to his assistant manager to order coffee and tea from the café on the second floor. He yelled, "Chocolate decadence cake for everyone!"

Savich said to Sherlock, "Perky's got to be forty, at least, just like Donley Everett said. Amazing." He leaned down, picked up her black wig.

"She was costuming," Sherlock said, "a very good disguise, too, for an assassin. She's about as hard-boiled as they get. I'll bet she's been at this for a very long time. I'll bet you Jack's old unit has a file on her. Well, at least she's out of business now.

"I'll tell you, Dillon, if the bitch doesn't make it, I'm going to punch her lights out." She swallowed, placed her hand on his arm, but she didn't say anything. Perky had tried to kill him twice. Close, too close.

Savich, oblivious, said, "I'm thinking if she pulls through this, we'll take her to Quantico. A nice visit with Dr. Hicks could be very helpful if he can get her under hypnosis. I'll bet my next paycheck she isn't going to give us the time of day, even if we offer her a deal."

Sherlock said, "She'll lawyer up, won't say a word. I bet hypnosis won't even be on the table.

"I don't want to deal with the media, Dillon. Let's get out of here. I called Mr. Maitland, gave him a quick overview. He isn't happy—I mean, we did shoot up a Barnes & Noble bookstore—but he'll deal with things. I told him Perky would be able to tell us who hired her to kill Senator Abbott and to kill Rachael. That cheered him up. Oh yeah, I asked Dane and Ollie to follow the ambulance to the hospital to get Donley Everett checked out. He was probably still moaning in the backseat of Ollie's car."

Savich and Sherlock went out the back of the Barnes & Noble, back to K-Martique. They walked up the steep stairs and stepped through the open doorway into Perky's apartment.

"Dillon, wait a moment."

He turned, smiled at his wife. He pulled her against him, stroked her hair. She said against his neck, "When we're through here, we're going to the gym. Yes, even before we spill out every single detail to Mr. Maitland six times. We're going to the gym. Get away from all this for a while. I've got to do something physical or I'm going to explode. You'd better look out—I just might take you down."

"In your dreams." He laughed as he walked to Perky's desk, turned on her laptop. He played around with it for several minutes, humming as he worked, then sat back in the desk chair, frowning.

"She's got the sucker passworded. It'd take me a while, but it would be a piece of cake for MAX." He unplugged the laptop, set it on the floor by the front door.

They looked through the desk drawers, found a checkbook, rubber-banded stack of paid bills, some invoices. The invoices were for repairs, for merchandise for her store, and the only checks used were written to utilities, nothing personal to help them. They found a couple dozen catalogs for Goth stuff, with some of the pages folded down. And an envelope filled with five thousand dollars in hundred-dollar bills.

"Her traveling money," Sherlock said, labeling the envelope and putting it in her jacket pocket.

In the kitchen they found three boxes of Grape-Nuts cereal, all unopened, and not much else in the cabinets. In the refrigerator were several dozen frozen bagels, fat-free cream cheese, and a half-gallon bottle of soy milk.

In the night table drawer by the narrow black-quilted bed, they found nipple rings in bright primary colors, black liquid eyeliner, three pairs of fangs, and two ornate bottles containing ruby red liquid, to simulate blood, they assumed. The best find was a paperback, the cover illustrated with a score of black knife slashes, titled *Sex for Vamps: How to Bleed Your Way to Pleasure.*

"Hmm," Sherlock said, picking up the book. "Pictures, you think?"

He laughed at her, grabbed the book, and began to thumb through it. "Now, would you look at this?"

They stared at a man wearing a black leather codpiece, a whip held high in his hand, a mask over his lower face. Beneath him, naked, on her stomach, tied with black leather straps to the four posts of the bed, lay a woman looking over her shoulder at the man.

Savich looked up. "Dare I turn the page?"

"Well, maybe better not. We're professionals, after all."

The most interesting thing they found in Pearl Compton's, aka Perky's, apartment was an address book, filled with numbers. No names, just initials beside every number.

Hallelujah.

THIRTY

World Gym
Georgetown
Wednesday evening

We've got information overload," Savich said as he increased the speed and incline of the treadmill.

"It beats not knowing anything." Sherlock matched his speed, but not the incline. She didn't want to push it, not when she still had plans to throw her husband to the mat at least a dozen times. Never had she considered a bookstore dangerous, particularly the Georgetown Barnes & Noble, but that was all changed now. Perky dashing up that down escalator, black boots pounding, waving a gun around, grabbing that teenage girl as a hostage—

the chaos, the screaming—it could have been a disaster. Dillon could have been killed. Perky had tried to shoot her, too, impossible to forget that. But that didn't bother her. She'd been terrified for Dillon.

Sherlock punched up the speed, viciously, to match her mood, a mix of fury and fear so corroding she thought she'd choke on it. She shot a look at Dillon. He'd already moved on, his run smooth and steady, his breathing easy, moved on just as she would have done if she'd been in his shoes, curse him. But she hadn't been anywhere near his shoes, and that was the problem. She owed Dane the world.

Sometimes—like right that instant—being married to Savich scared her to death. Because she was who she was, she'd far rather be pissed off than scared. She knew the only thing for it was to let off some serious steam.

Savich slowed a bit and turned to her. "Okay, what we know for sure is that Donley Everett is going down hard. The prosecutor had him sign his confession on the dotted line, so it's all wrapped up. It's a pity, but I believe him; he doesn't have a clue who hired Perky. But maybe he can give us a more specific location for where he buried Clay Huggins's body."

"Hypnotize him."

"Yeah, we could do that. Good idea."

All right, so he didn't have a clue that her insides were at the boiling point; he was a guy, after all. More to the point, and the point galled her, she hadn't said anything.

Everything's okay, it's over. Calm down. It's not like you haven't faced this before. She cleared her throat, said, "I wonder how Angel's keepers are doing with her attitude at Fairfax Juvie. Do you think she's been released yet?"

"Probably. Maybe Angel's got a chance. She's a bright girl."

"Yeah, yeah, so am I, and look what happened to me."

A black eyebrow shot up as Savich turned to look at her. What was with the snark? He said, "What happened to you is that you married your boss—a pretty cool guy—you get to chase down bad guys, and you get to stay in shape. It's like the perfect life for you."

She didn't laugh, as he'd expected her

to. She said abruptly, "It's a bummer about those phone numbers you got off Angel's cell phone. You were so happy to think your five hundred dollars paid off."

No more snark, that was good. Savich pushed the incline higher and breathed deeply, steadily. "Yeah, I was hopeful we might have Roderick Lloyd more in the loop, maybe calling Perky's boss, talking about killing Rachael in Parlow, but what we got are calls to Pizza Mac's, ordering double pepperoni, thick crust."

He still wasn't breathing hard, Sherlock thought, feeling a line of sweat snake down her back. She wanted to punch him for that, as well.

He said, "And the other three calls to bookies—three different bookies—and he owed all of them money."

Elvis belted out "Blue Suede Shoes." Savich pulled his cell off the clip on his waistband.

"Yes? Savich here." He slowed down and listened. When he punched off, he sped up again and said, "That was Dane calling from Memorial. He said Perky is still in surgery, but it looks good. She should be okay unless something unexpected happens. Then, just maybe, we can cut a deal with her."

"It could be a week before she's up to physically visiting Quantico. Maybe we can deal with her at the hospital, have Dr. Hicks visit her."

"That's a good thought."

Sherlock pushed the cool-down button, a bit on the violent side. "I like to impress the boss."

That black eyebrow of his went up again. "You do, every single day."

"You're a guy, so you're easy," she said, and stepped off the treadmill. "We need to get back to Dr. MacLean."

Elvis's voice crooned out again. "Yeah, Savich here. Hi, Jack. Talk to me." And Savich listened, asked a few questions, listened for a very long time, actually, then, finally, punched off, looking thoughtful.

"What? He and Rachael okay?"

"Yeah, no problem. He told me a bit more about Laurel, Quincy, and Stefanos. He said Laurel is the Big Dog, her husband is a slime, and Quincy probably has ulcers. He said Laurel hates Rachael's guts, doesn't try to hide it. About Quincy, Jack said that's a tougher call. Quincy

Abbott's all about packaging—he's flashy, a near prince in his nice Italian duds, and he's a coward, which probably also makes him a bully, but he's under his sister's thumb. He said Quincy's toupee is prime.

"If we need to reach Jack, he said he's staying with Rachael in her house in Chevy Chase."

Sherlock said, stretching, "I'm not at all sure I like the sound of that."

That eyebrow of his went up again.

"For heaven's sake, I'm not talking about sex. I bet they could sleep in the same bed and Jack wouldn't touch her. Well, that's optimistic. I was talking about the danger."

"You know Jack is good. Nothing surprises him. He's focused and wily. Don't worry, he won't let anything happen to Rachael. They're going to see Senator Abbott's head staffer, Greg Nichols, tomorrow morning. Nichols is already heading up another senator's staff. Jack said he can't wait to see what Nichols has to say to them."

"I'd like to speak to Nichols, too, feel out how much influence he had over Senator Abbott."

Savich nodded, sighed. "Jack asked me about Timothy MacLean, asked me what he could do. Unfortunately I didn't have anything to tell him."

Sherlock sighed right along with him, her righteous snark all gone in the face of what was happening to Timothy Mac-Lean.

Savich began to slow his stride. "I'm thinking you and I should focus on the two who appear to have the best motives—Congresswoman McManus and Pierre Barbeau. We've got to check out timelines, see if Jean David Barbeau drowned before the first attempt on Timothy's life. To be on the safe side, I'll have Ruth and Dane begin on his other patients."

"That sounds logical."

Savich said, "Let's visit the congresswoman first, see what she's got in the way of an alibi—not that it matters since she would have hired a thug to do the deed. I'll have Ollie check with the Atlanta detective who worked her dead husband's case, see if they had any leads. Maybe we can get a line on the thug she hired—in Savannah, was it?"

"That's what Dr. MacLean said." She

cocked her head to the side as Dillon ended his cooldown. "Do you believe she really had her trucker husband murdered so he wouldn't stop her run for Congress?"

"Yes, I do."

Sherlock chewed on that for a moment. "Maybe so. Still, I'm betting on Pierre Barbeau. Lots of wormy stuff going on there."

"We'll find out. How's your French?"

Laughter spurted out of her, from wherever it was hiding. "You've never complained before."

He grinned as he wiped his face with a towel. "You made me forget why I was asking."

Sherlock popped her knuckles. "You ready to come with me to the slam room?"

"Is that its new name?"

"Oh yeah. I'm going to make sure you'll relate to it shortly." She swatted at him with her towel as she walked past him.

Because he saw blood in her eyes and wasn't a fool, Savich allowed himself to be pummeled and thrown, and generally smacked around. The kick pad he'd held for her fared no better. He thought, at the end, it was worth it because Sherlock was laughing as she counted the number of times she'd thrown him. Violence, he thought, as he showered, appeared to calm the woman down and restore her perspective. He'd even called a halt several times during his royal butt-kicking to stretch and rub his muscles, and give her a chance to hoot and dance.

They stopped off at Dizzy Dan's for pizzas, one vegetarian for Savich and Sean, the other a pepperoni for the carnivore.

They ordered in two more when Savich's sister Lily and her husband, Simon, walked in right behind them. A short visit, they said, but neither Savich nor Sherlock believed them once they made a beeline for Sean, a new computer game in hand.

Lily was four months pregnant now, just beginning to show. "Practice is everything," she told Sean every time he challenged her to another game of *Treasures of the Ninja.*

They were finally asleep at midnight. Elvis sang in Savich's ear just as he was revving his race car at the Indy 500. He was instantly awake. "Savich here. Oh, no. Yes, I understand. Yes, I'm sorry, too." He clicked off. Sherlock was propped up on her elbow. "Who was that? What happened?"

"That was the hospital. Perky's dead. The surgeon said she came through surgery fine. She was in and out of recovery in an hour, still doing fine, and back in her room. No need for the ICU. When the nurse went to check on her maybe an hour later, she was simply dead." He slammed his fist against his night table. "I was going to assign an agent to guard her beginning tomorrow. I'm an idiot."

"It sounds like she died from a surgical complication."

"We'll know tomorrow, after the autopsy. But what if it wasn't from unexpected complications?"

Savich cursed, something he so rarely did he sounded faintly ridiculous. Then he got up, pulled on sweatpants, and said over his shoulder as he walked out of the bedroom, "I'm going to see if I can't come up with a plan to get things moving." He was talking more to himself now than to her. "Yeah, and MAX can maybe do something with all those initials and numbers in Perky's address book."

Sherlock didn't sleep again until he came back to bed. She didn't speak, simply curled up against him, her palm over his heart, and felt the strong, steady beat. She felt him begin to relax, and it simply all came out of her mouth. "You could have died. I was so scared this afternoon when she tried to kill you, Dillon, so scared I couldn't help you. I wanted to kill you."

He kissed her hair, her ear. "Don't you think it scared me spitless when she fired at you? And she looked at me the instant before she turned to you."

"I love you, Dillon. I loved you even when I kicked you into the wall mirror in the slam room."

"I won't forget," he said, and kissed her eyebrow. "We'll deal with this in the morning, Sherlock. Go to sleep."

THIRTY-ONE

Washington, D.C.
Thursday morning

Jack and Rachael were nearing the Hart Senate Office Building on Constitution Avenue for their nine o'clock appointment with Greg Nichols in his new position with the senior senator from Oregon, Jessie Jankel, when Ollie called. "Turn on your radio, Jack, you'll want to hear this. It's Savich holding an FBI press conference."

Jack said to Rachael as he flicked on his turn signal, "I bet he's speaking this morning because he has an agenda," and he turned up the volume on the radio. "He's got to address all the crap that went down yesterday at the Barnes & Noble, but then, it's his show."

Savich had an agenda. He stood at Jimmy Maitland's elbow, looking out over the sea of media faces from newspaper, radio, and TV, most of them familiar to him, seated in their plastic chairs, the TV people well-groomed, sharp, camera ready, the newspaper reporters looking on the seedy side in jeans, more like real people. He glanced over at Sherlock, gave her a smile and a nod. When Mr. Maitland introduced him, he stepped up to the mike, and looked out at the avid, hungry faces, ready to hurl their endless questions at him, eager for a sound bite or two.

"I suppose most of you have heard about the disturbance at the Barnes & Noble bookstore in Georgetown yesterday afternoon."

There was a wave of laughter since every reporter in the room had swarmed over Georgetown, interviewing everyone within ten blocks of the Barnes & Noble. Steve Olson, the manager, had closed the store and stood out on the sidewalk to take their questions. It had been a special report weaving in and out of regular programming throughout the evening, some of the speculation rivaling the truth, which was strange enough.

Savich said, "The woman we arrested in the Barnes & Noble died at Washington Memorial Hospital at around midnight. An autopsy is scheduled for this morning."

"Agent Savich, why an autopsy? Didn't she die of bullet wounds?"

"Did you shoot her yourself?"

Savich said, "So far, our preliminary information is that her wounds weren't fatal. Did she die from surgical complications? We'll know today."

"But she's still dead. Hey, wait a minute. You think she was murdered?"

"How many times did you shoot her?"

"What did she do? Who was she?"

"Why did she run into the bookstore?"

"What's her name?"

Savich finally held up his hand.

The room fell silent. "Her name was Pearl Elaine Compton. She was an established assassin, a very good one, according to our information, also a very long-lived one, given she was forty-one years old at the time of her death.

"She had three cohorts. One is dead, one is in the hospital, and the third is still at large. I'll say it again—we'll know the cause of her death today.

"As you might have heard, there was a lot of alarm and panic, all understandable, until one of the agents brought her down right after a teenage girl she was using as a shield was smart enough to bite Compton's forearm and escape.

"It took two shots to bring the suspect down, shoulder and arm. She stayed down and we evacuated her to the hospital.

"No one else was hurt—no customers, no employees, no one in law enforcement." He leaned even closer, cupped the mike between his hands. "The manager of the M Street Barnes & Noble is Steve Olson, a man I know personally. He was a great help at calming everyone down. He did complain to me, however, that they only now finished reshelving at least five hundred books."

A bit of laughter. All of them were straining to get closer.

"What this all boils down to is that we escaped tragedy on this one. I sincerely hope my next visit to the bookstore will involve only a cup of tea and looking through the new best sellers. Okay, does anyone have any questions?"

Every single hand shot in the air, voices already escalating. Savich gave them a look. He nodded to Mercer Jones, long-time crime reporter for the *Washington Post*. Mercer had planted a couple of stories for him over the years. Mercer said in his deep, plodding voice, "Agent Savich, why is the FBI involved in a shooting in Georgetown? Why not the Washington police? What's really going on here? Why were you after this Pearl Compton?"

Mercer was good, bless him; Savich had always recognized it. Mercer had given him the perfect lead-in. Savich said, "Good questions. Let me give you some critical information." He looked at Jimmy Maitland, who nodded.

"As you all know, Senator John James Abbott recently died in an automobile crash that was ruled accidental." He paused. "We now believe it's possible that Pearl Compton, the assassin who died last night, was involved in his death. We've reopened the case."

No need to mention Rachael, and Mr. Maitland had agreed. After all, this performance was to protect her. Why kill her if the FBI already knew everything she knew?

The media would go haywire, dig into all of it. They'd find Rachael, but it would take a while. Whoever in Senator Abbott's family was behind it, they had to be afraid. Fear meant mistakes. As he expected, there was a moment of stunned silence, then pandemonium.

Milly Cranshaw, host of *Night Lights* on PBS, yelled out, "Agent Savich, the official ruling was that Senator Abbott had been drinking and he lost control of his car. You're saying someone hired this woman to assassinate Senator Abbott? Who would do that? Why?"

Savich smiled at her. Trust Milly to load up with a half-dozen questions so he could pick and choose.

"Pearl Compton was hired to make it look like an accident?" added Thomas Black of CBS, bushy gray eyebrows raised nearly to his hairline.

"What I'm saying is, we're investigating whether Pearl Compton was involved."

"But who would want to kill Senator Abbott?"

"Do you think it was a terrorist act?"

Mercer shouted out, "But no one took credit."

Savich let the wave of questions flow over him. Many voices he recognized, but soon it became a cacophony, and they were beginning to argue with one another.

Time to bring it to a stop. Savich raised his hand. The room quieted.

"We're investigating everyone involved in Senator Abbott's life, both personal and professional."

"But what information do you have that raised doubt his death was an accident?" yelled Bert Mintz from Fox.

"We believe Senator Abbott had not taken a single drink for at least eighteen months before his death. And for eighteen months, he had not driven a car, either. We have a good deal of information in our ongoing investigation that we are not prepared to make public at this time." He knew what he'd just said would be his big sound bite.

Savich turned away in the two seconds of stunned silence, something he didn't realize was possible, then, of course, came more shouted questions.

Slowly, he paused, turned back. He said, "I will keep you updated as our investigation continues. Thank you."

Savich stepped away from the podium and walked off the dais amid the cacophony of voices, Jimmy Maitland on his heels. His boss was smart. No way was Mr. Maitland going to face that rabid pack.

Savich, Sherlock, and Maitland stood in the wing, listening to the questions being flung in their general direction. Director Mueller shut them down with his usual polite efficiency.

Maitland said to Savich, "We're putting the FBI's credibility on the line here, Savich." He plowed his fingers through his crew cut.

"We all agreed it's our best shot at protecting Rachael and getting to the truth."

Maitland nodded, then laughed. "The looks on their faces. I thought old Jerry Webber from the *Post* was going to fall out of his chair. That was some bombshell."

Maitland sighed. "It's still really tough for me to accept that someone killed Jimmy. I never noticed he'd stopped drinking, but then I only saw him every couple of months. Rachael is completely sure about this?"

Savich nodded.

Maitland said, "You know the media will

discover her in no time now they're motivated. They'll be camping out on the Abbott front yard. Like you said, the
announcement should protect her from
any more attempts on her life. Clean it up,
Savich, clean it up fast."

Director Mueller repeated what Maitland
had said. "Take care of it, Savich. Quickly.
The president is very concerned." He
smiled at Sherlock and left, three of his
staff surrounding him.

Sherlock asked Maitland, "Did Senator
Abbott tell you about his daughter, sir?"

"Yes, he was very happy, but he didn't
tell me too much about her background.
He seemed thrilled to have found her. His
spirits were good." Maitland shook his
head. "But then six weeks later, he's dead.
This is a deep black snake pit, boyo. The
director's right, it needs to be settled once
and for all."

"Soon, I hope," Savich said. "Why don't
you come over to my house this evening,
sir. You can meet Rachael Janes Abbott."

"Sounds good. How about Dr. MacLean? Any updates?"

Savich smiled. "We've got some good
leads there. In fact, if you'll excuse us, sir,

we need to follow up on something." Savich, holding Sherlock's hand, walked off, leaving Maitland to stare after him and shake his head. He was struck by a sharp memory of Savich's dad, Buck Savich, the wild cowboy who caught more bad guys than he had in his time. He remembered being in a bar in Dallas with Buck once when a paunchy guy in black leather came strutting in to pick a fight. He picked Buck, the fool. Maitland smiled when he thought of the guy stretched out on his back on the barroom floor, moaning.

He looked forward to meeting Jimmy's daughter. What did Jimmy's ex-wife, Jacqueline, and her daughters think about Rachael?

THIRTY-TWO

Hart Senate Office Building
Washington, D.C.

Jack shook Greg Nichols's hand, showed him his creds, and all the while Nichols stared at Rachael, the look in his eye, to Jack's mind, too interested. "It's good to see you again, Rachael," he said, and smiled, his voice too warm. When he shook her hand, he held it, his eyes on her face, on that braid.

Now this was unexpected. And Jack didn't like it.

Nichols cleared his throat and gave her that too-interested look again. He was tall, solid, fit, no fat that Jack could see. His tailored dark blue suit fit him well. His light brown hair was styled by a very talented pair of hands, and his teeth were as white as his shirt. He presented himself as a no-nonsense, rugged, supremely trustworthy man and had Rachael smiling back at him. Jack knew he was thirty-seven, and he wielded a good deal of power in his own right here on Capitol Hill. He even had enough juice to have gone from one top-dog master to another in under two weeks.

Nichols said, "I'm sorry, but as I said when you called, Agent Crowne, I have very little free time this morning. Senator Jankel has a vote before noon and I must brief him.

"Let me say I was flabbergasted by the FBI press conference and their speculations about Senator Abbott's tragic death. Do you . . . do they . . . really believe Senator Abbott was murdered, that his death was set up to look like an accident, and every local and federal agency was fooled?"

So you want to play, do you? Jack said, "That's about the size of it, yes. There's very little doubt at this point."

Nichols sat down heavily behind his

lovely mahogany desk, waved them both to the chairs in front. His back was to the window, naturally, with the sun flooding Jack's and Rachael's faces. Jack angled his chair, and Rachael did the same.

Jack looked around. "Nice digs."

"Yes, these offices are among the finest. A senior senator has usually garnered enough influence over the years for a large office. As chairman of the Ways and Means Committee, Senator Jankel is a major spokesman for the party. You should see the senator's office if this one impresses you."

Jack said, "Do you enjoy being the power behind the throne, Mr. Nichols?"

An eyebrow went up. "Power, Agent Crowne? Do you know, I've never really thought of it that way. No, rather, I think of myself as a facilitator, a person who keeps things running smoothly, a person the senator can trust implicitly to implement his ideas, to prepare him for whatever demands come up. But I only do what he wants done. Now, enough about me. Tell me what I can do for you."

"Mr. Nichols, you knew Senator Abbott possibly better than anyone, including his brother and sister and Rachael."

Nichols said, "That only makes sense since I worked closely with him for thirteen years before his death. As for Rachael, she only had weeks." He shrugged. "His siblings . . . well, here's honesty for you— only the Abbott name tied them together. There were never any bonds of affection, any genuine love or caring—at least that's how it always seemed to me. The senator's father—I met the old man exactly once. He looked at me like I was a mutt. He was an imperious old buzzard with an iron fist. He died less than five months before his eldest son. I knew he and his son rarely spoke. Senator Abbott said only that he and his father didn't see eye to eye about his career choice. I think that was an understatement. I thought it was probably a good deal more.

"When Rachael came into his life, not long after his father's death, I believe Senator Abbott hoped to get closer to his siblings, for Rachael's sake—wanted all of them to come together again as a family, but . . ." His voice hitched, his eyes blurred for a moment. He cleared his throat. "I'm sorry, it's difficult . . . I've just begun to accept his death, but now, to hear you say it wasn't an accident, that some crazy person actually murdered him, I ..." He stopped, shook his head, looked down at his clasped hands on the desktop.

"How did you come into Senator Abbott's orbit, Mr. Nichols?"

That brought his head up. "Call me Greg, please. Fact is, I met Senator Abbott when I was fresh out of law school, betwixt and between, I suppose you could say, uncertain what I wanted to do. I was sitting in the Big Raisin, an English pub and restaurant over on Platt Avenue, drinking a beer, wondering what I was doing here in Washington, of all places. I didn't know anybody, didn't have a single contact, and yet I'd taken the train down from New York to interview for a job that morning and was nursing a beer and thinking I was a great fool.

"Senator Abbott came in and sat down beside me, ordered a martini, two olives. He looked familiar, but I didn't realize who he was. He seemed like a nice businessman, friendly, passing the time while waiting for his lunch guest. He asked me what a young guy with a bad haircut was doing sitting at a bar in the middle of the day, and why I wasn't out building bridges or teaching children math.

"I laughed, told him it was all happenstance I was even in Washington, in that particular restaurant, drinking that particular beer, which I should point out was warm.

"He rolled his eyes, said, 'Ah, it's English.' We continued to talk, he kept asking me questions. Another man came in maybe twenty minutes later, evidently the fellow he'd been waiting for. I didn't realize it then, but it was the Speaker of the House. Senator Abbott got up and handed me his card. When I realized who he was, I tell you, I nearly choked on my beer. He even shook my hand, introduced himself. Then he told me to call him later that afternoon, he wanted to speak to me about a possible career change.

"I told him I didn't even have a career to change.

"He laughed, told me I wouldn't have to concern myself with former employers then, would I?

"I went to see him the next morning. He hired me. Over the years I took on responsibilities, I gained his trust. We became close." Nichols smiled. "I was his spear-head." Again, he paused, eyes filling with tears. "I'm sorry, but I know you under-stand, Rachael."

"Well, I certainly understand my own pain," she said. "I expect I'll feel it for a good long time."

Nichols glanced at an abstract painting on the far wall, huge red flowers, looking ready to explode. He said, "I certainly un-derstand that. Senator Abbott had cha-risma in spades. It's a natural talent, one you really can't learn. It's certainly not Senator Jankel's strong suit, but we're try-ing." He gave them a self-deprecating smile. "Please don't spread that around, all right? I really don't want another career change now."

"Of course not," Rachael said.

Nichols cocked his head to the side, looked thoughtful. "It's been so long since I've had these concerns, I'd forgotten. There's so much to learn. Believe me, Senator Jankel's likes and dislikes, his be-liefs, what's really important to him, they're very different from Senator Abbott's. What else can I tell you, Agent Crowne?"

Jack said, "Since I'm sure your time is

running short, Greg, you could cut the bullshit, that'd be good."

Nicholas jumped to his feet, planted his hands on his desk. "What is it you're implying, Agent Crowne?"

"Greg," Rachael said, "you and I are both guilty of not telling the investigators the truth. Both of us know Jimmy killed that little girl because he told us individually. And we both know he hadn't had a drink or driven a car for eighteen months because of it. Both of us remained silent. Neither of us wanted to ruin his good name. Of course, it might have led to your own involvement in the cover-up, but that's over now.

"I've told everyone the truth. It's time you did, as well. All of it."

He sat down again, looked at them over his steepled fingers. "When I spoke to the investigators, I did not cover up that the senator had stopped drinking and driving, I simply didn't emphasize it to the police because I didn't want the hit-and-run accident eighteen months ago to come out now that Senator Abbott was dead anyway.

"Evidently, the FBI believes the senator was murdered, because he'd stopped drinking and driving. I suppose this was based on what you told them, Rachael?"

"Yes."

To be honest, that sounds rather feeble to me, surely not enough to make the FBI reopen the case. There must be more." He looked pointedly at Jack, who only shook his head.

Nichols continued. "I have given this a lot of thought, and I don't believe he was murdered. No, that doesn't make sense. I believe he committed suicide. Of course, I haven't publicized that.

"And then you came to tell me you were going to make your father's confession for him, you were going to tell the world about it."

"Yes, that was what I was going to say, what I very well still might say."

Nichols said, "Do you want to know why he told me he was going public, Rachael?"

The braid momentarily curved around her cheek as she nodded, and Nichols stared at it. He said slowly, "I believe Senator Abbott told me because he wanted me to talk him out of doing it."

Jack said, "That's an interesting theory. Care to tell us what you said to him?"

"I told him it was the worst possible mistake to go public about killing the little girl because the media would devour him, make him into their monster of the month. He wasn't a monster and never would be, but that's how it would end up. The media would never take into account things like the man's excellent character, his caring for every man, woman, and child in this country, the legislation he'd gotten passed—thoughtful, far-reaching laws.

"No, the media would ignore all the good, wouldn't consider it relevant. I told him that ruining his own career was only the first bullet he'd take. Then they'd go after his family with gossip, half-baked stories and innuendos. His daughters and their families would be dragged into it.

"As for what they would do to the Abbotts, they'd dig up malcontents, interview anyone with an ax to grind against the family. Naturally, such a major scandal isn't anything the party needs."

Jack said, "But Senator Abbott realized all this. He'd thought it through, struggled with it for a very long time. He knew what would happen, he *knew*, yet he'd decided to act, no matter your arguments."

"Perhaps. But maybe hearing someone say it out loud—namely me—playing devil's advocate for him, made a difference. As I said, I think he really wanted me to talk him out of it. Look, Agent Crowne, I've struggled as well, wondered endlessly if keeping faith with Senator Abbott was the right thing, but you see, I knew the man, knew his heart.

"I also knew the death of the little girl was a dreadful accident, something that could have been avoided had he . . . well, had things been different for that split second, but they weren't, and so a child died needlessly.

"I tried to make him realize that it was an accident, tried to pull him out of his private hell. He wavered, and I was never sure what he would say from one day to the next, near the end.

"Let me be honest here. I'm simply not sure what his thinking was at the time of his death. I'll admit that I played the Rachael card—I told him the media would go after you especially, Rachael, you and your mom and her family. And was it fair to smear you in all this?

"Then he died, and now we'll never know

what he would have done." He paused, steepled his fingers again, a nervous habit, Jack thought, tapped them against his well-shaven chin. "In the end, would he really have resigned his office, confessed it all publicly? I don't know. When he died, it was all moot. I don't know what else I can tell you, Agent Crowne."

Jack said, "Well, we're still wading through it here, Greg."

THIRTY-THREE

Nichols's face spiked red with rage. "You think I'm lying to you? You want someone to blame for his death and you've selected me? That's nuts, you're nuts."

Jack said, "Fact is, we're running short on suspects here, Greg. You agree Senator Abbott told only you, his family, and Rachael. Do you know of anyone else he told?"

"No, I don't, but there could easily have been others. He had a lot of friends, all the staffers listen at every keyhole."

He was still breathing hard, his right hand in a mean fist. "Rachael, remember you told me you wanted to carry through with his wishes, you wanted to tell the world about his part in that little girl's tragic death?"

"Yes, I did," she said. "I still do. I believe to my soul he didn't change his mind, he wouldn't, and someone killed him to keep him quiet. Was it you, Greg?"

"No, it wasn't. Listen, Rachael, none of us know what your father's thoughts were in that split second before he died, what his decision was in that moment."

Rachael said, "I remember Jimmy was very quiet that evening. He gave me a kiss, patted my cheek, called his driver, and left, without telling me where he was going. His driver told the police he dropped Jimmy off at The Globe restaurant in Friendship Heights, where he was to meet some of his colleagues."

Nichols said, "I had nothing to do with setting up any dinner, and that's what I told the investigators."

She nodded. "But there were reservations in his name, for twelve. The guests arrived at the restaurant, but Jimmy never did, because he was dead, at the wheel of his own car, that's what the investigators told me—that the car was registered to

Senator John James Abbott, a white BMW. I'd never seen him drive it, it was always locked in the garage, so I couldn't even verify that it was his car.

"But the thing is, Greg, if Jimmy decided to drive again, why would he come back to the house without telling me? Why would he go straight to the garage, get into his BMW, and simply drive it away? I don't think he'd even seen his car keys in months. Better yet, how did he get back here to get his car? Investigators couldn't find any taxis that brought him back."

Jack said, "That's because the murderer had already gotten the BMW, probably forced your father into the car outside the restaurant. It was well planned."

Nichols asked, "What about Senator Abbott's driver?"

"Rafferty's in the clear," Jack said. "He said when he dropped Senator Abbott off outside the restaurant, the senator told him to take the night off, and so he did. He's very nicely alibied." Jack paused, studied the man's face.

Rachael fiddled with her braid. Jack said nothing, waited, his eyes still on Nichols's face.

Nichols said finally, not meeting her eyes, "As I already said, I think it's very possible your father killed himself. No, no, listen. I think he committed suicide because he couldn't live with the secret, but he didn't want to ruin your life, Rachael, or that of his family, and so he killed himself. This is what I believe. I think it was his gift to you. I'll tell you, I was relieved when his death was ruled an accident. I didn't want it ever said that Senator Abbott killed himself. Ever."

"Suicide?" Rachael repeated slowly. "You honestly believe Jimmy killed himself?"

Jack said, "You're saying he drank to bring himself to the sticking point, got in his Beemer, and drove over the cliff?"

"If he was ending his life, it seems to me it would make sense to ease things a bit."

"Jimmy did not kill himself," Rachael said. "He did not. He wouldn't, he simply wouldn't."

"You prefer to think that someone wantonly took his life because of what he was going to confess?"

Rachael sat forward, her voice becoming quite hard. "Jimmy was not that kind of man. Greg, you know Laurel, her slimy husband, and Quincy. Don't tell me they would hesitate to kill someone they believed would dirty their lovely worlds. Jimmy was planning to explode their world."

"Plan to murder their own brother? To actually follow through with it? No, that's pushing it too far, at least for me."

Jack said, "Shall I tell you the cases I've worked where family members have enthusiastically butchered each other?"

Nichols said, "I can accept that, Agent Crowne, if you're talking about psychopaths, about people with limited mental ability, the sort of people who have only their fists and the will to use them. That's not the Abbotts." He raised his hands, no longer clenched. "I know, you have the horror stories, Agent Crowne, but the Abbotts, no matter their behavior, their faults, their seeming lack of, well, humanity. I've known them a very long time. They don't abuse or murder their own blood."

Nichols sat forward, all his focus on Rachael. "You're still not planning to tell the world what your father did, are you, Rachael?"

"Yes, I think I am. I know you believe it might destroy your career, Greg, but you brought that on yourself."

He stared at her. "What do you mean by that?"

"I'm talking about your own involvement in the cover-up. Come now, Greg, Jimmy told me how you talked him out of calling the police after he struck the little girl. When he spoke publicly, of course he wouldn't point to your role in the cover-up, but you knew it would come out. The speculation alone about your connection would end your career and you knew it."

Nichols said, "Whatever passed between me and Senator Abbott is confidential, but I will say this. Even though I did know about the accident, I did not know the details, the particulars, until Senator Abbott told me days before his death. That is the truth." He shrugged and looked gravely disappointed.

Jack nodded, his voice approving. "I suppose denial of particulars is best. After all, Greg, no one would expect you to admit to being an accessory after the fact to a vehicular homicide. No one would expect you to send yourself to jail."

Nichols clasped his hands together, and his voice lowered, harder now. "I have told you the truth. I will not speak of it again." He turned to Rachael, raised his voice. "Who are you to destroy a man's name, to have the world judge him on a fraction of his life when he spent years—years—doing such fine work? That is one decision you cannot make for anyone. Especially not for him. You had only six weeks with him, Rachael, not enough time to know what he even liked to eat for breakfast. You did not know his mind, or his heart. You must accept that."

Jack saw Rachael's face was stark and pale, and said easily, "Where were you that night?"

"Me? All right, I suppose I am a suspect. Trust me, I don't need a calendar. That night is burned into my memory forever. I was to have dinner with Susan Wentworth—she works over in the GAO. But we didn't go, I can't remember the reason. So I don't have an alibi for the night of Senator Abbott's death." He looked down at his watch. "I must brief Senator Jankel. He needs my input before he votes." He rose, didn't offer to shake hands. He said to Rachael, "I hope you think long and hard about this, Rachael. Very hard."

Rachael didn't say anything. Jack thought she looked sad, and very tired.

Outside Senator Jankel's office, Jack said, "I expected you to tell him someone was trying to kill you, but you didn't."

"To be honest, I didn't see the point. He is very bright, Jack, and very smooth. His word against mine, and what good would it do? And he knows that." She shrugged. "I don't blame him, not really. He was only trying to clean up the mess; he didn't create it."

Jack said, "He's also a liar."

"Yes, he is."

Jack said, "Do you think he murdered your father?"

Rachael paused on the sidewalk in front of the Hart Senate Office Building and raised her face to the warm sun. She said, "Bottom line, who would hire him on Capitol Hill if it was known he helped my father cover up that accident? Oh, I don't know. My head hurts."

THIRTY-FOUR

When Savich called Congresswoman McManus's office, a staffer told him she wouldn't be in today, and that was all.

It was no problem discovering McManus's home address. They drove straight to her house in Tenleytown, past the business district along Wisconsin Avenue to Upton Street.

"No warning?" Sherlock asked.

Savich shook his head. "Nope."

"I would assume she's a very busy woman. I hope she's home and not off at some function."

Dolores McManus was home. Her

secretary, Nicole Merril, brought down her thick dark raised eyebrow when Savich identified them, then she led them to the congresswoman's home office in the back of the good-sized redbrick Georgian house set back from the busy street, surrounded by oak and maple trees. She knocked once, lightly, then ushered them into a room that wasn't all that large, but it was beautiful, covered with bookshelves, even a ladder to reach the ones on top, heavy dark furniture you could sink into, too warm for Sherlock's taste.

Nicole Merril said, "Congresswoman McManus, forgive the interruption. This is Agent Savich and Agent Sherlock from the FBI, here to see you about a Dr. Timothy MacLean."

As an intro, it did the trick. Savich saw McManus's hands fall off her computer keyboard and he'd swear she nearly rose straight out of her chair before she got herself together.

Then she straightened to her full height, and stood tall and still, facing them. In person, Congresswoman Dolores McManus was magnificent and well-dressed, standing close to six feet tall, with a sturdy, solid build and an amazing face, all angles and hollows, and deep lines seamed along the sides of her mouth. That mouth was opening right now, and Savich knew to his heels this woman loved to mix it up, no matter who or what the subject. Maybe he'd cheer her on if he agreed with her politics; at least he would if she hadn't paid some yahoo thug from Savannah to murder her trucker husband.

He looked into those dark eyes, saw both guilt and knowledge. He knew she'd done it. She'd thought about it carefully, gone through a dozen pros and cons, a dozen scenarios, then planned it meticulously, probably scared the spit out of the guy she hired to kill Mr. McManus.

He'd really like to have seen her with Timothy in the room, but of course there was no way she would have agreed to such an arrangement. If she was the one who tried to kill MacLean and indeed killed his tennis partner, Arthur Dolan, did she somehow manage to get out of Washington unnoticed and make the attempts herself, or did she hire someone like she did with her husband?

"Congresswoman," he said, striding

forward, his hand out, giving her an engaging smile. "Thank you for seeing us."

McManus shook their hands, gave them both a quick up-and-down look, offered them water, which they both refused, and said, "Agents. Let me say, this is unexpected. Nicole said you are from the FBI?"

"That's right, ma'am." Sherlock gave her a sunny smile. "We would appreciate your speaking to us, Congresswoman, about Dr. Timothy MacLean."

McManus was shaking her head as she looked down at the Rolex on her wrist. "I don't understand what this is about. I mean, what about Dr. MacLean? Look, I have no plans to sue him, so what are you doing here? I don't have any time right now, there's always a meeting, and I must go . . ."

Guilt and knowledge—Savich saw both again. She knew what MacLean had said about her—she'd just admitted to a motive. She was already flustered, talking all over the lot. He had to keep her off-balance. "This won't take long," he said, and his dark eyes became cold and flat. His voice went lower. "It's to your benefit, we believe, Congresswoman McManus."

"How could a visit from the FBI be to my benefit? How could anything about Dr. MacLean be to my benefit? I scarcely know the man."

"I suppose you weren't aware that someone brought down his plane? A bomb?"

"What's that? A bomb? No, of course not. It's regrettable, to be sure. Was it a terrorist act, do you think?" Her voice sharpened, the honey Southern accent became markedly clipped, and she slapped her open palms on the desktop. "Are you here because you believe I'm not tough enough on terrorism? Are you here because you don't believe I'm a patriot? Do you believe I don't love my country? Do you believe—"

"No, Congresswoman, not at all," Sherlock said, running over her smoothly, her voice nearly an octave higher, but it was difficult even with all Sherlock's experience. "May we be seated?"

"What? Well, yes, all right. But I don't have much time, as I told you."

She sat down herself and stared at them from across the expanse of her dark leather-surfaced partners desk.

Sherlock said, "We're here to speak with

you about Dr. MacLean's claim that you murdered your husband. Surely you remember, Congresswoman—under hypnosis you said you hired someone to murder your husband at a truck stop outside Atlanta?"

Congresswoman McManus jumped to her feet. Savich saw she did indeed have beautiful breasts, as Timothy had said. The lovely silk wraparound dress showcased them quite nicely. She was shaking, he saw, her face remarkably flushed—with rage? Fear?

"That is ridiculous nonsense! I want you to leave now. Do you hear me? I don't have to put up with this!"

Savich raised a hand. "A moment more, Congresswoman. I realize you can't begin to understand why Dr. MacLean told us about this, so let me explain. Dr. MacLean has been diagnosed with frontal lobe dementia, a pernicious disease that makes him say inappropriate, even extraordinarily damaging, things—in your case, breaking patient confidentiality—all without meaning to, all without malicious intent." He paused a beat. "Perhaps you know there have been other attempts on Dr. Mac-

Lean's life? That his office records were burned?"

McManus's voice was deep and vibrant, and shook with passion. "You're here to accuse me of having my husband murdered? That is monstrous nonsense, monstrous. His death, his murder, it was a horrible thing to have happen; my children were devastated. I loved my husband.

"You said Dr. MacLean claims I told him I killed my own husband? And now you say he's demented? And he didn't tell his patients that he was *demented*? I detest that man, he's an untrustworthy little *shite*. I abandoned him as an incompetent, but he was more, so much more."

"If he was only incompetent, Congresswoman, why would you think of suing him?"

That stopped her, but only for an instant. She planted large graceful hands on her desktop. "You listen to me, both of you. I was legitimately elected to the House of Representatives of the United States of America. Do you understand? I am a member of Congress. We do not kill. It simply is not done. All right, I will admit I chanced to hear that MacLean had said some horrible things about me. But that means nothing, do you hear me?"

Sherlock said, "Ah, but you hadn't yet been elected to Congress when your husband was killed."

McManus threw her head back and her voice vibrated low and hard now, but she looked only at Savich. "I did not kill my husband. I did not hire anyone to kill my husband. I am not trying to kill Dr. MacLean. I have not hired anyone to kill Dr. MacLean." Her palms smacked hard on the desktop, and she looked up at them, her eyes hot, sharp as glass. "He is a charlatan and a liar. He has slurred my good name, he has obviously told people I supposedly confessed murder to him. It's more than appalling! It's slander and malpractice. What else has he made up, and about whom?"

Sherlock raised her hand. "Congresswoman McManus, let me tell you something you obviously do not know. You may not remember Dr. MacLean hypnotizing you and eliciting such a story from you, but know that no confession made under hypnosis would stand up in court, even if it were recorded. The lawyers could tear it down in a matter of moments, if, that is, the judge even allowed it. So you see, there's no reason to deny being hypnotized by Dr. MacLean."

There was stony silence. *Well, that didn't work,* Sherlock thought.

Savich pulled out his small notebook and settled back in his chair. He asked pleasantly, "So you know nothing about rigging a bomb and putting it on the Cessna you knew Dr. MacLean would be flying in?"

"I know nothing about that! Nothing about the attempts on Dr. MacLean's miserable life! How many times do I have to repeat myself?"

Savich said, more steel in his voice now, "Would you please tell us your whereabouts on May eighteenth at about three o'clock in the afternoon? That was the afternoon Dr. MacLean was nearly run down by a dark sedan here in Washington."

She didn't spew this time. She became quiet and still. Her lips were moving, as if she were whispering a mantra, or ritual words, to get herself back in control. She said, slowly and precisely, spacing her words as if explaining something to an idiot, "I am calling my lawyer. I cannot imagine what you think you're doing bursting in on a representative in the Congress of the United States of America and conducting yourself in such a manner. I will have both of your jobs for harassing me. If necessary, I will ensure that your supervisors are fired, as well. Do you hear me?"

Sherlock said calmly, "Congresswoman McManus, can you begin to imagine what would happen to your public career if what Dr. MacLean is saying gets out? Just a whiff of it?"

"Now you have the gall to threaten me? You want to ruin me by spreading malicious gossip?"

"No, ma'am, we would not do that. But you know as well as we do that an allegation of that nature, even a mention of it behind someone's hand, could snowball and ruin you quite effectively."

Savich raised a hand before she could speak. "We don't know what the truth is about these matters, ma'am, but we felt it our duty to inform you of these allegations."

The door opened and Nicole Merril stepped in.

Obviously McManus had pressed a call button.

"Please see these people out, Nicole." She rose slowly, stared at them both with cold assassin eyes. "If you wish to speak to me again, you may not. You will speak only with my lawyer. Nicole will give you her name. If any of this absurd conversation leaks to the media, I will come after you personally. Good day."

After Savich fired up his Porsche, he turned to Sherlock. She saw he was grinning like a loon.

"That was more fun than outshooting you at the firing range. I guess that does it for our popularity with her at this point. You think she's running scared? Or is she planning our destruction?"

Sherlock said, "Oh, we got her all stirred up, that's for sure. And yes, she's scared. I could feel the tension pouring off her." Sherlock leaned her head back against the Porsche's soft-as-sin leather seat, closed her eyes.

Savich said as he turned into traffic, "Let's have some lunch, then pay a visit to Pierre Barbeau and his charming wife. I think we're on a roll." He nodded to the agent parked down the street. "I wish we could tap her phone. But at least we'll know if she meets up with somebody."

Sherlock smiled when the wind tore through her hair as the Porsche swerved gracefully around a big honking SUV.

THIRTY-FIVE

Sherlock said, "Remember how Sean was whooping and hollering, grabbed our hands and pulled us 'round and 'round that maypole at DuPont Circle?" Savich shot her a grin as he passed the circle and smoothly turned right off New Hampshire Avenue NW onto Eiger Street.

She was still smiling when they drove by the very ritzy modern condo building where the Barbeaus lived. "I guess I was expecting another huge Georgian set back in a beautiful yard. Although now that I think about it, is it possible their being French makes a difference?"

Savich laughed as he parked the Porsche a half block down, not far from one of the South American embassies. He gave Sherlock a grin, leaned over and kissed her. "You taste like the cheddar cheese from your taco." He lightly rubbed his knuckles over her cheek. He then ran his fingers through her tangled hair, his fault, she'd told him long ago, whenever she rode with him in the Porsche.

He sat back to admire his handiwork. She said, "You sure no one can tell I was riding in a convertible at wind-tunnel speeds?"

"Nah," he said, "you're perfect."

They looked over the immaculate grounds, at the blooming flowers planted in heavy ceramic pots and wooden flower boxes lining the walkways, everything swept and clean, the grass meticulously mowed. The sun was bright overhead and it seemed to Sherlock that the petunias and purple rhododendron were stretching up to reach it. She thought her deep red rhododendron at home was more brilliant.

"Maybe there's something to having someone do all the work for you. Every-thing's got a high shine."

Savich shook his head. "I like to sweat over my own lawn mower."

"A doorman, now isn't that uptown? And he's even wearing a spiffy uniform. I believe those are Green Bay's colors."

"The French National Police can't cover much of this expense," Savich said. "Lucky for him that his income is nicely subsidized by the large number of euros in Mrs. Barbeau's bank accounts."

"Her family is big into train construction and maintenance throughout Europe," Sherlock said, as they walked up the flagstone walkway to the glass-fronted building. "At least we know Pierre Barbeau didn't work today. You think he's lying low?"

"Maybe. I heard he and his wife haven't been seen much. They're still torn up about their son's death," Savich said.

The doorman glittered in his green-and-gold uniform. He was startled, clearly, when Savich showed him their FBI creds, but he recovered quickly. "You wish to see the Barbeaus?"

"Yes, please give them a buzz," Sherlock said. "We know they're both home."

When they stepped out of the elevator

on the ninth and top floor, it was onto pristine gold-white marble. The Barbeaus' condo occupied half of the floor.

On the second ring of the doorbell, they heard the sharp click of heels. A young woman, her complexion swarthy as a pirate's, and wearing, of all things, a classic French maid's black-and-white uniform, opened the door. She was a bit out of breath.

"*Oui?* May I help you?"

As she stepped forward, Sherlock wondered if the maid was the real French deal, or if she was amusing herself. Sherlock pulled out her ID. "I'm sure the doorman called up. As you see, we are FBI. We would like to see Mr. and Mrs. Barbeau."

The young woman turned quickly and disappeared through an arched doorway to the left. She immediately came back, heels loud and sharp on the marble floor, her face flushed. She apologized for leaving them in the entryway, and showed them into the starkly modern, entirely white living room. Savich hated white on white, but the view of all the historic residences through the floor-to-ceiling windows was very nice indeed. He saw his Porsche hugging the curb, boxed in now by a Beemer and a Mercedes, royalty, to his mind, surrounded by minions.

A good five minutes passed before Pierre Barbeau and his wife, Estelle, appeared in the doorway, both wearing casual chic, which for her meant tight designer jeans, a jeweled belt, and a silk blouse, and for Pierre, a short-sleeved golf shirt, black pants, and Italian loafers. He was holding a Diet Coke. Mrs. Barbeau looked like a thoroughbred—thin, sharp bones, the angle of her head arrogant, her chin high, and she stood straight and tall. She knew her own worth, Savich thought, and her opinion of her own worth was very high indeed. He looked more closely and saw the pain in her dark eyes, the new lines etched around her mouth. How fragile she looked in her expensive clothes. There was no doubt in his mind the woman was hurting.

Pierre Barbeau looked exhausted, like he was slowly bleeding, the life draining out of him. His black eyes were sunken and shadowed, his flesh loose on his face. There was no way this man could have planned and executed an escape for his son, not with his ravaged face and dead eyes. Pierre Barbeau looked like an old man who no longer cared about anything. He said as he paused in the doorway, "Tommy from downstairs told us two FBI agents were here. I do not understand. What would the FBI want to speak to us about?" Neither he nor Mrs. Barbeau appeared to want names or a handshake, which was fine by Savich.

Savich said pleasantly, "I believe you are both acquainted with Dr. Timothy Mac-Lean?" He didn't move from where he and Sherlock stood by a corner window that looked back toward DuPont Circle over the roofs of a dozen historic buildings.

Because Pierre Barbeau's face was already stark with misery, Savich saw only a small change at the mention of MacLean's name. He looked like he wanted to spit in contempt, but wasn't able to dial it up. He sneered instead. As for Mrs. Barbeau, there was instant dagger-cold viciousness in her eyes, her hatred for Timothy instantly overcoming her grief. Savich didn't want to, but he knew he should fan that hatred if he wanted to find out the truth as quickly as possible. They walked slowly into the living room and sat together on a white sofa, Pierre still clutching the Diet Coke. Savich and Sherlock sat opposite them.

Pierre Barbeau squared his shoulders, lifted his chin, but not to the same arrogant height as his wife's, and kept his sneer in place. He said, his voice low, an old man's tremor sliding through it, "Dr. MacLean? Well, yes, both my wife and I have known Timothy and Molly for many years now, but in reality who can you ever really know?" He shrugged. "Oh, we were friends, shared meals, talked about our families, our children . . ." He swallowed, and his hand trembled when he brought up the Coke can to rub his cheek. To wipe away tears he knew could roll down his face any moment? "We knew their children, they knew Jean David."

If Sherlock closed her eyes and only heard him speak, she'd have thought he sounded very sexy with that lovely accent, not so heavy that he sounded like a cartoon to an American ear. But looking at him, she saw a man utterly beaten down, like Atlas, holding the weight of the world, but ready to drop it.

"Yes, we are acquaintances," Estelle

said, her accent more pronounced. "Most everyone in our circle is acquainted with him. I will instruct Lissy to bring us coffee."

"We're fine, Mrs. Barbeau," Savich said. He watched them exchange a look, then move closer together—protection from more bad news?

Pierre said, "Now, what is this about? What is it I can tell you about Tim—Dr. MacLean?"

Savich said, "You visited Dr. MacLean at his office and told him your son had passed on classified information to a terrorist organization and then two CIA operatives were killed. You asked him if he would provide a psychological defense for your son. Dr. MacLean told you he could not do this, it was both unethical and illegal. He advised that your son turn himself in immediately or he would be constrained to go to the authorities himself since there were more lives at risk.

"You did not want to hear this—understandable, since Jean David was your son.

"A week later your son drowned in the Potomac. You went out despite a bad-weather advisory—winds, rain, fog. When the storm turned violent, you became ill. You said you and Jean David headed back to shore, but you didn't make it. A speedboat rammed your boat, not seeing you in the thickening fog. You went overboard, and your son went in to save you. The people on the speedboat did what they could. You were rescued but your son wasn't. Is that what happened, sir?"

"Yes, it is what happened," Pierre said. "His body still hasn't been recovered."

"We know. We're very sorry. We are here because there have been a total of three attempts on Dr. MacLean's life. Are you responsible for the attempts, Mr. Barbeau?"

Pierre looked as if he'd been kicked in the stomach, his pale face flushed a dull red. He jumped to his feet and began pacing in front of them, his hands twisting the Coke can. He yelled, "Timothy MacLean is a monster! He's never understood what it's like to live in a foreign country where everything is different, everything you do is questioned and doubted, everyone thinks differently and despises you for what you think, and there is always a rush to judgment. I did not wish to believe this of him, but it is true. Timothy was fully prepared to slander my son's good name, our good name! He is the one who should be in your American jail—not my son, not Jean David, who is now dead because of that man, who was supposedly our friend. Kill him? Gladly, but I did not."

"Mr. Barbeau," Sherlock said, "we appreciate that you would feel very strongly about this, that you are grieving. You assured Dr. MacLean that Jean David had no way of knowing the woman he was involved with fronted for a terrorist group headquartered in Damascus, and that she passed classified information to them that he had given her.

"I'm happy to tell you that two days ago, Homeland Security arrested her and most if not all of her associates, a lovely present to our country that Dr. MacLean helped make possible. She has admitted to seducing your son, to manipulating him to get information for her terrorist group."

"Yes, we heard of the arrests, naturally," Estelle said, dismissal in her voice, "but I paid no particular attention because that has nothing at all to do with us or France.

This woman—it does not matter what lies she tells."

Estelle rose to stand beside her husband. "None of this had anything to do with Jean David—nothing, do you hear me? He was an innocent boy, and whatever happened, it wasn't his fault. It wasn't. Don't you understand? Our son is dead."

Savich realized he'd thought Pierre Barbeau a strong suspect in the attempts on MacLean's life, but not now, not after meeting him, watching him, listening to him. This man looked shattered, he looked ready to bury himself in his misery.

MacLean was right. If anyone in this family was trying to off him, it was Estelle Barbeau. Her grief was as great and as consuming as her husband's, but there was violence and promise in her eyes. She said, her voice calmer now, more conciliatory, "This is very painful for us, Agent Savich. I do not know why you wish to dredge it up. My husband told you we had nothing to do with any attempts on Dr. MacLean's life. So what is your point? What do you want? Our son is dead, he is beyond your silly American laws."

"Silly?" Sherlock couldn't help herself,

she lost it. "I wonder how silly you would consider our laws if a terrorist group blew up the Eiffel Tower."

Estelle flipped her hand. "But such a thing would not happen. We live in peace with our Muslim countrymen."

Now that was a claim that wouldn't bear scrutiny.

Savich took a breath and said, "Mrs. Barbeau, if you would please give us your whereabouts on these two dates." He looked down at his notebook to confirm the dates when Estelle rode right over him. "Our son is beyond any pain you would inflict upon him for his youthful lapse in judgment. He was a boy, only a boy, an idealist, and a woman trapped him. An old story, to be sure, a tried-and-true one that will happen again and again. Jean David is dead. Let him and his name rest in peace. I hope Dr. MacLean dies. He should die, but neither of us is responsible for any attempts on his worthless life. How many times must we tell you that?"

Savich said, "The most recent attempt put him in the hospital."

Pierre looked bewildered, Savich

thought, no mistaking it. "You honestly believe that Estelle or I would try to kill Tim— Dr. MacLean? That is nonsense, absolute nonsense. Yes, we blame him for Jean David's death, but to actually try three times to kill him? That is absurd. Your FBI is absurd."

Sherlock said, "On the contrary, it makes a great deal of sense, sir. There is your belief that he is responsible and there is revenge. And what would happen if Dr. MacLean decided to go public with your son's activities?

"If this became known, would you still be received at embassy functions here in Washington? In New York? What about your job here?

"Indeed, sir, I can't imagine you could have happily continued your career with the French National Police. Tell me, sir, did you imagine what it would be like to return to France to face your family and friends, all of them knowing what your son did? Could you imagine bearing that? Could you imagine your wife bearing that?"

It was too much, and Sherlock wanted

to kick herself. If they were innocent, she had caused needless pain for these grieving parents.

Estelle waved a fist at them, the diamonds glittering madly off a huge ring on her right hand. "You listen to me. What our son did or did not do, none of it is important any longer. Jean David is dead, do you hear me? He is dead! All his thoughts, his deeds, his beliefs dead, drowned in a tragic accident—your damned Coast Guard couldn't even find him! And none of it would have happened if Dr. MacLean had kept quiet, as a doctor is supposed to do.

"Let me tell you, doctors in France are discreet, they do not preach. They do not make threats or issue ultimatums! But here? Obviously nothing is sacred here. The ethics of your American doctors, well, they have none, their behavior is inexcusable."

THIRTY-SIX

Someone found out that Timothy had spoken to his friend Arthur Dolan, and Dolan conveniently died. A coincidence? Savich didn't believe in coincidence. But how could the Barbeaus have found out about it?

He said, "You are right that Dr. MacLean spoke to several people about your son. Are either of you interested in knowing *why* Dr. MacLean betrayed your confidence?" Savich studied their faces as he spoke. Estelle's face was frozen in rage; Pierre looked like he didn't care, only wanted the earth to open up beneath his feet so he could slip away.

Estelle said, "We are not interested in any paltry excuses. The man is an abomination. We want you to leave now. We have nothing more to say." She jumped to her feet. Her husband, however, remained seated, rolling the Diet Coke can between his hands.

Savich said, "The last attempt on Dr. MacLean's life was a bomb placed on board a plane. He survived, barely."

Estelle shrugged. "What is this? A bomb? We know nothing of any bomb. We do not care what happens to him." She picked up a framed photo from a side table and waved it in front of their faces. "This is our son. This is Jean David. An elegant, brilliant boy, good, so very good. Look at him! He will never grow older, he will never have a wife and children."

He was indeed a handsome man, Sherlock thought, studying the photo. Dark hair, deeply tanned, his smile beguiling and utterly charming, his father's dark eyes shining out of his face. Such a waste, she thought, such a waste.

Savich decided not to tell them about MacLean's disease. He knew it wouldn't matter. It would mean less than nothing to them. He said, knowing it was a very risky roll of the dice, "Mr. Barbeau, I have read your statement to the authorities about the day your son drowned after saving you. After some dithering, it was determined to be a tragic accident. However"—he paused for effect—"however, I know that is not the truth. Please tell me what really happened that day."

Pierre grew very still, and Savich thought, *Bingo!* He'd known to his gut that something else was going on here. He waited, silent, patient.

When Estelle would have spoken, Pierre raised his hand to quiet her, shrugged, and said, "Why does it matter now? I say it no longer matters at all, nothing matters now that he is dead. Why not? I will tell you all of it."

Estelle stared at her husband. "What are you planning? No. Pierre?"

"I'm sorry, Estelle, but I knew it would come out eventually. And now, I'm tired, very tired, you see." He held up his hand to his wife once again and repeated, "It does not matter, Estelle. Agent Savich, Jean David did not die an accidental death."

Savich said, his heart racing at a fine clip, "Tell us what happened, sir."

Pierre raised his head, his face leached of color, but surprisingly, his voice was strong and steady. "My son came to me, told me what he'd done, asked me to help him. He knew, you see, knew his superiors would figure out soon enough he was the one responsible. I could not believe it. He gave me the details, convinced me. I told him I had to think about it.

"Two days after he asked me for help, I told him I'd spoken to Timothy, and I told him what he advised us to do, then I told Jean David of his threats. My son looked at me for a very long time, silent, and it broke my heart. He told me that he, just as I, must think about it. He left me. I feared he would try to escape but he did not. I am not lying to you. He did not.

"Two days later, on Friday, he asked me if I would like to go fishing, even though the weather was getting worse.

"And so we fished for striped bass in the Potomac, something we'd done many times, a ritual, a special time for us, to be together. But that day we really weren't fishing, we were silent for the most part, both of us in misery. I was afraid, Timothy's ultimatum rang in my mind. I finally broke the silence, told him I didn't know what to do. I loved him, but what he had done—I had to tell him I couldn't imagine his getting fooled so completely by that woman. And once again, I shook my head and told him I did not know what to do.

"Jean David leaned over and kissed me. He sat back, his fishing pole in his hand, and said he'd thought about it and decided he was going to kill himself, it was the only way, and that was why he'd wanted to come out in this storm. He told me he couldn't live with what he'd done, you see, and there were tears in his eyes when he spoke. The woman, he agreed, had made a fool of him, that was true enough, she'd led him to commit inexcusable crimes, to break sacred laws. He was a traitor, an unwitting one, but it was his own fault for being so gullible. He and only he was responsible."

Pierre's heavy breathing was the only sound in the large living room. Estelle said nothing, merely stared at this man who was her husband, this man radiating pain. There was no pity in her eyes, there was condemnation. Why? Because he'd told them the truth, and left them both naked.

Savich let the silence and Pierre's breathing hang thick in the air. He watched a dust mote sparkle in a shaft of bright sunlight.

Pierre said finally, "I told my son I would not forsake him, that I would hire the best lawyers, maybe I could even arrange for him to leave the country, but he only shook his head, smiled at me sadly.

"That storm, he had known it would be bad. The winds roared, the fog began to creep over us, and the rain pounded down, thick and wet, but to be honest, I didn't even notice. The waves were whipping up around our boat, but again, it simply wasn't important. Jean David said only, 'I cannot, Father.' And I knew in my heart that he was already gone from me.

"The wind became fierce. And I became aware that our boat was rocking wildly. Jean David stood up and I knew what he was going to do. Then a speedboat struck us as he jumped overboard. I jumped in after him. The people on the speedboat tried to help us, and they did save me, but not Jean David. Someone pulled me out, and I was screaming for my son, and then the Coast Guard was there, and they searched for him for hours.

"But he was gone, he killed himself, as he said he would. The truth is, Agent Savich, I was surprised my story was believed, it was so utterly unbelievable, silly really, but it was believed." He sighed. "But not by you. I suspect others are questioning it, as well. Perhaps they will believe something worse, that we staged the entire thing so Jean David could escape. But he didn't. He died, just as he'd intended.

"But it doesn't matter now. My son is dead. He paid for his crime. He paid with his life."

He looked down at the mangled Coke can in his hands, then raised his head once more. "They never found him. I wish they had found him."

Tears flowed down his cheeks. He didn't move, merely continued to stare at them, beyond them, really, his eyes dead and weeping. "It happened so fast, so very fast, as if someone had speeded up time. My son jumped into that cold rough water. He was not a good swimmer. I tried to teach him how to swim when he was a boy, but he never took to it. He said the water scared him because he knew it just went on and on, deeper and deeper, that there was no bottom. He always believed that. There was no bottom, he'd say. I have thought of that many times, Agent Savich, and I see my son and he is only a vague outline because the water is so deep and it is dragging him down.

"My son died that day. He took his own life. He is gone now, forever.

"I did not tell the police. I could not. The storm, the winds, the speedboat in the fog, all of that is the truth. All of that helped my fiction. Everyone believes it was an accident. *An accident*. But I have told you the truth and now I will tell you why I believe my son killed himself. He did it to spare his mother and me and his family. He did not want to see us shamed, did not want to see us reviled and humiliated because of what he did. My boy killed himself to save my honor."

THIRTY-SEVEN

Georgetown
Thursday evening

Sherlock opened the front door to Rachael and Jack, Astro jumping up and down behind her, barking his head off, his tail wagging so fast it was a wild blur, Sean at his heels.

Jack went down on his knees and stuck out his hand. "Sean, I'd know you anywhere. You look just like your father." Sean put out his hand and Jack pumped it up and down. "I'm Jack Crowne and I work in your dad's unit. This is Rachael Abbott. Hey, it looks like you've got a wild dog here."

"He's Astro," Sean said, staring up with

his father's eyes into Jack's face. He said to Rachael, "I'm Sean. You're pretty. I like your braid. You're almost as pretty as Mama."

"A wonderful compliment indeed," Rachael said. "Thank you, Sean."

Jack was scratching Astro's head. "Hello, Mighty Dog, how you doing, big boy?"

"Mighty Dog," Sean said, "we never thought of that name, Papa. *Mighty Dog*." He said to Jack, "We had fake grass for a while in the backyard and that's why he's Astro."

"Why don't we make Mighty Dog Astro's second name?" said his father.

"Astro Mighty Dog Savich," Sean said, and grabbed Astro around his belly and pulled him over to roll onto the floor. Jack laughed and roughhoused with the two of them, Rachael joining the chaos. Soon shouts and barks filled the house.

It felt good.

When everyone was seated in the living room, Astro on Rachael's lap, licking her hands, she said, "Jack told me Sarah Elliot was your grandmother, Dillon. That painting over the fireplace, it's magnificent."

"Thank you. I agree," Savich said. "She named it *The Lame Man in the Square*. I have eight of her paintings on display at the Corcoran. I change them out maybe three or four times a year."

"I'd want all of them around me all the time," Rachael said.

The doorbell rang again. Savich, Sean behind him, Astro leaping and barking on his heels, went to answer the door. In a moment, agents Dane Carver and Ollie Hamish walked into the living room.

After Rachael met Dane and Ollie and Astro Mighty Dog had been petted until he collapsed on his back, legs in the air, tongue lolling, Sherlock said from the kitchen doorway, "Mr. Maitland called. He can't make it. Let's eat first, then we'll sort things out."

"Sort what things out, Mama?" Sean asked.

"Come wash your hands, Sean," Savich said, and led him to the half bath.

"I'm sorry, Sherlock, I didn't offer to help you." Rachael immediately jumped to her feet. "Anything I can do now?"

"Sherlock cooked?" Ollie said, not moving.

"Tell us you cooked, Savich," Dane said

as he walked back into the living room. "Right?"

"Ingrates," Sherlock said.

Savich laughed as he wiped his son's now clean hands. "Yes, I did. Meat lasagna for you barbarians, vegetable lasagna for me and Sean."

"I made the Caesar salad," Sherlock said.

"Give her a lettuce leaf and she can make it dance," Savich said.

They all learned about Sean's first football game with three neighborhood kids, two on a side, and how he threw the best, longest touchdown pass ever, how Maggie had tackled Paul, bloodying his lip, and all the other convoluted details until it was time for dessert.

Sherlock sliced the apple pie into even pieces, every eye at the table on her knife. Between bites of ice cream and pie, Sean told them about his new computer game, *Dora the Explorer*. "I already know Spanish, so that's easy."

"He speaks Spanish with Gabriella, his nanny," Sherlock said. "I'm thinking Dillon and I should learn Spanish, to keep up with him."

There was a lot of laughter, something Rachael thought had disappeared from her life. There was no talk of business until Sherlock came back downstairs after putting Sean to bed and Savich came inside after walking Astro Mighty Dog for the night.

"All right," Sherlock said. "Let's get to it."

Rachael sat forward. "Dinner was such fun I forgot all the misery, but now it's coming back."

"That's not the half of it," Jack said. "We had a big surprise waiting for us when we got back to the senator's . . . to Rachael's house."

"What, for heaven's sake?"

Rachael said, "My ex-fiancé was standing on the doorstep."

Jack sat back on the sofa, his arms crossed over his chest. "Rachael came to a dead stop when she saw him, and I nearly shot him because for all I knew he was there waiting to kill her. I only made an insignificant move toward him and I thought the little wuss was going to puke."

Rachael said, "That's because his bookies were probably after him, and he was already on edge. You've got to admit, Jack, he did recover quickly."

"Yeah, he did, but only because he knew you were looking at him and he didn't want you to think he was a coward. Then the jerk acted like you were still going to marry him. He even tried to kiss you."

"You didn't clock him, did you, Jack?" Ollie asked.

Jack was silent for a moment, his brows drawn together. "For a moment there, I gotta admit it was close."

"What is the ex-fiancé's name?" Sherlock asked as she poured more of Savich's excellent coffee into Rachael's cup.

"Jerol Springer."

"I've been wondering what kind of name that is," Jack said. "I mean, it's almost like that guy on TV. I tell you, Rachael, I can't believe you ever considered marrying that idiot."

"Well, it never came to marriage, and not because of his name," Rachael said, sipped the coffee and closed her eyes a moment in pleasure. She said, "You know, Dillon's coffee's as good as mine."

There was a discreet snort; no one believed her.

Ollie said, "Why is Mr. Springer an ex? He wasn't faithful?"

"Oh no, he was faithful as a tick, as far as I know. The moron gambled too much and I found out about it. Actually, his bookie sent one of his yahoos to see me, something that makes a person see things very clearly, let me tell you. Evidently Jerol wasn't such a hot gambler. He was always looking over his shoulder."

"He was into the horses?" Dane asked.

"Horses, dogs, football—pro and college—beach volleyball, soccer, the first guy to belch after drinking beer, you name it, he'd bet on it, and lose. So when Jerol saw Jack, he thought he was there to break his kneecaps. When he found out Jack was only an FBI agent, I thought he was going to cry with relief. I hadn't seen him for a good six months."

Dane said, "Maybe he was there because he'd heard Rachael was the late Senator Abbott's daughter, and he saw cash registers ca-chinging in his brain."

Rachael said, "Do you know what Jack did? He pretended he was living there with me, cozied himself up all over me, even draped his arm over my shoulder while

Jerol was standing there looking hopeful."

Jack grinned hugely. "It sent him on his way fast." He frowned at Rachael. "You were being far too nice to him."

Rachael reached in her purse and pulled out a Smith & Wesson pistol. "If he'd hassled me, I would have shot him in the foot. It was my father's. It's got a nice feel to it."

"Then he wouldn't have been able to leave," Ollie observed.

"Oh dear, you're right." Rachael fell silent, sipped her coffee, her eyes on Astro, who was sleeping off vegetable lasagna from Sean's plate on a rug in front of the fireplace.

Jack liked the Sigma Series, you pointed at what you wanted to shoot and fired, but still . . . "I don't like your having a gun; it's not a toy."

"Jeez, you think? Jack, you've seen me shoot. I'm probably better than you. Be quiet."

"Moving right along," Savich said, "time to get you caught up." He and Sherlock proceeded to fill them in about their meetings with Congresswoman McManus and the Barbeaus.

"The thing is," Sherlock said, "neither Dillon nor I think Pierre Barbeau is the person behind the attempts on MacLean's life. Now, Mrs. Barbeau—she's something else, a real piece of work." Sherlock shrugged. "She's grieving hard, as torn up as her husband, but her level of anger at Dr. MacLean . . . I don't know. I simply don't."

Ollie said, "Did you guys pick up any vibes about McManus? Do you think she had her husband murdered?"

Savich nodded. "I think she's capable of having him killed."

Sherlock said, "She's got a real temper, but she's learned how to control it—had to, I guess, since spewing venom at her colleagues on the floor of the House of Representatives wouldn't make her any friends. She's an impressive woman, though. I'd rather have her on my side any day."

Savich shrugged. "Is she the one behind the attempts on Timothy's life? I hate to say it, but I don't think so. There's no motive, unless it would be revenge for his stirring everything up, maybe creating a scandal that could annoy her for a time."

"I think she has too much to lose for

that," Sherlock said. "Unless she knew there were too many loose ends surrounding her husband's murder, maybe worried a new investigation would turn up something too easily."

Rachael said, "Then where does this leave us?"

Astro Mighty Dog raised his head and barked once.

Rachael went over to sit on the floor beside him, petting him until he rolled onto his back, all four feet sticking in the air.

Savich said, "There's Lomas Clapman, the rich guy who stole his partner's ideas and may have committed fraud. But again, I can't see that as a motive."

Ollie said, "It always comes back to how the killer knew MacLean had talked. The bartender said he wasn't aware of any other customers listening, but he couldn't be sure. He said he never told another soul, so this remains a mystery."

Jack reached into his jacket pocket and pulled out a disk. "All Timothy's files are on this disk. If he hadn't backed them up, the fire would have destroyed all his patient notes. And just who set the fire?"

Ollie said, "We've reviewed all the files

with our forensic psychiatrists, done a lot of checking, but there aren't any other patients they can point to as having the motive to kill Dr. MacLean. Sure, there's some ugly stuff here and there, but murder?" Ollie shook his head. "And let's face it, who would kill his shrink on speculation—he hasn't told the world your secrets, but he might? It doesn't make sense."

Everyone thought about that for a moment.

Rachael said, "Tomorrow morning, Jack and I are going to see Jimmy's lawyer, Brady Cullifer. If there are skeletons, he may be able to tell us about them."

Savich sat back on the sofa, laced his fingers over his belly. "I spoke to the ME about Perky's unexpected death. Turns out it wasn't foul play. She died of a pulmonary embolism—a blood clot to her lungs. It's a major surgical risk, the ME said. So there you have it.

"I then paid a visit to our two wounded bad guys from Parlow and Slipper Hollow—Roderick Lloyd and Donley Everett. Lloyd still refuses to speak to us, and as for Everett, he's already signed a full confession. Unfortunately, he doesn't know who hired Perky. I don't think he's lying." Savich sat forward. "There's no reason for Lloyd to know that Perky is dead. Maybe we can convince him she rolled. What do you think, Sherlock?"

"I can't imagine Lloyd's lawyer not knowing she's dead, but it's worth a shot." She didn't sound optimistic.

"What about the fourth guy?" Jack asked. "What's his name?"

"Marion Croop," Sherlock said. "We've got an APB out on him, but no word yet."

THIRTY-EIGHT

Washington, D.C.
Friday morning

Rachael ladled hot, thick oatmeal into Jack's bowl.

He stared down at it, then up at her.

"What? Come on, dig in while the steam is still pouring off it. It's good for you, and I make the best oatmeal in Kentucky. Here's some brown sugar." She spooned some over the oatmeal.

He gave her a pitiful look. "Could I have some Cheerios instead?"

Rachael punched him in the shoulder. "What is this? Here I decide to cook you my very best breakfast since you're here as my bodyguard, and reward you because there weren't any break-ins last night, and you want Cheerios? Out of a box?"

"With nonfat milk?"

She crossed her arms over her chest.

"Maybe some sliced banana?"

She laughed, went to the pantry, and disappeared inside. She came out again a moment later. "Sorry, Jack, no Cheerios. It's either oatmeal or you're out of luck."

He took a bite of oatmeal and chewed slowly, then swallowed.

"Well? What do you think?"

"The truth?"

"Of course. Come on, Jack, I can take it."

"It's gotta be the best oatmeal in Kentucky."

"Yeah, yeah, but we're not in Kentucky, you jerk." She threw a napkin at him and dug into her own oatmeal. "All right, all right, I'll get you some Cheerios."

They ate in companionable silence. It was an odd feeling, Rachael thought, as she watched the morning sunlight pour through the window over the kitchen sink, having someone at the breakfast table with her. After Jimmy died, and the days were empty and passed slowly until she flew to Sicily, she'd begun to doubt she'd ever begin her morning with a smile again. And then someone drugged her and threw her into Black Rock Lake.

"Thank you, Jack."

He licked his spoon and held out his empty bowl. "For what?"

"You're here. I'm not alone. Did you sleep well?"

He'd slept in one of the antique-filled bedrooms three doors down from Rachael. Her father's bedroom remained untouched at the other end of the long corridor. The bed, in truth, had been hard as a rock and he'd had to stretch for five minutes that morning to get the kinks out.

"It was great," he said.

"I'm glad. You must be real macho. I slept in that bed once and I thought my back was going to break, the mattress was so hard. I'm so glad no one tried to get in and kill me." She refilled his bowl, not saying a word. "Truth is, I didn't sleep all that well because every single sound was a bad guy coming to get me, even though I knew you were close, knew I was safe."

"Understandable."

"I kept my gun right beside me. Yes, the

safety was on, Jack. Around three o'clock, I started hoping some idiot would show up and press his nose against my window. Question—if you shoot a gun through a storm window, does the bullet go straight through or does the glass throw it off target?"

"These windows? Straight through." He added without any consideration at all, "You could sleep with me."

As a simple declarative sentence with only five words in it, it should have flown high and proud. But it didn't.

Rachael's eyes fastened on his. "Sleep with you?"

"Ah, you know, as in sleep in my bed. I'd be close enough so that even if a bad guy did get in, he'd have to go through me first."

Rachael said matter-of-factly, "Yeah, he would. Okay, I'll think about making you the tethered goat."

"Well, I don't guess I was thinking of myself in exactly that way. Not really a goat. You know . . ." He shut his mouth.

She let him off the hook, but barely. He looked so interested, his eyes narrowed on her face, unblinking. She said, "I called my mom earlier, told her everything is peachy. She'd called Uncle Gillette and, bless him, he knew it was important to keep what happened under wraps, so he didn't spill the beans.

"Still, she's worried about me being all alone in Jimmy's house, no friends. I think she wants to sleep with me, too."

Jack choked on his coffee. He wiped the back of his hand across his mouth. "I hope you talked her out of coming here. Three in that bed wouldn't be good."

"I told her I'd visit soon. She's still in shock that Jimmy was murdered and I'm now a rich woman. She was stuttering when I told her Jimmy left me a full third of his estate. I still haven't called my sisters, and believe me, their mother Jacqueline hasn't called me. I want to wait to make contact until this is all resolved."

Jack said, "I checked for any leftover reporters camping on the curb. Evidently, they decided there'll be nothing exciting happening here, thank God."

"Yeah, but we should keep a close watch. You never know when one of the vultures will leap out at you from behind a garbage can."

He nodded, spooned in more oatmeal, frowned. He dropped his spoon. "Sorry, no more. I've tried, but it's the same taste, bite after bite."

"Doesn't Cheerios taste the same bite after bite?"

"Nope. The milk softens up the little do-nuts at different rates, so each bite is a surprise."

"You're nuts," she said, and grinned at him. "You look like such a regular guy, sit-ting here at the breakfast table, a bowl of oatmeal in front of you, but then I think about who you are, what you do, and what you did for four years—the Elite Crime Unit, that's what it's called, right?"

He nodded.

"What was that really like?"

He straightened his bowl, neatly folded his napkin, stared out the large window by the country oak kitchen table toward the lovely white gazebo in the backyard. He looked back at her. "Fact is, every sin-gle day brought new horrors, and you couldn't escape them. They followed you everywhere, even in your dreams. My dreams aren't so vivid and bloody now, thank God.

"There are scary people out there, Rachael, and you know what? Drugging you and tying a concrete block to your feet so after you drown you don't come back up to the surface—that qualifies big-time.

"In the ECU, we called them monsters and evil and psychopaths, all to dehumanize them. But what I kept seeing was each of those individuals as a baby—laughing, crying, innocent, and I'd wonder every single day, why? What happened to make that baby grow up to kill and destroy and inflict unimaginable pain and horror?

"We caught a good number of them, put most of them down, no choice. We saved some lives."

"Why did you leave the unit?"

"Because I knew something would die in me if I stayed. When I first joined the ECU, I was told the time to burnout was about five years, and they gave me a list of symptoms to look out for. One of the main symptoms was 'feeling death inside you,' and I knew I'd reached my limit. I only made it to four years. Savich scooped me up before I could go civilian again and return to a prosecutor's office."

"Are you glad you stayed in the FBI?"

"Oh yes. Savich's unit is special, all the agents are smart as a whip, the experience level is very high, and they care. It's a good unit—cohesive, everyone ready to cover everyone else's back. Sure there's the mind-numbing bureaucracy, some idiot agents who act like they should run the world, but most agents I know want to do a good job. They want to make things better. I'm sounding like a recruiting poster, sorry."

"That's okay."

Jack rose from the table, carried his bowl to the sink, and washed it. He wiped his hands on a towel. "First thing this morning, let's go to Black Rock Lake. I want to see firsthand where all this happened. I want to trace your footsteps back to your house."

THIRTY-NINE

An hour later, they stood together at the end of the wooden dock and stared down at the blue water lapping gently against the pilings, shimmering beneath the bright sunlight. It was beautiful, and Rachael thought, *I could be down there, tethered to that block, my hair waving in the water, dead and gone forever.*

She said, "As you can see, it's not very deep here, maybe twelve feet max."

He looked down at the water and felt such a punch of rage he nearly lost his breath. Even though he'd seen and heard just about everything one human being could do to another, this was different. This was Rachael. He said, keeping the violence out of his voice, "Two people carried you down this dock, one had your arms, the other your legs. You said you couldn't tell if they were male or female. Think about it a minute, try to put yourself back there, listen."

Rachael closed her eyes. She remembered the motion, remembered how she fought to come back, to get her brain working again, remembered them speaking, but what? Who?

She shook her head. "I don't know."

Jack said, "Okay, I want you to think about the weight distribution. Can you picture them carrying you? Is one of them carrying more of your weight than the other?"

She thought about that. "Maybe," she said, "maybe the person carrying my arms was female. I remember smelling some scent, close to me, not sweet, but not pungent enough for a man to wear it." She shook her head. "But I can't swear to it."

"That's okay. At least you were aware enough to pretend you were still unconscious. It gave you a chance." He paused, then lightly touched his hand to her forearm. "What you did, Rachael, it was amazing. You kept your head, kept the terror away, and used your brain. I am very proud of you."

"I didn't think I was going to make it. The pain in your chest, it's unimaginable. You want to open your mouth so badly, but you know it will be all over if you do. When my head cleared the surface—" She stopped, swallowed. "I knew they were still there. I could hear them talking, not ten feet from me, standing on the dock. When I got in enough air to convince myself that I was going to live, I slid back under the water and swam under the dock, and waited. I heard them walking back up the dock, heard the car engine. I came up to see the lights."

"You couldn't make out anything? Think back—did you see a profile? Male or female? Can you describe the shape of the car?"

"No, they were gone by the time I was getting out of the water."

"All right. Let's go back to that diner."

Mel's Diner was charming, right out of the 1950s, with windows all along the front,

Formica tables covered with red-and-white-checked tablecloths, and plastic menus. All along the windows were booths, the vinyl dark brown and cracked.

"I don't believe it," Rachael said as they walked in the front door. "That waitress, she's the same woman who was here last Friday night. Business is light, people in only a few booths, like it was on Friday night. The cook, you can hear him whistling from behind the counter in the kitchen."

"Hey," the woman said, doing a double take when she saw Rachael. "I remember you. Last time I saw you, you looked like a drowned rat. You look fine now, all dried out again. You all right, sweetie? Is this your husband?"

"He's my bodyguard," Rachael said, read the woman's name tag, and added, "Millie."

Millie whistled. "You know kung fu or jujitsu, foreign stuff like that?"

"All of it," Jack said. "You always gotta go with a pro."

"I'm thinking I'd like to hire a bodyguard, a hunky one like you, to keep that rat ex-husband of mine away from me. Could you kick him in the face for me? Can you kick that high?"

"Well, maybe a kidney shot instead?" Jack asked. "That's more in my range."

"You could start just about anywhere, honey."

They ordered coffee, and Rachael asked Millie about any customers she'd had last Friday night who were strangers to her. There'd been maybe a dozen tourists driving through who stopped in, but none of them had struck her as being weird or nasty.

She left to pour more coffee into a local man's cup, then came back, a thoughtful expression on her face. "I'm thinking, I'm thinking. Last Friday," she said. "Hmm."

She handed Rachael some creamer she didn't want.

"I remember this one gent, he came in to get two coffees to go, one black, one blond with three sugars. Now that I think of it, he looked kind of on edge. No nervous tics, nothing like that, but he was impatient, tapped his fingers on the counter while I was pouring the coffee. It was maybe thirty, forty-five minutes before you came straggling in."

"What did the gent look like?" Jack asked.

Millie pursed her lips. "He was maybe forty, longish black hair, sunglasses on, if you can believe that, like he was some sort of celebrity or some asshole wanting to look like one. He wasn't big, kind of thin, I think, and his clothes didn't fit him all that well." She screwed up her face, thought about it. "Sorry, that's about it. I can't think of anything else. But I remember thinking I wasn't sorry to see the back of him.

"I was pouring a refill for a guy next to the window and I looked out. I saw him sitting in the passenger seat of a big dark-colored car, maybe a Lincoln, but I'm not sure. He and another guy were talking, drinking their coffee. Then my boss called me and that was the last I saw of them."

"Did they seem angry?" Rachael asked. "Or pleased, congratulating each other?"

"Honey, I was too far away and it was too dark, sorry."

Jack asked Millie more questions, then asked the same ones again, using different phrasing until he knew the well had run dry.

Rachael hugged her before they left. "Thank you, Millie, thank you very much."

Millie patted her on the back. She looked at Jack again, up and down. "You being a professional bodyguard and all, you see to it you take good care of her, all right?"

"Yes, ma'am," Jack said, and smiled at her. "Millie, do you think you'd recognize the gent from Friday night?"

"I might be losing brain cells at a fine rate, but I still got enough to remember that face, even with the dumb sunglasses. He's the kind you wouldn't want to see in a bad dream."

"Good. I'll bring you some photos to look at."

A man shouted out from the kitchen, "Millie! I got the flats and strips for number three!"

"That's pancakes and bacon," she said. "I'm coming, Moe!" And she winked at Jack.

Once outside the diner, Rachael threw her arms around Jack, hugged him hard until he grunted. "You're a genius. I didn't say anything, but I never thought it would be of any use at all to come back out here. But Millie was here and she remembered me. And that guy. You are so smart, Jack." She went up on her tiptoes and kissed him. "I'm glad I laid out the big bucks and got myself a real pro."

He was laughing as his arms came around her. In the back of his mind, the FBI agent was screaming, *Stop it, you moron, are you nuts? Step away from the girl, now.* The FBI agent was loud and insistent, but he didn't make any headway. Jack didn't release her. In fact, he kissed her back and it felt so good he'd have given up his season tickets for the Redskins without a moment's hesitation just to keep his mouth on hers and his hands—but the unwanted agent finally kicked him in the butt. Jack set her away from him to keep from yanking her down into the backseat of the car.

She looked up at him, her mouth open, face blank, eyes wide. She was breathing fast, which his agent self demanded he ignore. She swiped her hand over her mouth. "What? Oh my God, Jack, I'm sorry, I didn't mean to do that. It's just that . . . I lost it. You're really smart, Jack. Oh damn."

"It's standard procedure, Rachael," and that was true, but wasn't that about the dumbest thing he'd ever said? He took a step back from her, had to. A beam of sunlight fell directly onto her and he saw the strangest thing. He saw her swinging a baseball bat. She walloped the ball and it flew and flew, and he realized it wasn't Rachael, it was a little girl with Rachael's smile and a braid in her hair—

"Stop being modest. I'm going to tell Dillon how brilliant you are."

"Great Balls of Fire" blasted out of Jack's jacket.

Jack had never flipped open his cell so fast. "Jack Crowne here."

FORTY

Jack drove down Wisconsin Avenue past a rare-cigar shop and an outdoor-gear emporium, looking for Brady Cullifer's law firm. It was in an older building, grand-looking, really, understated, standing proudly next to a holistic healer.

There were five names on the gold-etched sign on the front doors, two of them Cullifer.

A worried-looking receptionist led them to Brady Cullifer's office, knocked on the door, waited for the "Enter," and opened it. He stepped discreetly back, giving them a harried, nearly frantic look.

Brady Cullifer came around from behind a large, well-worn desk that looked like it had belonged to his grandfather, which, Jack supposed, was possible.

Jack said as he shook the man's hand, "What's with the receptionist? He looks strung-out."

"Oh, Rowley, he's the firm's major worrier, practically fingers worry beads whenever there's a big case being tried. One of our lawyers just left to hear the verdict in a big personal-injury suit, so Rowley's worrying big-time. Rachael, my dear, how are you? It's good to see you."

Rachael smiled, let Mr. Cullifer hug her. She liked him, probably because he'd always been so kind to her, always seemed to accept her. He was about Jimmy's age, with a bit of a paunch she remembered Jimmy kidding him about, lecturing him to get to the racquetball court. He was immaculately dressed, as always, in a lightweight gray wool suit, a pale pink shirt, and a dark blue tie that, surprisingly, tied everything together.

When he released her, she said, "I'm fine, sir."

"Like everyone else in this town, I heard

the FBI press conference yesterday morning about Jimmy's death being classified as murder, not an accident, and that a woman shooter was possibly involved. Now she's dead. Do you know why she died?"

"Complications of surgery," Jack said.

"I take it you are Agent Crowne?" He raised a brow at Jack.

"Yes, sir," Jack said, and shook his hand. "We appreciate your seeing us on such short notice."

Cullifer waved them to a burgundy leather sofa, offered them coffee, and sat himself in a chair facing them. "Rachael, my dear, tell me what I can do to help you."

Rachael said, "You remember I told you what Jimmy did, how he accidentally killed that little girl. You acted like you didn't know anything about it. I've been thinking that's not true. Please, sir, tell me what Jimmy said to you about that little girl."

Brady sat down and drummed his fingertips on his desktop. Finally, he said, "Why would you think I know anything more about that poor little girl than what you told me, Rachael?"

"You're his lawyer," Jack answered, "his longtime friend." He raised his hand. "Please don't invoke client confidentiality. I don't think it applies anymore. The senator is dead, and this is an official investigation. It's important, sir."

Cullifer slowly nodded. "Very well. Shortly before his death, Jimmy told me about his hitting and killing a little girl eighteen months ago."

Cullifer's eyes clouded. "I couldn't believe it, just couldn't. When he finished, when I couldn't think of another question to put to him, I asked him why he didn't tell me sooner, but he said only that he was telling me now to prepare me because he'd decided to go public. He wanted it in the open, he wanted it done and over with. He told me he'd also informed Rachael, Laurel, Stefanos, Quincy, and Greg Nichols of his intentions. He didn't know if there would be any blowback on me, but he was telling me just in case.

"And I played dumb with you, Rachael, because he *was* my longtime friend, my client, as well as the whole confidentiality issue. You're thinking I know more?"

Rachael said, "He wanted all those

close to him to be ready to deal with the media and any fallout, business and personal. He told me his family was furious with him."

"An understatement," Cullifer said absently. He sat back in his chair, crossed one leg over the other, and tapped his fingers together. "He also told me he'd told Jacqueline and his daughters. They were exceedingly upset, as you can imagine. Jacqueline wanted him to keep quiet. They had several extended phone conversations about it."

"Were you furious with him?" Rachael asked.

Cullifer said after a moment, "To be honest, I was devastated. You see, I knew something was wrong with Jimmy, knew it to my soul. I remember how distracted he was, how there were new lines on his face—a face, I might add, that was always youthful until the last year or so. But you know, I got caught up in a lawsuit and any concerns about Jimmy dropped out of my mind. Until it was too late. And then you came back from Sicily and told me what you were going to do, Rachael."

Rachael said, "The guilt was eating him

alive; that's why he was going to confess everything."

Cullifer said, "Yes, I know. Now, like everyone else who heard the FBI press conference, I wondered and wondered who would want Jimmy dead. Who would take such a risk? And believe me, killing a United States senator is a huge risk. The thing is, even after Agent Savich said he was murdered, for the life of me I couldn't figure out a motive, not for Laurel or Quincy, not for his ex-wife, who's very well off financially, believe me, or any of his colleagues. I honestly can't imagine any of them killing him to avoid a scandal—that's simply too far out there."

Cullifer looked thoughtful. "Tell the world what he did—I told him it would mean the end of his career, it would mean a huge scandal, a lawsuit to break the bank, it would have meant beggaring the estate, depending on the sharks the little girl's family hired. But most of all, I told him he would be tried and convicted of vehicular homicide and go to jail.

"Of course he knew all this. He also fully realized his family would be dragged into it—Laurel and Stefanos, and Quincy, all his staff on the Hill, me because I've been his lawyer for nearly forever."

Jack said, "Regardless, someone took it upon him- or herself to silence him. Rachael is convinced it's Laurel and Quincy."

Brady asked, "You're certain only these people knew what he was preparing to do?"

"As far as we know," Jack said.

"This was why Jimmy had stopped drinking and driving his car?"

Rachael nodded. "After he killed the little girl, he never took another drink, and never drove his car again. That's what he told me and I believed him."

"During the press conference, Agent Savich mentioned that a woman was involved."

Jack said, "Yes, we think so. But we don't yet know who hired her."

Rachael said, "Sir, do you think Laurel and Quincy could have murdered Jimmy?"

Cullifer arched a sleek eyebrow at her. "Laurel? Quincy? Kill their own brother? Evidently you believe it. As for me, Rachael, I don't know. Again, the motive isn't strong enough. I would prefer Greg Nichols, only because I don't know him well.

And he would indeed go to jail when Jimmy confessed."

He shook his head. "A real-life assassin, and you brought her down in the Barnes & Noble in Georgetown. Amazing."

Rachael said, "There's something else, Mr. Cullifer. Jimmy was committed to telling the truth. After he died, as you know, I decided to make his confession for him because it was what he planned to do, and what he wanted to do. And I told those same people, to prepare them, just as I told you."

Cullifer didn't say a word, just continued giving her that emotionless lawyer look until she said, "Someone has tried to kill me—three times."

It was rare to see a good lawyer caught off-guard. Cullifer leaped to his feet. "No! I can't believe that, no, Rachael, it simply—" He stopped dead in his tracks. "That's why you're with an FBI agent, isn't it? He's protecting you?"

"Yes," she said.

"Because you plan to make Jimmy's confession for him and someone is trying to stop you."

"Yes. I can think of no other reason."

"Are you still going to make his confession?"

"I don't know. I was sure about my reasons, sure about what Jimmy wanted, but now, I don't know."

"It is a difficult question," Cullifer said, and nothing more.

Rachael said, "Several people have pointed out that it's an ethical question. How can I presume to have Jimmy's entire life judged by one incident, and I'm assured that is what would happen. I don't know what to do, Mr. Cullifer."

"Are you still certain it's what he would have done?"

"Yes."

"Then do it and the fallout be damned."

They spoke to Brady Cullifer for another ten minutes. When he hugged Rachael good-bye, she said, "Thank you for accepting me as Jimmy's daughter, sir. Thank you for your kindness."

"Well, I didn't want to accept you, Rachael, not initially, despite Jimmy's enthusiasm. I should tell you I hired an investigator to do a thorough check on you and your mother. That was what convinced me. And I didn't charge your father for the investigator's time." He patted her cheek. "You're an Abbott now, Rachael, all right and proper. If you choose to be his spokesperson, then I'll be behind you one hundred percent."

FORTY-ONE

They ate lunch at a taqueria known for its guacamole and chips, then took an array of photos back to Millie at the diner near Black Rock Lake.

Millie was busy, and they waited. When she dropped into the seat next to them in a booth, Jack handed her a series of black-and-white shots. She looked at Donley Everett's photo carefully, the man Jack shot in the kitchen at Slipper Hollow. She shook her head and picked up Clay Huggins's photo, the man he shot and killed at Slipper Hollow, studied it for a good minute, then regretfully shook her head again. The same

for Marion Croop. Jack handed her Roderick Lloyd's photo, the man who walked right
into Roy Bob's garage in Parlow and started
shooting. She shook her head again.

Rachael was nearly out of hope when
Jack looked down at the last photo, then
handed it to Millie.

Millie studied it, then looked up at them.
"Now isn't this a kick? I would have sworn
it was a *guy* who came in last Friday night
and ordered the two coffees, but it's her"—
she stabbed the photo with her finger—"all
dressed up like a guy."

Jack and Rachael stared at Perky's—
aka Pearl Compton's—photo.

Rachael's heart was pounding. "You're
certain, Millie?"

"Yeah, all that blond hair—if you look at
her and think black hair, then it becomes
clear. Yes, Agent, it's her. I'm sure."

As they drove back to Washington, a
light summer rain falling, Rachael said,
"So Perky carried me by my arms down
the dock. Who was carrying my feet? Donley Everett or Clay Huggins or Roderick
Lloyd? Who's that fourth guy—oh yeah,
Marion Croop?"

"If so, then who hired them?"

"Or maybe it was Quincy or Stefanos carrying my feet."

"Or Laurel," he said.

The windshield wipers moved slowly back and forth, steady as a metronome. "I'm tired, Jack."

With no hesitation at all, out of his mouth came, "Sleep with me and you won't worry about a crook coming in through the window. You'll sleep soundly. With me."

Rachael turned in her seat to look at his profile. "How long has it been since you had a date, Jack?"

He laughed. "Fact is, I broke up with a very nice woman about a month before I flew to Lexington to pick up Timothy. It seems like ten years ago."

"It's only been a week."

He increased the wiper speed.

Rachael laughed. "I don't have an umbrella with me."

"Old Nemo here has everything in a box in the backseat. Including umbrellas."

"Nemo?"

Jack patted the dash. "Yep, I gave him that name when I drove into a swamp once. I thought he was a goner, but he started right up and steamed on down the road. I love Nemo, been with me eight years now, still runs faster than my dad when Mom chased him with a skillet."

Rachael pictured the Toyota Corolla steaming out of a swamp and laughed, then settled back and closed her eyes. "What are we going to do now?"

"How about we take off a couple of hours, take a nap, maybe on one of the sofas in the living room, anything but that rock-hard bed you put me in last night."

She didn't answer him. She was asleep. Slowly, she slid into him, her head on his shoulder.

Jack managed to extricate his cell without disturbing Rachael and punched in Savich, told him about Millie's identification of Perky as one of two people at Mel's Diner Friday night, not more than a ten-minute car ride from Black Rock Lake.

Savich was quiet for a moment. Then he said, "Things are beginning to come together. From what you told me about Laurel and Quincy, I can't see them killing Senator Abbott and Rachael themselves. Too messy for them. On the other hand, who knows? You done good, Jack. It won't be long now."

Jack hoped Savich was right, but he couldn't see any light at all himself. He wondered as he drove through the thickening summer rain, *Who hired you, Perky?*

FORTY-TWO

Georgetown
Friday evening

Savich closed and locked the front door, set the alarm. He was tired and stiff, bummed because it was too late to hit the gym. He rotated his neck as he thought about stretching out in his bed and sleeping deep and dreamless, forgetting both cases. He turned to see his wife standing on the stairs, looking at him over her shoulder as she shrugged off her white oxford shirt. He stopped cold. He went instantly from bone-tired to wide-awake, let-me-lick-those-beautiful-white-shoulders lust. Had he really thought he was so tired he was nearly brain-dead? That was very shortsighted of him. Well, perhaps he was brain-dead, but the rest of him was wide awake.

He didn't move, crossed his arms over his chest, a smile playing over his mouth, and watched the show.

Sherlock said nothing at all—what was there to say, anyway? She licked her tongue over her bottom lip as she unfastened the front clip of her bra. She waited, then slowly shrugged out of it while she shifted to stand nearly in profile to him. She gave him her over-the-shoulder smile while her fingers were busy, her movements slow and subtle, leaving just a bit to his imagination.

She pulled off the bra, one strap at a time, and tossed it at him over her shoulder, but it landed three feet short.

"Lightweight," he said, and she laughed.

"You're right, lace doesn't weigh much." She turned her profile to him again. Savich walked slowly toward her, all his attention focused on those hands of hers playing with the zipper on her pants. Then he saw the slow, downward slide. He did a fast fifteen-foot sprint, nearly tripping over her boots, which lay on the bottom step, her socks hanging out the tops. He saw she'd had the presence of mind to drape her navy blue blazer on the newel post. He loved those beautiful feet of hers.

Savich exercised great strength of will and stopped three stairs below her, waiting to see what she'd do next. He suspected he'd bite his tongue if he weren't careful, particularly now that she was wriggling out of the pants. She was doing a major tease, slow, really slow, and she knew what slow meant.

He got a glimpse of that beautiful rear end of hers, the white lace panties that matched her bra, cut high on her thighs, and it pushed him over the edge. He ran up the stairs, grabbed her up in his arms, felt her laughter wash over him, and felt her mouth kissing his ear, his eyebrow, her hands tangled in his hair. He wanted to laugh with the sheer joy of it, but the fact was he needed to concentrate on getting to the bedroom without tripping because he was so far gone he didn't know if he'd make it.

And he really wanted to make it.

It always seemed to him that time became both syrupy slow and galloped to hurricane speed when he was making love to her.

When at last he pulled her on top of him, when at last she had the energy to sit up, her strong white legs tight against his flanks, her palms flat on his chest, he marveled as he always did at the whiteness of her flesh against the darkness of his hands holding her.

She gave him a silly smile. "That was rather nice, Dillon."

"Oh yes." He looked up at her beloved face, saw her eyes were vague from pleasure, touched fingers to her fiery hair, tossed wildly around her head, and said, "I never tell you enough. You are my life."

As he was hers, she thought, but the words fell away when he came deep inside her and she was kissing him, and the words she whispered in his mouth were, "You are so hot I can't stand it," and it was enough, too much, really, and he didn't last as long as he would have wished, but she was with him, blessed be, so that was all right.

He was felled, so loose and relaxed it would have taken Sean jumping on top of him for a good three minutes before he moved. His breathing finally slowed, at least enough so he could think. His meager thoughts soon scattered when she began moving down his happy, lifeless body. He grabbed handfuls of hair when he felt her mouth on his belly, and he arched up, groaned.

"Music to my ears," she whispered against him.

She fell asleep stretched out on top of him, her head tucked into the curve of his neck, her hair against his mouth. He didn't feel it tickle, though, because his was the sleep of the dead.

When his cell phone belted out the *Monday Night Football* theme, he came instantly awake and looked with loathing at his cell phone half hanging out of his pants pocket on the floor beside the bed. Sherlock was stirring against him. He didn't want to move her, but a phone call late on a Friday night couldn't be good.

He managed to stretch out and grab his cell. "Yeah."

He listened as he leaned back to rub Sherlock's belly. She didn't want to pull away from that big warm hand of his, but she did. She managed to sit up, saying, "What's wrong, Dillon? What happened?"

"Someone just tried to kill Dr. MacLean."

They left a sleeping Sean with Lily and Simon, and arrived at the hospital sixteen minutes later.

He'd found hospitals to be eerily quiet at the witching hour, and truth be told, he hadn't expected excitement there on the main floor, but he heard some raised voices, saw two security people dashing up the stairs. To their surprise, the elevator was empty. When they reached Mac-Lean's floor, they had to dodge a gurney, then two wheelchairs being pushed out of the way, and a good half-dozen hospital personnel, running, yelling, or silent with shock. He saw several patients standing in doorways, one older man holding up his IV bag in his right hand, an orderly trying to talk him back into bed, but he wasn't buying it.

"Agent Tomlin," Sherlock said, grabbing one of the nurses. "Where is Agent Tomlin?"

"They're working on him. Someone walked up to him and shoved a syringe into his neck, but he didn't go all the way out and Louise noticed something was wrong—you know, he was kind of jerking in his chair, and she called out, but he didn't answer." The nurse was nearly hyperventilating. "Louise ran toward him. I don't know what happened—Louise was gone and there was a gunshot. I didn't know it would be so loud. It was like an explosion, and everyone was yelling and screaming."

Sherlock closed her eyes and prayed hard. Please, God, let Tom Tomlin be okay. She was right behind Savich when he shoved open MacLean's door.

There were half a dozen people around MacLean's bed, all talking, gesturing, some on cell phones, one security woman talking loudly on a crackling walkie-talkie.

When Savich shoved his way through, he saw MacLean lying on his back, the bed cranked up, his head on a pillow, and he was smiling impartially at everyone, the patriarch surrounded by his family. Hospital security was two deep.

"Timothy," Savich said, studying him even as he took his hand. "Are you all right?"

"I'm in fine fettle." MacLean grinned maniacally. "What with all the excitement, I'm ready for some fast music so I can do a victory dance with Louise here. Hot damn, can she ever move. You should have seen her, Savich. Runs in and BAM! Shoots the guy in the arm."

"Which arm, Timothy?" Savich asked.

"Hmmm, now, which was it? The right, that's it; it was his right arm. He dropped the needle."

"You're Agent Savich? I'm chief of security, William Hayward. I called you."

Savich quickly shook his hand. "Thank you for calling me." Hayward was a small fine-boned older man with a good build, nicely pressed pants, and smart eyes. Savich pegged him as a retired cop. "Hell of a business," the chief said, shaking his head. "I'm thinking I should check into the nurses' training curriculum—can you believe one of our nurses shot the guy?"

Savich then turned to MacLean. He heard Sherlock introduce herself to Hayward, heard his quiet voice telling her what they were doing.

Savich said, "Tell me what happened, Timothy."

"Well, the thing is, I was asleep. Then there was a sliver of light, right in my eyes. The door had opened, and the light was from the hallway. This guy walks in, a guy

I've never seen before. He just strolls in like he belongs, smiles at me when he sees I'm awake, says he's sorry to disturb me, but he's a neurosurgeon and my doctor asked him to see me, and sure enough, he's all dressed in green scrubs, a mask over his face, a stethoscope around his neck, those paper booties on his feet. I'll admit, at first I simply accepted what he said, so many white coats and green scrubs all over, in and out of here, like Grand Central.

"He comes toward me, talking all the time, telling me everything again, like I'm not a doctor and don't already know everything he's talking about, and even repeated how my doctor wanted him to check me out, and he's sorry it's so late but he just came out of an emergency surgery, didn't even have time to change, and I say, 'Why do I need a neurosurgeon? And what's with the mask?'

"And the guy stops cold in his tracks and I swear to you, he hisses, just like a snake. He pulls out a needle and I see it's capped, and right away I know there's something hinky in that needle, something real nasty bad for me in there. I yell out for

Agent Tomlin, but there's no answer. The man tells me I'm one lucky son of a bitch, but enough is enough. And he hisses again, amazing—like nothing I've ever heard before.

"I hear Louise's voice outside the door, and then the door slams open and there's Louise, a gun in her hand, and this guy whirls toward her, and bless her heart, she doesn't hesitate, she shoots him. The guy hisses again, drops the needle, grabs his arm, yells at me that I am a dead man, and bolts to the door. He knocks Louise flat on her ass. I yell after him to stop, and Louise raises the gun again to shoot him, but she hits the bathroom door."

"Yeah, she did," Hayward said. "A fine shot. That door's not moving."

MacLean said, smiling, "That wasn't bad, Chief."

"I've got the needle," Hayward said. He handed the needle, still capped and carefully wrapped up in his own handkerchief, to Sherlock.

Savich asked, "Did you recognize his voice, Timothy?"

"Well, no, he had that mask on. It muffled his voice."

"It was a man?"

MacLean looked at Sherlock. "I don't think it was a woman, but it all happened so fast—no, I'd have to say it was a man."

"Young? Old?"

MacLean looked at Sherlock. "Again, he had that mask over his face, mouth included. I don't know."

"All right, that's good, Timothy," Savich said. "Tell us again what happened then. Slow down."

Sherlock saw MacLean was beginning to come off his adrenaline high, and she began to stroke his forearm.

"I'll tell you, it was wild. Louise was yelling, *'Code blue! Get security!'* And then Louise was in here with me. She was panting, looking hard at me, and she was shaking all over like she'd had the life nearly scared out of her. Then she folded her arms over her chest, stared at Agent Tomlin's gun, which was still in her right hand, and she started laughing and crying at the same time. I watched her lay the gun very carefully on the table.

"She started examining me then, feeling me up, that's what I told her, and then she stopped and cocked her head toward the door. We saw all these hospital people working on Agent Tomlin. It sounded like pandemonium to me. I asked her to call you, Agent Savich, and she told me she'd tell Chief Hayward and he'd do it, that was better.

"Bless her heart, she was so upset, so excited, so relieved that I was okay. She hugged me, real hard, hurt my ribs, but I just hugged her back. She did really good. She saved my life."

"She certainly did," Sherlock agreed.

FORTY-THREE

Nurse Louise Wingo said from the doorway, "I've never been so scared in my life." She looked down at her watch. "It's after one o'clock in the morning, Dr. MacLean. You need to rest."

"Rest? For what reason, I ask you? Please don't tell me it'll improve my quality of life. You can come here if you want to, Louise, and you can hug me some more. You should have seen her, Savich. She came running in, brought the gun up, and shot the guy, no muss, no fuss. No, Louise, don't bother telling me I need to rest. My brain's working at a great clip, and I'm fine." He beamed a happy face at everyone. "I haven't had this great an adrenaline kick in a very long time."

Louise said to them, "Mine is probably higher than his." She fanned herself, and grinned. "Wow, was that ever incredible! No way my husband's going to believe it. He thinks the night shift is boring. Wait'll he hears this.

"Thank God you're okay, Dr. MacLean. I'm so relieved Mrs. MacLean wasn't here. She left about eleven."

"You're right about that," MacLean said. "Molly would have jumped on him, and he might have hurt her. I'm thanking you for her, too, Louise."

Sherlock said, "Jack told us that Molly looks after her own. If she saw anyone trying to hurt anybody in her family, she'd go nuts."

MacLean said, "That's the truth. Usually I'm the one on her bad side. Louise, she's going to bring you chocolate chip cookies for a year. Be prepared."

Louise said to them, "Actually, Mrs. Mac-Lean already brought us homemade goodies. She crochets afghans while she sits with Dr. MacLean. We let her stay as long as she wants to."

MacLean said, "Molly fusses and nags, she's always asking me how I'm feeling, what I'm thinking, as if she can stop the dementia from getting worse that way. I finally talked her into going home. She agreed, said I was someone else's pain until tomorrow, and she kissed me good-bye." MacLean closed his eyes, swallowed. "If she'd been here, that bastard wouldn't have hesitated to kill her, too." He looked over at Louise. "Thank you, Louise. Any of those yahoo doctors give you grief, you just give me a holler. I'll take care of them for you."

Sherlock said, "I'll call Molly first thing in the morning, tell her you're okay. No sense in worrying her tonight."

"Careful, Dr. MacLean," Louise said, "you've nearly dislodged the IV line." Sherlock saw that her hands were steady as she worked on the line. She straightened, lightly ran her hand over his forearm. "You're good to go now. Please, try to calm down."

MacLean said, "Yeah, yeah, I'll have enough time to be calm when I'm dead. How's poor Agent Tomlin?"

"I heard one of the doctors say it was

probably a load of sedative punched in his neck, but since he's already beginning to come out of it, it either wasn't much or he jerked away so not all of it went in. He's stable, still really drowsy. He should be okay, just out for a while. That's all we have so far."

Sherlock saw Dillon speaking to Chief Hayward. He looked up and said to her, "Chief Hayward's got all the hospital security searching the building and grounds, but he could use more people. I'm going to give Ben Raven a call, wake him up. He'll get more cops down here to help the security people."

They wouldn't find the man, Sherlock thought, and she hated that she was so certain. This was well planned, he knew how to get in and out. But maybe— "What about video?"

Chief Hayward said, "I called down to set it up."

Sherlock leaned down and whispered next to MacLean's ear, "All in all, none of us can complain."

"Poor Agent Tomlin can," MacLean said.

Ten minutes later, Savich and Sherlock went inside the small hospital security room near the front entrance. There were twelve video screens, ten of them running live feeds from cameras at locations inside the hospital.

Chief Hayward said, "We've got a camera at the entrance to the hospital, one camera on each floor. I asked Fritz to pull up two tapes of where the assailant would have had to walk to get to Dr. MacLean's room."

Fritz said, "I couldn't locate the assailant coming into the hospital. I will have to look earlier. This tape is from Dr. Mac-Lean's floor."

They all watched the screen. Chief Hayward said, "Stop. Look, that must be him, the guy in surgical scrubs, a mask over his face, and a cap on his head. If it was during the day, someone would have wondered who the hell he was since no one wears a mask in the hallway. There's no reason for that. He's also wearing surgical gloves, so no fingerprints. Sorry about the quality of the film, but we should be able to make him out okay."

They watched the man walk toward the camera. He turned a corner just past the nurses' station and disappeared.

"Okay," Chief Hayward said. "Fast-forward, Fritz."

"Stop, there he is," Savich said a couple of seconds later.

Fritz froze the screen.

Sherlock said, "Okay, three minutes have elapsed and here he comes. And she thought, *It took so little time.* In three minutes Timothy could have been killed. She said, "He's walking really fast, and he's holding his arm. There's blood seeping through his fingers. He's got his head down. About all I can say so far is he isn't fat."

"He's still got the mask and cap on," Fritz said. "Bummer."

They watched him until he disappeared.

Chief Hayward said, "Okay, let's see if he leaves through the front. Roll the other tape, Fritz." The film sped up, then slowly, Fritz brought it back to real time.

Chief Hayward said, "Stop, Fritz, you got him. I think that's him—the timing's about right, five minutes have passed. He looks about the same size, same build, and the loose clothes."

The man on the film was wearing a

watch cap pulled low on his forehead, touching the rims of dark sunglasses. He was wearing loose blue jeans, a large pale blue shirt that hung outside his pants, a baggy off-white linen jacket, and moccasins. For an instant, they were looking directly at his face, only they couldn't see him clearly.

Chief Hayward said, "He's still walking slowly and you can tell he's favoring his arm. It's gotta hurt like a bear. One of my men found a couple drops of blood on the floor of Dr. MacLean's corridor and marked the spot for you. It doesn't necessarily have to be our guy, but it's likely."

Savich said, "His blood will nail him when we catch him. He took a big chance, walking right up to Agent Tomlin, shoving that needle in his neck, knowing the nurses' station wasn't more than thirty feet away. I'd say he's really motivated, determined, maybe really angry."

They watched him walk out of the front entrance of the hospital. Chief Hayward said, "We didn't catch the guy coming into the hospital. He must have scoped out the camera locations, learned the hospital layout, all the particulars. He's not stupid. He came late, the optimum time. Sorry, but we don't have any outdoor cameras."

"It's something," Sherlock said. "Thank you, Chief. I'd say someone is more than motivated, more than just angry. I'd say they're obsessed."

Savich said, "We'll get you some photos of all the players we know of so your people can show them around. We might get lucky."

Chief Hayward nodded, but he didn't look hopeful. "This guy is careful. But maybe someone saw him near the OR. All I can say with any certainty is that he's about average height, average build, and wears really loose clothes."

Sherlock nodded. "Fritz, can you rewind it again?"

When he did, she said, "Okay, now watch. I'm thinking he looks young, too. Watch him walk, the way he moves."

"Freeze that frame, Fritz," Chief Hayward said. "Look, he's sort of slouching, bent over. Sure, he's hurting, his arm must feel like it's burning off, but I'm not as sure as you are."

"If he is a young man," Savich said, "he's probably hired."

Sherlock was shaking her head. "That doesn't sound right. From what Timothy said, it sounded like it was up close and personal to me, not like an impersonal hired gun."

"You're right," Savich said, and plowed his fingers through his hair, making it stand on end. "My brain's on default mode." He looked down at his Mickey Mouse watch. It was nearly three A.M.

Savich looked at Sherlock and said, "Let's check on Agent Tomlin, then go home."

FORTY-FOUR

Washington, D.C.
Late Saturday morning

Pierre Barbeau answered the front door, eyed them with resignation, and stepped back. "Tommy called me from downstairs. What is it you want now?"

"We'd like to speak to you and your wife, Mr. Barbeau," Savich said, his eyes on Pierre's right arm. He was wearing a ratty old blue velvet bathrobe, with thick, loose sleeves that could easily cover a bandage. He looked like he'd just gotten out of bed. He looked tired, defensive—shattered, and just maybe—afraid. But to Savich's eye, taking all of him in, he simply didn't look like he'd been shot in the arm.

Pierre said, "I don't know why. Listen, Estelle and I, we're—we're only trying to cope. We've told you everything. My wife won't want to speak to you, either of you. I can tell you that, and believe me, she usually gets what she wants."

Sherlock wanted to tell him that she usually got what she wanted, as well, but she merely smiled at him as Dillon said, "We checked with your night doorman. He said both of you were out from about ten o'clock until two A.M. Where did you go?"

"Why? Who cares?" He got two hard-as-nails looks and dead silence, and backed up a step. Then he gave them the French cop-out, a shrug that said nothing and everything. "Oh, I see, something else has happened, hasn't it? You think we're behind it, whatever it is, and it happened last night. Is that it?"

"Please tell us where you were, Mr. Barbeau," Sherlock said.

"Very well. I don't suppose it matters. My wife and I couldn't stand looking at each other's pain, and so we went out walking. It was nice, last night, the moon was nearly full, and so we walked in High Banks Park. Maybe an hour, give or take.

We went into a gallery that was having a special showing and was open late. We stayed there until nearly midnight, then we stopped at a bar. We drank too much, but it didn't help. We came back here. I didn't check the time. We went to bed. I woke up when Tommy rang up a few minutes ago."

"The name of the gallery, Mr. Barbeau?" Sherlock asked, her pen poised above her small black notebook.

"The Penyon Gallery on Wisconsin."

"What was the special showing?"

"American artists, modern stuff, you know, all squiggles and blobs of thick paint, something Jean David did with great enthusiasm when he was three, only he didn't use paints." He gave a brief ghastly smile, his voice hitching on his son's name. He raised his left arm to press his fingers briefly to his forehead. No bullet wound in that arm, for sure.

Sherlock waited a beat, then asked, "The name of the bar?"

"Who remembers the name of a bar? I certainly don't. We'd never been there before. I remember it wasn't very far from the gallery."

Sherlock leaned in close. "What did you and your wife talk about, Mr. Barbeau?"

"Nothing, really. Nothing important. We are both too miserable to do anything but exist right now. However, to be honest here, because we can't seem to help ourselves, we occasionally speak about our son, and we did talk about Jean David while we walked in the park last night. We spoke about how much we loved him, how this shouldn't have happened, how unfair it all is, how because of the threats from people like you, our son is dead."

Savich's eyebrow shot up. "Threats?"

Another shrug. "It would have come to threats if the authorities had gotten their hands on Jean David before he died. They would have threatened to deport us, freeze all our bank accounts, and send him to prison if he refused to sign a confession admitting to everything they could think of, even things he knew nothing about."

"You have quite an imagination, Mr. Barbeau," Sherlock said easily. "But the fact is, none of that happened. Your son's misdeeds died with him. I doubt the CIA will ever discover exactly what and how much your son passed on to the terrorists."

"He didn't help the terrorists! Maybe some of it got to them, but the point is, he didn't realize . . . It was all that woman's fault. She seduced him, twisted him up." He stopped, shook his head. "Jean David was so young, so innocent until she got hold of him."

Jean David Barbeau was twenty-six when he drowned. Savich and Sherlock remained quiet.

Pierre said, "At least it wasn't raining last night. Dreadful weather here, simply dreadful."

"Your English is excellent, Mr. Barbeau," Sherlock said.

"It should be. My father was always traveling here to the States with me and my mother in tow. He consulted with Amtrak, you know, and we lived here for long stretches of time. I attended American private schools, attended Harvard for two years before going back to France to finish my education."

"And your wife?"

"She, too, traveled widely with her family. She is one of those few people who can pick up a language like that." He snapped his fingers and looked sour. "She speaks five languages. *Five.* I've always believed three languages quite enough, but five? It's a bit over the top, I think."

Savich, who spoke only English, said, "So that's why Jean David was born in New Jersey. You are travelers like your parents."

"If you must know, we were visiting friends at their beach house in Cape May. Jean David came three weeks early and so he is an American citizen, something we never intended or wanted."

At that meaty insult, Sherlock said, "As it turned out, it might have been better for everyone if Jean David wasn't born here. The CIA would have been pleased if he'd joined his father at the French National Police, as well, Mr. Barbeau."

His breathing sped up. He looked at Sherlock like he wanted to hit her. Just as suddenly, the anger died in his eyes. No, Savich thought it was more like his eyes themselves died. He pictured Sean's beloved face, and couldn't begin to imagine the pain of losing his son.

Savich said, "We would like to speak to your wife."

He started to protest, then simply turned and yelled, "Estelle!"

Mrs. Barbeau, covered from neck to mid-calf in a thick white robe, her hair wrapped up in a white towel, appeared at the end of the hall. She'd known they were there, naturally, but she'd been staying back. "Go away," she called out. "I am not dressed. It is Saturday morning. Leave us alone. We have nothing more to say to you."

Sherlock called out, "I understand you and your husband visited the Penyon Gallery last evening. What did you think of the special exhibit?"

"It was pitiful. We saw nothing to interest us. I am not feeling well. I will not come any closer, I do not wish for you to become as ill as I am."

"Your illness, it came on very quickly," Sherlock said. "Since you were all about town last night."

"Yes, it came on quickly. Go away."

Savich stepped closer to Pierre, clamped a hand around his right arm, to check once and for all that he was not the one Nurse Louise had shot. He felt thick material, but no bandage. Pierre didn't jerk away, he very slowly pulled away. Had he flinched at all? Savich knew he'd tightened, he'd felt his muscles tense. Perhaps a very minor wound, Savich thought again, if Pierre was the man Nurse Louise shot.

Why couldn't anything be easy?

Sherlock called out, "So you didn't like the artists?"

"Not particularly," Estelle said. "It was all what I call commercial oatmeal—nothing of interest or import. Go away. Leave us alone. I am ill."

Savich said pleasantly, "If you wouldn't mind, Mrs. Barbeau, why don't you join us in the living room. We will be brief and we promise to stay three feet from you so you won't have to worry about being arrested for infecting an agent."

Estelle made no pretense of civility. She came to stand in the living room doorway, but no closer. It was true, she didn't look at all well. Her eyes were bloodshot, and she was very pale. And, Sherlock thought, that bathrobe was very thick for June. Could it have been a woman on those hospital tapes?

Estelle repeated what her husband had told them, probably because she'd listened to their conversation, Sherlock thought cynically.

Finally, Pierre threw up his hands. "Will you tell us what has happened?"

Savich said, looking Pierre right in the eyes, "A man pretending to be a physician tried to kill Dr. MacLean last night around midnight."

A moment of silence, then Estelle shrugged. "It is a pity, and a pity he failed.

"Oh, I see. You believe my husband is the one who tried to kill that miserable excuse for a doctor? For a *friend*? I will tell you, he did not. We were together—all night. I want you to leave."

Sherlock eyed Estelle's right arm. There could easily be a bandage beneath her robe. No, surely it was a man on the tapes—the walk, the posture, surely, but he wore loose clothing. Estelle was nearly as tall as her husband.

Short of having both Barbeaus strip to the waist, there was no way to be sure.

Savich wanted to go back to bed and sleep for a few hours or have Sherlock seduce him again. Both, actually.

There was light traffic on Wisconsin. Savich's foot went down heavy on the Porsche's gas pedal. Then he sighed, slacked off a bit, sighed again.

"You want to know what I'm thinking?"

She touched his hand, felt his fingers slowly relax. "Tell me."

"This persistence—obsession—you said. I simply can't see anyone we've spoken to being that dogged, that determined to kill Dr. MacLean. Maybe we should speak to Lomas Clapman, maybe he murdered a dozen people and Dr. MacLean's forgotten about it."

"I think our killer is right under our noses. We're missing something and that's because we're tired. It's been a wild week, Dillon. We've got to spend some time putting everything we know down on a timeline—and we've got to take some time to let it percolate."

Savich thought she was right.

She said, "I'm thinking we could arrange a little party tonight with Rachael's aunt and uncle, and maybe Stefanos. It would give us a chance to talk to them. You think they'd accept an invitation to the old family manse if Rachael asked them real nice?"

Savich laughed. "Yeah, maybe if we sent a SWAT team with the invitation. And if we brought them in for questioning, they would come with a half-dozen lawyers, refuse to answer any questions, and demand we arrest them or release them. Then they'd try to sue the FBI out of existence."

Sherlock said, "I guess we'd need some evidence for that—like fourteen eyewitnesses."

"They'd still sue. Actually, I've been thinking about another way to get together with them—a special invitation they might actually accept. I'll let you know if I can work it out."

Savich's cell phone sang out "Camptown Races." When he punched off, he turned to her. "Roderick Lloyd, the gun-happy yahoo at Roy Bob's garage in Parlow? Ollie says he wants to deal. He's willing to testify it was Perky who told him what to do."

"That's all well and good," Sherlock said, "but does he have a clue who hired Perky?"

"No."

"That's convenient."

Savich said, "Lloyd's lawyer found out Perky couldn't roll on him because she's dead, so why not sing? It always warms my heart to see a lawyer at work."

She grinned, leaned her head back against the headrest. She felt the wind tear through her hair, felt the sting on her face. She looked over at him and said, "It's Saturday. Let's get Sean and go play some touch football in High Banks Park."

Savich said, "Sean's getting pretty good. He doesn't try to jump on our backs any longer." Sex and a nap could wait. "High Banks Park? Why not?"

FORTY-FIVE

Rachael and Jack stood in the open doorway, Jack lusting after Savich's Porsche as he pulled out of the driveway. He looked around at the well-lit neighborhood. Everything quiet, nothing moving. Still—"I'm going to check around, okay?"

Rachael nodded. "Go ahead. I'll clean up here. Jack, be careful."

He nodded and headed around to the side of the house.

She went back into the living room, fluffed two English antique silk pillows, and set them carefully against the back of the sofa. She looked around the magnificent room. *This house is mine now,* she thought, still having difficulty believing it was true. But she hated what it had cost her. Only six weeks she'd had with Jimmy. With her father.

Rachael was stuffing pizza boxes into the recycle bin in the pantry when Jack called out, "It looks clear."

"In here!"

"You know," he said as he walked into the kitchen, only to stop cold, charmed by that skinny braid dipping around her cheek, "it was nice having Savich and Sherlock over. I can see Sean making a diving tackle on his mother to bring her down—"

"—and claiming he had to do it, didn't think a touch would stop her—"

"—and Savich standing over the two of them laughing his head off."

Rachael made tea while Jack loaded the few dishes into the dishwasher. "Do you know, what just came to me? I was wondering what Laurel would look like if she changed her clothes, colored her hair, maybe put on a bit of lipstick."

"I don't think that's going to happen as long as she's married to Stefanos," Jack said. "Seems to me that guy was a jerk from the very beginning."

"I wonder why she didn't kick him out? Divorce him and send him packing back to Greece."

Jack shrugged. "Maybe she will now that her father's dead. Maybe he forced her to stay with the guy."

Rachael handed him a couple of clean glasses. "You really think Mr. Abbott senior kept her married to Kostas?"

"Why else would she have put up with him except for threats from the old man?"

Rachael said, "Well, her father took my father away from my mother, threatened my mother while sending her a bloody check." She realized her voice had gone up. The old man—dear heavens, he was her grandfather—he was dead, his eldest son dead, as well. There was no changing that. And here she was living in their house, alone, a house she hadn't even known about until such a short time ago. "Jimmy told me when Laurel met Stefanos, she fell really hard for him, never saw any of the rot below the surface."

Jack turned on the dishwasher. "Seems weird to me the old man wouldn't have checked him out thoroughly, seen the rot.

So why did he let Stefanos marry his daughter?"

"Good question. Jimmy said Stefanos had a big problem—namely he needed a huge influx of money, and Laurel was his solution. And evidently she wanted him badly. She was thirty-five, her biological clock ticking."

Rachael took the two napkins Jack had wadded up and began to methodically smooth them out and fold them. He watched her for a moment, said, "They're dirty, Rachael."

"What? Oh, the napkins. It's just that they're so beautiful, so well made and . . . Oh, I'm losing it. I'll wash them tomorrow. By hand." She stacked them neatly on the counter. "Jimmy showed me some photos of Laurel when she was young. She wasn't particularly pretty, but she was smiling, full of hope. He said being married to Stefanos made her what she is today. It's sad."

A dark eyebrow went up. "Sad? Give her something sharp and she'd slit your throat, Rachael."

"Yeah, I know. I also know she's capable of a killing rage because I've seen her rage up close and personal. It's stark and ugly. I can see it breaking over her when Jimmy told her he was going public with what he'd done.

"She could have killed him—for herself, for her family, for the business, any and all of it. But her husband? Would he even care? Does he care about anything? And Quincy? I think he's got dark wormy things inside him, but kill his own brother? I just don't know.

"If Laurel was the ringleader, it only makes sense she would want me gone, too. I suppose I could tell her and Quincy that I'm not going to give Jimmy's confession for him, but—" Rachael shrugged. "I don't know yet what I want to do. I suppose I could tell them I've dropped it, lie straight out. I'm not very good, but I could practice until I convinced myself. Uncle Gillette, now, he would have made a great spy. He could lie his way out of a pig convention even with bacon grease smeared all over his mouth."

Jack smiled. "I've learned in my years with the FBI that many times people are never what they seem. We'll see. Don't forget, two people carried you down that dock, dumped you into the lake. We only know one of them for sure—Perky."

He added over his shoulder as he opened the refrigerator, and pulled out a wedge of Parmesan cheese, "Who was the other?"

Rachael pointed to one of the cabinets. "There are crackers on the middle shelf."

He placed a slice of cheese on a cracker and handed it to her, then made one for himself. He leaned back against the counter. "Savich said all those initials and numbers in Perky's address book— even MAX can't crack it. Who knows what it means?"

Rachael bit into a cracker.

"I've been thinking, Rachael."

She said around the cracker, "About what?"

He opened his mouth, closed it, fixed himself another cracker, and ate it.

"What, Jack?"

"Nothing. I'm tired. I think we should both sleep pretty good tonight."

"What are we going to do tomorrow?"

"I go back to some solid, boring every-day police work, like running in-depth checks on everyone remotely involved in the case, and take another look at Perky and all her merry men."

She washed and dried her hands. She stood facing the kitchen window, her head bowed.

"I'm sorry."

He pulled her back against him. "Don't be stupid. You've every right to be freaked out." He knew it was a mistake, but he did it anyway. He slowly turned her to face him and tugged her into his arms. He hadn't imagined the shock of her, not only how she felt, but the way she fit against him, like she was made for him, no other guy, only him. But that was plain stupid. He shouldn't be doing this. He wasn't thinking right. No, he was simply offering her comfort. She needed comforting, no harm in that. Maybe he needed some comfort, too. He said close to her ear as his hands rubbed up and down her back, "Don't stiffen up on me. I'm a friend, Rachael, and friends help each other. Remember how you helped me and Timothy when the plane crashed? You didn't even know at that time what a great guy I am; you just charged right in and saved our bacon."

She laughed against his neck. Then she kissed his neck, added a little lick, then froze. "Ohmigosh, I'm sorry, Jack, I didn't mean to do that. It just happened. I mean, you're here to protect me, not get involved. . . ." Her voice fell off a cliff.

Jack said, "I guess not." He knew she could feel exactly how much he wanted to be involved—actually, totally involved with her that very minute, maybe on that lovely oak kitchen table.

He kissed her, and, bless her heart, she kissed him back. He tasted cracker and Parmesan and something else, something elusive and sweet. Then, just as suddenly, she flattened her palms on his chest, pushed back, and said, "I can't do this. I can't lean on you like this, compromise you. You're an FBI agent. I'll bet you've got rules and regulations regarding people you're guarding. Right?"

"No."

He pulled her in close again, leaned his forehead against hers. "Not a single rule except common sense, and common sense isn't all that great a thing in every single situation, now is it? Hey, you're not a shrimp. That's good."

She said against his neck, "I'm so not a shrimp. I'd be licking your eyebrows if I were wearing heels. No, wait, I didn't say that, did I?"

She felt the laughter deep in his chest. "Yeah, you did. Anytime you'd like to, lick away."

She ran her fingers over his cheek, and he felt it in his gut. Jack knew he should release her this very instant, knew it, and knew he wasn't about to. He lowered his forehead to hers again. "I'm not a teenager with my hormones dive-bombing my brain. You're right, it isn't the smartest thing we could do at this point in time." And he cursed low, ripe, pungent curses. Rather impressive, she thought, and smiled. Uncle Gillette could curse like that. She could see him cursing at the rabbits who'd gotten through his tomato cages, digging underneath, hear her mom yelling at him that certain little girls had big ears.

Slowly, Rachael stepped back. She said, "I'm very glad you don't gamble."

He threw back his head and laughed.

He saw her to her bedroom, looked at her mouth a moment. "I'm glad you realize I'm nothing like that jerk ex-fiancé of yours.

But, Rachael, I'm hurting right now all the way to my heels."

"No, you're nothing like him. My heels are in pretty bad shape, too."

He reached out his hand, dropped it, stepped back. "See you in the morning, Rachael. Sleep well." To her surprise, and disappointment, he closed the door.

She felt so revved, so ready to rock and roll—with Jack—she doubted she'd sleep at all, but within minutes, she was out.

Black water closed over her head, something was pulling her down, no way to stop until she hit bottom and silt swirled up around her, blinding her until it slowly settled again. She knew she was going to die. It wouldn't matter if she held her breath for ten minutes, she would die. No, she didn't want to die, she didn't—

She lurched up in bed, abruptly awake, breathing fast and hard, sucked in air. But she wasn't at the bottom of Black Rock Lake. She wasn't drowning. She was here, in Jimmy's house, in her bed, but— What had awakened her? Whatever it was, she was grateful. But what was it? She must have heard something that shouldn't be there, something not part of the fabric of the house. She didn't move a muscle, listened.

It was Jack, she thought, trying to be quiet so as not to wake her. He was probably checking the alarm, the locks, or maybe he did his best thinking when he walked around.

Still, even as her muscles uncoiled and eased, she kept listening. She realized that ever since her thankfully brief trip to the bottom of Black Rock Lake, she had not completely let go, even with Jack close by. Her brain was always charged, always looking, weighing, assessing, wanting to know if anyone was trying to kill her.

Breath whooshed out of her and she realized she'd been holding it, just like when she was at the bottom of lake. She swung her legs over the side of the bed, ready to go to Jack, to . . . what? Have him protect her, chase away her fears, or make love to her until she couldn't think at all? She stopped cold, simply held very still and listened.

It was quiet outside in the corridor. The summer night air was sweet and still. The nightmare had conjured up the bogeyman, put him so close she'd popped awake, covered with sweat. She looked out the window. The quarter moon lit up the sky. She looked at that moon, kept listening, waited. A minute, another.

Nothing. She lay back down again, forced her muscles to relax, and she waited. She breathed deeply, but the question nagged her mind—*Who is trying to kill me*? Her brain squirreled around that until finally her breathing slowed, and her head fell to the side.

She heard a sound, a light footfall. Was Jack standing outside her door, his hand on the doorknob, wanting to come in and make love to her? Now, that was a fine lovely thought. . . .

It wasn't Jack. She knew it wasn't Jack. She leaned over and quietly slid open the night table drawer. It made enough noise to awaken the dead. *Easy, easy.* She reached in, felt the cold shock of Jimmy's gun against her palm, and curled her fingers around it.

Was that another footstep? Stepping away? No, there was nothing. Nothing at all. She was losing it. She had to get a grip, calm down, use her brain, not let the terror crush her. She heard it again. She swallowed spit and a scream. If a scream burst out of her, she knew Jack would come running as fast as he could to get to her. Would he have his gun? What about the person probably now pressing close, his ear against her door? Would he simply turn his gun on Jack and shoot him? No, no way was she going to take a chance like that.

She lay there, waited. Her fingers loosened on the gun. She stilled. *Where are you, you bastard*? Wait, maybe he wasn't outside her door, maybe . . . She jerked around to look toward the window again, at the yellow moon, the dark clouds webbing in front of it. Something moved, something at the edge of the window, near that huge oak tree, maybe someone was in that tree, coming toward her, coming to kill her. She didn't have her gun. Where was it? How could she save herself if she didn't have her gun? She'd taken it out of the night table, held it close, but it wasn't there.

She couldn't find her gun. Had she put it back in the drawer? She lurched to her side, grabbed for the drawer handle, but she couldn't find it, there was nothing there except blackness that was coming toward her, somehow through the closed window.

She screamed.

The screamed

FORTY-SIX

Rachael! Wake up! Dammit, wake up!"

She screamed again, out of control. Jack slapped her, then shook her. "Wake up, Rachael! Come on, wake up."

She choked, stared at him with panicked eyes.

"Breathe, dammit, breathe!"

She sucked in air, heaved a huge sigh. She fell forward against him.

"It's all right, baby, it's all right."

She burrowed in, her hands clasped tightly behind his back. No way was she letting him go, even if he had called her—

"Baby?" she whispered against his shoulder. His bare shoulder. Her hands were against his bare back.

Reality flipped on like a light switch.

"Yeah, well, baby's okay, isn't it?"

"You don't have a shirt on, Jack."

"No, only boxers. But they're quite modest."

He kissed her temple. "Rachael, you were having a whopper of a nightmare. Can you tell me about it?"

She heaved a breath and held on. "Give me a moment, just another moment."

He held her, rubbing her back, then after a while she said against his shoulder, "I heard him outside the window. I knew he would come in and I couldn't find my gun, the night table wasn't there, nothing was there, only blackness, and I was sucked into the middle of it, and I couldn't see, but I knew he was coming to kill me—damn, I got hysterical and lost it. I've never been hysterical before. I've always scoffed at people who get hysterical."

"Hysterical's okay sometimes. You were dreaming. Breathe lightly, don't talk, that's it. Keep breathing, slowly, in and out. Good girl."

She concentrated on breathing, on

blocking out that waking nightmare so real she could still feel it.

"That's it," he said against her hair. "Center yourself, you know how to do it. Feel me, I'm real here, not that damned dream."

"Yes," she said, "you're real."

He smiled as he rocked her a bit, and he looked toward the window. The night had been quiet, a light breeze, nothing more than that. But now the wind was picking up, gusting tree branches against the house. Maybe leaves had hit the window.

The alarm went crazy, whooping loud and long.

She lurched back, the braid slapping against his cheek. "Someone's in the house. Jack, we've got to hurry, someone's in the house."

"It's okay, Rachael. Go disarm it, now."

Jack was out the door even before she scooted off the bed and ran to the keypad on the bedroom wall. He yelled, "Stay put!" She couldn't get her fingers to work. She tried again, punched in the five numbers. The alarm cut off instantly.

She heard him running. Then nothing. She stood in her bedroom, Jimmy's gun held tightly in her hand, until she couldn't stand it any longer. She pulled on jeans under her sleep shirt, and ran out onto the second-floor landing, bent over, her gun at the ready. The entrance hall lights were on. The front door stood open. She threw on all the lights as she ran down the stairs, fanning the gun around her like she'd seen on TV. She felt a sheen of sweat on her forehead. She was so afraid she thought she'd choke on it. *Calm down.* She ran to the front door and looked out. The moon was directly overhead, and the wind was up, swirling through the leaves, ruffling her hair. She saw a light in the Danvers' house across the street. It went out. The alarm must have awakened them, but they'd figured it was an error on her part and gone back to bed. She stood on the front steps, the flagstone cold beneath her feet, and she didn't move.

"Jack? Where are you?"

"Here," he said a foot from her elbow, and she jumped. She whirled around, thought her heart would leap out of her chest. "How'd you do that? I didn't hear you. Are you all right? Did you see anyone?"

"He was gone by the time I ran outside.

I found an open window in the guest bedroom at the end of the hall. I guess it's not in the alarm system because it's not an entry. There's an oak he could have used to climb in—a big one. He was already in the house when you screamed. He ran down the front stairs and out the front door, and that triggered the alarm.

"In the morning, I'll check for footprints, particularly by that oak tree. He could have ripped his clothes, maybe left some threads or material on a branch. We might get lucky. Rachael?"

She was shivering now from reaction. "What?"

"Come inside. You're cold."

"I shouldn't be. It's a warm night. I was even sweating." She started trembling. Jack took her arm and led her back into the house. "Give me your alarm code."

He shut the front door, punched in the code to reactivate the alarm. He turned to her. "I'm glad you got hysterical, glad you screamed your head off. You heard something. It was real."

She walked to a sideboard, poured a shot of brandy for herself and one for him. "Here." They both drank.

A moment later the phone rang in the living room.

"Yes? Rachael Abbott here."

"Rachael? It's Dillon Savich. Are you guys all right?"

She stared at the phone. "How did you know something happened?"

There was silence on the line, then Savich said calmly, "A feeling, a gut feeling, that's all. Talk to me."

She told him what had happened, then handed the phone to Jack. The first words out of his mouth were, "What did your gut tell you, Savich?"

"That you were running around Rachael's house in your underwear."

FORTY-SEVEN

At ten o'clock Sunday morning, an FBI evidence team converged on Rachael's house and set up shop around the big oak tree outside the guest-bedroom window, Agent Clive Howard the team leader.

Savich, Sherlock, and Sean sat at the oak kitchen table, Sean next to his mother drinking cocoa and eating a vanilla scone slathered with peach jam, Rachael and Jack opposite him.

"He's like you, Dillon, a sucker for scones." A big dollop of jam fell onto the table and Sherlock scooped it back into his scone. She said to Rachael and Jack,

"They were releasing Agent Tomlin when we got to the hospital. They said he was fine, he said he was fine, he was great, he wanted to kick himself, but Tom very much wanted to go back to guard Dr. MacLean."

Savich said, "Poor Sherlock. Agent Tomlin's no longer looking at her with such tenderness. Now it's Nurse Louise who's got his eye. He couldn't stop talking about how fast she was.

"I sent him back to relieve the agent guarding Timothy. You can bet from now on Tomlin won't let any hospital staff he doesn't know come within ten feet of MacLean's room."

Sherlock said, "Unfortunately, he didn't get too good a look at the guy who shoved the needle in his neck, and couldn't identify the photos we showed him."

Jack said, "Tomlin's one tough mother, I hate to see something like this happen. It was too close. For both him and Timothy, it was too close. I wish you'd called me, Savich."

"I thought about it, but the fact is, you couldn't have done anything, Jack, so let it go."

"Imagine," Rachael said, "someone going

after Dr. MacLean in the hospital. That's insane." She stopped cold, gave them a twisted grin. "I guess there's a lot of insanity going around lately."

Sherlock nodded. "After hours of interviews at the hospital, we still don't have a viable witness." She carefully selected a scone and bit in. She rolled her eyes. "Goodness, this is wonderful. Hey, Sean, can you pass me the jam?"

"The GoodLight Bakery on Elm Street," Rachael said. "Jack found it, and didn't hesitate to bring home about fifty thousand calories."

Savich gave Sean a quick sideways glance, saw that he was focused on trying to trap the evil king Zhor in the Forest of No Escape, and said, "The guy who broke into your house last night—what he did was dangerous for him, and that really worries me."

Sherlock said, "Dillon's right. If we can't predict what he'll do, we can't protect you, and that means we need a new plan."

"Your screaming, Rachael," Jack said, "for no apparent reason, must have scared the bejesus out of him. That was excellent timing for a nightmare. It scared the bejesus out of me, too."

Rachael sat forward, her hands clasped so tightly her knuckles were white. "Why can't we get a search warrant for the Abbotts' financial records? You know we'd find a record showing payments to Perky and her thugs. Probably huge cash withdrawals, near the right dates."

Savich said, "I'm sorry, Rachael, but we don't have enough proof to get a warrant to search the Abbott pool house. With people of their stature, you've always got to have every single duck in a row before you go after them.

"So that means we have to go another route, find some way to bring this to a close. Here's what I propose. I got permission to speak to the vice president before we came over this morning. I told him we know every member of Congress and the president are concerned about the recent allegations that the senator was murdered. He laughed, said I was right. I told him I have a plan to get some closure. He's decided to help us.

"The vice president has agreed to reschedule the Jefferson Club's speaker tomorrow night and change the agenda of their dinner meeting. It's now going to be a remembrance and a tribute to your father, Rachael. Many senators will speak. If you're willing, you can speak, as well. When I told him it was imperative the Abbotts be present, he didn't say a word. The vice president agreed to extend a personal invitation to them. And that's part of what we want.

"The break-in last night—in spite of your having protection right here with you—shows the killer seems to have thrown caution to the wind. He didn't seem to care about the enormous risk he was taking. Like I said, he's doing precipitous things, and that makes him even more dangerous. We either get this resolved, or I can see you hidden away in the Witness Protection Program, Rachael. What we're doing is providing the killer with another physical opportunity, but under controlled circumstances—our control. The killer might suspect it's a trap, but he also might go for it. What's happened here makes me think that although our killer might be playing with all his marbles, there's something out of control driving him.

"If you agree to speak tomorrow night at

the Jefferson Club, we'll alert the media about your father's commemorative dinner, and the fact that you will be there and you will address the group.

"The media are fascinated already, licking their chops over you more every passing day because Jack's managing to keep you away from them.

"So, the question is, Rachael, are you willing to take this hopefully final step? Are you willing to be bait?"

Rachael said, "When you announce I'm going to speak about my father, the Abbotts will think I'm going to tell everyone what he did. They'll feel compelled to have another go at me, is that what you think? Even for them, wouldn't that be short notice?"

"No," Jack said, "not if they have the contacts. Admittedly, Perky and her band are out of commission. Can they come up with something by tomorrow night? I guess we'll see."

Rachael said, "You don't think they're still trying to keep me quiet, do you? It no longer applies."

Savich said, "We all agree that the possibility of your 'going public' no longer holds much of a threat—we already know everything you know, and killing you now would make it more likely, not less, that the story would come out. If keeping that story secret is the killer's motivation, his only hope is that you decide not to go public and that the FBI can never gather enough evidence to indict anyone. And they would be right."

Rachael said, "Then why is someone still trying to kill me?"

Savich said, "Given his behavior last night, I'm thinking we haven't cottoned to his real motive yet."

Jack said, "I know it's the way to go, my brain recognizes that, but I'll tell you guys, the whole thing scares me. I guess it's preferable to being on the defensive. At least it's proactive. But, Rachael, it'll still be dangerous."

"After last night," Rachael said, "I'm ready to do about anything. I found a gray hair this morning. In my braid. Show me the dotted line. I'll do it."

Jack grinned at her, gave her braid a tug. Savich leaned closer to speak, then paused when he saw Sean was at a dead end on his computer game. He reached over and punched two buttons. They listened to a trio of whistles, two loud beeps, and one long, deep *bong.*

Sean jumped up and down in his chair. "Wow! Look at that! Papa, you got Zhor to run right into the magic prison in the Forest of No Escape! He's toast now."

"He could still escape, he's smart and cunning, so be careful," Savich said, his eyes on Rachael's face. He added quietly, "If Laurel or whoever can't find you tomorrow, and you can bet she'll try, she'll have to go after you tomorrow night. Before you speak? I don't know."

"Can I carry Jimmy's gun in my purse?"

"You can carry a machete as far as I'm concerned," Jack said. "If you decide a gun's what you need to make you feel safe, I'll carry it in for you since they'll be checking bags at the door."

"We'll give it a go then," Savich said. "I have this feeling the Abbotts will act, Rachael."

Rachael bit into another scone, listened to Sean yell that he'd dumped Zhor into a bog, and hoped she'd still be breathing come Tuesday morning.

She stood up, planted her palms on the

tabletop. "Would you look at the time. I've got a speech to write. And I've got to figure out how to keep myself from getting too scared in front of all those big shots."

There was a knock on the back door.

FORTY-EIGHT

Jack held up his hand and walked to the door, looked out, and opened it wide. "Hey, Clive, you got something?"

Agent Clive Howard, a twenty-year FBI veteran and one of its top forensic specialists, was six feet six inches tall, looked like a windowpane at 160 pounds, and had his grandma's huge smile. "Of course I've got something," he said in the thickest Southern accent Rachael had ever heard. "Lookee here." Clive handed him a small rough-edged piece of material. "Our guy should have been more careful when climbing that oak tree to get into the house.

Now, this guy has either noticed the rip in his jacket, in which case he's already deep-sixed it, or he hasn't noticed, and we might use it to identify him later. Now, I'm thinking this is off a lightweight jacket, and that makes sense since it was pretty warm last night. The material's a synthetic stew, everything in it but good ole cotton."

"I know it's real small, but does the material look new to you, Clive?" Sherlock asked.

"Hard for an average untrained professional to say, but me?" He grinned real big at her. "I'd say it's gotta be fairly new. We'll test it, but I'm willing to bet it's never hit the dry cleaner's. Given he wouldn't wear it during the winter, it's probably a spring buy, maybe three, four months ago."

Savich toasted Clive with his oolong tea. "Thank the good Lord for you, Clive."

Clive beamed. "And we know our boy is a boy—a size ten shoe, heavy in the heels, a good-sized guy, maybe one eighty, but not too tall—that's according to Mendoza, who can tell you the foot size of a gorilla swinging through the forest."

"Forest?" Sean said, coming to attention. "Is someone else trapped in the Forest of No Escape?"

Life never stopped happening, Rachael thought, and laughed as Savich quickly explained to Clive about Sean's computer game. "Hey, Sean," Clive said, "my little girl really likes Zhor and the Forest of No Escape, tries to zap him whenever she gets done eating her vegetables."

Sean sighed. "Papa had to help me."

"That's okay. I sometimes help my little girl, too."

"She isn't big like me?"

"Well, yeah, actually she is. She just turned eighteen."

Sean giggled.

Savich stood, and the two men shook hands. Savich said, "Thank everyone for coming out on a Sunday morning, Clive."

"All in a good cause." Clive nodded to everyone, said to Sean, "Yo, kiddo, good luck cutting off Zhor at his evil knees," and walked back into the yard.

"That material," Rachael said. "May I see it?"

Savich handed it to her.

It was dark brown, a smooth fabric, sharp, she thought. Rachael said, "Synthetic stew or not, the guy who'd wear this dresses sharp."

Savich's cell sang out the *Harry Potter* theme. "Savich here. What? Okay, Tom, escort Dr. MacLean back to his room and make sure he stays there. Keep the reporter away from him and on ice until I get there. Yeah, okay, I understand. Yes, we'll be right there."

Savich looked at them. "Dr. MacLean is talking to a reporter about Congresswoman Dolores McManus murdering her husband."

FORTY-NINE

Washington Memorial Hospital

It was nearly noon when they stepped onto the elevator in the hospital. They'd dropped Sean off at his grandmother's house. She promptly hauled him off to church, whispering in his ear that she'd made potato salad for him, which made Sean beam at her and say in a confiding voice, "I'll teach you how to fry Zhor, Grandma. You gotta get him into the Forest of No Escape and wrap a monkey vine around his neck."

"My day will be perfect."

The six people on the elevator obligingly moved to the side so they could enter. Savich said quietly as he punched the

button, "I've got Ollie going through pur-
chases made by Laurel, Quincy, Brady Cullifer, Greg Nichols, and three of the senator's
former staffers. We'll see if a nice brown
jacket shows up."

"It could be a hired thug, Dillon."

There were still two people on board
when the elevator reached their floor.

Sherlock said, "I'll speak to Dr. MacLean, Dillon; you take the reporter. Scare
him spitless, okay?"

"That's the plan."

The reporter was the *Washington Post*'s
Jumbo Hardy, a smart-ass the size of a
well-fed linebacker with both a brain and a
mouth. He always looked droop-eyed and
worn-out, like he hadn't slept in a week,
only Savich knew better.

Jumbo gave Savich a grin, fanned his
big hands in front of him. "Hey, isn't this
something—I got one of the big guns."

Savich said easily, "I'm surprised to see
you again so soon, Jumbo. Don't you ever
sleep?"

"More than you do," Jumbo said. "I didn't
think you could outdo your press conference, but having you show up in person to
get rid of me—what's going on, Savich?"

"Yeah, you got my attention. Glad you could stick around."

"Your guy gave me no choice, said he'd arrest my butt and toss it in a janitor's closet on the fifth floor of the Hoover Building. He said I wouldn't be found until next month." Jumbo gave Savich a big toothy smile. "I was just checking out Congresswoman McManus." He patted his laptop. "It ain't MAX, but I can still find most stuff, like the details about the death of her husband. Now I hear from her very own shrink that she admitted paying some hit man in Savannah to take out her old man. Now, that's news, Special Agent Savich, big news."

"I know you're not about to write about this until you've got verification. And you also know you're not going to get it. Listen, Jumbo, you know very well Dr. MacLean is suffering from frontal lobe dementia, a disease that makes him talk about all sorts of stuff he shouldn't, even stuff that didn't happen. You also know there have been attempts on his life—"

"Nearly more attempts than we poor representatives of the people can keep up with," said Jumbo. "That deal last night, what a fiasco for you guys. I mean, an FBI agent getting stabbed in the neck with a needle, not to mention a nurse saving the day. What's that all about?"

"Hang that up, Jumbo. We've already made a statement."

"The people got a right to know, Savich, that's all I was saying. I heard rumors about this disease of his, but no one ever confirmed it. To tell you the truth, that's why I didn't mind staying. I know he's real sick, know what he says is likely libelous, and that he can't control himself. Talk to me, tell me what's coming down here."

"Off the record?"

"If I agree, when do I get to go on the record?"

"When everything is over. All right, Jumbo, I need your help."

Jumbo whistled, sat back, his arms behind his head, and crossed his legs. "What is this? You need *my* help? When did the sky fall? What's going on here I haven't already guessed?"

FIFTY

Sherlock found the good doctor sulking in his room.

A neurologist, Dr. Shockley, was checking MacLean's reflexes, humming under his breath. MacLean was ignoring him. His eyes narrowed when Sherlock came into the room. It looked to her like he was ready to yell his head off.

Dr. Shockley straightened. "Well, you're good to go, Dr. MacLean, despite the excitement."

Sherlock introduced herself, waited for him to leave the room, which he did, with one last very long look at MacLean.

Before he could spit at her, Sherlock intoned just like she would to Astro, "Bad dog, Dr. MacLean, very bad dog."

"Bad dog?" MacLean said slowly, "*Bad dog*? That's pretty funny, Agent Sherlock, but that's exactly my point. I'm not your damned dog. It's none of the FBI's business if I want to talk to a reporter. It's just talk, a bit of conversation with another sentient human being—wait, he's a reporter, but at least I was sentient."

"Hey, that was pretty funny, too. Are you done?" When he would have continued, Sherlock raised her hand. "I understand, Timothy, I really do. But you've got to believe me now. It was wrong—you broke patient confidentiality, and to a reporter. Try to think clearly about this for a moment. This is exactly why someone is trying to kill you. Do you understand that your speaking to Jumbo Hardy was inappropriate?"

MacLean shrugged. He looked petulant.

A different tack then. Sherlock punched him in the arm. "I hear your wife was pretty upset about what happened last night. She didn't want to leave you alone."

"Yeah, right. Oh, that stupid Molly, she's always hovering, always checking my pulse, my eyeballs, my goddamned feet. She says my toenails need trimming. I didn't do anything to deserve it—well, hardly anything, at least in cosmic terms."

"You told her to go find a lover because you found her disgusting."

He shrugged. "Well, fact is, she smelled funny."

Down the rabbit hole, Sherlock thought. "She loves you."

He was silent for a very long time. Then, "No, she doesn't."

"What do you mean?"

MacLean leaned his head back against the pillow and closed his eyes. "When she found out what finally happens to people with this disease, she nearly left me.

"Everyone thinks she's a bloody saint for sticking so close to me, but I know the truth. I know she's siphoning off all the money she can out of our joint accounts. I know she's got a lover, you see. Only thing is, she can't very well leave me in this sucky condition, now can she?" He paused, shrugged. "It isn't Pierre or Dolores behind this. No, Molly's the one who's trying to kill me."

Whoa.

"That's the biggest crock of shit I've ever heard out of you, Tim, and you know it and even the good Lord knows I've heard more than my share from you over the past twenty-seven years!"

Molly MacLean stood in the doorway, hands on her hips, her face nearly scarlet with rage.

"Mrs. MacLean," Sherlock said, smiling at her, "would you please come with me for a moment?"

"If I stay in the same room with this ... individual, I just might kill him," Molly said, and waved her fist at her husband. "Lead on, Agent Sherlock. Save this idiot's miserable lying hide by removing me."

Savich found Sherlock and Molly in the nurses' lounge, Molly in tears. He paused in the doorway. Sherlock raised her eyes. "Hi, Dillon. I think we've got things in some perspective. Do we, Mrs. MacLean?"

Molly knuckled her eyes. "Yes, I've got it together again. It's so easy to forget he doesn't realize what he's saying, doesn't begin to comprehend how his words twist and turn the knife. He doesn't even know there is a knife. And when I heard him talking about me to you like that—I'm sorry. Oh God, he's so sick, so unlike himself. Sometimes I can't stand it." Molly lowered her face in her hands and wept.

Sherlock lifted her to her feet and held her in her arms, murmuring nonsense to her, really, but kept it low and soothing.

Molly pulled back, sniffed, and wiped her eyes. "I'm sorry I lost it like that. I've got your blouse all wet. I'm a miserable human being for losing it when I know—I understand—he can't help it."

"You're doing remarkably well under the circumstances, Mrs. MacLean," Savich said, and he meant it.

Sherlock said, "Dr. MacLean was wound up today, probably as a result of last night. He called a reporter and he verbally attacked you, probably because Dillon and I ruined his fun. We're so sorry." And Sherlock hugged Molly. "You're hanging in there as best you can."

She sighed and walked away from them to the window. She hugged herself. "Yes, I am. Poor Tim, to be trapped like that in this nightmare, and a lot of the time he doesn't even recognize he's in one. I spoke to his doctor at Duke, read what they gave me. It's not going to be pretty, what happens from here on out."

Thirty minutes later, when Savich pulled his Porsche out of the hospital parking lot, he said, "Jumbo Hardy agreed to keep this under wraps. He's going to put Rachael's announcement in the *Washington Post* right away."

"What did you promise him?"

He gave her a quick smile. "Not much. Jumbo sobered up real fast when I told him the course of the disease. He also knew he didn't have a source he could quote. I did, however, promise him a one-on-one, with the FBI's approval, of course, when we catch who's trying to kill Timothy.

"I've removed the phone from Timothy's room. From now on, he'll have to ask a nurse to dial any phone numbers for him to ensure he doesn't pull something like this again. The nurses will have to be hard-nosed with him."

Savich said as he wove the Porsche in and out of traffic, "Hey, you want to tell Congresswoman McManus how she barely escaped the big bullet?"

"That means she'd have to thank you. Fat chance." She patted his shoulder. "It's going to end soon, Dillon, both cases. But I've got some ideas of my own I want to check out."

"You wanna share?"

She shook her head slowly.

FIFTY-ONE

Rachael was restless, and yes, she admitted it, scared out of her mind—a feeling she hated because it was so debilitating, a feeling that had been a part of her for more than a week now, ever since she'd been dropped into Black Rock Lake to drown. She remembered the coarse wet texture, the strength and stiffness of the rope as her fingers worked it. She closed her eyes for a moment. What was worse was that she was becoming used to the fear, a sort of vacant humming in her head that made her muscles clench. It should make a difference that she survived, but it didn't seem to. She drew in a deep breath and looked around. At least she hadn't been sitting lock-kneed on the sofa, her brain paralyzed. No, she'd cleaned Jack's large corner apartment thoroughly, although, she had to admit, it hadn't needed it.

Before Jack waltzed out the door, he'd had the nerve to tell her to take it easy, check out his music, and eat, she was getting too thin, maybe take a nap, and he'd held her face between his hands and kissed her fast and hard, and left without another word, the jerk.

She turned on his flat-screen TV and listened to the local newscaster while she watered plants—five azaleas and one ivy. She stopped when she heard the guy segue into a report on Senator John James Abbott's memorial dinner at the Jefferson Club tomorrow evening. She stared at the TV while he listed some of the senators who would be there, mentioned Jimmy's family, and at the very end, he finished by saying, "There's an interesting aside here. Rachael Janes Abbott, Senator Abbott's recently discovered daughter, will be one of the speakers."

The local channel skipped to the

weather. Summer rain, nothing new there. Rachael turned off the TV and began pacing Jack's very nice living room. No antiques, but lots of big, overstuffed pieces in rich browns and golds, touches of turquoise. He needed a couple of bright throw pillows, the designer thought, a focal point, and the room would be perfect. He had good taste, she'd say that for him, and that special "knack" most people didn't have. He was also, she noted, an extremely good kisser.

She wandered into Jack's good-sized kitchen, all modern, appliances sparkling, and so they should because she'd shined them with a soft cloth for a good five minutes while she was off in never-never land. The walls were painted a pale yellow, the wooden cabinets the same yellow, the result bright and warm. She walked into the hallway, this time pausing to look at all the black-and-white photographs he himself had taken, photos of southwestern national parks, stark and wild, and a close-up of two mammoth elks fighting. And there were the pictures of people—diaper sized to ancient, faces lined and smooth, bodies twisted and straight. Her favorites were a teenage girl laughing hugely, her head thrown back, long hair blowing in a stiff breeze, white iPod wires in her ears, and an old man in baggy tweeds, his head bald as an egg, sitting on a bench, a meatball hoagie in his hand, smiling up into the bright sunlight, a drop of tomato sauce on his mouth.

Jack's world was eclectic, but entirely his. Here was a big-time FBI agent who was also an excellent photographer, an artist, and owned a house he was fixing up. What were the odds? She was struck, as she had been several times before, how you thought you knew someone, but many times you really didn't have a clue. Take that gambling son-of-a-bitch former fiancé of hers, for example. She sneered at herself for being an idiot. Jerol Springer. She shuddered.

She wandered back into the living room to one of the two big bay windows. His building was vintage 1930s, well maintained, as were the grounds, an amazing example of art deco, with oodles of atmosphere and style. But it was the magnificent views that made it prime, she thought, as she looked toward the Lincoln

Monument. There were several photographs of the monument on the wall beside the window, one taken in the winter with snow piled everywhere, two determined, bundled-up tourists trudging up the monument steps, heads down, fighting a strong headwind. She wondered if he took the shots with a zoom lens from his living room window.

Where was he?

Rachael wandered into the guest bedroom, a room she'd only dusted lightly because it had indeed been pristine. It was small, tidy, spare, with a double bed covered with a sleeping bag spread on top, not a spread. She roamed back to Jack's bedroom with its high ceilings and beautiful art deco moldings. She studied the Diane Arbus and Ansel Adams photographs on the white walls, obviously two artists he admired.

The bed was nicely done, a big king with a navy blue and white quilt, two bright red pillows covered with red sequins tossed against the navy blue shams. Hmmm. The pillows added a nice punch. Who had added the bling? A former girlfriend? Why hadn't this same person added bling to the living room? Hadn't she been around long enough?

Don't go there. Maybe whoever she is, she'll hook up with my loser of an ex-fiancé.

Rachael sat down on the side of the bed and twitched. She was driving herself nuts, she couldn't help it. Her mind took her right back to her near drowning, that black water closing over her head as the concrete block dragged her down, then skipped to the very close call at Roy Bob's garage, that man standing in the bay opening, shooting at her and Roy Bob, Sheetrock raining down on them. And Slipper Hollow, so many bullets, death, raw and ugly, in their faces. If not for Jack being such a useful guy, things might not have ended so well. But at Roy Bob's garage she survived because of her own skill, and she planned to keep reminding herself she wasn't a helpless victim. She'd survived all three attempts. She supposed the incident at the house the night before didn't really count because it hadn't terrified her like being thrown into Black Rock Lake or being shot at. But now she was safe; whoever wanted her dead had no idea where she was. She knew that, knew it—but somehow it didn't quite reach to her center, where all her doubts and fears crashed about endlessly.

Rachael's eyes went to a photo sitting on his dresser, obviously his parents, four siblings, and a slew of kids. She said aloud to the empty room, "No one knows where I am. No one. Not even you guys."

She repeated it. Finally, she accepted it enough to allow her built-up fatigue to get a toehold in her manic brain.

Rachael lifted the blue patterned quilt to find beneath it a blue-and-white striped duvet cover. It was sharp, elegant. This was very serious, very cool coordination. A former girlfriend? His mother?

Where was he?

She lay down and closed her eyes. She'd called Uncle Gillette and told him the plan, about which he was markedly silent, then her mother, lying cleanly yet again. She'd listened to her half brother, Ben, tell her about how buff he was getting for the upcoming football season. She hadn't known there were grade school football teams. Life didn't just continue, she thought, marveling, it galloped forward. She remembered Ben at eight years old, tossing a Frisbee to her, rolling on the ground with his dog. The last time she'd seen him, he was fishing with his dad at Lark Creek Lake.

Her own life wasn't galloping. She was lying in a strange bed with nothing happening, nothing resolved, and no Jack. She closed her eyes and her brain sped up again and she remembered:

"It wouldn't do you any good to announce to all of them that you've decided not to tell the world about what your father did, Rachael," Dillon said, Jack nodding in agreement. "You wouldn't be believed because there'd always be the chance you would change your mind. It no longer seems to be about that, anyway. We have no choice but to go forward."

Forward it was, she thought. No other direction, really. She was very grateful it might all end tomorrow night at the Jefferson Club. She prayed it would.

Where was Jack? For that matter, where was his house?

Then Greg Nichols had called her cell.

"Hello, Rachael, where are you? I went by the senator's house, but no one was

there. Well, there were some FBI guys wandering around in the backyard, but they wouldn't tell me anything. What's going on? I can't find you. Where are you? I'm worried."

"I'm preparing my speech for tomorrow night at the Jefferson Club. I hope you'll be there, Greg. I know it would mean a lot to my father."

"What about Jacqueline and your sisters?"

"They sent their regrets."

She was deeply asleep when Jack found her an hour later in his bed, a small smile playing on her mouth, her head turned slightly to the side. Her braid was lying against her cheek.

He eased down beside her and kissed her.

She didn't jerk away, only turned her head toward him and slowly opened her eyes. She looked up to see him leaning into her, not an inch from her nose. "I'm sure glad you're not the bad guy," she said, and raised her hand to smooth his hair, "or I'd be in big trouble."

"When I was a little kid," he said, stroking her hair, "I always wanted to be the robber, wanted to be the major badass when we played, but my big brother said I couldn't snarl and talk jive well enough, so I had to suck it up and be the cop. I guess I got used to it." He kissed her again. "So that means you're not in big trouble."

"Where have you been?"

"I was doing that old-fashioned police work I told you about, and I talked to some people. I stopped off at Feng Nian, brought us some Chinese."

He saw the spark of panic in her eyes.

"Absolutely no one knows you're here with me. No one followed me, believe me, I checked often enough. You're safe. Tomorrow night, this will be over."

Will it? she wondered, and let him help her up. It was all too simple, too straight-forward, too *planned*. She knew Laurel wasn't simple. She didn't know about Quincy and Stefanos.

Rachael smiled when he turned to smooth down the covers. Her mom would pronounce him a good man.

"You've got a lovely apartment."

"Thank you. My mom was my interior decorator."

A mom supplying bling was okay.

"But the photographs are yours."

"Yes," he said, "they are."

"You might not snarl and growl enough for a badass, but you're an excellent photo artist."

"Ah, well, not really . . . well, anyway, thank you. You should see Savich's pieces. He whittles."

She ate the entire carton of kung pao chicken but didn't read him her speech. "I'm still thinking, and rewriting," she said.

"As you should. It's quite an honor."

She sighed. "Yes, I realize that."

Jack's cell rang.

FIFTY-TWO

The Jefferson Club
Washington, D.C.
Monday evening

When it came down to it, you placed good people around you and trusted them to do their jobs. If you couldn't, it was time to hang it up. The six undercover FBI agents working the big room were the best—smart and focused.

Savich spotted Director Mueller standing with Rachael. Jack, he didn't see. He was checking out the catering staff imported for the event. He'd already arranged checks on the extra waitstaff the club had brought in for tonight's shindig, and the permanent staff for that matter.

Savich smelled a mellow, woodsy perfume

and turned to see Laurel Abbott Kostas coming toward him, a flute of champagne in her hand, dressed in an undoubtedly very expensive black dress that did nothing for her. Odd how well he thought he knew her, yet this was the first time he'd ever seen her in the flesh.

She wasn't wearing a long gown, like most of the women. Instead she wore potentially sexy black fishnet stockings on her heavy legs, but her feet were in low-heeled pumps, a real clash in message. Her coarse graying hair was pulled back and clipped at the nape. She wore a touch of lipstick, nothing else. But the diamonds—she was wearing mounds of them everywhere, her ears, throat, wrist, fingers. She looked like she'd cleaned out a display case. De Beers had to love her.

Her husband, Stefanos, another player whose character Savich thought he understood fairly well, was at her side, dressed in an expensive tuxedo, his black hair slicked back from his swarthy heavy face, a handsome dissipated face Savich didn't like or trust. He watched Kostas's eyes roam and assess. He looked bored and restless, and on edge. He held a whiskey in his hand and used it as an excuse not to shake hands when Savich introduced himself.

"Mr. Kostas," Savich said, and nothing more, very aware that Laurel was giving him the once-over. When he turned back to her he saw a spark of interest in her flat cold eyes. What was that about?

Laurel said in a smooth, dismissive voice, "I know who you are. I saw you on TV, running that ridiculous FBI press conference."

He smiled at her. "I'm Agent Dillon Savich. And you are Mrs. Laurel Kostas?"

She nodded. "I see you're wearing a tuxedo, Agent Savich, and it is expensive. A surprise, I suppose, given you're a policeman."

Stefanos was looking at a woman's cleavage. His eyes slid past Savich to his wife, and he said with world-weary contempt, "The whiskey is watered down." Then he turned on his heel and made his way through the crowd toward the bar, where the woman and her cleavage were standing.

Laurel said, "I suppose you're here because Rachael is. She isn't actually going to tell everyone what the senator did, on an occasion like this, is she?"

"You will have to ask her, Mrs. Kostas. I really don't know."

He motioned to the waiter carrying a silver tray of champagne flutes. At her nod, he handed her one, took the empty one and put it on the tray.

"Where is Quincy Abbott, ma'am?"

"I left him speaking to the vice president about the current power struggle between the French and the Germans, nothing new there. Actually, no one seems to get along with either of them. In business, as in war, I've learned it's always best to pit them against each other. Where is Rachael? I don't see her. Perhaps she's decided not to make a spectacle of herself, not to make us all the butt of malicious gossip?"

He smiled his vicious smile that Sherlock told him could freeze your heart, but it didn't seem to work on Laurel. He said, "If you look to your left, you'll see her speaking to Senator Mark Evans. There was a break-in at her house Saturday night. The intruder was careless and left us some evidence."

She went stiff, her cold eyes suddenly

needle sharp on his face, and he'd swear he could see her thinking. He knew she had a formidable mind, and wasn't easily rattled. She said in a bored voice, "Evidence? Well, it's about time you found something, isn't it? What did you find?"

"Sorry, ma'am, I can't tell you."

"Why not? Who cares, after all?" He heard it then, fear in her voice, a thick undercoat of it. She moved closer, the movement making her diamonds dance and glitter madly.

He leaned close, as well, and went with his gut. "Do you know who shimmied up the oak tree to climb in through a second-floor window, Mrs. Kostas? Did her scream scare him away? Or was it the alarm going off?"

She took a quick step back from him and looked toward her husband, who was speaking now to a senator from Arizona. She turned, said to him over her shoulder, "Can you really see one of us climbing a tree, Agent Savich? I think not. But it seems to me Rachael has to run out of luck sometime."

"Everyone eventually does," Savich said. "You included, ma'am. Ah, here are Agent Sherlock and your niece."

"She's not—" Laurel shut her mouth, something, Sherlock imagined, she did neither often nor easily. But she was smart enough to get the lay of the land before she charged into battle.

Savich introduced Sherlock to Laurel, who ignored her to land squarely on Rachael.

"So," Laurel said, looking Rachael up and down, "you have to have an agent sticking to you now?"

Rachael said, "Yes. I've found I prefer it."

Quincy and Stefanos joined them, probably, Savich thought, because they believed Laurel needed reinforcements. Laurel made begrudging introductions.

Sherlock shook the men's hands. Stefanos held her hand a bit longer than he should have. She cocked her head at him. "You have such lovely hair, Agent Sherlock," he said, that accent meant to warm and seduce. "There is no red hair like yours in my country. It is glorious."

Boy, you lay it on with a trowel, don't you? She smiled at him.

Quincy Abbott looked like he wanted to bolt, but inbred civility won out and he shook Savich's hand. He gave only a mildly displeased nod to Jack, who was standing at Rachael's shoulder. When he took Sherlock's hand, his eyes went hot. Now that was interesting. It wasn't lust, not at all like the message Stefanos had broadcast to her. What was it? Was it anger? Did his look mean he hated female cops? She'd heard Rachael say he was a misogynist. She looked at Dillon. He was stone-faced.

Stefanos said, "You look magnificent, like a cabaret singer from the thirties, Agent Sherlock."

"Thank you," Sherlock said.

Savich agreed with Stefanos. Sherlock was wearing a long black skirt, a black top that bared her shoulders, and her hair was loose, a sunset of curls around her head, pulled back from her face with two black clips. She looked good, that was Savich's remark when he saw her, and she'd known he wanted to haul her back upstairs. Even Sean, standing at his father's side, had stared at her. "I wouldn't know it was you if it wasn't for your hair, Mama."

She'd laughed and kissed him soundly. But Savich bet she had no plans to kiss Stefanos Kostas.

Stefanos said, "You're really an FBI agent? You?"

"You were thinking I was perhaps a runway model?"

"Maybe that's not too much of a stretch."

Rachael said, "Agent Savich and Agent Sherlock are married. They have a little boy."

"What?" Stefanos asked. "You're actually married to him? But, I—"

Laurel rolled over her husband. "Married? I've never heard of FBI agents being married to each other before, but I suppose our government allows just about anything."

"Not really," Sherlock said.

"I have two boys," Laurel continued. "The elder is nearly grown up now. He met a girl in New York City and is convinced he's going to marry her."

"How old is he?" Jack asked, though he knew very well.

"Damian is sixteen."

Quincy said, "Stefanos isn't happy about this, even though it's only a young boy's crush, isn't that right?"

Stefanos shrugged. "He can have his

fun. I only hope he doesn't contract some disease from her."

Quincy said, "You're an expatriate xenophobe, Stefanos—you want both your sons to marry into old Greek families."

Stefanos smiled at his brother-in-law, sipped at his whiskey like an elegant sloth.

Jack asked Laurel, "What did you think of the FBI press conference?"

Her heavy face froze. "I already told Agent Savich it was ridiculous. To me it smacked of conspiracy theories, which are generally nonsense. It is like saying the Warren Commission lied. How can you disprove a negative? I suppose the FBI will continue prodding and poking about, annoying us until we have our lawyers manage to cut you off at the knees."

Savich said pleasantly, "I certainly agree with you about conspiracy theories. However, do you really believe, Mrs. Kostas, that your brother took up drinking again, that he got into a car after not driving for eighteen months?"

"Perhaps the senator considered cutting back on his drinking, even spent some time not driving, but in the end, he seems to have been doing both. There seems no doubt about that. Stefanos, Quincy, do you agree?"

Stefanos looked bored. Quincy, in a very discreet one-finger move, adjusted his toupee.

Laurel said, "No matter what the senator said, he would not have called a press conference and made a grand announcement of his guilt. He knew if he spoke up, he would lose everything—the prestige and power of being a senator, all the privileges of being wealthy and sought after, of being endlessly feted and admired."

Jack said, "And last but not least, he would probably have gone to jail for vehicular homicide."

"That is not possible. The senator had excellent lawyers," Stefanos said. "He would never have spent a day in jail."

That might be the truth, Sherlock thought.

"No matter," Laurel said. "The senator lived for those things. He did not like to lose. What happened the night he died was an accident. All these theories—and that's all they are—they sound like those ridiculous conspiracy theory blogs."

"Jimmy told me he was going to do it," Rachael said. "There was no reason for him to tell you if he hadn't made up his mind." *Was that the truth? To say it, flat-out, it sounded so simple and straightforward.* She said, "Besides the three of you, he also told Greg Nichols. Yet you still doubt it, even after Jimmy told you the misery he'd been living with for eighteen months?"

Quincy said, his voice dismissive, "I will say this one more time: it was a phase, nothing more. The senator was self-indulgent. He liked to analyze things to death—business, politics, a specific piece of legislation, how he was going to get back at another senator or congressman or staffer who got on the wrong side of him.

"Look, I'm sure he felt very sorry about what happened to the little girl, he had a conscience, after all."

There was a malignant look on Laurel's face, a look filled with cold rage, and it was aimed at Rachael. "If you have convinced these three FBI agents that we murdered our own brother, you have done the senator and our entire family, Jacqueline and her daughters included—not to mention the entire country—a grave disservice. You are contemptible, Miss Janes. And no, I will not call you an Abbott; you will never be an Abbott to us."

Laurel turned on her low-heeled pumps and walked away, Quincy and Stefanos, after one last caressing look at Sherlock, following in her wake.

"I hadn't expected them to speak so freely," Savich said thoughtfully, watching them begin to work the room, the tall well-built man whose ego was bigger than his brain, and the dowdy woman covered in diamonds, with her powerful, vicious eyes. And Quincy, looking like a beautifully dressed royal adjunct.

Sherlock said, "Do you know, the three of them have one thing in common. They all radiate clout. Look, there's the senator from New Hampshire going over to them."

"They're a big deal," Rachael said. "They're American royalty, rich—oozing confidence, used to getting what they want."

Savich said to his wife as he touched his fingertips to her ear, "I really like the jet-black earrings."

"You should, you bought them for me."

He could feel the tightly coiled energy rolling off her. "Yes," he said slowly, "I did."

Sherlock said to Rachael, "You look perfect. You've struck the right note— classic outfit with a hint of pizzazz."

She did indeed, Jack thought. Rachael was wearing a long black gown, as were many woman in the room. Unlike them, Rachael wasn't showing very much skin, but what showed was potent. She looked beautiful and pale and dignified. Jack imagined she was wound tighter than his grandfather's watch, a ritual Jack had watched countless times when he was a little kid.

Champagne flowed along with the stronger stuff. He saw Laurel and Stefanos speaking with the vice president. As each of them spoke, the vice president nodded solemnly. Several times, he leaned in to say something.

Savich spotted Greg Nichols entering the room, three women and two men with him, former Abbott staffers all. He was wearing a tux, and should have looked buff and competent, but he didn't. Something was wrong, something was off with him.

He was moving slowly and awkwardly. Nichols looked up and met Savich's eyes across the room. He caught Jack's eye and nodded slowly. Then, strangely, he rubbed his stomach. What was going on?

Greg Nichols felt sick to his stomach. He thumbed another Tums from the bottle and discreetly slipped it into his mouth. How many was that so far? Six? Seven? He hoped it was nerves. Nerves he could deal with, he'd had a lot of practice. No, he was going to have to face it, this was for real, probably the cioppino he'd had for a late lunch—a mistake, his secretary Lindsay had told him, what with the hullabaloo happening tonight with the movers and shakers, and he with his nervous stomach. All right, so the cioppino had been off, he'd known it after a few bites and stopped eating it. Curse Lindsay, she was right.

He'd already had massive diarrhea and vomited twice. He thought there'd been a bit of blood, prayed he was mistaken, because that was scary.

But maybe he was feeling a little better now. No, he felt like crap. For a moment, he watched the FBI agent Dillon Savich, the one who'd led the FBI press conference, and chewed faster on the Tums. And that damned agent Jack Crowne, who was sticking to Rachael like glue. Nichols knew he'd been checking on him, and if he didn't know everything about him already, he would soon enough. He'd know everything about all of them. It wasn't fair, just wasn't.

He looked around at the sea of powerful people, spouses hanging onto senators' arms, staking claim to power. So much power concentrated in this one room—it was a terrorist's wet dream. He easily spotted Secret Service agents from long practice. They were everywhere. There had to be FBI there, as well; they were better at fading into the woodwork.

He realized he no longer cared if Rachael spoke out or not. He was a lawyer, he knew how things worked. He'd roll over on Senator Abbott, no problem with that, since he was dead. Then he'd take the bar exam, and set up his practice in Boise.

He didn't need this aggravation that was going to escalate into a shit storm. It was time to cut his losses. It was time to get out of Dodge.

He saw Laurel Kostas speaking to the

ancient senator from Kansas, and at her elbow, nodding occasionally at something his sister said, stood Quincy, that good-for-nothing whiner the senator had tolerated only because he'd felt sorry for him.

His stomach was roiling, but the cramps had lessened a bit. He nabbed a glass of carbonated water from a waiter's tray and sipped it. Maybe it would help settle his stomach, that's what his mother had always preached. He saw his boss, Senator Jankel, all earnest, bending to eye another congressman's wife, the old fool.

Dammit, he couldn't think, his belly was on fire.

FIFTY-THREE

Savich saw a man out of the corner of his eye, a small man, dressed in a waiter's uniform, duck behind a grouping of black-gowned women and tuxedoed men.

Savich moved quickly and, he hoped, discreetly. But he wasn't as fast as Jack, who already had the man's arm and was pulling him toward the kitchen.

Good. Jack would get it sorted out.

The evening rolled on. A distinguished man Savich recognized but couldn't place, wearing a black bespoke tux that disguised his paunch, stepped onto the dais to stand behind the podium. He adjusted the microphone and greeted the guests, and announced dinner. Everyone migrated to their tables, and for three minutes Savich couldn't see anyone clearly in the crowd. Ah, there was Director Mueller. He had Rachael's arm and was leading her to a table at the front of the room where he sat on her right. Jack was to be seated on her left, only he wasn't there.

What was happening in the kitchen?

Savich was at the point of heading back there when Jack came through the swinging dark-paneled doors, straightening his tux as he made his way to his table. He spoke briefly to Director Mueller and eased in beside Rachael.

Savich and Sherlock stood for a moment by the doors to the large, dark-paneled nineteenth-century gentlemen's club, which turned coed in the late fifties. Interesting how it still retained the original smell of countless cigars puffed inside its walls over the decades, sort of sweet and old, like lace in an antique trunk.

Savich sat at one of the front tables with Laurel, Quincy, and Stefanos, four couples separating them, Sherlock at one of the back tables with Greg Nichols.

Jimmy Maitland, to cover all the bases, sat with Brady Cullifer.

Savich listened to the rock-hard political conversations going on around him and wondered when the rubber chicken would make its appearance. He wondered how they would rubberize his vegetarian dish.

To his surprise, he was served spinach lasagna, a tossed salad, and green beans dotted with pearl onions, all delicious. For the predators, they brought out what looked like a Thanksgiving dinner with all the fixings.

A gentleman at the microphone announced that Thanksgiving was Senator Abbott's favorite meal of the year. There was appreciative laughter. And more laughter when he announced there would be gelato for dessert, because pear tartlets prepared for more than two hundred people never made it to the table tasting quite like fruit.

Forty-five minutes later, the vice president walked to the podium and adjusted the microphone upward. He spoke of his long friendship with John James Abbott, of his major legislation and his ability to work with both sides of the aisle, no matter the party in power. There was a low buzz of conversation about that statement until the vice president managed to get off a couple of old golf jokes, then turned it over to a senator from Missouri. It went on from there, each speaker with an amusing or touching anecdote about Senator Abbott.

When the crowd was feeling no pain at all, what with the waitstaff serving the hard stuff as well as rivers of wine, the vice president said, "I would like to introduce all of you to Jimmy's daughter. As you know, he didn't know she existed until she knocked on his door. In the last six weeks of his life, his happiness shone like a beacon. He once said to me she was the daughter of his heart. Many of you have had the opportunity to speak to Rachael this evening, to experience her kindness, her sense of humor, and her charm, doubtless inherited from her father. I give you Ms. Rachael Abbott." He stepped forward to hug her when she gained the dais.

I'm still alive. The turkey was good, the cranberry sauce homemade and delicious, better yet, no one has tried to get near me with a knife. No one has tried to lure me to the men's room.

She looked out over the room at the men and women who ruled the world. She knew her mascara had smudged a bit because she'd cried at some of the stories told by her father's colleagues.

She looked at older faces, lived-in faces, faces that held both knowledge and secrets, and at that moment held a good deal of benevolence. And she saw clearly their sense of self-satisfaction; it was tangible, seemed to fill the air.

The lights were dim, the scents of discreet perfume mixed with the rich smells of the Thanksgiving dinner.

She caught Greg Nichols's eye, cocked her head at him, gave him a tentative smile. Strange, he looked frozen, and more than that—he didn't look right.

She said into the microphone, "I only knew my father for six weeks before he was killed. As you know, his death was originally ruled an accident. Now there are very real questions about that. However, tonight we are here to talk about the senator's life." There was a faint stirring in the group until she continued.

Greg Nichols took another sip of sparkling water, eyed the nearly empty bottle of Tums. All his staffers were looking at him like he was going to explode. Agent Sherlock had spoken to him during the long dinner, asked him repeatedly if he was all right. Upset stomach, he'd told her, nothing more, just an upset stomach from something he ate. And he'd give her a weak smile, say he was feeling better.

It had to get better, didn't it? Food poisoning lasted just a few hours, didn't it? He remembered the potato salad he'd eaten once as a teenager that had left him moaning on the bathroom floor, puking up his guts for eight hours. Then it was over. Would this be over soon? Dammit, he hadn't eaten that much of the damned cioppino. A violent cramp slashed through him again, doubled him up. He gasped with the force of it. It kept getting worse until he thought he was going to die. There was no hiding anything now. He heard voices but didn't recognize any words, he was too deep in the pain. He wasn't about to puke in front of United States senators. He lurched to his feet, groaning, holding himself, and ran toward the door.

"Mr. Nichols, wait!"

It was Agent Sherlock, but he didn't acknowledge her, he couldn't, everything in him was focused on the god-awful pain ripping and tearing through his belly.

He heard Rachael say in a loud voice, sounding strangely far away and deep, like from the bottom of a well, "Senator Robertson spoke about his ability to nudge opposing sides into compromise, his ability to persuade without backroom bloodshed . . ."

People were coming at him, men in dark suits, FBI, Secret Service, his friends, but it didn't matter. He was going to vomit, he was going to—

The lights seemed to go out around him, turning the huge room black as a pit.

He stumbled and went down.

He knew men were leaning over him, touching him, speaking to him, but he was caught in the agony and couldn't say anything, could only groan, tears running down his face, and he knew there was blood flowing out of his body, and it was dark, so very dark. Was the dark on the inside or the outside? Why was someone yelling?

He lurched up as blood gushed out of his twisting mouth, the tears streaming from his eyes tinted red, two snakes of blood running out of his nose.

Sherlock yelled, "Dillon! Come here!"

Savich saw Secret Service agents surround the vice president and chivy him back against a wall. Four FBI agents converged on Rachael at the podium. There were more agents and a dozen other people knotted together. Something was very wrong.

He shoved his way through and looked down to see Greg Nichols lying on his side on the floor, blood trickling from his open mouth. There was blood everywhere. He was soaked with it. Sherlock was on her knees beside him.

"The EMTs should be here soon. He's very bad, Dillon. All this blood. I knew something was wrong with him, I knew it."

"We thought he was up to no good," a Secret Service agent said, straightening over Nichols. "But no, this guy's very sick."

"I'm guessing poison," Savich said. "He's drenched in blood. What else would it be?"

A Secret Service agent said, "Yeah, you're right, sounds like coumarin, rat poison."

"Yeah, probably," Savich said, and felt for Nichols's pulse.

Sherlock rose to look at Lindsay Culley, Nichols's secretary. She was wringing her hands, her face as white as Savich's shirt. "I told him not to eat the cioppino, because there'd be a big meal tonight, but he did, only a few bites. It must have been bad. Really, he didn't eat all that much. I thought he was better, he kept saying he was fine."

She burst into tears. Sherlock patted her shoulder and nodded to Grace Garvey, Senator Abbott's former secretary, who told her, "I didn't know he was ill. We spoke about tonight, and I told him how nice it would be, how pleased we all were they were doing this for Senator Abbott. He and Senator Abbott were so very close." She put her arms around Lindsay.

Savich said, "His pulse is thready, nearly nonexistent." He sat back on his heels. "I don't think he's going to make it."

A Secret Service agent opened the doors and paramedics rushed in carrying medical bags and a gurney. Savich listened to Sherlock tell them his symptoms as they worked over him. He heard an older man say abruptly, "Would you look at all that blood!"

They had him on the gurney quickly, white cloths draped over all the bloody clothes.

Two FBI agents accompanied the group. "Keep me informed," Savich said, then turned back, saw the vice president looking over the heads of the crowd at him, and nodded.

Another three minutes and all the senators had turned to face Rachael once again at the podium.

The vice president nodded to Rachael. "As you all know by now, ladies and gentlemen, someone has fallen ill. I'm told it was Greg Nichols, the former senior staffer for Senator Abbott. He is being seen to, and we certainly hope he will be all right. Ms. Abbott, after all this excitement, do you feel like continuing?"

She nodded, stepped again to the podium, adjusted the microphone. *Greg, what happened?*

FIFTY-FOUR

She looked out over the group, met Laurel's cold, malicious eyes, and nearly recoiled. Then Laurel smirked, no other way to describe that small, self-satisfied smile. Her father's sister—how could that be possible?

She looked around at the group, cleared her throat, and said, "I'm very sorry my father's chief of staff, Greg Nichols, has taken ill. I hope he will be all right. I will keep this brief.

"My father loved our nation's capital, and it disturbed him that alongside the beautiful granite buildings, the stretches of perfectly maintained parklands, just beside the towering monuments, there is squalor and poverty, their roots dug deep for more years than anyone can remember. It both angered and embarrassed him.

"Therefore, in his honor, I will be creating and endowing the John James Abbott Foundation, which will address first and foremost our local citizens' problems. You are our nation's lawmakers, our movers and shakers. I would appreciate any and all expertise you can throw my way. Together, we can make a difference in his name, I'm sure we can."

She picked up her glass of water, raised it high. "I would like to toast Senator John James Abbott, a compassionate man, and an excellent father." She raised her glass, and the rest of the room quickly followed suit. "To making a difference!"

There was a moment of silence while people drank, then, slowly, the members of the Senate stood, clapping, their eyes on her, nodding.

When she returned to the table, Jack said, "I didn't know what you were going to say, but a foundation—that's an excellent idea, Rachael."

She took his hand and said, in a low voice, "I couldn't do it. I thought hard about it, Jack. I argued with myself, taking one side, then the other. I finally decided you were right. What my father would or would not have done became moot the moment he died. It was his decision and only his, no one else's. It would be wrong of me to change how history will judge him. I don't have that right or that responsibility. Only he did."

FIFTY-FIVE

Washington Memorial Hospital
Monday night

One of the emergency room doctors, Frederick Bentley, turned tired eyes to the clock on the waiting room wall. His green shirt was still covered with blood. He said, more to himself than to the people standing around him, "Isn't that strange? It's ten o'clock, straight up. It always seems to be ten o'clock straight up when the freight train hits. You'd think midnight, the witching hour, would bring that choo-choo, but no. All right, I can tell you Greg Nichols is still alive, but I doubt he will be for long.

"We poured blood, plasma, and fluids into him to resuscitate him. His PT—that means prothrombin time—measured off the charts, meaning his blood wasn't clotting, and his hematocrit just wasn't compatible with life.

"He has remained unconscious. We've intubated him, meaning we put a tube into his trachea through his nose to allow him to be hooked up to a respirator. We'll be moving him to the ICU in a minute.

"We're not yet certain why his blood isn't clotting, but I'm thinking poison or an overdose. Most commonly it's coumarin, or something chemically related to it like a superwarfarin, which is used as rat poison. It must have been a massive dose.

"We took stomach and blood samples, which will show us what was in his system, and maybe how long ago he ingested it. It will take a while for the results, though.

"To be blunt, I'm surprised he's still alive. Even if he regains consciousness, he may not be able to talk. I strongly doubt his brain survived the anoxia, the lack of oxygen. Would one of you like to see him?"

Savich followed Dr. Bentley into a screened-off section of the emergency room.

"You're the boss, right?"

"Yeah, I get all the perks."

"Good luck."

Nichols lay alone and still, his face white as a plaster saint's. Dried blood and vomit caked the side of his mouth. His eyes were closed; his lids looked bruised, like someone had punched him. There were two IV lines tethered to his wrists. The obscene wheezing of the respirator was the only sound in the room.

Savich leaned close. "Mr. Nichols."

Savich heard Dr. Bentley suck in a breath behind him when Nichols opened his eyes. Savich saw the death film beginning to creep into them. No, Greg Nichols wasn't going to live through this.

"Do you know who poisoned you, Mr. Nichols?"

Savich was losing him. His eyes were darkening, the film creeping slowly over them, like a veil. His voice was urgent. "Who, Mr. Nichols?"

He was struggling for breath to speak but couldn't.

His eyes froze. He was gone.

Nichols was dead and Savich wanted to howl. There were alarms, the heart machine flatlined.

Two nurses joined Dr. Bentley in the cubicle. Savich stepped out and returned to the small waiting room. There was an older black couple there now, their faces blank with shock, holding each other.

"Come with me," Savich said to Jack and Rachael. He took Sherlock's hand and led them into a long empty hallway, away from the emergency room and the soul-deadening silence of that waiting room.

"He's dead. He regained consciousness, but it was only for a moment."

"They killed him, Dillon."

"Yes, Rachael, I think they did. And they did it dramatically, something I think pleased their vanity."

"But why?"

Savich was quiet for a moment. Sherlock sighed. "I'm sorry, Rachael, but I think Greg Nichols was involved with them. After you and Jack met with him, maybe he spoke to them. Whatever he said must have made them realize he was a weak link, that he'd break, and so they killed him. I'll bet you we'll find out from Greg's staff how they got to him."

Savich's cell sang out "Raindrops Keep

Falling on My Head." He checked to see who it was, frowned. "Savich here."

He was shaking his head as he said, "No, no, that can't be, it just can't be. Yes, we'll be right there. We're in the ER right now."

He closed down, looked blankly at them. "That was Agent Tomlin. We've got to go to Dr. MacLean's room."

His voice was flat, but his eyes were dilated with shock. It scared Sherlock to her toes. She shook his arm. "Dillon! What in heaven's name has happened now? Did someone try for Dr. MacLean again?"

He looked beyond her and said, "Timothy MacLean is dead, two floors up."

FIFTY-SIX

It was chaos—medical staff walking about, seemingly without purpose, the hallway jammed with hospital security, and above it all the fury of Agent Tomlin's deep voice, trying to establish some order. He looked up, nearly yelled in relief at the sight of Savich.

Sherlock grabbed his arm. "What happened, Tom?"

"It appears Dr. MacLean had a gun. He put it to his temple and pulled the trigger. Chief Hayward's inside with the medical staff, trying to figure out how this could have happened." Tomlin swallowed. "Mrs.

MacLean had just left when it happened. She came back up again, I don't know why."

Jack said, "Rachael, you stay put. Don't come in, you hear me?"

She nodded, looked toward Molly Mac-Lean, who was leaning against the wall opposite the nurses' station, her hands over her face, weeping.

"Molly?"

Molly looked up, saw Rachael through a curtain of tears, recognized her.

"I'm so very sorry," Rachael said, and pulled her into her arms. Molly's pain swamped Rachael, drew her into the well of familiar grief she'd lived with since her father's death. It was the hardest thing a human had to bear, she thought. She'd only known her father such a short period of time, a moment really in the long skein of a normal life, but the pain was constant and still throbbed inside her, like a beating heart. She couldn't imagine Molly's pain. She'd lived with her husband for more than twenty-five years. She'd lost someone stitched into the very fabric of her life.

Jack was walking toward them, and

Rachael realized he was struggling to put his own grief away. She admired him greatly in that instant as she watched him get it together and the cop in him took over. He nodded to Rachael. Then he gently touched Molly's shoulder. "Molly? It's Jack. I'm so very sorry." When Rachael's arms dropped, Molly turned to collapse against him. She wrapped her arms around his back, held on hard, and wept against his neck. He held her, murmuring meaningless words, really, hoped it was comfort, but he doubted it. Nothing could make this mortal wound magically better. He said against her hair, "Molly, let's go to the waiting room."

The waiting room was empty, as he knew it would be. All the excitement was down the hall. It was relatively quiet in there. He closed the door, motioned Rachael to sit as he led Molly to a small sofa. He eased down beside her, continued to hold her, rubbing her back, and spoke quietly to her.

When she hiccupped, Jack gave her another squeeze and a Kleenex from a box on a side table. Rachael handed her a cup of water from the cooler in the corner. They waited in silence while she collected herself.

Molly raised her face, looked straight at Jack. "I know you've got to know what happened." She squeezed her eyes closed for a moment and another tear slid down her cheek. She opened her eyes, wiped a hand over her cheeks again. She drew in a big breath, held it. "All right. This afternoon, first thing when I walked into his room, Tim asked me to bring him his gun. He's kept it for years in the bedside table; thankfully he's never had to use it. I stared at him, terrified of what he was going to say, but when I asked him why, he looked at me like I was nuts. He said some guy had just tried to murder him and if it hadn't been for Nurse Louise, what was left of him would be sitting in a lovely silver urn. He said he wanted to be able to protect himself, and if I really cared about him, I would bring him the gun. When I continued to resist, he shrugged, looked away from me, and said maybe it would be better if the guy came back and gave it a second try. After all, he was going to end up a vegetable, why not spare himself the indignity and welcome the guy back, maybe point to a good spot on his head where he should shoot him. It didn't matter, nothing was going to change for him.

"I smacked him on the arm, called him an idiot. You never knew, I told him, simply never knew when medical science would come up with a new drug to help him. He listened to me, at least I thought he was listening.

"Then he looked up at me and said, 'Bring me a gun, Molly, let me take care of myself. I don't want to feel helpless.'

"I finally agreed. I went home and came back about an hour ago. I watched him check out his gun, then he slid it under his pillow and smiled at me. 'Thank you, kiddo, I feel better now,' he said. He was quiet for a while. Then he spoke of our family, his parents, our kids, and his patients—many other things, as well, bad things, painful things, but when I left I thought he seemed more centered, more like the old Tim, bright and funny."

She viciously wiped away the tears. "Oh, Jack, no one managed to get to him, no one murdered him. He did it himself, and I brought him the gun so he could do it."

Her words hung heavily in the room.

Finally, Jack said, "Molly, we'll get back to that. You told me he was himself again, the old Tim. Can you think of anything specific that could have been the catalyst for his killing himself?"

She raised her white face, tears scoring her cheeks. "Yes, I realize now that it was me. I pushed him to it, Jack," she said. Her eyes blurred and she choked. "I pushed him to do it."

Jack said, "Tell me."

Jack was aware that Savich and Sherlock had come into the room. They didn't say anything, stood back against a wall. Molly said, "Tim started talking about his patients, the same three he'd spoken about so freely to Arthur Dolan, his friend and tennis mate, you know, the poor man who was murdered by that maniac up in New Jersey?"

"Yes, I know."

"Tim said, 'Molly, I didn't even realize what I was saying was wrong. It all tripped happily out of my mouth, all of it, every confidential filthy detail, and I sang it all out, happy as a lark. I broke every ethical code I've lived by all my professional life. I accepted my patients' trust and crushed them with it.

" 'Look at what happened to Jean David—Pierre loved his son, Molly, both he and Estelle adored Jean David. He was their only child, they would have freely given their lives for him, and here I actually enjoyed telling Arthur—with that bartender listening in—what Jean David had done.

" 'And now Jean David has drowned, and Pierre is wild with pain and grief and hatred for me. If Pierre is the one who's been trying to kill me, then I hope he succeeds. I pushed him to it.

" 'I am responsible for this tragedy, Molly, no one else.'

"He stopped talking, just stared off at nothing in particular, like he was alone, like he no longer cared about anything."

Molly looked down at her twisting hands and clasped them tightly together. Jack laid his hand over hers. She continued after a moment. "I told Tim he was not the one who chose to betray his country. He only shook his head, and his voice was so . . . accepting. He said to me, 'Yes, Molly, that's true, but not to the point. This disease—it's only going to get worse, you know that as well as I do, but I'll probably escape the worst of it myself because I'll be oblivious to what is real, to what it feels like to be real, to be connected. I won't know my kids, I won't know you and that you're my wife of forever, and all my love, all my experiences, the pains, the joys— even the meaning of it will be gone for me.

" 'I can't bear knowing I'll go through that, Molly, now that I can still see clearly. I can't bear knowing I won't have any balance in my mind, that I won't even recognize that what spills out of my mouth might destroy someone.'

"I recognized the look on his face. He said, 'Do you know, I told one of the doctors here about your affair with Arthur all those years ago? I didn't remember saying anything about that, but the doctor told me what I'd said.

" 'I thank God that He's left me some moments of lucidity so I can remember all the hurt I've already caused, and decide what I want to do about it.' "

Molly choked on a laugh, said to Jack, "Fact is, I did sleep with Arthur a couple of times, years ago. I didn't even think Tim knew about it. I never told him. Funny thing was, both Arthur and I realized it was dumb, realized the truth of it was that all three of us were friends, very good friends, and had been for more than twenty years.

"But Tim saw his speaking of it as the final betrayal, spilling out secrets about our own personal life to strangers.

"All I could do was think about that gun under his pillow. I asked him what he wanted to do and I was terrified of his answer. But he gave me one of his old Tim smiles, said he was going to think, really think about where all this was leading and the consequences of it. He was going to think until the ability escaped him, probably in the next thirty minutes, he said, who knew but God?

"Before I left him a few minutes ago, one of the nurses brought him a pint of pistachio ice cream, his favorite. He grinned at me as he spooned it down. He looked calm. He told me he loved me, then smiled and offered me a bite of ice cream. I took a very small bite, but he teased me and told me I could even have one more small bite. We laughed, and I squeezed his arm and told him we were going to be together for a long time, it didn't matter what came down the road and he'd best accept that. And he said, yes, he liked the sound of that."

Molly raised her face to Jack. "He kissed me, Jack, the sweetest kiss you can imagine. I can still taste the pistachio ice cream on his lips." She fell silent for a moment, looking down at her twisting hands.

Then she nodded toward Savich and Sherlock, smiled at Rachael, and said, "I got all the way downstairs when I remembered I'd forgotten to tell him it was Kelly's birthday tomorrow. I wanted to tell him what we were giving her. Perhaps he'd remember when she came to visit him.

"I heard the shouts when I stepped off the elevator." She stopped, stared at a Monet water lily print on the wall. "I knew, Jack, I knew instantly what he'd done, what I'd enabled him to do." She lowered her face into her hands and wept. The room was quiet, the only sound Molly's ugly, raw tears. She raised her face. "Do you know I signed the birthday card from both of us, as always? It's a funny card—

it says she needs a new bedmate, her teddy bear is all used up."

Jack touched his fingers to her face. He wanted to tell her maybe it was better this way, but his heart couldn't accept that.

She said, "Whoever was trying to kill Timothy—he doesn't have to bother now."

Jack said, "If he killed Arthur, he has to pay for it, Molly. He tried to kill Tim—what is it now?—four times? He's got to pay for that, too."

Molly said clearly, "And what about me, Jack? I wanted to believe him, you see, he knew I wanted to believe the gun was for his protection. He gave me a way out." She paused, and Jack could feel her grief and her awful guilt. She placed her palm over her chest. "But in my heart, I knew he was going to kill himself. I knew it. I am the one responsible for his death, not this maniac."

Savich walked to her and sat down beside her. He took her hands in his. "Molly, listen to me. What you know in your heart, it must stay in your heart. It would do no good to burden your family with this."

Savich rose. "You couldn't have known,

not for sure. What Timothy did, it was his own decision. You made it easier for him, that's all.

"When I walk out this door, Molly, the investigation into Dr. Timothy MacLean's death is closed."

FIFTY-SEVEN

Tuesday afternoon

Rachael walked into Jimmy's study and stood in the middle of the room. The rich brown draperies were partially drawn, framing only a bit of afternoon sunlight. She smelled him still, the aroma of his rich Turkish cigarettes. She sank down onto the burgundy leather sofa, leaned her head back, and stared at the bookshelf behind his desk. She could see the dust beginning to gather on the bindings. Books could be dusted, she thought, but you had to live at close quarters with them to keep them fresh, keep their pages alive.

She looked down at her watch. Nearly

four o'clock. Jack would be back by six, he'd said, and she knew he hated leaving her alone, even in the middle of the hot, sunlit afternoon.

She looked again at Jimmy's desk, the few papers on top in neat piles, the computer screen dark and silent. She drew in a deep breath and forced herself to sit in the wonderfully comfortable high-backed burgundy leather desk chair. She straightened in the well of the desk.

She had time. It was something that had to be done. She opened the top drawer and began sorting through papers. She made piles that had to be handled when his will went through probate, invoices to be paid, a few catalogs he'd evidently marked for order.

She'd sorted through the papers in most of the desk when she opened the bottom drawer and found a beautiful hand-carved bubinga wood pen box. She lifted it out carefully. Sure enough, there were a good dozen pens inside, some of them gifts from foreign countries, from ambassadors he'd visited in his travels. There was a slip of paper at the bottom of the box with three pairs of numbers written on it. A safe combination.

Rachael hadn't even thought about a safe. She looked around but didn't see one. If she owned a safe, she'd keep it in the room where she spent most of her time. She searched the bookshelves, looked under the carpet, and when she lifted a Durbin Monk Irish countryside painting, there it was, built into the wall. She dialed in the numbers and it opened easily.

Inside she found an accordion file that was filled with insurance documents and a journal from the year before showing all his appointments for twelve months. Behind the last page of the journal, she found an envelope labeled "Will & Testament of John James Abbott."

His will. She hadn't thought about whether he had a copy. Jimmy had told her she would inherit a third of his estate, her two sisters the other two-thirds, and this included his shares in the family business. He'd said once, she remembered now, that when he was sworn into the Senate, he turned his proxy for the voting shares over to Laurel, to distance himself from his financial interests while he was in office. She began to read.

It couldn't be right.

She read it again, and yet a third time.

She found Brady Cullifer's number in Jimmy's Rolodex and dialed. He'd just returned to his office from court and came on the line.

"Brady, I just read Jimmy's will. There's something very wrong here."

An hour later, she heard a car pull into the driveway. Not Jack—not yet. It was Brady, walking swiftly up the flagstone path to the house.

She met him at the front door.

"Rachael, I couldn't believe it when you called me. There must be some mistake here, there must be. I've brought the original will. We'll compare them, all right? Jack isn't back?"

"He'll be back soon. He's still at that meeting at the FBI."

Rachael spread the will she'd found on Jimmy's desktop. Brady lay his beside it. "Let's see what we've got here," he said, and the two of them bent down.

"Rachael? Where are you?"

Rachael straightened, a smile on her face. "In here, Sherlock. Come in." She walked over to the door to the study. "Hey, what are you doing here?"

"Jack asked me to come. What's going on? Oh, hello, Mr. Cullifer."

"It's Agent Sherlock, isn't it?"

Sherlock smiled at him, nodded.

Rachael grabbed Sherlock's arm. "I found Jimmy's will, only it doesn't say what it's supposed to say. I called Brady and he brought over the original so we could compare them."

"A forgery, Mr. Cullifer?"

"I don't know, Agent Sherlock. We've just begun to study them."

All three of them leaned over the desk to compare the two wills.

Sherlock read the first page and looked at them. "They're different, Mr. Cullifer. We've got a forgery here." She shook her head. "Wouldn't you know it? This was all about money. Why does it always have to be about money?"

She should have detected something in Cullifer's steady, monotonous voice, but she didn't until she tensed at a dark voice close to her ear. "Somedays I think the angels aren't on our side. You're very unexpected, Agent," and at the moment the last word sank into her brain, he struck her hard with the butt of his gun.

She heard Rachael yell as she fell to the floor.

"Stefanos! What—"

He struck Rachael, and watched dispassionately as her eyes went wide with shock, then blurred with pain, and closed, and she fell beside Sherlock. A trickle of blood snaked down her cheek.

FIFTY-EIGHT

Hoover Building

Savich frowned, lightly tapped his fingertips on his cell phone. "What's wrong?" Jack asked in a low voice, leaning close, momentarily blocking out the mellifluous voice of federal prosecutor Dickie Franks.

"Sherlock isn't answering. We have a deal. Anytime one of us calls the other, we always pick up, doesn't matter if we're in the shower or out running. Her phone's on, so she should answer. This is the second time I've called."

He was ready to seize up when Faith Hill sang out "The Way You Love Me." "Sherlock? It's about time, where—Dr. Bentley?"

Every eye at the conference table swiveled to look at Savich.

When he punched off his cell, Savich said, "That was Dr. Bentley. Greg Nichols was poisoned by a massive dose of superwarfarin, a rat poison. Dr. Bentley said there was still a lot of it in his bowels, so he may have ingested it with a recent meal, maybe the cioppino they talked about. Jack and I need to head out, find out who served him his lunch yesterday."

The three federal prosecutors began debating alternatives again. Dickie was saying, "I was thinking it's time we simply hauled the Abbotts' butts down here. We can handle their lawyers."

Janice Arden, the veteran of the three, said, "Or we could wait to see if Savich finds proof of who poisoned Nichols."

Savich wasn't listening. He was too worried. "Jack, try Rachael's cell phone."

"I did. She's not picking up."

"Try her landline."

There was no answer. Savich didn't say a word, simply dialed his own landline.

Again, no answer. "Sherlock said she might go over to see how Rachael was doing when I told her you and I would probably be late. I wanted coverage even though it's daylight. I was hoping maybe she brought Rachael back to our house." He drummed his fingers against the conference table. "Evidently not."

FIFTY-NINE

Sherlock didn't want to open her eyes. She knew if she did, she'd want to vomit, or pass out again from the god-awful pain, or both. *Well done, kiddo, you let the nice lawyer pull you right in with that will business. A civilian, no, less than a civilian—a lawyer.* But who had struck her? Stefanos, she thought—or Quincy—but there was Stefanos Kostas's face in her mind. She knew somehow it had been him, she could hear the echo of his voice. She'd been hit on the head before, a long time ago, really, but the pain was familiar, like an old enemy. She recognized it instantly, and hated it. *Don't open your eyes, let it stay dark a moment longer. Don't open your eyes.*

"Sherlock?"

Rachael's voice, far away—blurred, vague. She was alive, thank God. Sherlock wanted to forget she heard her, but her quiet voice came again. This time, she heard fear in it. "Sherlock. Please, wake up. Talk to me."

One eye opened, and Sherlock shuddered with the pain of it.

"I'm sorry, but you've been unconscious too long. Wake up, please wake up."

"Well, all right," Sherlock whispered, and opened both eyes. Flashing pain sliced through her head, and rising bile clogged her throat. She swallowed, still wanted to vomit, and swallowed again.

Rachael said, "I was nauseous, too, but it's almost gone now. At least I can control it. You will, too."

"Rachael?" Was that her voice? That thin little thread of sound?

"Yes, I'm right beside you. I woke up maybe five minutes ago. Are you all right?"

Now that was a joke. "Yes, but give me another moment."

"We're both tied up."

"Yes." Sherlock felt the ropes digging into her wrists. They'd tied her ankles, too, but around her slacks, so there was some protection. "Brady Cullifer," she said, "he's a real showman—all that concern about your father's will. He staged it like a pro, sucked me in like a raw rookie. I'm sorry, Rachael, I didn't protect either of us."

"Stefanos Kostas hit you."

"I know. I wasn't fast enough."

"I'm the lousy judge of character here. I trusted Brady completely," Rachael said. "He seemed to like me, right from the beginning, and he'd worked for Jimmy for at least two decades. Jimmy trusted him, felt he was completely loyal."

She sighed. "I never believed for a second he was involved. I liked him so much, he was so comforting, so sympathetic. It's beginning to look like every single person Jimmy introduced me to is involved in this thing. And Brady Cullifer's in the thick of it. He sucked Jack in, too."

"Yes, he got all of us. I wonder where we are?"

"I woke up briefly. Before I went under again I realized we were moving, in a car.

I think we were stuffed in a trunk. This room is too dark to see much of anything, so I don't know where we are. Has Brady brought us to his office? His house?"

Sherlock heard voices. "Keep quiet. Play dead."

A door opened and light speared into the dark.

"Looks like they're still out," Stefanos said, and came down on his knees. He placed two fingers against the pulses in their necks. "Strong. They're not dead."

Laurel said, "All right, then. They're alive, no bullet wounds or injuries, we can go through with what we discussed. It will be an auto accident. It is too bad, though, that we now have to deal with this damned FBI agent, as well."

Stefanos said, "I didn't have a choice. But we're good at this. We'll stage it just like Nichols and I did with Jimmy."

"I'm not a murderer," Cullifer said, his voice suddenly austere. "Stefanos struck both of them down. I helped bring them here as you asked. You can deal with them as you choose."

Laurel laughed. "So you draw the line at slipping barbiturates into Rachael's wine?

You didn't think she was supposed to die? We will all deal with this, Brady, and don't forget that. You're certain that the real will the senator made is now in his papers?"

"Yes, everything's as it should be."

Laurel said, "Not ideal, but at least there will be no smoking gun for the FBI to discover when Rachael and the FBI agent are found dead in an automobile accident."

Quincy said, "I still can't believe we're ending up leaving Jimmy's will to be found there and not our own version. After all that's happened, we'll have nothing at all to show for this, not majority control, not even a way to prevent an audit. I still think we should leave our version of his will. Why not? I mean, everyone can be suspicious, wonder why Jimmy didn't leave anything to his adopted daughter, but what can they do?"

"We've been through this," Brady said. "I was very particular in my wording, emphasizing it was his father's deepest wish that all stock remain in his children's hands. But now—"

Laurel said impatiently, "But now having our version of the will surface would be like waving a red flag at the FBI and confessing our guilt. Look, Quincy, all the stock will go to our two nieces and Rachael's family. Yes, it's a damned tragedy to have to deal with people like that, but perhaps we can buy them out. It will cost us, admittedly, but at least the will the FBI will undoubtedly find won't be our forgery. They can prove nothing about the senator. They can prove nothing about Greg Nichols. As for Rachael, we've been extremely fortunate. We will be harassed, but I don't see how they'll be able to indict us. We will salvage this mess yet. Rachael has given us a golden opportunity. We will use it. Then we can go back to our lives, the nightmare behind us."

It had nothing to do with my father's confession. Sherlock was right, it was about money the whole time, money and control of the company. Unfortunately for them, I didn't die. When I showed up with the FBI, they knew they were in deep trouble.

Rachael managed not to move when someone toed her in the ribs. Quincy's voice came from above her. "I can't believe this damned girl survived. I'll tell you, I thought it was all over when she showed up with the FBI."

Keep it down, dammit, keep it down. But it wouldn't stay down, wouldn't— Rachael sneezed.

"Well now, look who was playing possum," Quincy said. "You trying to be cute, too?" He kicked Sherlock hard in the side. Her breath whooshed out at the sharp blow. "Come on, Agent Sherlock, time to rise and shine, as my nanny used to say." He drew back his foot again.

"Leave her alone," Rachael shouted as she struggled to sit up. "Don't, Quincy."

Laurel stared down at her. "You didn't drown. Perky showed me the nice stout ropes, the block of concrete, and yet you still managed to get free, even full of those barbiturates. Imagine Quincy's surprise when he went to the senator's house to make certain everything was set. Pity he didn't have time to get to you before you drove off."

"I guess you and Perky screwed up, or whichever one of you was with her at Black Rock Lake. But it didn't matter much, did it?" Rachael said. "You found me fast enough."

"It took a bit of research to turn up that backwoods town Parlow, but you managed to survive that, too," Laurel said.

It was difficult to be conciliatory—no, it was impossible. Rachael was filled to overflowing with hatred. She looked up at Laurel, her coarse hair haloed in the light. "Greg Nichols didn't survive. You appear to be getting better at poisoning people."

Quincy kicked her in the ribs.

Rachael saw Cullifer move back to stand in the doorway. Was he afraid of what he'd done?

Laurel dropped to her knees beside Rachael, grabbed her by her long hair, wrapped it around her fist, and jerked her head up. "How did you get out of Black Rock Lake? All of us were surprised, particularly Stefanos and Perky, who were sure you were dead."

Why not tell her? It didn't matter. "Stefanos and Perky didn't tie my wrists, only wrapped the rope around my chest. And they didn't bother to check me out, Laurel. I was awake, and I can hold my breath for a good long time."

Laurel reared back a bit, and a hank of hair fell alongside her cheek. She brushed it back, shook her head. "Bad luck, it was just bad luck."

"And bad luck that two of the assassins

you sent after me are dead, and two others are headed straight to jail, once they get out of the hospital. I don't think I'd want to work for you, Laurel, even with a good life insurance plan."

Laurel struck Rachael across the mouth. She felt her lip split, felt the blood well up and dribble down her chin.

Laurel screamed at her, "Shut up! Now, you look at me, you miserable whelp. Damn you, you look like the senator, don't you? How he loved that stupid braid you wear. It makes you look like a teenage hooker." She shoved Rachael onto her back, and rose.

Stefanos closed his hand over her shoulder. His voice softened. "Don't let her get to you, Laurel. It's all right. We won't have to worry about her any longer. Her luck's finally run out."

Sherlock's cell vibrated in her jacket pocket. She tensed, but managed not to move. If there was only some way she could open her cell phone, but she couldn't. Not yet. Was it Dillon? Had he tried before, while she was unconscious? If he did, he had to be worried.

"You might as well drag them into the

living room, Stef, get ready to go. Quincy, make sure the windows are shut and the drapes pulled."

Quincy asked, his voice contemptuous, "Tell me, Stefanos, when did you last use this hidden bordello of yours?"

Stefanos said, sounding amused, "A good week now, Quincy, a good week. You know you love the decor, don't be shy about it."

Being dragged about thirty feet into the living room hurt, but that was all right; it wasn't as bad as the alternative. Rachael's stomach ached from the blow from Quincy's foot. She looked over at Sherlock, who lay on her back, her eyes closed, and, it seemed to Rachael, barely breathing. Then Sherlock's eyes opened and she blinked in the bright light. They weren't at Cullifer's office or at his house. They were in a bungalow that indeed resembled a bordello, just as Quincy had said—Stefanos Kostas's hideaway for his many mistresses?

The living room walls were covered with flocked red velvet wallpaper, gold brocade draperies over the window. They were lying on a Persian carpet beside four chaise longues and large deep chairs.

It was tacky, Rachael thought, and called out, "I'm very thirsty. Could I have some water, please?"

She was ignored.

Sherlock said, "You poisoned Greg Nichols, didn't you? You didn't trust him anymore?"

Stefanos threw back his head and laughed. "You were awake the whole time we were talking, weren't you? Well, it doesn't matter. Actually, Nichols planned how to kill his boss. He approached us to talk about the senator. He was more than willing to buy in since he didn't want to go to jail with the senator, have his own life ruined. I went along for the ride since Nichols already knew everything he had to do to make it look like an accident. Then the fool lost it after you and Agent Crowne went to see him, Rachael. You must have really scared him. He whined how everything was crashing down, and he knew we were all going to jail. He wanted to leave town. He wanted money, can you believe that? Well, he left town all right, didn't he?"

Laurel walked to her husband, put her arms around him, and kissed his cheek. "That was well done, Stef."

Stef? Laurel called her philandering husband *Stef*?

His arms went around her. "It will be all right, *matia mou*," Stefanos said, and kissed her hair. "I always snip loose threads."

"And why not?" Laurel said, eyeing both of them impartially. "Does everyone agree? We can't have an FBI agent disappear. Agent Savich would never let that go, never. It would have been hard enough to have Rachael disappear. Our only choice now is an auto accident, fitting, I think, particularly for Rachael."

Quincy nodded.

Stefanos stepped away from his wife and pulled a small blunt-nosed .38 from his jacket pocket. "Ladies, we will untie your feet. You will stand up and we will go out to Agent Sherlock's car. You needn't concern yourselves about anything else." He turned to his wife. "I believe we'll drive to those cliffs near where Rachael's father died. There's never much traffic there, even this time of day."

"Yes, that's good. Let Brady help," Laurel said.

Quincy said, "Brady must have slipped out, the shitty little coward."

"No matter," Stefanos said, and smiled at Rachael and Sherlock. "We don't have to worry about Brady. He has a very strong sense of self-preservation."

SIXTY

Dillon shut MAX's top and rose. He said, "Excuse me, sir, but Agent Crowne and I have to go. There's trouble."

He and Jack were halfway to the conference room door when Maitland called out, "But, Savich, where are you going? What happened?"

"Sherlock's in trouble," Savich said over his shoulder, never slowing. "MAX helped me track down her cell phone GPS coordinates."

"But how do you know she's in trouble?"

There was no answer because Savich and Jack were gone. Savich roared out of the Hoover Building garage, only to hit the afternoon traffic on Pennsylvania Avenue. The Porsche preferred to fly, but Savich also knew how to skim around other cars, slip in and out whenever there was a sliver of an opening. Too many people, Savich thought, and turned onto Seventh Street and picked up some speed as they passed the National Mall. He caught Pennsylvania Avenue again, heading toward the Potomac, and crossed the John Philip Sousa Bridge at a crawl, but was soon speeding north on 295, the Baltimore-Washington Parkway still light with commuters.

"Looks like we're heading to Hailstone," Savich said. "Eighteen minutes, if traffic stays light and the cops stay away."

"I can't believe she and Rachael are at Stefanos's mansion. Why? How'd they get from Rachael's house to Hailstone, Maryland?"

"We'll find out. Jack, have one of our people check out Rachael's house, see if her Charger and Sherlock's Volvo are there. Is your seat belt fastened?" There was a break in traffic and Savich let the Porsche hit one hundred miles an hour, smooth as a slide of silk.

Jack nodded and used his cell phone.

A clear stretch ahead. Savich hit the hammer. The Porsche glided to 110, passed a speeding Cadillac. Savich saw the guy's white face flash by.

A black Ferrari danced with them for a mile or two, then let them go, Savich smoothly pulling around it. The driver sent Savich a look of surprise and a thumbs-up.

Traffic thickened up and the Porsche growled back down to sixty. "They got both Rachael and Sherlock, Savich, you know they did. But how? Sherlock's more careful than the Secret Service." *What are they going to do to them*? But he didn't ask that, his jaw locked so tight he couldn't get the words out. "Why now? In the middle of the day? It's a huge risk. What happened to make them move now?"

The Porsche ate up the miles. Savich said, "Jack, I've never believed people like Laurel Kostas wouldn't commit murder based on strong emotions. Everything has happened so quickly, we never really thought this through. I don't buy they murdered the senator because he was going to talk, even harder to believe they were trying to murder Rachael because she was going to confess what her father did. It simply isn't enough of a motive. And then even after she's with us and they know we must know everything, they still tried to get to her, broke into her house. It doesn't make sense."

Jack said slowly, "Okay, if the guy who broke into the house wasn't there to kill her, then why was he there?"

Savich said, "Money."

Jack said, his eyes locked on the highway ahead, at the blur of cars, "All right, something to do with money. But what?"

"I have a feeling we're going to find out right now."

The Porsche's sexy female GPS voice told them the Hailstone exit was in 3.2 miles. "Good, good," Savich said like a mantra. "Almost there. We'll make it in a couple of minutes."

Savich took the exit in a tight, controlled turn. After another right turn onto Nimere Avenue into the town of Hailstone, he said, "Rachael said her father left her a third of his estate, including the company stock and the house." He smacked his palm on the steering wheel. "Why is that worth so much to them?"

"Maybe it's about control of the Abbott empire," Jack said.

The Porsche took a left on Clapton Road as smooth as spreading butter, doing sixty.

Jack said, "Wait, the Kostas mansion is back to the right. Where are we going?"

The GPS announced the location was 0.5 miles ahead.

"I don't know," Savich said.

An old gray Chrysler pulled onto the road directly in front of the Porsche.

SIXTY-ONE

Laurel said, "Just a moment, Stef." She looked down at Rachael. "Tell me why you didn't make the senator's grand confession for him last night when you had the perfect chance."

Quincy said, "That's clear enough, Laurel. She finally realized she'd be considered a traitor to her father, and her idea for that damned foundation she wants to run would be trashed."

Keep them talking, keep them talking. Rachael saw it in Sherlock's eyes, and so she said, "No, none of that. Fact is, Aunt Laurel, I decided that only Jimmy could make public a revelation with such far-reaching consequences. His decision, no one else's."

"Are you telling the truth?" Quincy asked her.

"I'm lying here at your feet. Why would I lie?"

Suddenly tears appeared in Laurel's eyes. The prison matron was suddenly remorseful about murdering her brother? *Tears?* Rachael stared at her. What was going on here?

Laurel said, "It means I didn't fail. And do you know, I'd already accepted that I had? I despised you so much, Rachael. Daddy would never have forgiven me if you had spoken out. Never. He believed there was never any excuse for failure."

Daddy? Her father? That profane old man who took my father from my mother? But he was dead, months and months dead, dead before they murdered Jimmy. *Daddy?*

"That old bastard," Quincy said. "How did he even find out what Jimmy did? I didn't have a clue until Jimmy told us." Quincy banged his fist against his palm.

"Dammit, he should have told me, too. I

was his loyal son. I stayed, didn't go haring off to the damned Senate. I was the son who did whatever he asked. Damned old bastard."

Rachael and Sherlock barely breathed.

"Calm yourself, Quincy. Daddy never told me how he found out about it," Laurel said. "I do know he had Jimmy followed now and again, had detectives check on him. He liked to know where all the pieces were on the chessboard—you know that was always his way. Plus, he was very angry that Jimmy ignored all his ideas for new legislation."

"Stop your whining, Quincy," Stefanos said. "It is really unattractive, doesn't go well at all with your patrician image."

"Shut your trap, you suck-up—"

Stefanos laughed. "Is that envy I hear?"

Quincy shouted, "Envy of what? That the old man invented your image to suit himself and his own purposes, and you let him?"

Stefanos said, "I always thought it was one of your father's better ideas."

Sherlock was working the knots at her wrists. *Please, let them keep talking, let them thrash it all out, go for each other's throats, for all I care. Three more minutes, that should do it.* She worked until her wrists were raw and she felt the sting and wet of her own blood but it didn't matter. They'd found her ankle holster and taken her Lady Colt, but they hadn't searched her inner jacket pocket with its single Kleenex and her Swiss Army knife.

Quincy said, "Yeah, right, making a fool of Laurel for fifteen years! I never liked it. I knew what people were saying about you behind their hands. But Father used to laugh when he'd hear gossip about your mistresses, about your barhopping, your partying with hookers in this little bungalow, not even five minutes from where you lived with my sister. Did you laugh with him, Laurel?"

She said, her voice light, "I've always loved the theater."

Sherlock felt her cell vibrate again. Dillon, it had to be Dillon. He'd come, she knew he'd come.

Stefanos turned to Rachael, smiled down at her. "You have no idea what he's talking about, do you?"

"I only know you're a philandering jerk."

Laurel said, "But that's only what everyone was supposed to believe. Stefanos's reputation as a womanizer—that was my father's idea. He got a real kick out of building that reputation for my dear Stef."

Stefanos picked it up. "It worked to our advantage, what with business associates believing I was nothing more than a simple-minded playboy he'd bought for Laurel. I got so many of those old jackasses to invite me to their weekend retreats where they paraded their mistresses about, talked openly about the women they were screwing, about this business expansion or that merger. They couldn't imagine I was a threat to them. All the booze, the sex, the stupid schemes. I recorded all of it, even managed to videotape some of it when those old codgers came over to my own little place here. They loved all the red velvet. They never saw the cameras. The old man was very pleased. He enjoyed watching the films I made."

Laurel said with a smirk. "Business took a marked upswing."

"I haven't done so much of that now that

the old man's dead," Stefanos said. "It was getting tiresome."

Laurel said, "Before Daddy became really ill that last time, he told me what Jimmy had done. He asked me to promise I would never allow anyone to find out. He was worried because he said Jimmy had this tender girl's conscience, he hated to say it out loud since Jimmy was his oldest son, but the truth was the truth. He'd bred a weakling. Jimmy had all our mother's flaws. It shamed him."

"Dammit, Laurel, our old man was nuts. You know what else? I think he turned on Jimmy when he broke away to run for the Senate. You know why—it was Jimmy's idea, not his. He hated that he couldn't control Jimmy, hated that Jimmy wouldn't do what he told him to."

"It doesn't matter," Laurel said. "Not now. When he was dying, he asked me again to promise, to accept it as my responsibility. And so I did."

Quincy said, "And look where that's led. Jimmy's dead. Greg Nichols is dead. These two bitches will shortly be dead, and we're fighting for our lives here."

A lot of bodies piling up around you, aren't there, Laurel? Rachael held very, very still.

Stefanos looked at his wife's white face. "The promise you made to your father was honorable, Laurel. As to what he really was, it no longer matters, just as you said. It's only us now, and we will do what we must to survive. To win."

Laurel said, passion thick in her voice, "Daddy mattered. He mattered more than anyone." She walked over to Rachael and went down on her knees beside her. "After Daddy died, your mother thought she could cash in at last, make her move, and so she sent you to the senator, and that ridiculous fool decided you were a gift from the gods."

"He adopted the bitch," Quincy said. "I couldn't believe he did that, and so fast."

"Yes, well, Jimmy never cared about money, now did he?" She looked up at her brother. "In the end, he didn't care about the family, either. He became a threat to us." She touched her fingers to Rachael's cheek. "And now you will die in a car accident, just like he did, and we will survive."

Laurel got slowly to her feet, strode over to where Stefanos was standing next to the fireplace. Without her shoes, she looked smaller, a frumpy, heavyset matron in fishnet stockings. She looked tired, old, her lipstick long gone, a spiky band of coarse hair hanging along her cheek.

Stefanos took her hand, kissed it, then smoothed his thumbs over her eyebrows. "All will be well now, *matia mou*. Quincy and I will take the ladies to the agent's car and send them on their final journey. The FBI will howl and bitch, but what can they do? They have no proof against us. They have suppositions, they have a wish list, but nothing our lawyers can't handle."

Stefanos turned to look at Rachael and Sherlock. A dark brow went up. "Time to see if there's an afterlife, ladies," he said, and raised his .38.

SIXTY-TWO

Savich saw the woman's deathly white face the instant before he would have slammed into the driver's side of her Chrysler. He turned the Porsche's steering wheel hard to the left, pumped the brake, fed in a bit of gas, and that magnificent machine responded perfectly, but the road simply wasn't wide enough.

The Porsche came to a stop, the front wheels dangling over a ditch.

The ancient Chrysler slowly moved forward again. Savich looked up to see the woman give him the finger. He laughed, couldn't help it.

Jack was cursing as he opened his door and looked out. "Well, the damned ditch is only six feet deep. We've got to get the Porsche out of here fast, Savich."

Savich carefully opened the driver's door and eased out. "Stay put, Jack, we're a bit wobbly." He dialed 9ll, asked for immediate assistance. He punched off, punched in Sherlock's cell. She didn't answer. He looked around, watched at least six cars roll by, people looking, but nobody stopped. Savich raised his face. "Where's a cop when you need one?"

Time, Jack thought, time was running out. Savich dialed Sherlock's cell once again.

There was no answer.

SIXTY-THREE

Rachael said, "There's something I don't understand. When you broke into my house, you weren't there to kill me, were you? I mean, there was no reason any longer. You took a huge risk."

Stefanos said, "We needed to replace the forged will with the will the senator had made and told you about. When we believed you dead in Black Rock Lake, disappeared forever, it was all much simpler. The forged will was in place—with no mention of you. You know the rest of it. We had to salvage what we could. We had to protect ourselves. But it didn't work out, did it? Why the hell did you scream? I was no-where near you."

Rachael said, "I was having a drowning nightmare, thanks to all of you."

The ropes on Sherlock's wrists split apart. Her wrists hurt, her hands were numb.

She didn't look at Rachael. It was all on her, no one else.

Stefanos said, "All right, no more talk. Quincy, let's get this over with. We'll haul them out to the car. Don't you move, Agent, or I'll kill you here." And he raised his .38.

When he bent over to grab Sherlock's feet, she kicked him hard in the chest. He couldn't yell, he had no breath. He fell backward, grabbing his chest, and the .38 flew out of his hand. Sherlock flipped open her Swiss Army knife and sliced through the ropes on her ankles in a sin-gle motion.

She heard the .38 hit the carpet but didn't know where it landed. There wasn't enough time. Quincy was on her, yelling, hitting her, then his hands were around her neck. She sent the back of her hand into his Adam's apple. Quincy fell back, gagging, clutching his throat.

Sherlock rolled over to Rachael, flicked the knife over the ropes tying her ankles, then sliced through the ropes on her wrists.

Laurel was moving, fast, but Sherlock didn't stop, she couldn't stop.

"That will be quite enough."

Rachael was finally free. They both looked to see Laurel holding Stefanos's .38. Sherlock said right in Rachael's face, "Get out of here. Now." She rolled upright and threw her knife at Laurel.

The knife went deep into Laurel's shoulder and she screamed.

"You bitch." Tears streamed down her face as blood flowed down her chest. Laurel made a strange growling sound, and pulled the trigger.

Sherlock felt the sharp punch of the bullet. She wanted to pull the knife out of Laurel's shoulder and slam it into her black heart. But she knew she couldn't do it. She was on her knees, couldn't seem to stand. She stared at Laurel, and fell onto her side.

Was that Rachael yelling? At Laurel? "You bloody bitch! That's it, I've had it with you, do you hear me?" She heard a door slam in the distance, fast footsteps, heard a struggle, then Rachael screaming, "I've got the gun! Quincy, Stefanos, don't you two move! No, wait, *move*—I want to wipe you off the face of the earth! You murdering bastards, you murdered my father!"

Even though she couldn't move, Sherlock heard the sound of men's voices, then Quincy yelling. Why? Maybe to save himself from Rachael?

Sherlock smiled. One of the men's voices was Dillon's. He'd taken his time, but he was here now. Finally he was here. She heard Rachael shouting, heard Dillon's voice, quiet and close. Everything was all right now.

She felt cold suddenly, but it didn't matter. Dillon would see to things. She closed her eyes and let her brain shut down.

SIXTY-FOUR

Savich lightly rubbed his fingers along her palm. He hated that her beautiful hand was limp, the flesh flaccid. But he'd put cream on her hands and they were soft. *Two days, two whole days since that crazy woman shot you. Two days, but at least you'll live. I've prayed so much I'll bet God has closed down the switchboard. Do you know how close Laurel came to killing you? Jack was squeezing your side so tight you're still bruised.*

Savich looked up to see Mr. Maitland standing quietly in the doorway.

"The pain was pretty sharp so they gave

her some more morphine," Savich said. "She's out. Before she closed her eyes, she asked me if she'd gotten Stefanos's ribs. I told her three of them were busted, that he was hurting pretty bad. She said her aim with her Swiss Army knife wasn't what you'd call real accurate—small wonder since it isn't made for throwing. I told her Laurel wasn't feeling too hot, either, and wasn't it better that she'd stand trial and lose everything?

"Then she told me she really doesn't need her spleen. I agreed. What was a spleen in the face of all the problems in the world? She was out again before she could laugh."

Both of them considered this.

Maitland said, "We've got Brady Cullifer in a stylish orange jump-suit in a nice cell. He's demanding to make a deal, ready and willing to roll big on Quincy, Stefanos, and Laurel because he claims he never killed anyone. The prosecutors—particularly Dickie—want him to sweat big-time before they offer him anything."

Savich said after a moment, "That shoot-up we had in the Barnes & Noble in Georgetown—Sherlock was so angry at me because Perky could have killed me. To preserve my marriage, I let her throw me around at the gym."

He sighed. "Now, look at her, flat on her back, minus her spleen, and I'm the wreck."

"It's over now, everyone's alive, and all your agents are working double to cover your cases for you. We've got auditors going over all the Abbott corporation books. Be interesting to see what we find."

Savich thought about it for a moment, then said, "There's something I should tell you about the senator." And Savich did, every detail of what happened eighteen months before.

Maitland said, "Thank you for telling me, Savich." He sighed. "I know none of us want it, but it's going to come out anyway at the trial. Hell of a thing. I am sorry about all of it."

There was a light rap on the door. A nurse stuck her head in. "Agent Savich? Your mother-in-law begged me to come in and pull you out of here so she can see her daughter."

Savich kissed Sherlock's mouth, straightened, and said, "Okay, she can have five minutes."

The nurse smiled at him.

Maitland said, "They're all here—your mom, your boy, your sister, your in-laws from San Francisco, half the unit. I wonder when Director Mueller will show up. We even have some media. No, don't worry, we'll deal with them when the time comes."

Maitland closed a big hand on Savich's shoulder. "When Sherlock wakes up, you've got to bring Sean in to see her. He's scared, but he's doing okay." He looked back at Sherlock. Her brilliant red hair spilled onto the white pillowcase, but her face was still pale, too pale.

He wondered when Savich was going to tell her that Sean's terrier had chewed up her best and only pair of fancy high heels, the ones she'd worn at the Jefferson Club.

SIXTY-FIVE

Jamaica
Four days later

Savich and Jack made their way along the limestone cliffs to the narrow promontory where a man wearing baggy shorts, sneakers, and a Redskins T-shirt sat next to a mango tree, his arms around his knees, staring out over the water.

The spot wasn't civilized and touristy like Negril, the closest town. The air smelled wild, the winds blew fiercely, the land baked hot and dry, and the cliffs rose a good seventy feet above the blue blue water that dashed against black rocks below, spewing white foam upward, the sound mesmerizing.

He didn't move, didn't say anything, didn't acknowledge them when Savich sat down on one side of him, Jack on the other next to an ackee tree, although they both knew he'd heard them coming over the loose rubble that crumbled toward the cliff.

He said, "I wondered when someone would come. Are you CIA or what?"

"I'm Special Agent Savich, FBI, and this is Special Agent Jack Crowne."

The man still didn't move. He said, "Tourists dive off the cliffs at Negril, but not here. All those rocks below, sticking up like black teeth, and there are more hidden below the surface. They'd tear the flesh off your bones even if you managed to miss the others."

Savich looked at the young man's profile, dark complexion, thick straight black hair, a nice, wholesome-looking man who resembled his father, but he couldn't be completely sure because they hadn't yet seen him full face.

Savich said, "We haven't told your father and mother that you're alive and well and living in Jamaica."

Jean David Barbeau finally turned to

face him. He did indeed look a great deal like his father, but, unlike his father, he didn't look ghastly pale from grief, his dark eyes weren't desolate and empty. He looked calm, almost indifferent, as if he didn't care they were there, and it was all over for him. He said, "How did you find me?"

Jack said, "Since your body was never found, I started thinking about the speedboat that rammed the boat you and your father were in, and why was it there exactly. The reports stated the boat's name was *River Beast.* I checked into it and discovered the owner had a nephew who attended Harvard with you. Don't think he rolled on you easily. We brought young financial analyst David Caldicott to the fifth floor of the FBI building, scared the crap out of him, and he finally admitted that he'd helped you stage your suicide."

Jean David said, "David called me last night, told me how you threatened him, his parents, said he had to, no choice. He was sorry."

"I know," Jack said. "We gave him the phone."

Jean David's head whipped up at that. "Why?"

Savich said, "To triangulate your location. We wanted to know if you really were where Caldicott said you were."

Jack said, "We found out you have a passport under your mother's maiden name. You used it to come here, the day after you tried to kill Dr. MacLean in Washington Memorial Hospital."

"I was afraid you'd accuse my father of that."

"Didn't fit," Savich said. "You're a young man, you move like a young man, and your father isn't a young man and no way could he move the way you did on the hospital security video. You had us chasing our tails there for a while, but then again, you're quite the student of strategy, aren't you, Jean David?"

His laugh was ironic. "Yeah, that's me, the strategic expert. I always was smart; people used to tell me so in school and at the CIA. My bosses were grooming me because of my brain, but I'll tell you, when it came to what was really important to me, my brain didn't count a damn."

"You're talking about Anna Radcliff," Savich said.

"Yes, Anna."

"Her real name is Halimah Rahman, not Anna," Savich said.

"No, damn you, her name is Anna. That bastard MacLean told you her name, didn't he? And that's how you got her."

Savich said, "Dr. MacLean said your father had mentioned an Anna. It wasn't difficult to find her and a half dozen of her terrorist friends."

Jean David's voice shook a bit. "If only she'd listened to me. I told her Dr. MacLean was blabbing about us. I told her she had to leave the country. I swore I'd join her, but she didn't leave."

He looked off into the distance, but Jack didn't think he was admiring the Caribbean. Jean David said, "You know, I still think of her as Anna. That's how she introduced herself to me in that coffeehouse in Cambridge." He gave a sharp laugh, pointed to the single petrel swooping down to the surface of the water. "I know her real name is Halimah, but to me she will always be Anna. She confided in me, praised me, was *interested* in me, interested in what I thought. And she was so damned beautiful. I fell for her, fell hard. The sex was great, but you know, it was how she spoke to me, how she listened to me, laughed with me, admired everything I said. I fell completely in love with her."

He turned to look at a huge cormorant that had entered the scene, not six feet from the petrel, hovering a dozen feet above the water, lazily scouting lunch. He spotted a surface fish and dove clean and straight. "I've watched him before," Jean David said. "He's really good. He's smart. See, that's a wrasse he's got. He never misses."

"Your parents are a mess," Savich said. "As Agent Crowne said, we haven't told them you're alive."

"Yes, well, I did what I could, now didn't I? My father was planning to send me into hiding, God only knows where. He kept making excuses for me, saying it wasn't my fault, it was this evil woman's fault, and what did it matter anyway since it was only a bit of American intelligence gone awry. I'm French, he said, who cares?

"But I know my parents, particularly my mother. The disgrace would have been more than she could bear. Hell, I couldn't deal with it, either." He shrugged.

Jack said, "You're saying you tried to kill

Dr. MacLean to keep him from talking about Anna?"

Jean David laughed. "Finally, something you've got all wrong. Those two attempted hit-and-runs, and the bomb on his plane, I didn't do those things, I wouldn't know how. It was Anna's associates, as she called them. Like I said, Anna didn't leave the country. She and her friends were doing well here. They believed they could contain any fallout, and so they started off by killing that friend of Dr. MacLean's. They found out about him because they were already following Dr. MacLean."

"Anna told you that?" Savich asked.

"She told me everything. Then you arrested her, and she was gone from me, forever. I guess I went nuts. Those guys had three chances to get MacLean and failed. I wasn't going to fail. But I did. You know, I couldn't believe that nurse shot me.

"By then I'd already staged my own suicide, of course, to solve the CIA's problem, my parents' problem, my problem. Everyone would be happy. Using Caldicott's speedboat was the only weak point in the plan, but I had no choice. I had to hope the authorities wouldn't doubt what had happened and dig too deep. They didn't. But you did."

Savich said, "Telling your father you were going to kill yourself, that was an excellent touch. You were gone, your parents were safe."

There was surprise on Jean David's face. "You got my father to admit I killed myself? I thought he'd go to the grave with that."

Savich nodded. "He was devastated, he no longer cared about much of anything because his only son was dead. He saw no reason not to tell me. Your mother, however, didn't want him to."

Jean David shrugged. "It was better with me dead than standing trial as a traitor. Trust me on that.

"As for my life, it was over once you took Anna. She is the only woman I have ever loved. I'll bet you've got her jailed and being interrogated as a terrorist in some place like Guantanamo."

"She is a terrorist," Jack said. "What's even better is we got her whole group along with her."

"Yeah, well, I love her. All I wanted to do was kill the man responsible but I even failed at that. I saved myself but I couldn't save her." Jean David fell silent, watching two pelicans follow in the cormorant's trail. He said finally, "I understand that if it wasn't for you, Agent Crowne, MacLean would already have died, scattered in a hundred pieces in the Appalachians."

"Both of us would be," Jack said.

Jean David whirled around to face him. "Dammit, my parents were his *friends*! He betrayed all of us." He gave a harsh laugh and threw a pebble over the cliff. "I should have been the one to execute him, but I didn't. I even told Anna I wanted to kill him, but she said I wasn't trained, I'd fail. As if training made a bit of difference when her friends tried to kill him.

"But she was right. And would you look what happened—that corrupt bastard killed himself. I wonder if he saw any irony in that. After all, he believed that I'd killed myself."

Jean David spat onto the rock just beyond his toe. "He knew me nearly all my life. Damn him, I was fond of him. Do you know he even visited me at college when I was a freshman? Just to see how I was doing, he said." He struck his fist against his thigh. "I tell you, he deserved to die, deserved it. That trip to the hospital to kill him, I knew that was crazy. I knew it even as I was doing it, tried to talk myself out of it even as I walked up the stairs to his floor. But there was Anna's face in my mind, and I knew I'd do it anyway." He kicked a rock with his foot. "It turns out vengeance isn't all it's cracked up to be."

Savich said, "Do you know why Dr. Mac-Lean killed himself?"

Jean David picked up a pebble and tossed it from hand to hand. More cormorants flew in and swooped down to the water for lunch. He said absently, "These guys prefer the bigger fish, like snapper, but they'll take wrasse. I guess Dr. MacLean killed himself because he finally realized he was to blame for all this misery, realized he didn't deserve to live."

That was close enough, Jack thought. Why bother to waste his breath explaining about the disease that had robbed MacLean of himself? Jean David undoubtedly already knew about it, and didn't believe it, or didn't care.

Savich reached out and grabbed Jean David's arm.

He winced. Savich dropped his arm. "It got infected, didn't it, but it's better now. You saw a Dr. Rodrigo in Montego Bay. He said you left it until it was nearly too late."

"Yes, it's better, but who cares?"

Jack said, "Did you know Dr. MacLean was also a longtime friend of my family?"

Jean David said, "I don't suppose he tried to ruin you and your family, too?"

"Well, you see, I didn't betray my country and refuse to take responsibility for it."

Jean David twisted around to face him. "Look, I know you're thinking I'm a selfish asshole. I'm not sorry about Dr. MacLean, but believe me, I regret passing secure information on to Anna because of what she did with it, sorry about all of it. But I did it, so anything I say comes across as a pitiful excuse, as self-serving, as meaningless to anyone who counts."

Jack said, his voice emotionless, "It seems you were ready and willing to risk the lives of any number of people. I wonder how many more CIA operatives have died and will die because of the information you passed to your girlfriend.

"This woman you claim you love—she

is a terrorist. She kills people. Her name isn't Anna, it's Halimah. She's a Syrian fundamentalist. She's been trained to seduce young men, to use them. She used you, played you to perfection. What she gave you was a fantasy, and you bought into it. Love? It wasn't ever about love, and you should know that by now.

"You're not only an asshole, Jean David, you're pretty stupid. Talk about letting a woman lead you around by your dick. Aren't you done with that?"

After a moment of acid silence, Savich said, "But you'll always be smart to your parents, Jean David—their beloved, precious son who was seduced into making a few bad judgments. I don't think they'll ever allow themselves to accept that their son is responsible for the loss of countless innocent people."

Jean David said, "One of the excuses my father made for me was that I couldn't be a traitor to this country—I was only born here by accident, after all. No, France is my country, and I owe my allegiance only to France.

"The thing is, he's dead wrong. Hell, I'm a Redskins fan. America is my country. I would never have done what I did on purpose." He sighed. "I don't suppose it matters now. You want to take me back, don't you?"

"Yes," Jack said. "We do."

He was fast. Savich managed to grab his Redskins shirt, but it was so old, it ripped off him. He saw the white bandage on his arm as Jean David Barbeau leaped off the high limestone cliffs on the far west coast of Jamaica. He didn't make a sound.

Savich was breathing hard, shocked and furious that he'd let him get away from him. He and Jack stood at the edge of the cliff. They saw him floating facedown seventy feet below.

"Do you think he hit those hidden rocks?"

Savich said, "I don't think it matters."

"His parents," Jack said. "They're going to be destroyed all over again."

"Only if they find out about it. Let's retrieve his body, see how we can get him buried here in Jamaica, and try to keep what happened here from getting back to them."

He heard a loud squawk. Savich looked at the group of cormorants hovering some fifty feet above Jean David's body. They hovered a moment, then winged their way out over the Caribbean.

Savich turned to Jack. "It's odd, isn't it, how both these cases involved obsessions with family honor and family shame. So much needless tragedy."

"No, not in this case," Jack said slowly, looking down at Jean David's body, waves pushing it back and forth against the black rocks. His body would be torn to shreds, he knew, and he didn't care. "I think it's about a spoiled young man who found out he wasn't as smart as he thought he was."

"All right, let's get this done." Savich pulled out his cell phone and called the local police captain.

EPILOGUE

It was a fine day in Slipper Hollow. By count, nearly half the population of Parlow, Kentucky, had made the five-mile trip to a place few of them had even known about a few short months before.

It certainly wasn't at all hidden now. There'd been a two-dozen-car caravan driving the two-lane road, winding and turning back on itself, trees pressing in on all sides, mountains hovering, then, all of a sudden, there was a wide turnoff to the right onto another, narrower road, beautifully paved and landscaped with bushes and flowers on both sides. It was a very wide driveway, really, and it led to a beautiful hollow of land in the midst of which sat a magnificent house, built almost entirely by Gillette Janes himself.

It wasn't to celebrate a wedding that half the town came out on this beautiful, warm fall day, it was the installation of a new cell phone tower right on the property. Now everyone had cell phones, and glory be, they worked. All the time. Deals had been made, Dougie Hollyfield knew, between the newly established Abbott Foundation and the cell phone company.

It was the middle of September, a vivid day, blue sky, the leaves beginning to change color, and the golds and oranges mixed with the remaining green made you weep with the beauty of it.

Rachael and Jack Crowne were engaged now, Sheriff Hollyfield knew, and they sure looked it, always standing close, always touching, even as they greeted people and directed them to the two huge open-sided tents, loaded with tables of food, circular tables and chairs, and hired waiters serving champagne and beer. There was even a band and a dance floor made of plywood.

Agent Dillon Savich stood with his wife, Agent Sherlock. She'd been shot, she'd admitted to Sheriff Hollyfield the day before when he'd asked her about it, and had lost her spleen, but she looked fine now. Their son, Sean, was throwing a football with half a dozen other little boys in the meadow outside the tent.

As for the engaged couple, they'd announced a Christmas wedding here at Slipper Hollow and invited everyone. Sheriff Hollyfield could imagine a White House–sized tree all decorated with lights standing in the middle of the hollow. A bit of snow would be nice.

Dougie Hollyfield, as was his habit, kept his eyes open, watching, and when a little girl ran after a Frisbee and stumbled, he immediately ran toward her. He was so fast he even beat her mother. He looked up to see Gillette Janes speaking to Jack Crowne's older sister, dark-haired, tall and leggy like her brother, a lawyer. They looked mighty interested in each other.

He remembered how badly the house had been shot up, and he'd had to deal with the aftermath of all those people trying to kill not just Rachael, but Jack Crowne and Gillette Janes himself. What a mess that had been. But it seemed to have changed things here quite a bit, beginning with the huge building project Gillette had begun two weeks later when he'd opened up Slipper Hollow to the world around it.

Dougie Hollyfield's cell phone blasted out "Born Free," programmed especially for him by Agent Savich the previous day. He answered it and grinned hugely at the clear, crisp voice of one of his deputies. "What did you say? Mrs. Mick's car broke down and she's in labor and alone? Well, why didn't you call Dr. Post? You don't have his cell number?" Dougie gave it to him. "Look, he's here, so I'll tell him his fun is over and to meet you at the hospital with Mrs. Mick."

He flipped his cell closed, accepted a glass of very nice champagne from a passing waiter, and walked toward Dr. Post, who was laughing at something Suzette from Monk's Café was saying to him.

Funny how life worked, he thought, and waved to Dr. Post, who turned and lost his smile.

The cell tower party lasted until midnight. Everyone was calling everyone else, even when they stood three feet apart, and everyone was exchanging cell numbers.

It was a glorious night, a half-moon high in the sky, the music slow and dreamy now, couples dancing.

Dougie Hollyfield didn't think there was any more champagne in Slipper Hollow.